KAGE BAKER

Mendoza in Hollywood

A NOVEL OF THE COMPANY

TOR®

A TOM DOHERTY ASSOCIATES BOOK
NEW YORK

This is a work of fiction. All the characters and events portrayed in this novel are either fictitious or are used fictitiously.

MENDOZA IN HOLLYWOOD

First published in the United States by Harcourt, Inc.

Copyright © 2000 by Kage Baker

Book design by Linda Lockowitz

A Tor Book
Published by Tom Doherty Associates, LLC
175 Fifth Avenue
New York, NY 10010

www.tor.com

Tor® is a registered trademark of Tom Doherty Associates, LLC.

Library of Congress Cataloging-in-Publication Data

Baker, Kage.
    Mendoza in Hollywood: a novel of the company/Kage Baker.
        p. cm.
    ISBN 0-765-31530-0
    EAN 978-0-765-31530-4
    I. Title.
  PS3552.A4313M46 2000
  813'.54—dc21   99-14949

First Tor Trade Paperback Edition: May 2006

Printed in the United States of America

This book is dedicated to Phyllis Patterson,
Instigator, with respect and affection;
And to the village she founded under the oak trees
And to its people. *Et in Arcadia ego.*

CONTENTS

PROLOGUE

*I*N THE TWENTY-FOURTH CENTURY, *about halfway through, it was said there was a fabulously powerful Company that could obtain virtually anything, if one had enough money.*

A Shakespeare first folio for your library? A live dodo for your aviary? An original sketch by da Vinci for your bedroom wall? Recordings of every performance Mick Jagger ever gave?

What about a necklace once worn by Cleopatra?

Have you a favorite historical figure? Would you like to have his baby? Or have your wife have his baby? Guaranteed authentic off-spring of Julius Caesar, Napoleon Bonaparte, Elvis Presley.

As it happened, the Company actually existed, and it called itself Dr. Zeus Incorporated.

It began with two goals: to render human beings immortal and to develop time travel. Success in either goal was incomplete, though with all the money Dr. Zeus was making, it hardly mattered.

Time travel, for example, seems to be possible only backward, and then forward again to your point of departure in your present. Nor can you bring anything forward out of its own time into yours. And, by the way, history cannot be changed.

You can get around this somewhat by establishing indestructible warehouses in the past, where you stash all the loot you acquire there,

*to be retrieved in your present time. But you will need a workforce to
maintain these sites, and run your errands through time...*

*Immortality is another matter. It's absolutely possible to confer it
on a human being. Problem is, what you have when you've finished
won't be a human being any longer, it'll be a cyborg, and how many
people want to pay millions to become one of those things?*

*Somebody clever at Dr. Zeus came up with an idea that solved
both problems at a stroke: Make your workforce immortal.*

*Since they'll live forever, there's no need to ship them back and
forth through time: look at the costs you'll cut if you just create them
at the beginning of time and let them work their way through it, day
by day, like everybody else. Transmit your orders to your cyborgs
using that subatomic particle you've discovered that exists everywhere and in all times at once. You're in business.*

*Every epoch has its abandoned children, its orphans of war or
famine. Won't they be grateful to be rescued and gifted with immortality and lifetime jobs? And what jobs: rescuing precious things from
the relentless sweep of oblivion. Of course they'll be grateful...*

This is the third volume in the unofficial history of Dr. Zeus
Incorporated.

In the Garden of Iden *introduced Botanist Mendoza, rescued as a
child from the dungeons of the Inquisition in sixteenth-century Spain by
a Company operative, Facilitator Joseph. In exchange for being gifted
with immortality and a fantastically augmented body and mind, she
would work in the past for the future, saving plants from extinction.*

*On her first mission as an adult, Mendoza was sent with Joseph
to England, at that time under the repressive Catholic rule of Bloody
Mary. Disguised as mortals, she and other operatives were to loot the
private gardens of an eccentric collector, Sir Walter Iden. Her goal:
obtain samples of* Ilex tormentosum, *a species that contained a powerful anticancer drug and that would be extinct in the future.*

*Superior and snide as only a teenaged immortal can be, Mendoza
looked down on the mortals among whom she had to labor—until
she met Sir Walter's secretary, Nicholas Harpole, a Protestant heretic.*

Mendoza and Nicholas engaged in a contest of wits that led them into bed. Passionately in love despite Joseph's warnings about the folly of becoming attached to a mortal, Mendoza attempted to juggle her heart, her mission, and her secret. She failed spectacularly.

Nicholas ended up being led to the stake. Mendoza was heartbroken, numb. Joseph came to her rescue again and got her transferred to the Company research base in South America: New World One.

Sky Coyote *opened 144 years later, as Joseph arrived at New World One for a brief holiday before going on to his next mission in Alta California. The project—persuading a village of Chumash to let the Company relocate them to one of its research bases—would be immense, requiring the services of operatives of all disciplines. Mendoza was also drafted for the mission.*

Unpleasant surprises awaited them in California. The immortal operatives met a number of their mortal masters from the future. They were appalled to find them ignorant and bigoted, fearful of their cyborg servants. Joseph learned unsettling facts about the Company that brought to mind a warning given him centuries earlier by Budu, the immortal who recruited him.

Why was it that, though the immortals were provided with information and entertainment from the future, nothing they received was ever dated later than the year 2355? The Company's official answer was that in 2355 Dr. Zeus would be able to go public with its great work and reward its operatives for their ages of service. But could the Company be believed?

Mendoza, back in contact again with the mortal world, found that her heart had not recovered from Nicholas. Despising the mortals and uncomfortable even with her own kind, she found comfort only in the vast wilderness of Alta California. In its forests she was able to leave her painful humanity and focus on the only reliable consolation: her work as a botanist.

Then, after 160 years, ...

Mendoza in Hollywood

TRANSCRIPT ACNW032063 PRIVATE HEARING

Subject: Botanist Mendoza. March 20, 1863.

Five kilograms Theobromos administered.

Auditors magisterial: Labienus, Aethelstan, Gamaliel.

YOU WANT THE TRUTH from me? It's a subjective thing, truth, you know, and you could easily get all the damning evidence you need from the datafeed transcripts. Oh, but you wouldn't understand my *motive*, would you? I see the point.

Will it help if I freely confess? I killed six—no, seven—mortal men, though I must say it was under provocation. I acted in direct violation of the laws that govern us, of the principles instilled in me when I was at school. I betrayed those principles by becoming involved in a mortal quarrel, supporting a cause I knew must fail in the end. Worst of all, I stole Company property—myself, when I deserted the post to which I had been assigned. I don't expect mercy, señors.

But it might help you to know that what I did, I did for love.

I had an unfortunate experience when I was a young operative, you see; I was baptized in the blood of a martyr. No, really. Did you know those things work, baptisms? I didn't. I was given the same education we all get, sanity and science and reasonable explanations for everything that happens in the world. Faith and its attendant rituals sound like a good deal, the whole eternal salvation thing, but inevitably they lead to fear, oppression, the rack and flames. I knew that much was true firsthand.

I was blindsided, as I'm sure you would have been, by the discovery that the experience actually left some kind of psychic mark on me. The mortal man smeared his blood and shouted his incantation, and there I stood like an animal that's been collared and let go, to wander bewildered among my own kind wondering what had happened. I was never right again after that. For a long time I thought I'd shaken off his spell. I was almost happy there in the mountains all alone. But you wouldn't let well enough alone. You sent me back into mortal places, and he found me again, tracked me by the mark he'd put on me for that purpose.

He will never let me rest.

Thank you, I certainly will have some more Theobromos. This is excellent stuff, by the way. Keep it coming, and no doubt you'll find out everything you want to know, with me a weepy mess at the end of it.

Okay, señors, are those tapes rolling?

ANY OF YOU GENTLEMEN ever served in Los Angeles? No? Rough place. Murders and fighting all the time since the Yankees came. No good reason to put a city there, on that clay bluff above the river; but Spain was so certain the Russians were going to invade Alta California, they had to go stick little pretend towns along its coast, like pins on a map. That way they could claim white settlement, because the mission Indians didn't count.

White! That was a laugh. What happened was that Felipe De Neve sent his goons riding up from Sinaloa with anybody he could bribe, threaten, or deceive into coming along as prospective settlers. There were maybe one or two Spaniards in that bunch, but the rest were mestizo and mulatto ex-soldiers, the mingled blood of New Spain and Africa with their wives and little children. De Neve's men dragged them up through the desert and over the mountains and set them down by that dry wash of a river, with its big sycamore trees. And after a mass was duly celebrated, they left them there, rode away and left them staring out into that night, and what an empty, empty night it must have been. No neighbors but the local Indians, and nothing to shelter them from the bears but brush huts. The settlers, huddled together listening to the coyotes howl, must have wondered what on God's earth they had got themselves into.

But they made the best of things, built a little adobe village, got some Indians to be their slaves, and in a generation or two they were gentlemen rancheros, with thousands of head of cattle on estates the size of small kingdoms, estates that would have made the threadbare gentry of the Old World sick with envy.

Of course, if one wanted a chamberpot or a carving knife or a bolt of cotton cloth, one had to wait for the supply ship from Mexico, which put in an appearance once every five years or so. This situation did not improve after the Revolution, either; a free and democratic bureaucracy moves even more slowly than a viceregal one. So in came the Yankee traders, smuggling consumer goods in their trading brigs, and the Californio rancheros were only too glad to do business with them. You know where *that* led. Richard Henry Dana wrote home about the fortune waiting to made by anybody with the ambition to build mills and factories here. Emigrants from the United States came struggling over the Rockies to see if it was true, some lady found a gold nugget in a sluice, and in no time at all we were all Americans, thanks to a little strong-arm work by John C. Fremont.

Not a bad thing, entirely, at first. It was the making of San Francisco. Los Angeles, though, sort of festered. It filled up with drunks and outlaws, white trash from the States who'd failed at gold prospecting, men on the run from civilization generally. There was nothing down there, you see, except dry brown hills and cattle, plenty of space to get lost in. Soon there were lots of saloons to get lost in too, and drunken shoot-outs in the streets. There were so many murders, people began calling Los Angeles the City of Devils rather than the City of Angels. *Los Diablos.* The old ranchero families huddled in their fine haciendas, listened to the gunfire, and wondered what in hell had happened to their town.

So you can see, señors, why I wasn't exactly thrilled to be posted down there. Monterey, green and gracious, that was where I preferred to be when I had to work near mortals; better still, the wild coastal mountains, the Ventana and Big Sur.

When you're coming down from the north, Los Angeles looks horrible at first: all brown rolling monotony. Hasn't got the redwoods, hasn't got the green mountains or the air like wine. It's a sad, trampled place. But let me put it on the record that my distaste at my assignment played no part in what happened. I went where I was told and did my job. I always have. We all do.

Weren't you briefed on this part? All right, I was sent to the HQ in Cahuenga Pass, close by La Nopalera. The cover is that it's a stagecoach stop. It's far enough out from Los Angeles to give us privacy, but being on the stage line, it's convenient for getting agents in and out. Agents and other things.

But that's all beside the point. Give me more of that—it's Guatemalan, isn't it?—and I'll try to stick to the story. You know, it's amazing, señors, but you bear a striking resemblance to certain inquisitors I knew in Old Spain. All of you. It's your eyes, I think. They're too patient.

PART ONE

CAHUENGA PASS, 1862

I ARRIVED DURING a miserable winter. It had rained most amazingly; the locals had never seen such rain. The canyons flooded. The new sewers down at the pueblo were a total loss. Roads washed out, and the stages were late or never arrived at all. There was, I understand, a little mining town up in the San Gabriels that was washed away completely—whole thing wound up down on the plain in scattered soggy bits. Only the rancheros were happy, because of the good grazing there was going to be from the rain. They thought. Little did they know that that was the last rain they were going to see for years. Before it rained again, Señor Drought and Señorita Smallpox and a few shrewd Yankee moneylenders would pretty well end the days of the *gentes de razón*. Ah, Los Angeles. One disaster after another, always has been.

Those particular disasters were still somewhat in the future on the day I finally walked into HQ. I'd followed the coast down as far as Buenaventura and then swung inland to follow El Camino Real through the hills and along the valley floor, traveling mostly by night to avoid the mortal population. The rain never let up the whole way, and I was soaked through. I crossed innumerable creeks swollen with white anger, roaring their way out to sea and taking willow snags with them. I saw smooth green hillsides so saturated, their grassy turf slid, like a half-taken scalp or a toupee, and left bare holes that the rain widened.

So much for Sunny California. All I saw of it that dark morning was water, brown water and creamy mud, and black twigs bobbing along in the hope of someday washing up on a white beach. You can imagine how grateful I was to see a plume of smoke going up between one foothill and the next. I checked my coordinates. *Cahuenga Pass HQ?* I broadcast tentatively.

Receiving, someone responded.

Botanist Mendoza reporting in.

Okay. You see the smoke? Follow it in.

And in another minute I'd come around the edge of a rockslide, and there it was, back under some oak trees, a long low adobe building and stable thatched with tules. A couple of cowhides had been stitched end to end and strung up in the trees like a tarpaulin, and under this nominal shelter an immortal crouched, attempting to build up a small fire with what looked like fairly damp wood. Arranged on the ground beside him were a blue graniteware coffeepot and a couple of skillets. The idea of grilled beef and frijoles drew me like a magnet.

"Hola." I jumped the last brown torrent and made my way up the sandy bank to the inn.

"'Morning." The immortal looked up from under the brim of his dripping hat. "Welcome to the Hollywood Canteen."

"This *is* where Hollywood's going to be, isn't it?" I asked. I dropped my bag and held my hands down to the little fire. "Funny thought."

My informant stretched out an arm to point, trailing the fringe of his serape through dead leaves. "Chinese Theater and Hollywood Bowl right down there. Paramount Studios out in that direction. If you've got eighty years to hang around, we can go for breakfast at the Warner Brothers' commissary."

"I'll settle for what you've got." I eyed the skillets: last night's leftovers, cold and congealed. I looked around for something dry to add to the fire.

"So you're Mendoza?" inquired my host. He was lean and dark, with a thin black mustache and a sad, villainous face villainously scarred. The scars were all appliance makeup, of course, but they gave him the look that sends liquor store owners diving behind counters for their shotguns. I nodded in reply.

"Porfirio." He reached across the fire and shook hands with me. "I'm your case officer, subfacilitator, and security tech. Nice to meet you."

"Thanks. Is it dangerous here?"

"Oh, yeah," he said. He took up an oak log and tried stripping the wet cork layer off. "We don't get much trouble over this way, but you want to be careful when you ride out." He broke the log between his hands and fed it carefully into the coals. "Especially where you'll be working. Your temperate belt passes through some nasty bandit nests." He was referring to the climate anomaly that was my present assignment, a long terrace roughly following the future route of Sunset Boulevard, where an unusual weather pattern had evolved some plants unique to the area, several of which had potentially remarkable commercial properties. Unfortunately they were all scheduled to go extinct in the next big drought, grazed out of existence by starving cattle.

"Bandits?" I was profoundly annoyed. "They told me I was going to be working in Beverly Hills!"

He was really amused by that. "Oh, you will be! It just isn't *there* yet. What, were you planning on having a cocktail in the Polo Lounge? You've got a while to wait if you want to see the mansions and the swimming pools." The fire blazed up at last, and he edged the skillets in toward its heart. "Come on, little fire, come on, we want some breakfast. Where's your horse, by the way?" He looked up in surprise as it occurred to him that I'd walked in.

"I don't have one."

"You're kidding me! *Nobody* walks down here. We've got a good stable you can choose from," he said firmly.

"That's okay. I don't care for horses, actually."

"I don't myself, but I ride them here. Trust me. You may need to get out of certain situations in a hurry. This is Los Diablos, after all." He put up a hand to stop my objections. "And don't think you can deal with the situation by just winking out at a speed mortals can't see. That may have been all right in the old days, but there are a lot of people out here now. It's too conspicuous. You'll need a horse. Everyone rides them. You'll need a gun, too."

"A gun?" I said, sitting back on my heels. "I've never carried a gun! You mean you've actually had to shoot people?"

He nodded somberly.

"But we were always trained—"

"I know," he said as he pushed the coffeepot over wavering flames. "The rules are different down here. You'll see."

"Who are you talking to?" Another operative emerged from the adobe, stooping below the wooden lintel of the door. He stood, sleepily scratching himself through a suit of long underwear worn under blue jeans. He gave a yawn that turned into a shiver.

"The botanist's here." Porfirio gestured with the skillet. "Mendoza, this is Einar. Einar, this is Mendoza."

"Zoologist grade 5." He came forward and shook my hand, then crouched down beside us. "Fire's not doing so good, is it?"

It wasn't. It had sunk away from the coffeepot and was smoking out.

"Wood's wet," he said.

"No kidding," we told him. He was tall for one of us, with white-blond hair and eyes like ice caves. Spectral coloring aside, he was a nice-enough-looking fellow.

"I was just giving her the safety lecture," Porfirio explained, handing him an oak log to break.

"Uh-huh." Einar snapped it into fragments. "Hey, chief, did you tell her about where we are? The movie studios and everything?"

"Yes. I thought you could issue her one of the Navy pistols and give her a short training session with it." Porfirio took the kindling from him and fed it into the coals, where it caught.

"No problem." Einar poked up the fire and coaxed a few tongues of flame to rise. "Come on, I need some coffee. There. Yeah, and I can show you where all the neat stuff will be. A lot of early cinema is shot in these very canyons. DeMille, D. W. Griffith, Hal Roach. Tinseltown!"

"But there's nothing there to actually see yet, is there?" I said.

"Well, no. Except the familiar landscapes, you know. I just enjoy the atmosphere of it all." Einar waved another oak branch in the air. "I mean, here we are in the mundane West, as far west as you can go, if you think about it, and everywhere around us the West of the cinema—the true West, if you will—is just sort of immanent. Hovering in these canyons like a spirit, waiting to be born. Ghosts of the future. All this greatness just about to happen, but not yet. We are the actors on a stage where the curtain hasn't risen!" His eyes were alight with enthusiasm.

"We're behind the scenes, you mean." Porfirio watched the fire doubtfully. A little thread of steam was rising from the mouth of the coffeepot, but the grease on the beefsteaks was still cold and waxy.

"Good morning, gentlemen," said yet another of my kind, stepping out into the courtyard. This one looked like a little Yankee lawyer or congressman, in a black suit and polished boots, with a cosmetically induced receding hairline that featured a sharp widow's peak. His eyes bulged slightly when he saw me. "*And* lady. Why, you must be our new botanist. Pleased to meet you, ma'am, I'm sure. Mendoza, isn't it? Yes. Oscar, grade 2 anthropologist, at your service."

I nodded at him. He put his hands in his pockets and came over to stand looking down at the fire. "Say, you know—"

"The wood's wet," said Porfirio.

"It is, isn't it? No, I was just thinking, wouldn't some of my corn bread go good with those steaks and beans? I'll just go fetch it out." He ran back indoors, and Porfirio and Einar exchanged a disgruntled look.

"What?" I said.

"He tried making corn bread out of masa," Porfirio said. "He's very proud of it."

There was a gloomy silence. The trees dripped. There was a distant rumble of thunder; from the sound of it, the storm front was approaching the future site of the Whiskey a' Gogo.

"This is Raymond Chandler country too, isn't it?" I said.

"Yeah." Einar brightened. "Laurel Canyon, Hollywood Boulevard. I could show you—"

"Here it is." Oscar came bustling out with a pan. He dropped the bread beside the guttering fire—there was an audible thud—hitched up his trousers, and crouched down to cut slices. "Miss?" He offered me a slab of solid gray cake.

"My, isn't this substantial" was all I could think to say.

He beamed. "Real stick-to-your-ribs food for a chilly morning, yes indeed." He stood again with his hands in his pockets, rocking back and forth in his shiny shoes. "So, Miss. You're in botanicals? What are you going out for, if I may presume to ask?"

"Um—rarities. I was told there's a lot of good specimens of *Striata pulchra* I need to collect, as well as some mutations of common plants. Snowberry, Artemesias, that kind of thing. Creosote bush," I said. My job always sounds unbelievably boring to anyone but another botanist, so I didn't take offense when he blinked and forged on:

"You don't say so? I'm in notions, myself. Of course that's just my cover, ha ha! Actually I'm here to report on the impact of Yankee settlement on the local inhabitants—the decent ones, I mean—and document early Anglo-Californian culture."

"I see."

"I've got the sweetest little cart back there you ever saw." He nodded in the direction of the stables. "Just a wonder of clever design. Only requires the work of one mule—seats two—sides unfold for display of anything the locals could want to buy, from threepenny nails to dancing pumps, plus a complete photographer's apparatus, *plus* I can sleep in it, if I'm benighted somewhere and the weather's foul. I have but to fold down the seats and slide out the patented Collapsi-Cot!"

"Gosh, how clever."

"And, you know something? It's not Company issue! Not at all! The whole thing was made by a firm in Boston, Massachusetts!"

"Speaking of cots," said Einar, grinning. A female operative appeared in the door of the house and yawned expansively, stretching up her arms like a dancer. All I could see was a flowing wave of white ruffles on a fancy nightdress, of the kind I hadn't owned in years. When she brought her arms down in a slow dramatic gesture, I saw that the bosom was cut low enough to make her look like the heroine of a romantic novel. She gave a little toss of her head—lots of dark-ringlet hair whooshed from side to side—and raised startling green eyes to regard us.

"Imarte." I placed her.

"Would that be Mendoza?" She paced forward, pretending to peer at me through the gloom. "It *is* the botanist Mendoza, isn't it? I believe we worked together on the Humashup mission?"

"Yeah," I said.

"You were a friend of, ah, Joseph's." The corners of her lovely mouth turned down.

"That's right." I grinned with all my teeth. "And you're an anthropologist." She hadn't got on very well with my old pal and erstwhile mentor, as I recalled. In fact, there'd been a truly nasty incident, hadn't there? Well, this was going to be a fun posting.

"An insertion anthropologist," she corrected me, and Einar fell over in helpless giggles. Even Porfirio smiled under his mustache. Oscar turned red and looked at his shiny shoes. "I'm stationed in this culture on a semipermanent basis, interacting with the mortal element in Los Angeles in order to observe them more closely, as opposed to an anthropologist like Oscar, who merely interviews," she said primly.

"She, uh, her cover identity is as a sort of a—" began Einar, but Imarte finished:

"A whore. And there's really no need to make a dirty joke out of it. I've been a temple prostitute on numerous occasions during my career. Men speak the truth in bed, as the proverb goes, and what better place to gain valuable insights into the *real* life of a culture? And this is an astonishingly rich era for study. In one night I might have a conversation with a Yankee from New York who came west to pan for gold, followed by a Mexican outlaw whose family were massacred by Indians, followed by an Australian ex-convict who failed at piracy, followed by—well, followed by *anybody*." She tossed her head. "Why, during this period in history the whole world is passing through the Golden Gate!"

I don't think she meant the one in San Francisco. I blinked.

"You actually go to bed with all these people?" I asked.

She lifted her chin at me. "What, I should feel degraded? Should we not consider it, rather, as a way for me to experience their lives more fully, more meaningfully? Particularly in view of the fascinating material I'm compiling on mid-nineteenth-century mores and sexuality in California."

"Besides, any good stagecoach inn has at least one hooker," argued Porfirio. "It makes our cover more authentic, and contributes to our operating budget too."

This was more than I cared think about. I turned to Porfirio. "So, okay...I'd like to see my quarters after breakfast, if I could. I'm pretty tired."

"I'll bet you are, after walking all that way," Porfirio said.

"She walked here?" Oscar asked, staring. Imarte looked appalled.

Then there was another person standing beside our almost-fire, so silent in his approach, he seemed to have materialized there. He too was an immortal, but a young one; if you knew where to look, you could still see the scars of his augmentations. Remarkably enough, he had been made from an Indian. I hadn't seen many of these. My guess was he'd been among the few survivors of the Channel Island tribes, because he had their silver hair. It used to be a fairly common color for Native Americans, but smallpox was swiftly winnowing it out of their gene pool, the way the Black Death had rendered extinct similar exotic strains in Europeans.

"Hi," he said.

"Where've you been this morning? You were out early," said Porfirio.

"I heard him crying," the boy said, and held up in his cupped hands a tiny writhing monster from outer space. "It's a baby condor. *Gymnogyps californianus*. The mother hadn't come back to the nest in a while. I guess somebody shot her. I had to climb way, way back up the canyon to find him. Are you the new botanist?" He looked at me.

I nodded. "Mendoza. And you're—?"

"Juan Bautista." He came closer to the fire and peered down at it. "We need some dry wood or something, huh?"

"Wait, I have an idea," said Einar, and jumped up and ran inside. A moment later he emerged with a case bottle of a clear liquid. "Home-brewed aguardiente." He strode toward us, uncorking it. "We tried it on a plum pudding, and the damned thing burned for two hours. This'll do the job."

"Careful how you—" said Porfirio.

I threw myself flat and rolled. I heard Imarte scream. The fireball took out the cowhide tarp, but when I looked around cautiously, there was certainly a merry blaze going, all right, flames five feet high. And breakfast was cooking at last: in fact, the frijoles were on fire.

"SORRY ABOUT THAT," called Einar from where he had retreated about thirty yards up the hillside.

"Couldn't you have been more careful?" complained Oscar, squelching up from the mouth of the canyon. "Now my shoes are wet."

Later Porfirio showed me to my quarters. I had a cot all to myself in a board-and-batten lean-to next to the adobe stable. It smelled of horses, it had a dirt floor, and water was seeping up the wooden legs of my cot; but the stretched cow skin over the frame was dry, and so was the woolen blanket, and there was a dry ledge on which to put my bag. As field accommodations went, not too bad. I sat down and pulled off my wet boots.

Now, señors, I think some of the reason for my subsequent lamentable behavior is evident right here in the next scene. I hung up my oilskins and shrugged into dry clothes, meditating smugly to myself that it didn't take much to make me happy nowadays. I was an old hand now, wasn't I? A couple of tamales and a dry place to put up my feet and read a novel were enough. I could make my own space anywhere they posted me, as a good operative should. Wisdom at last. Perhaps I'd attained enlightenment after tramping through that beautiful desolation all these years collecting specimens alone. Certainly I had equilibrium.

Well. Where pride flaunts such scarlet banners, blares such brazen trumpets, you know what follows.

I had turned in early, after walking up on the ridge above the house to get a feel for the land, making friends with the oak trees, exploring the rooms of the coaching inn, chatting a little more with my fellow operatives (the male ones anyway) most amiably and normally. I had endured a few hands of gin rummy with Juan Bautista and an hour or so of anecdotes from Oscar about his mortal customers before I excused myself on the grounds that I'd been conscious for forty-eight hours and needed some alpha waves badly. And so I retired to my spartan room, pleased with myself. I'd done well for my first day back among people, I thought. I ought to be able to handle this posting just fine.

Maybe it was having an actual bed to lie down in that did it. See, I'd got out of the habit of sleeping like mortals, all those years in the mountains. I know, we're not supposed to do it—but it's so convenient just to lean into a tree limb or an angle of rock and fugue out for a couple of days, especially when you're on your own schedule. You have no idea how restful it can be. You just sort of tune in to the patterns moving in the tree or the rock, and you forget you even exist.

One feels so vulnerable, undressing and getting into a bed. It summons up memories. The memory that it summoned was not one I wanted. I lay in the dark listening to the rain drip, to the wind sigh in the oak leaves. Because of the downpour, there were no coyotes howling, so you didn't necessarily know you were in California. With just the wind and the rain, it might have been anywhere. It might have been England.

Then I thought it had to be England, because my door was opening and there was green and sunlight beyond, that wet sunlight and drowningly intense green of an English garden. And *he* was there, standing in the doorway and looking at me. So tall, he had to bend to look into my narrow little room, and his black scholar's robe trailed in the lush summer grass. He was smiling, smiling at me in the old way, and held out his hand to me.

"*Talitha koum*," he said, in that voice I'd have leaped out of a grave for. "Up and haste my love, my dove, my beautiful and come, for now is winter gone and rain departed and past!"

Who was he, señors? My martyr, who do you think? Nicholas Harpole, the mortal man with whom I fell in love when I was a young operative who should have known better. He died on April 1, 1555. This was either a dream or a haunting.

A haunting, I think.

I was so glad to get up and run to him where he waited in that doorway, to quit my dark cold room and run into the summer garden. Time must have turned backward, because there I was in my peach-colored gown with all the petticoats and my placketed bodice and stiff sleeves, and my hair falling loose. I never braided it back then, I was too vain. I leaped into his arms, and he made a little pleased chortling noise in his throat, and we were kissing, staggering backward and bumping into the orange tree, so his scholar's biretta was knocked forward over his eyes. I pushed it back, and we kissed and kissed, and oh the taste of his mouth and the scrape of stubble under his jaw and the hungry noises he made, I hadn't forgotten one detail in three centuries of trying desperately to forget.

We kissed until we were blind and gasping and his breeches

needed to be unfastened, so I did it for him, and he pulled his long shirt up and out and freed himself, and I hadn't forgotten one detail about *that* either. Nor had I forgotten what to do next: one didn't just grab the front of one's skirt and haul it up, no, that was sluttish, one gathered it at the two sides as though one were going to sit down, and one lifted it in a discreet and genteel manner just far enough for the purpose. No bloomers, no underwear at all, only my fine-woven stockings gartered at the knee, and he was bending down to gather me up in his big fine hands and lift me against him.

Every detail was perfect and exact, the rustle of my gathered petticoats, the texture of his clean linen shirt and woolen doublet under my cheek, and how they smelled with the full hot sun on them releasing the scent of washing soap, and the green feverish privet-fragrance of the garden at high summer. I had my arms around his shoulders, my face pressed into the side of his neck, and a trickle of his sweat came coursing down as he labored, and I kissed the sweat away. And how we strove there together, in our mutual delight, as he growled his pleasure and I felt the vibration of it in his throat, and how soundly we knocked the trunk of the orange tree, until golden fruit fell all around us in a shower.

Oh, I thought, jackpot, surely that's a favorable omen. And as we rested, sobbing for breath, I felt a little stab. We both looked down, surprised. Protruding from my heart was the haft of a bodkin, and my heart's blood was welling out around it like a cut pomegranate. I laughed, joyous, incredulous, and he laughed with me. We both knew what this meant: I was free of the world now, I could stay in that garden with him eternally. Impossibly, wonderfully, my weary heart had stopped beating.

But I was slipping somehow, he was losing his hold, and the pain became terrible as I opened my eyes into darkness and felt the chill, heard the rain.

I hadn't gone through the doorway to him after all.

It took a long moment of struggling for air to be able to voice my

agony. I wasn't loud, even so; but within seconds I heard hurrying feet
crunching through the oak leaves.

Mendoza?

Go away!

He wouldn't go away. The door opened, and Porfirio looked in on
me, all concern, a black silhouette against blacker night. Good God,
I thought, what's he got that gun for?

You okay?

Yes! Don't you ever have bad dreams? I transmitted. He looked at
me in irresolution a moment before nodding and shutting the door.

I guess, señors, if I were somebody else, I might have called him
back and begged some kind of physical comfort as a favor, that I
might not lie alone there in the dark. But I was and regretfully am myself, and I was not alone. The dark thundered around me like a pal-
pable presence, and I belonged to it.

Next morning, Porfirio didn't mention the disturbance, and neither did I. I ran a diagnostic on myself, but everything tested out
normal.

For the first couple of weeks that I lived at that stagecoach inn,
there were no stagecoaches at all, and precious few travelers, because
the roads were in no condition for going anywhere. This situation
didn't improve much the whole time I was there, in part because Butterfield had decided to cancel its stage lines to California for the du-
ration of the American Civil War, which left its rival Phineas Banning
with a lot of territory to cover all by himself.

At about the point where there were no dead trees left to float
down the canyons and you thought all the topsoil had washed out to
sea, the rain stopped. The sun came out! And abruptly we were living in a paradise. The hills were green and purple and silver with
sagebrush, the grazing land was brilliant lime-green with good grass,
and everywhere there were banks of wildflowers. I stepped out under
the dripping oak trees and looked up at the puffy white clouds in
the blue sky. What a fine place, I thought. What a *beautiful* place.

Murder? Robbery? Social dysfunction? Surely not in sunny southern California.

I was humming Rodrigo's *Concierto de Aranjuez* (first movement) as I went indoors to collect my field kit. Temperate belt, here I come! My ghost had not returned to haunt me, and my work was waiting. Who knew what botanic anomalies lay there waiting to be discovered?

But when I shouldered my pack and emerged from my quarters, Porfirio looked up from the cookfire he had just got going. "Where are you off to?" he asked with a frown.

"I thought I'd go get some work done at last, now that the rain's let up." I gestured at the enchanting sky.

"Not alone, you're not. Not over in that neck of the woods." He shook his head decisively. "Too many damn bandits. Wait until Einar gets up. He'll go with you."

"Oh, come on," I said, almost too surprised to be annoyed. "I've been on my own in California for years. I've outrun bears, Indians, and every one of the Joaquins. I worked in San Luis Obispo, where they hang so many outlaws, there's a gallows at the end of every street. I don't need an escort, thank you very much."

"It's different down here," he said, and something about his tone made me slip off my pack and find a dry place to wait as he got a pot of coffee brewing. Presently Einar came out, hopping on one booted foot as he pulled the other boot on.

"Hey, folks," he said. "Sunlight, huh? I guess I'll go out looking for a coyote or two today."

"You can go out with Mendoza," Porfirio said.

"Sure." He grinned at me. "You want the Grand Hollywood tour? Show you where the homes of the stars will be."

"I hope there's something useful growing there," I said grumpily. "And did I hear you say you were collecting *coyotes*?"

"Uh-huh." He poured a mug of coffee and handed it to me. "Don't laugh. The particular subspecies in this area will disappear after a couple of centuries. First they'll crossbreed with settler's dogs.

Then they'll crossbreed with wolves that escape from the zoo during a riot—that's during the dark ages of L.A.—and they'll get so huge and vicious, they'll start eating street beggars when the winters are bad."

"Jesus." I shivered, looking up at the sky. It was such an innocent shade of blue.

"But these little guys we have now are real sweet," he told me seriously, sipping his own coffee. "Sort of foxy. Nothing to worry about. Not like when I go after a bear."

"Bears?"

"California brown bears, like the one on the flag," he said. "They're already on the way out. Last known survivor in California will be shot right here, or actually out there"—he pointed down the canyon—"in 1912. Then they're extincto. Supposedly. They take some catching!"

"I can imagine." I looked into the bottom of my graniteware cup. "Tell me, are we likely to encounter any bears today?"

"Only if we're lucky," Einar said. "Since you have other work to do, I thought we'd keep things simple for now."

"Wonderful."

After a breakfast of velvety frijoles and steak rolled in tortillas, we saddled up and went to explore. Einar wore fearsome-looking bandoliers and a pair of shotguns, one behind either shoulder, like samurai swords. He showed me a trail that led through the back of the canyon and up a series of switchbacks to the top of the ridge. We followed the rimrock above the foothills, and down below us the plains swept out to the east, where there were big white snowy mountains, and south and west, where beyond the sprawl of adobes that was Los Angeles the land terminated in the blue line of the sea. Paler blue and farther out, lay a floating mountain.

"Is that an island?" I asked, squinting at it.

"Catalina," Einar said. "Location shots for *Mutiny on the Bounty,* *Treasure Island,* and a couple of versions of *Rain,* to name but a few. And check this out." He leaned over in his saddle, pointing into a steep valley to our left. "Know what that is, down there? Hollywood Bowl!

Imagine a big white half shell right there, with a reflecting pool in front of it, and a fan of seats sweeping up and up, rows and rows of pearly gray wooden benches, and thousands of screaming girls filling the amphitheater. Right down there is where the Beatles will perform. I've been up here at night, alone, and I swear to God I can hear them."

I stared down, impressed, though all I could see was a wilderness of sagebrush and toyon holly. "That's when, the 1960s? Only a century off. Where's the Hollywood sign?"

"Look across there." He pointed east, where a red mountain thrust up against the sky like a rippled wall. "Under the crest. It'll say *Hollywoodland* first, for the real estate park below it, and then when the last four letters fall off, they won't be replaced. There'll be two sister signs as well, for a couple of other developments, one down on that lower ridge that'll say *Bryn Mawr* and one over here that says *Outpost,* but they won't last long, and nobody will remember they were ever there. Neat, huh?"

"You certainly know the area," I said. We urged our horses on, and they continued to pick their way down the trail. "What are you going to do when it finally starts to happen, though? You're a zoologist. Dr. Z isn't likely to keep you here once the bears and the coyotes are gone."

"I have a double discipline," he said. "Programmed for zoology *and* cinema. I can stabilize a silver-nitrate print with one hand and do a genetic assay on a musk ox with the other. I've been in the field for millennia, though, so all my experience is with animals. Reindeer, caribou, wolves, those guys. The wheels of time roll swift around, though! When this assignment's up, I'm off to Menlo Park and then on to Melies in France. I'll be in on film from the beginning. I just hope Dr. Zeus sends me back here once the industry's up and running. Wouldn't that be swell?"

We both heard the shot, a little *pow* from somewhere down in the canyon to our right, and in a tiny fragment of time the bullet came zipping up through the bushes at us. We were off our horses and flat on the earth by then, however.

"Aw, shit," Einar said. He unslung one of the rifles and pointed it in the direction of our assailant; then he went into hyperfunction, firing and reloading faster than a mortal eye could have followed, sending a volley into the canyon below that cut a swath through the pretty purple sage. The echo boomed off the opposite ridge like thunder on Judgment Day. The mortal must have wondered what war zone he'd stumbled into, but he didn't wonder it for long; as I scanned, I felt his vital signs flutter and fade out.

"You killed the guy!" I gasped, rising shakily to my knees. The horses stood calmly cropping scrub, as though nothing had happened.

"Gee, I wish he hadn't done that." Einar stood and peered down the hill. "I thought he was going to leave me alone this time."

"You mean he's taken shots at you before?" I was incredulous. "And we rode up here anyway? Into *danger?*"

"What danger?" Einar loaded another couple of shells. "Stupid bastard knew he couldn't hit me, after all the times he's tried it. I'd shown him what I had to throw at him, too. When you're too dumb to learn, you're out of the gene pool, man. Down here, anyway."

I stood staring into the silent canyon. Cool air currents brought up a smell of cut sage and fresh blood. I half-expected sirens or shouting, but all I heard was the wind. "Shouldn't we go down and do something?" I suggested.

"Nope." Einar slung his gun back over his shoulder. "That's what buzzards are for. Turkey vultures, actually, according to J. B." He bent and offered me his cupped hands to climb back into the saddle. I vaulted up and sat there, bent forward nervously as he got back on his own horse.

"Let's get off the skyline, shall we?" I said. He nodded, and we moved on, descending the gentle ridges through the aromatic brush. After a moment I asked, "But who was he? He had to have had some family or somebody, someone we should notify."

Einar shook his head. "He killed 'em. That was why he was hiding out up here. Thirty-year-old Caucasian male psychopath from St.

Louis, Missouri. Also killed two Mexican hookers and three Chinese guys of assorted vocations. I don't know why."

"Oh," I said. We rode on.

After a while, I ventured, "Are there many like him down here?"

"Some," Einar said. He got a loopy grin on his face. "But mostly lions and tigers and the California brown bear!"

"Oh my," I responded faintly. What sort of crazy place was this?

"Come on." He turned in his saddle to look at me, all alight with an idea. "I know that was a pretty grim scene up there. I'll show you something nice. You want to see? Come on." And he spurred his horse down the trail in front of me, and I followed while he chanted about the lions and tigers and bears all the way. Nobody else shot at us.

Below the foothills we came upon a sandy wagon track that ran east and west, in a fairly straight line through clumps of wild buckwheat and chaparral. We took it east, as I stared around in cautious expectation.

"Road to nowhere in particular," Einar said, "at the present time. But in a couple more decades, it'll be Prospect Avenue, when the genteel folks from back east build a little community here. Shortly thereafter they'll change the name to Hollywood Boulevard. Right here, to the left and right, the Walk of Stars will run. The neatest part, though, the *really* neat part, most people will never know about."

"And that would be?"

"This way." He urged his mount forward, counting off nonexistent cross streets on his interior map: "Highland, McCadden, Las Palmas, Cherokee..." Abruptly he turned his horse's head, and we left the trail a few yards north into the trackless thicket. "Here." He looped up the reins, slid from the saddle, and stood beaming at me, as though the Holy Grail was pulsing over the nearest cactus clump.

"Okay, señor." I looked from side to side. "What am I supposed to be seeing?"

"You're seeing the nice little streets laid out just like back east, with shady trees and picket fences and charming rose-covered cottages. Okay? All the white latticework and clapboard and ginger-bread that relocated Yankees gotta have. It'll all be here. And right here, on this very spot, will stand the very nicest house with the very nicest garden, and you know whose house it'll be?" He held out his hands, as if framing a picture for me. "L. Frank Baum's. Ozcot, he'll call the place. This is where he'll settle down, this is where he'll write most of his books about the Tin Man and the Scarecrow and the rest of 'em. How many generations of children will read every word he wrote? How many kids will dream about escaping to Oz, and keep on dreaming about it when they're sick and old?"

"You're kidding." I dismounted and stared around, trying to see the fairy-tale house and its flowers in the midst of this wild place.

"I'm not. He'll even build a movie studio out there and produce his own Oz movies, years before MGM even exists. But then he dies, eventually, and guess what his wife does? *She burns his original manuscripts.* She doesn't think they're worth anything, so she piles them into the backyard incinerator, and they're reduced to ashes. All that magic, all those winkies and witches sift down in a fine silver dust through the grate and lie there forgotten, under an incinerator in a ne-glected garden behind a house that eventually gets sold and bull-dozed." He made a leveling gesture with his hands.

"Neighborhood changes. Little houses get torn down, one by one. Gardens are paved over. A cheesy apartment building is built on this site. Right over there, the limousines zoom by, stars go to dinner at Musso & Frank's Grill, tourists wander the Walk of Stars and see the names of Judy Garland and Ray Bolger and everybody, and all the time this powder of dreams is buried and forgotten."

I stared at him, almost hearing the blaring horns of the traffic, al-most breathing in the smell of expensive cigars and auto exhaust.

Smiling, Einar raised an index finger. "*Until,*" he said, "a young artist named Lincoln Copeland—"

"Oh, come on, not *the* Lincoln Copeland."

"Yes, *the* Lincoln Copeland comes out to Hollywood in 2076 to sketch the ruins. His timing's real bad. The Billy Tahiti riot breaks out while he's there. Bombs are going off all around him. He finds a bomb crater and dives for cover under a tipped-up piece of concrete that used to be a garage floor. He finds he's sitting in the middle of all this amazing gray dust.

"Now, by an incredible coincidence, L. Frank Baum is his favorite author, and luckily there's a street sign still standing. Copeland *knows* where he is, he knows this bomb crater was a magician's garden once, and he knows the story about the burnt manuscripts. What does he do? *He fills his pockets with dust.* With bullets whizzing and souvenir stands burning all around him, the guy crams all the gray dust he can carry into his pockets. And as soon as it's dark, he makes his way to Sunset Boulevard and follows it all the way to the beach, where he manages to thumb a ride out of the riot zone."

"I don't believe this."

"I swear to God! And as soon as he's out of harm's way, he finds a glass jar and shakes out his pockets, takes off every stitch he's got on and beats out the gray dust, and fills the jar. He takes it home with him. It's after that that his career takes off, that he suddenly begins painting those fantastic landscapes and allegorical murals that make him so amazingly rich. He doesn't know why he sees the things he sees when he picks up a brush, but he suspects it's because he dabs a tiny pinch of that gray dust on his palette every time he starts a new piece. He says so in his autobiography, written in 2140."

Einar bent and scooped up a double handful of sand, and let it sift through his fingers. "Right here. It's all right here, waiting to happen, man. Immanent. The air is on fire with it. Jesus, I love this town."

I started and stared, because for just a second I had seen it all: the pretty houses, the ruined city in flames, the Yellow Brick Road curving away up the wall of a soundstage.

"You are nuts," I said. "But I'll bet the Company brings you back here."

"Gotta hope." He grinned. Suddenly his gaze focused on a point in the distance behind me. He reached up for one of his shotguns. I dove for the dirt. "No, it's okay!" he said. "This is the trank gun." He aimed and fired. There was a dull bang and a plaintive little yip, and destiny had found another coyote.

We returned to the inn as darkness was falling. I had a couple of specimens of rare members of the artemisia family in my collecting kit, and Einar had a neatly trussed coyote sleeping peacefully in a wicker creel behind him. There was a loud argument going on around the cooking fire. The principal raised voice was female.

"That man had actually participated in the Bear Flag Rebellion!" Imarte was wailing. "Do you realize what a unique opportunity has been lost? Have you any idea of the insights he could have given us into the mind-set of the Anglo-American rebels?"

"I said I was sorry." Juan Bautista sounded as though he would have liked to crawl into a hole in the sand. "But Erich will die if he doesn't get the right food. It's not like I was chewing it up and vomiting it for him, anyway."

"Oh, my goddess." Imarte flung up her arms in disgust.

"The thing stinks, Juan. You're going to have to feed your bird someplace else, okay?" Porfirio said. As we rode into the clearing under the trees, it became obvious what he meant: someone, presumably Juan Bautista, had dragged a carcass into the clearing. It had been either a large dog or a small deer. I wasn't a zoologist, so I didn't know which. It had been worked over by coyotes already, so I doubted whether anyone else could have told either. Erich von Stroheim (that was what the baby condor had been christened) was sitting on it, looking bewildered. When Imarte raised her voice again, the bird ducked his head and shook his wings desperately, squeaking.

"I don't care what the little horror needs, he doesn't have to have it here when I'm bringing home a client," she said.

"Oh dear." Einar swung out of the saddle. "You lose another john?"

It seemed that the stagecoach had made a stop, and while the horses were being changed and the drivers were refreshing themselves, Imarte had sallied down and offered refreshment to the passengers.

One gentleman had felt confident enough in his appetite to be able to do justice to her offer in the comparatively brief time allotted, and so she'd led him up to the adobe. Unfortunately the first sight that met his eye was Erich von Stroheim pecking at his supper, watched fondly by Juan Bautista. Not only had the gentleman been unable to avail himself of the refreshment offered, he'd lost the lunch he'd partaken of earlier in the day, and departed hastily.

"This *cannot* happen again," raged Imarte. "That creature *cannot* be allowed to interfere with my work, do you understand? It's not even as though he can be trained to live in the wild. He's nothing but a pet."

"That's enough." Porfirio held up his hand. "Juan, take the carcass away now. Downwind, please. We can work out a supplement with chopped beef and an enzyme formula, okay? He'll be fine."

"Okay." Dejectedly Juan picked up the little condor and buttoned him inside his shirt. The bird made happy sounds. Juan took the dead thing by one leg and dragged it away into the darkness. Imarte went flouncing off to her room.

"Ay-ay-ay." Porfirio put his face in his hands. "And was your day good? Tell me your day was good."

"It was good," I said. Einar took down the creel—the coyote twitched and growled in its sleep—and unsaddled our horses. He led them off to the stable, whistling a little tune.

"Hell-oooo, everybody, I'm home," said Oscar as he strode into the circle of firelight, leading his mule. Behind them the patent peddler's cart lurched from side to side, catching its roof on the lower branches of the oak trees.

"And you had a good day too," Porfirio said.

"Oh, first-rate. Finally persuaded Mr. Cielo over at the walnut orchard that he absolutely required the civilizing influence of music in his home. He took a flageolet and six pieces of sheet music. Any day now his neighbors (when he gets them) can expect to hear the strains of popular selections from *The Bohemian Girl* wafting through the walnut trees."

"Nice going." Porfirio poked up the fire. "Get any good material on him?"

"Oh, certainly." Oscar set the hand brake on his cart and let the mule out from between the traces. "Got a fair holo of his kitchen and a splendid one of the parlor, all furnishings in situ. Extensive vocal recordings, too. Got him to tell me half the story of his life. The archivists will be pleased with yours truly, I shouldn't wonder." He patted his mule fondly.

"So that's what you do?" I asked. "You go around pretending to peddle stuff, and while people are talking to you, you record details of historical interest about them?"

"Yes indeed! Though I hasten to add that no pretending is involved. I am a true and bona fide salesman of the first water. It's more than a matter of personal pride with me, you see, that I can play the golden-tongued orator with the best of them when it comes to persuading a reluctant dweller in adobe that he or she wants—nay, *must* have—a patent cherry-pitting device superior to all previous models." Oscar was completely serious.

"Yeah, you are one nickel-plated Demosthenes, all right," Einar said, emerging from the stable to take charge of the mule. "Hey, Amelia, sweetie! How we doing, babe? How's our little hooves today?"

"No trace of lameness, I'm pleased to report," Oscar said. "She appears to have regained her customary surefootedness."

"Great." Einar led her away, and Oscar strutted up to the fire, hands in pockets.

"Yes, a most successful day. Might I inquire what's for supper this evening?"

"Grilled beef, tortillas, and frijoles," Porfirio said. "I just haven't had time to put it on yet."

"H'm." Oscar stood there in the light of the fire, rocking back and forth, a small frown on his bland face. "No chance of any cabbage, I suppose."

"What do you want, man? It's February."

"Oh, quite, quite, I see your point. You know what I'd like to do, though, when we can get a little more garden produce? I'd like to serve you folks a real authentic New England boiled supper. Yes, *sir.* You'd enjoy it no end. I daresay I could make the brown bread to go with it, too. I've got cans of molasses and a cake of raisins in my cart. Just the thing for a nippy night."

"Sure," Porfirio said without enthusiasm. He gave a narrow-eyed smile. "I meant to ask you: have you managed to sell that Criterion Patented Brassbound Pie Safe yet?"

Oscar's face lost some of its aplomb. "Well, no, not yet."

"Aw, that's a shame." Porfirio's grin of sympathy was very white under his mustache. "I can't think why nobody's interested in that thing."

"Neither can I," Oscar said. "You'd think, in this wild country overrun with mice and insects, that the natives would fight for a chance to possess such a marvel of guaranteed safe storage for all manner of comestibles, whether fresh-baked or fried, complete with buttermilk well and yeast compartment!"

I leaned forward, genuinely intrigued. "What is this thing, señor?"

"Ah! Let me show you," said Oscar, running to his cart. Porfirio rolled his eyes at me, but I got up and went to look anyway. Oscar unfastened a couple of latches and opened out one whole side of his cart. Glass jars glinted, and various hanging utensils and tools swung and shone in the firelight; but Oscar gestured past them to a big cabinet kind of thing that took up the entire back wall.

"There you have it. Positively the last word in preservation of fine baked goods. All drawers lined with plated tin to prevent the unwelcome attentions of minor pests such as mice, rats, or voles. And! Regard the patented securing latches designed to foil the marauding efforts of coons, polecats, or possums! Why, given the superb solid-oak construction and high-quality brass reinforcement, I daresay the Criterion Patented Brassbound Pie Safe could withstand even the predations of our friend the bruin."

He didn't know bears very well. Still, I had to admit the thing was impressive. It gleamed with fanciful brass trim all etched and inscribed with curlicue patterns of dizzying complexity. The various locks and latches looked formidable, and in addition to the drawers and cabinets were features at whose purpose I could only begin to guess: weird upswept or recessed sections.

"Gee, Oscar, that's really something," I said.

"Isn't it? And yet—can I interest even one member of the native populace of Los Angeles in this modern marvel? You'd think any one of them would jump at the chance to call it his or her own. Yet here it remains, unpurchased, unowned." Oscar shook his head in bewilderment.

"Well..." I hunted for the words. "You know, Oscar, I've been in California for a hundred and sixty-two years now, and in all that time I don't think I've ever seen a pie. Maybe that's part of the problem? I mean, nobody even grew much wheat here until recently. And this safe was designed for real Yankee-style pies, right? Two crusts, blueberry or rhubarb filling, that kind of thing?"

"True." Oscar looked wistful. "I could go for some rhubarb pie myself this very moment."

"San Francisco," Porfirio remarked from where he was stirring the frijoles. "That's where he could sell it. Not in El Pueblo de la Reina de Los Angeles."

"I beg to differ," Oscar said hotly. "I have sold these people maple syrup, quilting frames, and birch beer extract. I *will* sell this fine item. I simply haven't found the right customer yet."

"There must be plenty of gringos in Los Angeles," I said.

Porfirio grinned. "They don't make many pies. Too busy shooting one another."

"I'll sell it, I say, and not to a fellow Yankee," vowed Oscar. "Do you hear me, sir?"

"What, is this a bet?" said Porfirio, sitting back on his heels. "You want to wager on this?"

"By the goddess of consumer goods, yes! Name the stakes."

"Okay." Porfirio looked thoughtful. "Let's say...I get one of those snappy patent pearl-handled shaving razors you carry, if you don't sell that pie safe before you're transferred out of here. If you *do* sell it to a nongringo, I'll personally prepare that New England boiled supper for you. I'll even eat it with you."

"Then dig yourself a root cellar and lay in the rutabagas and parsnips," said Oscar, eyes flashing. "For I'm at my best when given a challenge, sir, I warn you."

Porfirio turned his attention back to the grilling beef. "Go for it, man" was his reply.

Personally I thought Porfirio would lose the bet. Los Angeles was becoming more of a Yankee city with every passing year. I learned from our copies of the bilingual *Los Angeles Star* that bullfights had at last been outlawed, to be replaced with the more humane pastimes of baseball, Presbyterian prayer services, and debating the outcome of the Civil War.

That Civil War raged on, over on the other end of the continent, at Mill Springs, Pea Ridge, and similar quaint-sounding places. Los Angeles was a world away from that, mired in its own problems. (Literally mired: the new brick sewers were proving a slightly more complicated engineering feat than had been expected.) To my amazement, though, the local Yankees—I must get out of the habit of calling them that, now that about half of them take it as a deadly insult—the *Americans* among us actually staked out sides and fought the war here in their own way, right in front of their bemused Hispanic neighbors. The older Yankee element, the sober sea captains and shopkeepers, were staunchly pro-Union. Banning, the stagecoach fellow, actually took time out from building his fine new house to donate land at San Pedro for a Union army barracks, so his side would have a military presence in California. The trash, the white boys from the States who'd failed at gold prospecting and trapping, were ramping stamping secessionists, so I guess Banning was wise.

Maybe I'll go on calling them Yankees anyway. The Union will win the war, after all. And it's less offensive than calling them Americans, to the people of South America, who have a claim to that word too; and less offensive to the Yankees than calling them Anglos, when so many of them were shipped into this country as Irish bond slaves. Come to think of it, I guess most Latinos don't like being called Hispanic, after the way the conquistadors treated their grandmothers. You can't win, can you?

To me, the whole issue seemed irrelevant, living back in that canyon as I was with the stagecoaches arriving and departing as time and mud permitted. I was more amused by the fact that Mexico was now in danger of becoming French. It should have warned me that I was out of touch, that I'd been in the hills too long. But for three hundred years now, the only political reality had been the long slow ruin of Old Spain's fortunes in the New World. These Kentuckians, these Narragansettians, these absurd Cape Codders, I knew they too were destined for their part on the world stage. But I was perhaps too slow in realizing that the curtain had already risen on their act. How could it affect me, after all? Nothing in the pageant of mortal fools had been able to affect me since the English Reformation, and I'd sworn never to let anything else get to me again.

"OUT OF MASA," announced Einar, rummaging through the storeroom. "Out of brown sugar. Out of coffee. Half a bag of pinto beans. You want me to go to the store, chief?"

"Good idea. You can take those damn coyotes to the transport depot too, how about it?" Porfirio said.

"Okay, okay. I didn't think they'd make that much noise. The last batch didn't."

"You're going into town?" Imarte stuck her head out of her room. "Will you wait until I'm dressed? I'd like to go down to the Bella Union."

"I wasn't planning on staying overnight," Einar said.

"Don't worry. I'll catch the next stagecoach home." She ducked back into her room, and there was a great rustling of silks and creaking of whalebone. I was wondering why she didn't walk back—I would have, because the pueblo didn't look that far away from up on the ridge—when Einar turned to me and asked:

"How about it? You want to come?"

I blinked at him in surprise. "Okay," I said, deciding to continue my program of readaptation to human company, though it did seem a bit reckless. If there were bloodthirsty crazies hiding out in the chaparral, how many more of them would be in the infamous saloons and gambling dens? On the other hand, I'd have to visit the place some-time, and Einar seemed able enough with a gun.

I went to put on my best shawl and pin up my hair. By the time I came out, Einar had hitched a pair of horses to our wagon. Imarte came sashaying from the adobe, complete with painted face, scarlet satins, and feather boa.

"Wow, you really do look like a whore," I complimented her, with my most naive expression.

"Thank you. You won't mind riding in the back with the coy-otes, will you, dear?" She vaulted into the seat beside Einar. "This satin crushes so terribly, the least little thing makes wrinkles that simply won't come out. I envy you that plain broadcloth. And how lucky you are to be able to wear that color. Dirt and stains are almost invisible on that particular shade of—what would you call it? Olive drab?"

"Matches your eyes, doesn't it?" I said, clambering up into the back, where the month's catch of *Canis latrans* slept soundly in their crates.

"Break it up, ladies," Porfirio snapped at us. I shelved my next re-mark, which had to do with the bitches I was riding with. You know, in the twenty-second century the feminist Ephesian Party will bid for political power on the grounds that if women ran the world, there would be less senseless aggression. Strangely, they'll never be able to get a consensus within their own party. Can you imagine why not?

"Let's have a nice happy little drive into town, shall we?" Einar said. He clucked to the horses, and we bumped and rolled away down the canyon, to turn right on the dirt road that was El Camino Real and would one day be the Hollywood Freeway.

"Check it out!" Einar pointed with his whip as we rumbled along. "Hollywood Bowl, back up in there. *Symphonies under the Stars*. That hill over there? Whitley Heights, where all the movie stars live before Beverly Hills is fashionable. Rudolph Valentino will have a house right *there*."

"I've never seen one of his films," I said. "I really ought to, sometime."

Einar half-turned in his seat as an idea hit him. "We should have a film festival! We can show them after dark. All the great Golden Age of Cinema stuff. I wonder if I can get films that were shot right here in town."

"Probably." Imarte sniffed. "You could try to find the interesting ones. There are only a few with any historical value, in my opinion."

"We'll do it," said Einar, bouncing on his seat. "We'll have the first film festival in Hollywood, how about it? I'll see what I can order from Central HQ."

We emerged from Cahuenga Pass and swung left down the track of the future Hollywood Boulevard, where Einar gave us a running commentary on the famous sights we couldn't see yet. I remember the corner of Hollywood and Vine, not for any precognitive vision of Clara Bow zooming around it in a fast car but because we had to bump through a particularly vicious seasonal creek that cut across it, and mud splattered Imarte's scarlet finery. I was proud of myself for not smiling.

As we entered the plain below the foothills, the land opened out more and changed: low green hills gently rolling as far as the eye could see, dotted with oak trees and starred everywhere with golden poppies. Here and there wandered herds of longhorn cattle, grazing and growing fat.

"See those guys?" Einar's voice was sober. "This is their last hurrah. Nobody knows it yet, of course, but this drought will pretty much wipe them out. And when they go, the old Mexican gentry go too; they'll lose their revenue, get into debt to the Yankees, and sell off their estates. Boom, whole way of life gone. The Yankees will run cattle after the drought, but not these longhorns: they'll bring in their own stock, Jerseys and Holsteins—Eurocows. All kinds of useful genetic traits scheduled to disappear from the bovine gene pool when these longhorns nearly go extinct. It'll be a bitch collecting specimens—expensive, too—but I really should get started on it."

"Why expensive?" Imarte asked. "I should imagine the rancheros will be desperate to sell, once the drought is in progress."

"Yeah, but by then the specimens will be weak and stressed out. The Company wants healthy, happy cows." Einar shook his head.

I sat up and stared at the gentle landscape, so pastoral, such an idyll. Cracked earth and skeletons soon, to be followed by another Eden, this time of prosperous little Yankee orange groves, to be followed by a gray wasteland of diesel exhaust, concrete, and steel. Paradise and hell, boom and bust, together forever in Los Angeles. I shivered and wished I was back in Big Sur.

We followed the Hollywood Freeway route all the way into the city, creaked gradually uphill, and paused at the top of a long low ridge. Einar pointed at the vista below us, a wide gesture taking in the whole horizon. "There you go, Mendoza. The original wretched hive of villainy and scum."

It didn't look particularly dangerous. What surprised me was the space it took up. It sprawled and sprawled, out to the edges of the sky, and yet you could count the number of two-story buildings on the fingers of one hand. Right below us was a squat brick thing like an armory in a weedy central plaza crisscrossed with dirt paths. I found out later that it was a cistern for dry years. There was a solid-looking church with its back to us—recently repaired, to judge from the two-tone plaster. There were a couple of stately adobes with pink tile roofs and peeling whitewash. But the vast majority of structures were little flat-topped shacks with tarred roofs, rows of them leaning on one another and single ones peeping out from orchards or ranged across fields. I couldn't see a single living soul moving in that vast panorama. You could have fit every other city in California into the space Los Angeles took up, and yet it looked like nothing so much as somebody's big cow pasture, with an unusual number of cowsheds. A dark line of willows and cottonwoods snaked through it, and one particularly big sycamore: the trees must have marked the bed of the Los Angeles River, which actually had water in it this year.

Crack! A bullet tore up weeds a few yards down the hill from where we were parked. Oh, here was somebody. We looked down into the belligerent stare of a man who had come out to the edge of his little orchard. He was lowering a long rifle.

"Thass a *wahnin'*!" he called hoarsely. "Y'all stay *outa* mah orchard. Come down some *otha* place!"

Einar grinned and signed tipping his hat. "You bet, Davy Crockett!" He shook the reins and turned us around, and we followed the trail along the ridge and down into town. Well, it was clear where all the people must be: hiding. My knuckles were white as I clenched the sides of the wagon.

"Does everybody shoot at perfect strangers here?" I asked between clenched teeth.

"If they think you're going to trespass on their property, yeah," said Einar. He began to sing a ballad about Davy Crockett, waving one arm for dramatic emphasis.

"Oh, shut up," said Imarte, and for once I agreed with her.

There actually was a business district, with some Yankee-style stores of brick and of timber, and a couple of adobes Yankeefied with false fronts. Here was where all the people had got to. There were wagons like ours rumbling to and fro, driven by Mexicans or Yankees. There were white boys leaning in the doorways of saloons, looking out at the world through painfully narrowed Clint Eastwood eyes. There were Mexican dons on elegantly caparisoned horses pacing along, and some of these were distinctly African in appearance: dignified old gentlemen whose great-grandfathers had bought their way out of slavery by joining the Spanish army and exploring the New World. And here was a genuine Indian begging in the gutter, with eerily empty eyes. Imarte leaned over and said a few words to him as we passed. His gaze snapped into focus for a moment and locked on her. He shouted something in a desperate voice and stumbled after the wagon, dragging one foot. Imarte made a face and tossed him a coin. He fell flat, covering it with his body. I looked away. Imarte shook her head.

"That man's race once conquered all their neighbors, for hundreds of miles to the north and east. They had a sophisticated monotheistic religion the equal of Christianity or Islam. Look at him now." *Sic transit Chinigchinix,* I thought.

In the next block, we passed another prostrate beggar, drunk and wailing out "Flow Gently, Sweet Afton" in ghastly Southend Cockney. Two gutters over, an obvious native of Georgia was murdering "Sweet Betsy from Pike." And a Mexican crawling along on hands and knees implored his little white dove to return to his embrace. The mud is a democratic place, at least.

And here were *señoritas de mala vida,* dressed like our Imarte, liberally represented by the assorted races, swinging along with the set smiles, upper-arm bruises, and blank eyes of the true professional. And a Chinese fellow going somewhere in quiet, self-effacing haste. And an august old shopkeeper standing just inside the door of his emporium and jingling his keys as he watched the passing scene: a Jew, to judge from the name painted on his sign. He looked exactly like Uncle Sam. Put him in a striped top hat and long tailcoat, and he could have posed for a twentieth-century war bond poster.

On Calle Principal we pulled up in front of a little place whose sign read BELLA UNION. It was dark and dirty. Imarte jumped down from her seat with the grace of a cat and made straight for the door, a gleam in her eye.

"Wait a minute," Einar said, sliding down. "Marcus has something in his hoof. Whats'a matter, boy?"

I climbed down while he coaxed the horse to put its foot up for him. Was the hotel as bad inside as it looked from the street? I ventured close enough to peer inside. God, it was worse. That couldn't be a dirt floor, could it?

There at the long bar was Imarte, advancing on the British tar who had just been served a local beer and was now staring at his glass with horrified wonder.

"Hello there, sailor. In town long?" she said, flexing a tit at him. "Got time to tell me your life story?"

He turned to meet her eyes. "It's like piss, for Chrissake!" he complained.

Silly me, to stand in the doorway of a lesser class of hotel looking amused. A regular customer mistook my smile and was suddenly in front of me, breathing rye whiskey through the fringe of his mustache.

"Well, now, señorita, you looking for someone to dance with? You want me to show you how we dance the fandango out Durango way, huh? Nice earrings. They real gold, Chiquita?" He reached for my face.

I took two hasty steps backward and summoned up my best Katherine Hepburn imitation. "Sir, if you *ever* presume to lay hands upon me, I assure you legal action will follow! Do I make myself clear, you palsied, imbecilic, and alcoholic cretin?"

He staggered back, very surprised. "Lady, I'm sorry," he gasped. "I thought you was Spanish."

Mental note: Leave the gold hoops at home next time you visit sunny downtown Los Angeles. And ditch the rebozo, too. I turned on my heel and stalked out. Einar was just releasing Marcus's hoof. He stared at me openmouthed. "You went in there?"

"Stupid, wasn't it?" I agreed, climbing up on the seat. "Let's get the hell out of here, shall we?" I didn't like mortals, I *really* didn't like mortals. In fact, I hated the sight and the smell of them.

"Come on, I'll buy you a drink," he said.

"Not in there, you won't."

He got his crazy smile again. "How about a cocktail in the Lost City of the Lizard People?"

It turned out that if you went to a drab-looking little adobe on Calle Primavera and knocked, a mortal man would let you in and obligingly help you unload your crates of tranquilized coyotes. He would then slide back a section of the floor, revealing a service elevator, on which the coyotes descended toward a new life following air transport to a Company zoo. The man would then bow you to an ornate wardrobe, which, when opened, proved to be a passenger elevator. Once you entered it, it dropped with unnerving speed thirty stories to a short length of tunnel tiled in gold enamel. At the end of the tunnel was a first-rate Company cocktail lounge, beyond which was a Company transport terminal, also tiled in gold enamel.

"There's miles of tunnel, running all the way to the undersea base in the Catalina Channel," Einar told me over a couple of margaritas. "And one long tunnel runs out to the Mojave base under the sand."

"Nice." I bit into my wedge of lime. "But what's with the lizard motif?" I waved a hand at the decor. There were lizard patterns on everything, woven into the carpet, tooled into the booth leather, printed on the cocktail napkins.

"Joke," he said. "In 1934, this guy will claim that an old Indian told him about a highly advanced race of lizard people who retreated underground following a global catastrophe in 3000 B.C.E. They built a city in the shape of a giant lizard and a maze of gold-filled tunnels right here under Los Angeles, supposedly, using magic chemicals that melted through bedrock. Rooms crammed with gold and sacred tablets, all kinds of weird shit. So anyway, this guy claims he's found out where the gold chambers are, using an invention he calls the Radio X-Ray, and he actually gets permission from the city authorities to drill. Tells them he's located a treasure room a thousand feet down. He only goes about three hundred fifty feet before the shaft starts to collapse. Tells the city he's putting the dig on hold until he can solve the technical problems, which he expects to do in no time. Then he vanishes. Drops out of sight. Never heard from again. Obviously the lizard people got him."

"Obviously."

"It gets weirder. This'll be in 1934, right? But by 1932 the Company will have abandoned this base and filled in the tunnels. Earthquake in Long Beach the next year, remember? By the time the guy claims to detect the tunnels, *they won't be there anymore.* Last call at the old Lizard Bar was months beforehand. Nuts, huh?"

"Nuts. Unless maybe the man is an undiagnosed remote viewer."

"Could be." Einar tilted his glass. "Want another cocktail?"

*A*FTER THAT VISIT I was content to stay close to Hollywood, venturing out to collect specimens when Einar's schedule allowed him to go with me. No more argument on my part that I didn't need an escort. Hot lead seemed to be the language of social encounter down there, and I felt squeamish about becoming fluent in it, though I dutifully practiced hyperfunction with a Navy pistol.

We were by no means so isolated as I had thought. We got mail; we got magazines. We subscribed to the *Los Angeles Estrella/Star,* to a couple of back-east papers so we could follow the Civil War news, and Porfirio had a subscription to *Punch,* of all things. I read it for the humor, though the British slant on the war was strange. They played both sides of the diplomatic fence with a prissy hypocrisy that I took to be Victorian. I wasn't impressed. I had known the brilliant savages of the Tudor period firsthand, and, though I'd never thought I'd say it, I preferred them to their smug descendants.

Yes, we really had our window onto the world, despite the lack of radio for the local Company news—no reception back in our canyon, because those granite hills kept the feeble broadcast out. And we made our own nightlife; we even had movies. Not holos, you understand, movies.

I woke from uneasy dreams one bright morning to find a card stuck in my boots. Yawning, I examined it, sitting on the edge of my cot. It was cream-colored pasteboard, inscribed by hand in purple ink, with nice calligraphy, and it told me that I was invited to the Cahuenga Pass Film Festival, which was to take place tonight at 2000 hours sharp. This evening's featured film: Hollywood's first premiere of the director's cut of *Greed,* based on Frank Norris's classic novel *McTeague,* a tale of mortal doom. Approximate screening time nine hours, so refreshments would be provided. Formal dress optional. (Good; the closest thing I had to evening wear was a black rebozo.) Location: suite B of the Cahuenga Pass Hilton. (Yuck yuck.) My host: Einar.

I pulled on my boots and wandered out to the fire, where Porfirio was frying breakfast. "Did you get one of these?" I held the card out to him. "What's it all about?"

"Didn't you hear him chortling when the afternoon stage left yesterday?" Porfirio said, handing me a mug of coffee, which I accepted gratefully. "He got a big box he'd ordered from Central HQ. He was fussing around in his room all last night. He's in there now, as a matter of fact. This should be some party."

"I guess." I looked at the card doubtfully. "Will we all fit in his room? I'm not much for parties, really."

"It's not a party party, it's a film screening. He's working like a dog to create a sense of occasion. I'm going, and you should too." Porfirio looked at me sternly. "What else have you got to do tonight? Sit in your room and look at plant DNA? This will be good for you."

Actually I enjoyed sitting in my room in front of a cozily glowing credenza, but I didn't want to disappoint Einar. Accordingly, at 2000 hours that evening I wrapped my black shawl around me and ventured into the adobe. I could see lamplight coming from Einar's room; and was that music? It sounded like a selection of famous film themes by Hollywood composers, tinnily played on a battery-powered portable, and that in fact was what it was. But I barely noticed the music once I crossed the threshold of Einar's room.

He *had* worked to create a sense of occasion. It was a small square room with bare adobe walls and rough furniture of peeled logs and cowhide; but he had borrowed Imarte's red velveteen bedspread and tacked it up in hanging swags against one wall, and a dusty oriental carpet had been rolled out on the floor, and a fairly clean sheet had been tacked up on another wall. That had to have come from Imarte's bed, too. In fact, there was a lot of her finery draped around to give the room a film palace look. She was being an awfully good sport about this, wasn't she? And there she stood in a ballgown of Arrest Me Red, holding forth sententiously to Oscar:

"...outrageous what they did to von Stroheim, but it's a classic case of the fate of great literature in Hollywood. Of course it was bound to happen, given the incredible social significance of Norris's work. Audiences simply weren't ready for the grim realism, the pitiless examination of hopelessness among the uneducated working classes, the dwindling of the American Dream to despair, the ugly realities of passion."

"You don't say?" Oscar raised a graniteware coffee mug to his lips and took a cautious sip of the contents. He looked startled. "Good Lord, Einar, is this gin we're drinking?"

"Sure is," Einar said, welcoming me with a bow and handing me my libation for the evening. He was resplendent in a black tailcoat, stiff collar, and flowing foulard tie. He'd greased and combed his hair back, and so had Porfirio, also dressed to the nines. They looked like a couple of cast members from a melodrama. "It's a martini, complete with olive. Don't worry, the gin hasn't been anywhere near a bathtub. Mendoza, you look lovely this evening; pray be seated. A space has been reserved for you in the balcony." He gestured grandly at his cowhide bed, which had been dressed up with needlepoint cushions. "You too, Imarte; and as highest-ranking cyborg here, Porfirio, you have the seat of honor between the ladies, okay? The rest of us gentlemen will be seated in the loge. Well, we're only waiting for J. B. to make his fashionably late entrance—"

"Here I am. Sorry," murmured Juan Bautista from the doorway. Apparently he had no shirts that weren't plain calico, but he'd made a pasteboard shirtfront, inked a bow tie and little buttons on it, and pinned it to his chest. He'd made a little shirtfront for Erich von Stroheim too, and tied it around the bird's repulsive neck with string. Erich huddled in his arms, looking at us doubtfully.

"Cool! The director himself, here to attend his first Hollywood premiere!" Einar welcomed them in. "Have a seat, gentlemen, down in the loge—or maybe that's the mezzanine." It amounted to a row of pillows on the floor in front of the bed. Juan Bautista settled down comfortably crosslegged, and Oscar lowered into place beside him, grumbling about having to press his trousers tomorrow. Erich von Stroheim took an experimental peck at his own shirtfront, but Juan Bautista reproved him gently, closing his fingers around the nasty-looking beak. The bird lowered his head to be scratched, making a little pleading noise.

"Well, the appointed hour is upon us," said Einar, stepping to the front of the room, before the white sheet. He took his six-gun from his holster, and I half-expected him to shoot out the lamps, but he reversed it and held the butt to his face, pretending he was speaking into a microphone. "Ladies and gentlemen..." He altered his voice to sound as though he were speaking into a twentieth-century PA system, complete with the boom and squeal of badly adjusted speakers. "Ladies and gentlemen and, uh, condor, welcome to the first installment of the first-ever Cahuenga Pass Film Festival. And what a glittering turnout we have here tonight. We're pleased to present, as our first offering, Director Erich von Stroheim's immortal classic *Greed*, starring Jean Hersholt and Zasu Pitts. Do I see the director in the audience? Stand up and take a bow, Mr. von Stroheim!" Juan Bautista held up the bird and dipped him forward in a little bow. Erich gronked querulously and pecked to have his head scratched again. We all applauded.

"Thank you, Mr. von Stroheim. All right. Now, tonight's offering is one of the truly great films cinema has produced. Unlike most of our future offerings, it was *not* filmed primarily in Hollywood, mostly because the director was a raving fanatic about location shots. Notable examples are the authentic San Francisco sequences shot on Polk Street and the climactic scene in Death Valley, which nearly killed the cast and crew as temperatures soared to 120 degrees Fahrenheit and the camera equipment had to be iced down.

"The location shots were necessary, because von Stroheim insisted on a literal interpretation of the book, which meant he filmed *every single scene*. Unfortunately, the age of the miniseries had not yet arrived, and the resulting nine-hour spectacle was edited down by Universal executives to a much smaller masterpiece. Von Stroheim never forgave the studio, and they never forgave him either, which was why the rest of his cinematic career was pretty much limited to his role as Gloria Swanson's butler in *Sunset Boulevard*.

"Anyhow, Doctor Zeus will have a quick-fingered operative in the cutting room, with the result that we are able to present tonight the full-length director's cut, made from the original silver nitrate print, complete with the Variety Theater scene in its original version and the subplot involving the crazed Mexican cleaning woman and her Jewish pawnbroker boyfriend. I should warn the more sensitive in our audience that some of the material is really, *really* racially offensive, okay? So I apologize to our Hispanic audience members in advance, and also to anybody who might have been Jewish when they were mortal—?" He looked inquiringly at Imarte.

"I was *Chaldean*," she corrected him.

I put up my hand. "I was arrested by the Inquisition. Does that count?"

"I think that makes you an honorary Jew," Porfirio said.

"Okay," continued Einar, "just don't get sore. Now, before we begin, I'd like to serve refreshments." He went to the corner table and took down two big bowls of popcorn and handed them out. "Eat hearty. There will be brief intermissions when I change reels, because, no, ladies and gentlemen, this is not a holo! Tonight's entertainment comes to you in the authentic and time-honored medium of reel cinema." He gestured dramatically to the corner, where he'd opened out the primitive-looking projector and connected it with alligator clamps to a solar battery unit. "So without further ado, distinguished audience..."

Einar blew out the lamps one after another, killed the music, and stepped over Oscar to reach the projector. A click and a buzz, a white light on the screen briefly occluded by his head and shoulders as he groped his way back to his seat; then the flickering images held our attention, and the only sound was the faint whirring of the projector and the crunching of popcorn.

It was a great film. Horrible unrelenting tragedy, but you couldn't be depressed watching it, because you were constantly exhilarated at what a work of bloody genius it was. Have you ever seen it, señors? From the opening scenes in the mining town, where you meet this appalling, tender-hearted ogre who protects little birds but is willing to kill his fellow men with a backhand blow, to his astonishing transformation into a *dentist*, for Christ's sake, to the banal and doomed love story with the girl who won the lottery—their degeneration, she into a grasping harpy, he into a bestial drunk—and the murder, the chase across the desert, the final scenes where the poor monster finds himself handcuffed to a dead man on the floor of Death Valley, the last frames where he watches the expiring flutters of the damn canary he's brought along with him, cage and all, on his flight from justice— I tell you, it beats Hamlet for craziness and black humor in tragedy. Not a ray of hope in a frame of it.

So why did we sit there enthralled for nine hours, never saying a word? The last frames unrolled, the progressively longer shots of the wretched mortal's end winked out, and the screen went white. It was 0500 hours. There was silence but for Juan Bautista's stifled sob.

"That poor canary," he gasped.

Imarte began to applaud, and we all joined in, even Juan Bautista. And I think our applause counted for something. We're immortals, after all. We've watched history itself unspool before our eyes. It takes a lot to impress us. So even though the real Erich von Stroheim had yet to be born on the night we watched *Greed*, I hope his shade heard our ovation for his butchered masterpiece. I hope he was appeased, somewhere, somehow.

I WAS SO IMPRESSED with the film, I accessed the text of *McTeague* and read it through in the following days, as the inn drowsed between stagecoach visits.

On a good day we got two passing through, pausing long enough to let off or pick up mail or passengers. If one of the horses was in need of attention, Porfirio got out his farrier's tools while the passengers wandered up and down our little canyon or availed themselves of our remarkably clean and tidy outhouse. Imarte would hurry to entertain them; if it was a group of mixed couples, she'd leave off the feather boa and play gracious hostess rather than daughter of joy. She'd do whatever it took to get them talking to her about themselves. There were in-depth interviews with an Italian opera singer headed for San Francisco, a Scot in a genuine kilt (sporran and all), two Basque wool magnates who might have been identical twins though they weren't, and a Mormon patriarch from San Bernardino, who proposed marriage to Imarte on half an hour's acquaintance. She was genuinely regretful at having to turn him down. ("What an incredible opportunity to study a fascinating mutation of American folk morality!") I mostly slunk away into the oaks when passengers were around. Mortals got on my nerves, these days.

They never spent the night, unless they were Company operatives passing through. Porfirio would explain politely that all our rooms were presently occupied, and the *señores y señoras* would most certainly find lodging at the Garnier brothers' inn farther up the highway. If the *señores y señoras* got ugly about it, a bottle of aguardiente was offered for the road; if that failed to mollify them, Einar would swagger into sight with his bandoliers and look menacing.

But once in a while one of our own would climb out and have his or her trunk handed down, and there'd be anecdote swapping and aguardiente far into the night. Usually the trunks were full of high-tech stuff we'd ordered, processing credenza replacement parts or refills for Einar's tranquilizer gun. When they left on the next stage, they took with them DNA material, coded transcripts, and anything too solid to transmit or too small to bother shipping from the Lost City of the Lizard People.

I was out behind the stable one afternoon helping Einar crate up an antelope (obtained in Antelope Valley, where else?), when Juan Bautista came running to find us, hugging Erich awkwardly. The damn bird was growing.

"You guys! Come see, the stage just pulled in, and it's a Concord!"

"No kidding?" Einar dropped his pressure sealer, and we both ran to look, eager to admire the lines of the Rolls-Royce of stagecoaches. Butterfield had used *only* Concords, of course, which was maybe why it didn't want to risk them cross-country with a war on. So how had Banning managed to get his hands on the gorgeously engineered thing we saw sitting at our humble embarkation point? I never found out; and I never had much leisure to wonder about it, either, because while Einar and Juan Bautista were checking it out ("Body by Fisher, man!"), I realized with a start that I actually recognized a friend among the passengers.

Have you gentlemen ever noticed how rare that is with us immortals? Of course we run into acquaintances now and again—I had known Imarte before, unfortunately—but why is it that we almost never get stationed anywhere near old *friends*? Does this have something to do with one of the Company's famous secret agendas? Not that I'd ask if I wasn't higher than a kite. It's the Theobromos talking.

The mortal passengers saw a rather bulky and foreign-looking gentleman help his drab wife out of the passenger compartment, and then raise his hand to assist their colored servant down from her seat by the driver. If they noticed his gallant gesture toward the black lady, they probably raised an eyebrow. But California was a Free State, and people didn't care as much about race relations out here, between blacks and whites anyway.

She was a beautiful woman. Tiny and elegant, with ebony skin that glowed as though polished and fine West African features. Her hair was braided up, but I knew that if she let it down and shook it out, it would wave around her shoulders like a storm cloud.

Nancy? I transmitted in astonishment.

She lifted her head, saw me, and smiled, and she still had the tiniest gap between her front teeth when she smiled. There had been a boy in our graduating class who wrote an impassioned poem to that little gap.

Mendoza? Can that be you?

I nodded dumbly, feeling every one of the years since the last time I saw her, at our commencement party in 1553. I was on a transport to Spain shortly after, and she went to do research work at a base under the Sahara. I heard later on that she'd had a very successful career in Italy and Algiers, but we never kept track of each other; you don't keep track when you're busy in the field. I never have, at least.

She lowered her eyes and played the docile maid for the mortal passengers, fetching the drab wife's reticule and parasol from where they'd been forgotten, while the big fellow saw to their trunks. Porfirio led up the change of horses, and I could see him double-taking on the wife, though she looked like Miss Kansas Corn to me. She turned to him, too, and there was evidently an exchange of some kind; for as soon as the stage rattled away, leaving the three immortals there, she screamed like a steam whistle and fell on him in an embrace.

"Porfirio! You goddam son of a whore, you look *great!*" she said.

"Eucharia!" he said, and they staggered around and around in a prolonged hug. The big man, meanwhile, took Nancy's hands in his

and was leaning over her, evidently murmuring anxious queries as to
her well-being during the ride. She smiled and said something reas-
suring. He bent and kissed her face.

I gawked. You see, *he was an immortal too.* In all the years I'd
worked for Dr. Zeus, I never, ever saw a pair of immortals in love
with each other. I thought it just didn't happen. Our teenaged neophytes have crushes on anything that moves, of course, but full-
grown immortals put all that behind them. Don't they? Plenty of
affectionate friendships, even noisily affectionate ones like what Porfirio and the bleached-out lady from the Midwest apparently shared,
but romance? No.

She was leading him by his big bear paw up the slope to me, her
eyes sparkling. "Dearest," she said to him, "allow me to present my
oldest friend. Mendoza and I have known each other since we were
neophytes together. How many years has it been?" She put out her
arms, and we hugged. I hadn't hugged anybody since 1700. It felt
strange.

"Three hundred and nine," I said. "But who's this?"

The big man bowed. "Vasilii Vasilievitch Kalugin, mademoiselle, at
your service. I am indebted to you for an excellent botanical survey of
the Novy Albion region, though you may not recall the occasion—?"

I accessed hurriedly and suddenly placed the name. "In 1831. *You*
were that operative up at Fort Ross?"

"The very same. My eternal thanks." He took my hand and
kissed it. The clothing was aristocratic Russian; but the accent was ex-
quisitely Continental, as was hers now. She wore her servant's calico
with her customary grace and style, and believe me, they didn't in the
least look mismatched as a couple. Some of Kalugin's bulk was his
Russian coat, but he was genuinely a big guy, with sort of harsh sneer-
ing features in a round pink face framed by amazing muttonchop
whiskers. His eyes were timid and kindly, though, and he couldn't
keep them turned from her for long.

"I'll just go bring up the trunks, shall I, my love?" He squeezed
her hand. "Your pardon, mademoiselle. I return directly. I daresay

you ladies have much to discuss, no?" He turned and bustled after the trunks like an anxious husband. Gosh, he was cute.

"Well!" I burst out laughing, and she just stood there looking happy. "When did *he* happen to you?"

"We've known each other since 1699," she said. "It's a long story."

Sixteen ninety-nine? That was just before I'd been posted to California. "I'll bet. And you're really—? He's really—? It's love?"

"Yes," she said, turning to watch him. "Oh, Mendy, it is."

Mendy. God, the years were rolling back. "So, like, are you married?"

"In a manner of speaking. Not as mortals marry, of course. We've exchanged certain vows of our own. Our work has parted us frequently, years at a time, on occasion. Fortunately the Company is understanding and arranges our work near each other whenever possible."

"What's he do?"

"He's a marine salvage technician," she said, and I nodded, because she was an art conservation specialist. I couldn't think their jobs would overlap much.

"So he's away at sea a lot? But what are you two doing here in California?"

"All those San Francisco millionaires are returning from Europe with art treasures for their mansions," she said. "Half of them will be beggars within the next five years, and their collections will be blown to the four winds. I'm doing a preliminary survey before Beckman's sent in. It should be easy to get domestic positions. I have several letters of recommendation from persons of the highest quality, all giving me an excellent character." She smiled, narrowing her eyes. "As you are doubtless aware, although California is technically a Free State, it is inadvisable for a Negress to travel alone. Kalugin has been assigned duties in San Francisco, and dear Eucharia agreed to travel with us to lend *respectability* to our journey."

Eucharia was stepping back from Porfirio and regarding him, hands on hips. "We'll have a high old time tonight," she said. "Got any tequila?"

"No, and no Southern Comfort, either," replied Porfirio, and that set both of them roaring with laughter. I guess there was some history there. I hadn't seen Porfirio smile like that in the whole time I'd been there, not a real smile like he was enjoying himself.

"But what of you?" Nancy took my hand. "Have you been happy?"

"Happy? I—well, of course. I've mostly worked alone, you know, back in the mountains. Remember how I wanted to come here after I graduated, how I made New World grains my specialty? Well, the Company finally noticed. Here I've been, years and years now."

"I heard about what happened in England," she said quietly, looking at my hand. "I was so sorry. I wrote to you."

I shivered. "I was in therapy for a while. I probably never got your letter. Well, it was a long time ago, and I'm over it now. But thank you for writing."

"Here we are!" Kalugin came puffing up the trail, a trunk under either arm. "Everything seems to have survived the journey, Nan. Will you do me the kindness of showing me where I can stow these, mademoiselle?"

"This way." I gestured, and took one of the trunks from him and swung it up to my shoulder. He made a little dismayed sound but followed me to the adobe, where I led them down the long corridor to the guest room that was kept for visiting operatives. "Here you are. Don't be scared of the cowhide bed, they're actually very comfortable," I said. "Dinner at 2000 hours, alfresco. The menu includes such authentic regional delicacies as grilled beef, frijoles, and tortillas, but I should warn you that a tortilla here bears no resemblance to the Spanish item of the same name."

"Yes, I've discovered that." Kalugin hastened to relieve me of the trunk. "Allow me, that really is too heavy for a lady."

I could lift a horse, let alone a trunk, if I had to, like any cyborg; but how sweet of the man.

I left them alone to get the dust of the journey out of their teeth, and went to pace around in the oak trees for a while. Was I happy for my old friend? Yes, unquestionably; but I didn't want to be reminded of being young, or of England, or of the mortal man who had died there so long ago. He was after me again, following me relentlessly from shadow to shadow through the trees.

Eucharia helped Porfirio prepare supper for the rest of us, but then the two of them disappeared into the night with pistols, a small box of ammunition, and a lot of aguardiente. Imarte was away on one of her sleepovers at the Bella Union, thankfully, and Oscar had trekked far afield on his quest for a buyer for the Criterion Patented Brassbound Pie Safe; so the company around the cookfire was fairly intimate that evening. Juan Bautista even brought out his guitar.

"But how charming," Nancy said. "That was made in Old Spain, was it not? And by a master, to judge from the inlay work."

"Yes, ma'am," said Juan Bautista in a tiny voice. He'd fallen in love with her, desperately, of course. "One of the mortal travelers left it. Lucky chance, huh?"

"Can you play it?" I peered at him across the firelight. "I've never seen you actually play it, Juan."

"Sure he can," said Einar, putting another log on the fire. "I hear him practicing sometimes."

"I play for Erich von Stroheim," Juan Bautista said. When Nancy and Kalugin stared at him, he hastened to add: "My condor. Baby condor. I rescued him. It helps him get to sleep sometimes when he's nervous."

"Ah, of course," Kalugin said with a nod of understanding. "Would you perhaps do us the honor of playing for us now?"

Juan Bautista hung his head and fiddled with the tuning pegs. "Sure," he muttered. I braced myself, expecting him to clutch painfully at the frets in a beginner's "(I Can't Get No) Satisfaction,"

but to my astonishment he went into a classic Segovia piece, and it
flowed out on the night air smooth as coffee with cream. He kept on
with beautiful classical stuff all evening, Rodrigo and de Falla and
Five Jaguar, quiet and unobtrusive, the background to our talk.

"I have to know," I said, leaning forward, "how the two of you
met. It's so rare, you know, for any of us to find...what you've
found."

"It was terribly romantic," Kalugin said, smiling where he lay
with his head in Nan's lap. "I'd been in a shipwreck, and washed up
on the coast of Morocco. She was all in silks and bangles, third wife
to one of the sultan's corsairs."

Einar leaned his chin on his fist and grunted. "Our anthropologist
will be disappointed she didn't get a chance to talk with you."

Nancy opened her reticule. "I'll leave her one of my calling cards.
It is, after all, the correct thing to do in these circumstances in polite
society."

"Calling cards," I said. She nodded serenely and handed me a tiny
square of pasteboard, embossed, beautifully engraved. I read:

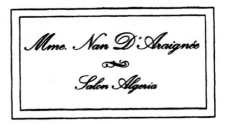

"D'Araignée?" I asked.

"An artistic decision," she said. "French for *spider,* you see. I have
always retained the clearest memories of the folktales of my mortal parents. Indeed, I can scarcely recall anything else from my mortal life."

I remembered the angry four-year-old girl that she'd been, telling
me how the spider god of her tribe had deserted them, saving only her.

"Anansi," she said. "The friend and helper of men, as I understand
from my researches into the work of M. Griaule and Mr. Parrinder."

I stared into the fire. The immortal operative who'd rescued the child must have named her for the word she repeated most often, thinking it sounded like Nancy. Had the little girl been calling on her god? Had she finally made her peace with him now, since she'd taken his name for her own? I'd never made peace with mine.

But how wonderful, what style she had, to what good use she'd put her anger.

"What's Salon Algeria?" I asked.

"One of the Company safe houses in Paris," she said. "I reside there when Dr. Zeus has no pressing errand on which to send me. And it's useful, too; a certain segment of the artistic denizens on the Left Bank know that I am always interested in seeing canvases, and perhaps paying cash for them. Regretfully, members of the criminal class are also aware of this, and I'm afraid I have purchased stolen paintings on more than one occasion." She shrugged. "One has the consolation of knowing that everything one purchases in this way will survive for the ages rather than burn in the political upheavals with which France is so frequently visited these days."

I nodded. God, she even had a home.

"What were you doing in a shipwreck?" Juan Bautista raised his head and looked at Kalugin. "I thought we always know when a ship's going to sink."

"We do," Kalugin told him ruefully. "But when history records that a ship's going to disappear with all hands, young man, she becomes fair game for the Company. And when history records that she carries valuable cargo, the Company acts. Most people suppose a marine salvage technician is some sort of diver, and it's true; but, you see, I don't go down after the wreck. I go down *with* it."

This extraordinary statement was followed by a distant salvo of gunfire, followed by wild laughter from somewhere up the canyon. Porfirio and Eucharia were apparently target shooting by infrared.

"Anyone can dive down to retrieve gold or jewels," Kalugin explained. "They aren't spoiled by a little seawater. But what about manuscripts, paintings, Stradivarius violins? You need someone there, on the scene, someone with the knowledge of what's to come, who can secure all those perishable treasures in sealed containers before the ship sinks. You need someone to ride the poor wreck to her final resting place, and transmit exact coordinates on her location to a Company salvage team. You need someone to stay with her on the bottom, lest she drift, lest she break up and any of those carefully sealed boxes float away. And you need someone there to guard her, in her grave, lest the chance fisherman or swimmer should find her before the Company team arrives."

"You mean you stay in the wreck with all the dead guys?" Juan Bautista asked, horrified. His music faltered for a moment.

Kalugin nodded sadly.

"How can you stand that, man?" said Einar.

"I go into fugue," said Kalugin. "I shut down. I respond only when there's a threat to the ship. When the Company divers come, they pull me out, and I go bobbing up to the surface to breathe again. Wretched business, isn't it? To do one's work by impersonating a bloated corpse." He gave a little embarrassed laugh. Nancy took his hand and kissed it.

"But living on board with those guys, knowing all the time that they're doomed..." Einar shook his head.

Kalugin seemed to be choosing his words carefully. "Well, it's rather like what we all face every day, isn't it? Every mortal who stops here is doomed, eventually. All our fellow passengers in the stagecoach, every one of them bound for the unknown. I just...try not to think about it." He turned his face up to Nancy and smiled. "Fortunately, when not thinking becomes impossible—as it does—I have an angel to pray to."

A silence fell. Juan Bautista had stopped playing. I suppose we were all sitting there with identical expressions of appalled sympathy on our faces.

A voice began to sing, somewhere up on the hill, a woman's voice powerful and harsh, raw with emotion and alcohol, echoing in the night.

You hear no sound but my silenced voice.
You feel no heat but the fire that burns me.
You draw no breath but I come into you.
Before you, behind you, I am the sea and the rock.
I AM THE SEA AND THE ROCK!

Juan Bautista lifted his head, recognizing the song, and so did I. It was by the twenty-first-century composer Whelan, from *The Unquiet Dead*, his Celtic reinterpretation of de Falla's *El amor brujo*. Juan Bautista flexed his clenched hands and improvised on the melody, and as the flow of guitar music began again, we all drew breath.

That night in bed, I tried to occupy my mind with how much better off I was than poor Kalugin, but all I could do was envy him and Nancy their good fortune. Whereas I was alone on the shore, like the girl in the song waiting for my lover to return from the other side... And now here he came, from the east, out of the sea. From the east? What coast was I on?

There was the track of foam breaking the water as he emerged. The white horse bore him up, he was coming on the wave, armored like a knight but all in seashells, and his charger in seashells likewise. Oh, the beautiful arrogance of his big body in armor, and how well he sat a horse! His lance was a narwhal's horn, a twisted ivory spear, and he wore no helmet but a tall hat banded with a trailing ribbon of seaweed. His eyes were the color of Spanish glass in his stern face, yes, and fixed on me as he came on, and he came faster now and was lowering his lance at me. Yes! I knew what he meant to do and tore at my clothing, baring my heart to his assault.

"Strike!" I screamed. "Strike, in God's name!"

He struck true, and what a great relief it was.

I awoke in darkness.

*E*ARLY THE NEXT MORNING, I staggered out to make coffee, under the assumption that Porfirio wouldn't be in any condition to do so; but I was mistaken.

He was sitting beside the fire with Eucharia, and they were both watching the blue graniteware pot like pilgrims waiting for a miracle to happen. She looked pretty bad; she was clutching her whalebone corset, which I guess had been removed at some point during the target party for convenience, and her mauve taffeta ruffles were torn. As for him, I didn't think our eyes could sink that far back into our heads.

I noticed them only for a split second, because my attention was immediately drawn to the dead bear.

"That's a dead bear!" I yelled. They both winced.

"I'm sorry, okay?" Porfirio put his hands to his head. "I'm really sorry. Just keep your voice down."

"But we're trying to keep the damn things from going *extinct*," I hissed.

"It was my fault," Eucharia said shakily. "Wasn't it, babe? We were shooting at targets, and he just popped up against the skyline. Thought for a minute I was in a shooting gallery."

I paced around the bear. He had a neat bullet hole between his eyes. "That was some nice shooting, anyway."

"I thought Einar could salvage it for DNA," Porfirio said, reaching for the coffeepot with a trembling hand. "Oh, man. I need to metabolize some glucose. Mendoza, is there any of that pan dulce left?"

"I'll go see," I told him, and as I was entering the adobe, I passed Einar coming from his room. A moment later I heard his howl of dismay at the sight of the bear.

Nancy and Kalugin emerged slightly later, managing to look like an Arabian Nights illustration despite their primly Victorian morning wear. Nancy took one look at poor Eucharia and led her away, shaking her head. By the time they came out again, Eucharia had been dusted off and freshened up, and you wouldn't have known her for the gum-popping honey of the previous evening. She looked a lot like the farm wife in *American Gothic.* By the time the morning stage rolled in, the three of them were back in their roles completely: vaguely foreign gentleman, dull-eyed wife, and meek servant girl.

As Kalugin was seeing to their trunks, Nancy turned to me and reached out her hand. "Mendoza, will you be all right?"

Who, me, ashen-faced after a night of erotic death dreams? But I wasn't the one facing a stagecoach ride with a hungover fellow passenger. "Sure I will. I mean, here I am in the New World. I got what I wanted. Granted, this is a lousy place, but I've already put in my request to go back to the Ventana when this tour of duty's over. It'll be great. Green wilderness, Nancy, oak trees older than we are and not a mortal soul for miles. You should go up there sometime."

"I should love to," she said. "But, you know, my dear, it's going to become more difficult to find places in California where there aren't mortals. Nearly impossible, in another few decades. Where will you go then?"

And I realized, only then, that I had no clue, none at all. I guess it showed in my eyes, because she gave me a hug. "Oh, Mendoza, find something to make you happy! It's easier than it seems. You'd be surprised."

"Okay," I said, for lack of anything better to say, and the driver shouted, and we hugged again, quickly, and she was away and running to clamber up on her seat. I wondered how many centuries it would be before I saw her again. With the crack of a whip the stagecoach was off, up Cahuenga Pass, on its long journey to San Francisco.

Imarte had disembarked and brought a customer with her, her arm wound firmly through his, leading him up the trail to her lair.

"You're going to love it here, Mr. Kimberley, the climate's real nice," she was telling him. "I bet it's real cold in England, huh?"

"Wretched, dear lady," the john assured her, and he was definitely English. I shuddered at the sound of his voice. "Though England does have the advantage of a certain amount of stability. I trust there are no civil disturbances hereabouts? Relating to the present war, I mean?"

"No, honey, none at all," Imarte said, lying through her teeth, because there was a regular secessionist crowd that hung out at the Bella Union, and they not infrequently took potshots at fellow Americans whose accent sounded a bit Down East. Not that I understand how Maine can be *down* anything when it's as far north as you can go in the States.

She led the Englishman away with her, assuring him they had plenty of time before the next stage came through. I thought sourly that if the man had any inkling of how much talking he was expected to do in bed, he'd be running after the departing stage. I wandered away up the canyon to the little brook where you could occasionally find trout and sat there awhile, looking into the brown water, wondering where I *would* go when California filled up with mortals. Canada, I decided at last, and made a mental note to do some studies on the botany peculiar to our neighbor to the north. Yet I loved California; I was even beginning to like this ghastly corner of it, with its killers lurking in the sagebrush and its yet unborn movie industry.

And I thought to myself that things weren't that bad. I had my work, didn't I? There was my problem! I wasn't working enough, what with needing an escort for every field trip. That was why Nicholas was haunting me. Well, if I practiced harder with the Navy pistol, maybe Porfirio would decide it was safe to let me go out on my own. In the meanwhile, another good collecting trip was just the thing to chase away the blues.

By the time I mulled all this over and wandered back to the inn, the afternoon sun had fallen behind the ridge and the dust of the last stage had long settled. Nobody was in sight. I scanned and detected Porfirio and Imarte in the inn, and followed their signals to the pantry room, where Porfirio was kneading dough for a fresh batch of pan dulce. His eyes had come out of their caves a little. Imarte sat with her elbows on the table, watching him. She had a bitchy line between her eyebrows.

"Where is everybody?" I asked, pulling out a chair and sitting down.

"The kid's around here somewhere. Oscar, I don't know. Einar went off to Antelope Valley again."

"Nuts." I sighed. He probably wouldn't be home until the next afternoon. "I wanted to go out collecting tomorrow."

Porfirio shrugged. "You could go with Oscar," he suggested hopefully. Now there were two women with bitchy expressions in the room with him. "So, Imarte, what was the deal with the Englishman? Get any good material from him?"

"Virtually none," she said. "He never stopped asking *me* questions all afternoon! In fact he shut up for exactly five minutes, and I leave it to you to guess why. The rest of the time, I might as well have been a tour guide."

"Maybe you met up with a kindred soul," I said. "Dueling anthropologists."

"Very funny. I learned nothing of his home region or native customs. The best I could get out of him was that he's a mining engineer with the Albion Mining Syndicate. Apparently some confidence man persuaded a group of foreigners that there's been a gold strike on Santa Catalina Island, of all places."

I remembered the blue island I'd seen, way out there in the sea. "And it's a con, you think?"

"Certainly. Who ever heard of gold out there?" Imarte leaned back in her chair and stretched.

I actually asked Oscar about his rounds the next day, I was that desperate for work. He was only too happy to oblige; he hadn't made the West Hollywood sweep in a while, it seemed, and so next morning I crowded onto the seat of the peddler's cart with him, and we rolled off down the canyon.

"So, is it hard to get your foot in the door when you're making your pitch?" I asked as we turned right and headed west.

"Goodness no, not at all," Oscar said. "Not like in the States. I mean, the original thirteen. The local inhabitants are charming people, with a keen appreciation of the solid worth and delightful abundance of general merchandise offered by your humble servant. They'll welcome a salesman into their homes, indeed invite him to dine with them, which is certainly more than I can say for the inhabitants of Rhode Island. The folks here will sit patiently through a complete demonstration of every ingenious and laborsaving device I have to offer. Only problem is, they have no money."

"Really?"

"Nobody here has," he said. "All these Californio gentlemen, and the Yankee fellows too, have pitifully little cash. All they've got is the land and cows. The land's dirt cheap, but most of it's mortgaged to the last square inch, with the highest interest rates you've ever seen. Why, it's plain crazy." He shook his head in commiseration.

"Boom and bust, huh?" I said. Finance had never interested me, but I craved trivia just now, anything to tie me to the present place and time.

"And take this new silkworm business." He gestured angrily with the whip. "Fools planting mulberry trees, thousands of the darned things, everywhere, and importing cocoons from the Orient at great expense. Will it ever produce so much as a handkerchief's span of silk? No, sir! The whole enterprise is a sham, a bubble, a speculator's airy impertinence, and the end result will be *ruin*, you mark my words. And a lot of mulberry firewood."

Was that why my orders had included collecting samples from mulberry trees? I'd wondered about that; they weren't an indigenous plant. Sounded like another tulip fiasco: when speculation on bulbs wrecked Holland's economy and prices plummeted, nursery stock was destroyed en masse, and lots of genetic diversity disappeared.

"Will we be passing any mulberry plantations today?" I asked.

"More than likely," Oscar said.

"Good. I can take some cell samples. Got a customer lined up for your Criterion Patented Brassbound Pie Safe yet?"

"Just about," he said, brightening a little. "If my careful analysis of my customers is correct."

We followed the rocky track, which paralleled the foothills and continued west in a fairly straight line toward a tiny cluster of adobes, all facing one another on opposite sides of what would undoubtedly one day be an avenue, boulevard, or drive. Tilled fields and orchards took up a few acres around the hamlet; straggling fences of nopal cactus raised formidable paddles against bears, wandering longhorns, and chicken thieves. The place appeared deserted save for a dog lying in the dust in the middle of the avenue, boulevard, or drive, and I'm not sure he was alive.

"Now this," Oscar said, "is the ill-fated village of Sherman. I don't believe it's named after the redoubtable general of the same name. No, indeed, and it certainly won't live to be as famous. West Hollywood will obliterate it completely, as a matter of fact. Nevertheless, these people are as receptive to the improvement of their lives by beautiful and useful merchandise as any you'll find in more progressive communities."

"Really. Look, there's a grove of mulberry trees." I pointed at a double row of miserable little whippy seedlings, each with its green flame of young leaves waving at the top. "Do you know these people? Think you could get me permission to take samples?"

"Undoubtedly," he said, and clucked to Amelia to stop just in front of the first house. Describing it now will save my having to describe nearly any other structure in southern California from here on: a long adobe, its former whitewash peeling and cracked away in places, all of it badly eroded by the winter rains. Flat roofs of pink tile, cracked or missing here and there, held on by thick tar from the nearby La Brea pits. Wooden doors and window frames, closed shutters painted faded blue if they were painted at all. Most were of bare wood silvered and cracked with the weather.

"I don't think anybody's home," I said, as a chilly breeze whirled through the cactus.

"Nonsense. Always looks like this. Decent people stay indoors and mind their own business around here, that's all." Oscar hopped down and ran around to offer me his arm in descending. I looked up at several pockmarks in the nearest wall; if they weren't bullet holes, the place had damned big hailstones. Oscar didn't notice, seemingly; he strode right up to the door and knocked briskly. "Hello there! Buenos días, Señora Berreyesa, might I have a moment of your time?" I followed him slowly, ready to throw myself flat if a hail of shot came from anywhere. After a moment we heard a bolt drawn, and the door opened a trifle. A woman peered out at us.

"What do you require, señor?" she said in Mexican Spanish.

"Ah, Señora Berreyesa, what I require is not the issue at all," said Oscar, matching her Spanish pretty well. "It is what *you* require. Perhaps you recall me? I was here last autumn, before the rains. You purchased a splendid shaving razor for the señor of the house, which perhaps you will also recall. Doubtless you will be pleased to discover that I have returned, bringing even more splendid wares for your inspection."

"In that case, consider my house your own," she said, with great courtesy but less enthusiasm, standing aside to open the door. Oscar threw me a triumphant little smile and stepped inside, and I followed, murmuring my thanks to Señora Berreyesa.

The interior was typical of a reasonably well-to-do working-class family. A dirt floor, packed hard and pounded smooth, and smoothly plastered walls shading to an olive brown near the ceiling, from smoke, and almost black over the household shrine, where a couple of candles winked in jars of ruby glass before a little wooden figure of the Virgin of Guadalupe. This was a house of two rooms, and the fine oven and cooking hearth were built into the wall between the rooms, so as to warm both. There were stoneware jars with heavy lids ranged along the wall, and shelves above them displaying graniteware dishes. Several wooden chests; a solid table; and on it a chunk of fresh pork loin and a carving knife, which the señora had apparently been using when we arrived. She eyed the knife now, and looked at us in the hope that we'd be polite enough to leave soon and let her get back to her housework.

"And may I introduce Señora Mendoza, who was kind enough to accept my offer of transportation when her horse went lame? Very good. I know your time is valuable, señora, so I won't waste it," Oscar said, interpreting her expression correctly. "You should know I have cakes of shaving soap available that fit precisely into the mug your husband uses. And, if I recall correctly, you must be nearly out of Morning Glory Laundry Bluing, and that was a particular favorite of yours, was it not?"

"It is, señor," she said.

All this while, subtle unseen miniaturized cameras and recording devices on and in Oscar's person were noting every detail of the house and of its inhabitant. "Very good." He rubbed his hands together cheerfully. "I have all you could require. Now, let's see, your husband, do I err in remembering that he's a vaquero?"

"No, señor, you do not," she said. "At the Rodeo de Las Aguas."

"Yes, so he is. And he's, ah, twenty-eight years old?"

"Twenty-six, señor."

"A good age for a man to begin looking after his teeth, wouldn't you say? I don't believe I've ever shown you the fine assortment of American brushes I carry for that very purpose. Regard this!" From seemingly thin air he produced a bone-handled toothbrush. The señora did not seem impressed at the sleight of hand, but the tiny brown boy who had been watching from her skirts yelled with delight and pointed at us.

"Well." Oscar hitched up the front of his trousers and crouched down, smiling, turning his head for a good camera angle. "And who's this little fellow? I don't believe I met *you* on my last visit, no, sir."

The child retreated a bit, staring in fascination. "He was asleep then, señor," the mother explained. Oscar produced (again, from apparent thin air) a little wooden jointed doll and offered it to the boy.

"Well, here you go, sonny. Here's a dancing Uncle Sam to keep you busy while your mama does the household chores, eh? No, no, señora, it's a free gift, a trifle. And I'd like you to consider this brush I was about to show you." He stood again, proffering the brush in one fluid movement. She must have wondered how she found it in her hand without consciously accepting it, but there it was; and he pulled out a can of tooth powder and held it up before her puzzled eyes.

"Now, señora, I can see you've been favored by Nature with exceptionally beautiful and durable teeth. How fortunate you are. But as a dutiful wife and mother, it falls to you to see to the well-being of your spouse and little ones; and they may not be as dentally gifted as yourself, if I may say so. Were you aware that it is the opinion of most modern physicians that an astonishing number of diseases, distemperatures, and infections find their root and origin in *poor dental hygiene?*"

"I know," she said. "Gingivitis."

"Er—well, yes, exactly so, señora. And yet, by following the simplest of daily regimens, one can preserve glowing dental health and, incidentally, the beauty of a radiant smile."

"It's true," she agreed. "You chew on sage leaves. Keeps away the gum sores, and your breath doesn't stink either. And they're free. They grow all over the hills here."

"To be sure," said Oscar, not missing a beat, "and I can see you're *exactly* the caring and concerned parent and mate who does her best to see to it that her family follows that oh-so-careful daily routine for their own good. For that very reason, I know you'll be interested in this splendid dentifrice applicator, manufactured out of the very finest materials by the Superior Brush Company of Ogdensburg, New York, USA, and guaranteed to withstand the most rigorous use. Only regard it, señora! Observe the bristles, designed to delve into the crevices between difficult-to-reach back teeth, where home remedies can so seldom penetrate. Now these bristles are derived from the splendid native American wild boar, and they have a particular flexibility unknown to the inferior European variety, which makes them the material of choice for delivering a sufficient dose of this excellent nostrum to the teeth and gums of the gratified user. Now this, señora, is Cleopatra's Smile Tooth Powder, not merely a solution to ensure dental health but a restorative of the natural whiteness of the tooth enamel itself. Tell me, señora, your husband's a vaquero: does he ever chew tobacco?"

"Never!" Señora Berreyesa said with a scowl. "I'd throw him out of the house if he took up a dirty habit like that."

"You would, of course, like any right-minded wife, I don't doubt it, but do you know that Cleopatra's Smile has removed stubborn tobacco stains even on those depraved unfortunates who practice the tobacco vice? Now let's address the question of tea and coffee, which we all enjoy from time to time. Cleopatra's Smile has been proven to remove tea or coffee stains from the teeth and restore snowy whiteness *after only one application*." I think he was sweating just a little, but Fate smiled. Señora Berreyesa put her head to one side and considered the bright logo on the can.

"Will it do that for tablecloths too?" she asked.

"Well, why wouldn't it?" Oscar said. "If it was brushed in sufficiently, I bet it would! Now I'll tell you what I'll do, señora. I'll make you a complimentary gift of that very brush you hold in your hand. Society matrons in the eastern States can't get Cleopatra's Smile for less than ten cents a can, but I'm able to offer it out here for a mere three red cents."

She thought about it. "Three cents? You will excuse me one moment, señor?" And she went into the adjoining room, with the little boy following her like a shadow.

"A can of tooth powder isn't a pie safe," I said to Oscar. "And you had to give away a doll and a toothbrush, plus a seven-cent markdown on the tooth powder."

"That's not the point," he murmured. "I'm building a clientele, don't you see? The point of the game is getting them to *want* this stuff. After want comes need, and once they need what you have, all you have to do is supply the demand."

"Will you remember to ask about the mulberry trees?"

"The what? Yes, yes, of course. And we'll just see about that pie safe, shall we?" He stuck his thumbs in his waistcoat pockets, looking mighty pleased with himself.

Señora Berreyesa returned and held out her hand. "Three American cents, señor. I will try a can of that powder."

"You won't regret it, señora," he assured her, pocketing the money and presenting her with the can. "And may I add that this is also a superlative remover of the stubborn and unsightly stains caused by the consumption of mulberries? Of which I notice you shall soon have abundance, by the way."

"Those?" She rolled her eyes. "If we ever see a berry from them, I'll fall over dead. My husband let Señor Workman plant them, after some crazy talk about silkworms. Chinese shawls growing on trees, he told him."

"Well, isn't that just like a man? But I wonder, señora, if you would allow my friend here to collect a couple of leaves from the young trees? She studies such things."

"You can take the whole damned orchard, as far as I'm concerned," she said to me. "Please, señora, help yourself. This way." She scooped up the little boy in her arms and led us out the back door to the garden beyond.

As I walked among the little trees, clipping off a likely-looking

shoot here and there, Oscar cleared his throat. "I couldn't help noticing that our arrival interrupted preparations for a meal," he said.

"That's true, señor, but I can spare the time to speak with you,"
Señora Berreyesa lied graciously.

"Ah, but, busy woman as you are, you must frequently suffer in-
terruptions in the course of your culinary duties, and food intended
for human consumption may then be unintentionally exposed to the
assault of common household pests. I'd like to suggest a means of ensuring that your foodstuffs stay safe and unmolested. Now I happen
to have in my wagon a miracle of modern design: the Criterion
Patented Brassbound Pie Safe! I believe it may be the answer to all
your problems, and if you'll just step out to the cart and let me
demonstrate its assorted features, I'm sure you'll—"

But Señora Berreyesa had stopped in her tracks, her face registering outrage as the import of his words sank in. "Are you suggesting
that I have rats in my kitchen?" she said.

"Uh—why, no, certainly, but—"

She seized his sleeve. "You think I keep a dirty house? You think
I leave food lying around to draw rats? You come in here and see."
She dragged him back into the house, and I ran after them hastily,
tucking trailing mulberry cuttings into my collecting basket. She
gestured dramatically at the row of stone jars, each with its heavy
stone lid.

"*There.* That keeps the food safe and cool. There is never any
food left lying unprotected in my house, except when annoying little
white men come to sell me things."

Oscar gulped and scuttled for the door. "Point taken, señora,
point taken. I'll just be on my way, I guess. Buenos días."

"Buenos días, señora, and please excuse the discourtesy," I said as
I followed him. She inclined her head stiffly in acknowledgment. The
little boy stared at us with solemn eyes.

"Well, at least she bought the tooth powder," I said when we
were out in the street.

"Tactical error," he admitted, taking out an immense spotted handkerchief and mopping his face with it. "Ought to have seen she was house proud. Well, well, I'll do better next time. Got your sample cuttings, did you? First-rate. Let's be off to the next customer."

Down the street we went, the mule sighing audibly.

Nobody answered our knock at the next few houses. Near one there came a little whine and a *ping*, and a puff of adobe and plaster flakes jumped off a nearby wall; so we kept on going, until we got to a board-and-batten shanty sitting by itself in a field. Smoke whirled from its tin chimney.

"Can this be a new customer?" Oscar stared at it keenly. "That place was abandoned, and somebody's been and fixed it up. Well, well. Cameras and audio at the ready! Care to come in with me?"

"Why not?" I said, scanning the house. I could pick up only one occupant, a female. No, there was a cat, too.

So we got out, and Oscar rapped smartly at the door. There was a silence and a scurrying, then someone tugged the door open from the inside, scraping it across the warped sill.

"You will excuse please," said the lady who had answered. "My door, it is wretchedly made. There are no good carpenters here, like in my country."

We beheld a mortal woman in her mid-thirties, with a plain freckled face and intense blue eyes. She had a vaquero's red bandanna bound tight on her head, like a Gypsy scarf, and the rest of her appearance produced that effect also: calico blouse and skirt of violently clashing colors, red morocco slippers with pointed-up toes, and brass hoop earrings so big, a mouse could have jumped through one. Around her neck were numerous strings of beads, some of crystal, some of cheap trade glass, some of bones and shells and little unidentifiable oddments. She wore a lot of rings, too, gimcrack stuff, the costume and curtain variety.

For once, Oscar was speechless; but not for long.

"And what country would that be, ma'am?" he asked, removing his derby.

"Grumania-Starstein," she said. "I am princess there. You are addressing Her Highness Sophia Sylvia Rodiamantikoff. Filthy conspirators brought about the downfall of the royal house. But I fled to safety through snows aided by loyal servants, chased by wolves all the way. I have come to this country to await restoration of monarchy by my secret friends in the palace."

Right. My guess, analyzing her accent, was that she'd been born in Pennsylvania (possibly Shamokin) and probably known some immigrant families. Oscar blinked, turned his derby around in his fingertips, and smiled.

"Why, isn't that interesting. It didn't leave you much time to pack a bag, did it? Is Your Highness provided with all the minor necessaries a lady requires for good health and hygiene?"

"I *had* such," she said with a melancholy sigh, lifting the back of her hand to her forehead. "Had beautiful set of tortoiseshell combs, given to my great-great-grandmother as a present from Ivan the Terrible, who was her godfather, you know. Alas! They are lost, along with solid gold comb-and-brush set I was given by my uncle the archduke. Gone, gone with my jewels and my crown!"

"Golly, that's really too bad," Oscar said sympathetically. "Fortunately, I happen to have a complete assortment of the finest toiletries and toilette accessories a lady could require, ready for your inspection. I'd be honored if you'd care to purchase any, ma'am—Your Highness, I mean."

She bunched the fingers of one hand together and set them in the middle of her forehead, frowning thoughtfully. "One second, if you please," she said. "I must consult spirit guides. Chief Running Deer! King Elisheazar! What you say, boys?"

In the silence that followed, I transmitted to Oscar: *So, is she nuts or a con artist?*

Your guess is as good as mine, he replied.

"We will consider your wares," she said at length, and stepped forth into the light of day. Behind her an evil-faced cat came to the doorway, peered out at us, and fled back inside. Oscar hastened to open up the side of his wagon, displaying a gaudy splendor of ribbons, brass thimbles and scissors, pack thread, playing cards, cheaply bound books, and various items for personal grooming.

"There, now, Your Highness, what d'you think of this?" he said, as though he expected her breath to be taken away by the glory of it all. I decided they were both nuts and turned my attention to a nice little specimen of *Lupinus* lifting spires of blue and purple from the edge of an irrigation ditch. Her Royal Highness Rodiamantikoff fussed and sniffed at the items on display, remarking plaintively that these things were very shoddily made, not like wares in dear old Grumania-Starstein, and occasionally her two spirit guides threw in their two cents about the quality of this bottle of toilet water or that pair of silver-plated sugar nippers. Oscar just poured on the ingratiating charm, bowing and scraping as though she were standing there in her royal finery.

She'd decided on three yards of scarlet ribbon and a deck of playing cards, explaining that her mother had been a Gypsy and taught her to read the future with them—this, by the way, was why the evil conspirators had not wanted her to inherit the throne and stole the crown for the prime minister's baseborn son Otto, who was the offspring of a chambermaid—when Chief Running Deer and King Elisheazar got into a fight over whether or not she should buy herself a peppermint stick. Chief Running Deer (she informed us) said she oughtn't to deny herself such a small pleasure, poor exiled creature that she was, but King Elisheazar told him he was a savage without any breeding and it showed, because *everybody* knew that royalty didn't buy themselves candy; such luxuries were given to them by loving subjects and by foreigners out of respect for the aura of rulership that hung about their persons despite unfortunate circumstances.

Oscar took the hint and presented her the peppermint stick with his compliments, which restored the good humor of the spirit guides, much to Her Highness's relief, for it *so* embarrassed her when they went at it like that. She paid a whole thirty-five cents for the cards and the ribbon, delving into her skinny bosom for it, and I guess it was more money than Oscar had made in days, because, encouraged by his success, he made so bold as to say:

"Now I wonder, Your Highness, if you'd be interested in purchasing a certain item I have here—and I've only the one, you see, you won't find its like this side of the Rockies, but you being royalty and all, I'd like to offer you first crack at it. Step this way if you please, Your Highness, and I'll give you a private viewing."

She followed his outstretched hand around to the other side of the wagon, where he opened up the panel and revealed the Criterion Patented Brassbound Pie Safe.

"You see here?" His face was shining with desperate hope. "*Your* eye, trained as it is in discernment and accustomed as it is to superior craftsmanship, *your* eye will surely appreciate the magnificence of this prime household appurtenance. Note the panels of polished rosewood. Note the decorative brass figuring: pineapples, the ancient symbol of abundance and hospitality. Now, I don't pretend that this is any match for the fine kitchen furniture they've got in your country, but I'll tell you plainly, Your Highness, that this is positively the finest the U. S. of A. has to offer, and no other lady in all of southern California has the like. Now, down east where I come from, the wives of millionaires would pay as much as twenty-five dollars for the likes of this—*if* they could get it! And of course out here, where everything has to be brought by ship, it's worth a lot more. Yet to you, Highness, to you I'll offer exclusive ownership for a mere token sum of eleven dollars—why, that won't even cover the shipping and handling—and the priceless privilege of numbering royalty among my customers." My God, he was actually getting down on one knee. "What do you say, eh? Shall I take it down for you?"

Ooo, he'd come so close. She'd been transfixed, listening with mouth half open, fascinated. But she didn't have that kind of money. She wrinkled her freckled nose in slightly disdainful regret.

"I think not, at the present time," she said. "Spirit guides advise that stars are not presently auspicious for buying furniture. Perhaps later, when vibrations are better."

He looked so crestfallen that she hastened to add, "Yet you may use my name. Yes, you may say truthfully that you are purveyor to Royal House of Rodiamantikoff." She swept past him to return to her shack. "In exile," she said, just before crossing the threshold. "Good day, mister. You are excused from the royal presence."

"Well, you've made thirty-eight cents so far," I said to Oscar as I helped him close up the panels on the wagon.

"Be-elzebub!" he said, grabbing his buggy whip. "I nearly had her, do you realize that? She saw it, she wanted it, she could envision its rich cabinetry making that dreary hovel a refined and gracious retreat. Nothing was lacking but *money!*"

"Well, that's always the way it is with mortals, isn't it?" I climbed up to my seat. "And think of the footage you got of her. Genuine California eccentric, wherever she's supposed to have been born. She's one for the archives, all right. But you know what? She's a gringa. If you sold it to her, you'd still lose the bet."

"I think not," he retorted grimly. "She says she's a refugee from a foreign land, and would any true gentleman impute falsehood to a lady? No sir, if Her Highness says she's not an American, I'll take her at her word."

A bullet came whining out of nowhere, drifting in to clip the top off a young oak tree nearby. Oscar whipped out a pistol and fired off three furious shots at the unseen gunman.

"I'll prevail, I say!" he shouted. "Do you hear me? I'll *sell* the darned thing! I say I will, by thunder!"

But he didn't, at least not on that day's rounds, and he was dull and taciturn—taciturn for him—by the time we returned to the inn that evening. He accepted his plate of grilled beef, tortillas, and frijoles from Porfirio and retired early.

Even though I was eager to get the mulberry samples to my processing credenza, I lingered over the food, because it was particularly good that evening, the beef fiery from a red chile marinade, the frijoles especially creamy, the tortillas unusually redolent of earth and corn and rain. I was still sitting in the clearing when Porfirio rose to his feet, stared off into the canyon and the night, turning his head for a better signal scan, and announced:

"Stranger approaching on horseback. Mortal male. Emotionally excited." He had a gun in either hand before he finished speaking, and Juan Bautista rose in haste to carry Erich von Stroheim indoors out of harm's way. The bird had got too big to button out of sight inside his shirt, though it kept trying to climb into its old refuge in times of stress. It croaked in protest as Juan Bautista passed Einar, who was emerging from the house with a loaded shotgun.

"Company, chief?" said Einar, cocking his weapon.

"Maybe," said Porfirio, though as the mortal drew nearer, we could tell that the excitement registering on the night air was the harmless, pleasurable kind: anticipatory, nonviolent. When he finally rode into the light of our fire, the mortal saw no weapons of any kind in evidence. Porfirio took a few steps toward him, hands outstretched in a peaceable gesture.

"You come for a room, señor? But we have no empty beds tonight. Bad luck, eh? Perhaps you'll ride on to Garnier's? Plenty of room there."

"Thanks, but that ain't why I'm here," the mortal said politely. "I come to see a lady, mister. Met her at the Bella Union. Said her name was Marthy, and she lived hereabouts. You wouldn't know where a man could find her, would you?"

"Ah. Marthy," said Porfirio, just as Imarte herself came sweeping to the door of the adobe, magnificent in her Love's Purple Passion negligee. She paused there in the doorway, holding up an oil lamp like one of those fancy figures that lift a lighting fixture on a newel post.

"Why, who is it at this time of night?" she said throatily.

"It's only me, Miss Marthy," said the stranger, dismounting and tying his reins to our hitching post. He stepped forward out of the shadows, hat in hand. "Only me, and perhaps you remember my name? Cyrus Jackson, ma'am. We met at the Bella Union, and you was so kind as to listen to my troubles."

"Why, to be sure," she cooed, "the *very* interesting man who hunted Apache scalps for bounty." She threw us all an arch glance as if to say, See what a trophy I bagged? "How well I remember your thrilling tales of adventure in old San Antonio! But what brings you here, sir, at this unaccustomed hour?"

He blushed. "Why, ma'am, I hope not to give offense—I sort of thought that you might receive callers after sundown, your trade being what it is. And, you know, I wasn't at my best when last we met—but I'm sober now, and I did remember that you was so taken with my recollections, that I wondered if you mightn't like to hear about when I was down in Nicaragua in '56."

"You rode with Walker in Nicaragua?" Her eyes lit up. She surged forward, bosom first, and placed a coy hand on his arm. "Why, sir, how fascinating! I wonder if you'd be so kind as to share the treasure of your eyewitness memories with an interested listener? In my private chamber, of course."

"Aw, ma'am, I'd be..." Words failed him, or perhaps they just couldn't make it through the barrier of his enormous foolish grin. He let himself be led by the arm into the house. Staring after Imarte, Porfirio shook his head.

"*Anthropologists,*" Einar muttered in agreement.

*M*ORE BOXES ARRIVED on the next stage, and Einar ran off gleefully to his room with them. The next edition of the film festival featured hours of Charlie Chaplin, of Fatty Arbuckle and Mabel Normand. We sat in our finery in the dressed-up room and played Hollywood premiere again, sipping gin martinis and crunching on popcorn as the silver light flickered and Einar read the titles aloud in his master of ceremonies voice.

Now and then there were a few frames of a landscape we recognized: a smooth-backed elevation with a single line of trees, or a dirt road ascending a steep canyon, or tiny toylike frame houses perched high on the sides of hills and wide empty country all around them. Such a raw new place Hollywood would be, and how unlike the chaparral wilderness we inhabited. For, just as Einar had told me, it would be an eastern Yankee settlement in that time: there were the clapboard houses and the shop fronts and the front porches. It looked like any little town in Connecticut or Maryland, save that it sprawled over endless rolling hills. Edendale, Sunset Park, Lankershim, Burbank, the names to assure new arrivals they were back home and not in some barren wild place where coyotes trotted down the streets at night.

I didn't enjoy the comedies, as a whole, because so much heartache went with them. That world didn't even exist yet, that innocent place, and it was already lost. Those comedians weren't yet in their mothers' wombs, but their fates were known. It was hard to watch pretty Mabel and not look for the icy vivacity of cocaine, hard to watch Fatty hide his face in comic shame, knowing the doom one rowdy party would bring on him. Chaplin wasn't so bad; you knew he'd get off relatively easy for a mortal: long life, fame, lots of family—also scandal, disgrace, exile, quarrels. But the comedians were nearly as immortal as we were, and we gave them our applause.

*T*HE DAYS GOT LONGER, and the green hills silvered and then went to gold. The wildflowers vanished as though somebody had rolled up the magic carpet and whisked it away, except for a few bright orange poppies that decorated the edges of roads. The heat of summer browned everything else. Even the eight-foot-tall thickets of wild mustard, which had bloomed in an electric Day-Glo yellow you could see for miles, went to brown; and the country took on a dry, businesslike look. The arriving and departing stages traveled in a permanent cloud of white dust.

The dust got everywhere. It covered every surface in the inn, and you shook it out of your blankets at night, and it greeted you in a fine sediment at the bottom of your morning coffee. The low-hanging branches of the oak trees, heavy with leaves, were thick with it, and dewy morning cobwebs in the grass looked like little brown rags by nightfall, they'd collected so much dust. And what had happened to all those burbling rills and freshets that had been so picturesque a couple of months earlier? Dry and dead; and in their places bone-dry trackways of sand and gravel, or deep piles of dead sycamore leaves. The cicadas started up a drone about 0700 hours in the morning, when the day would begin to heat up, and they rang in your ears like fever until sundown, when the crickets started up *their* song in the cool of the shadows.

No way you could have mistaken the place for England now, not a sight or sound or smell that was anything but Californian. You might think my specter would leave me alone now, and in truth I had no more gasping visitations that made Porfirio stare at me suspiciously the next morning; but the darkness was still there, beating like a sullen heart when I was alone in my room. I woke up one morning and realized I'd give anything for a breath of sea air.

"So, what's it like at San Pedro?" I said to Porfirio at breakfast.

"San Pedro?" He frowned. "Muddy. Used to be dangerous in the old days. It's not so bad now that Banning's running the place."

"It's the local seaport, right? Any chance Einar could take me down there for a visit, if he's going that way? I haven't seen a good-sized body of water in months."

Porfirio shrugged. "We've got some cargo due to come in. I've been meaning to send him down to the warehouses to see if it's arrived yet. You want to go with him? Nothing growing down there that I know of, though."

Einar, when approached on the subject, thought a day at the beach sounded like a great idea, so he busied himself hitching up the horses while I packed my collecting gear. In the midst of our preparations, Juan Bautista came out of the lean-to he shared with Erich von Stroheim, rubbing his eyes.

"What's going on?" he asked.

"Field trip to San Pedro," Einar said, giving me a hand up to the seat.

"The *beach*?" His eyes widened. "Can I come too? I haven't been swimming anywhere since I've been here!"

"San Pedro isn't exactly surf city, man," Einar said. "But if you want to come, sure. What will you do with Erich, though?"

"Oh," Juan Bautista said, turning guilty eyes to the condor, who had come staggering out after him. He wasn't a mature bird yet, according to Juan, but he was enormous. "I don't guess he should come. The seagulls might scare him. But I've never left him alone before.... Would you mind watching him for me?" He looked hopefully at

Porfirio, who was just sitting down with his six-shooter, preparing to clean it.

Porfirio looked about as enthusiastic as one might expect. "Look, I've got work to do," he told the kid. "Put him in a cage for the day. I'll see to it he gets food and water."

Juan Bautista ran off to shoo the bird back to his room. Einar and I waited, listening to the croaks of protest as Erich von Stroheim was coerced into the aviary Juan had built for him. A moment later, Juan came running out with his towel and a short broad plank, planed smooth and rounded off at the corners. Behind him we heard a plaintive scream.

"Okay!" he said breathlessly, vaulting up into the back of the wagon. There was another scream, louder than the first.

"Is he gonna be all right?" asked Einar, releasing the brake and starting us down the canyon.

"Yes. He's just never been alone for very long," Juan said, turning around to get comfortable. Another scream rang out on the still morning air, echoing off the canyon walls. We could still hear the condor when we turned onto the road, and in fact the sound of his outrage carried for a good mile out into the plain.

"I hope he doesn't do that the whole time we're gone," I said, looking over my shoulder as the foothills receded into the distance behind us.

"Nah. He'll settle down and sleep. He likes to take a nap every morning," said Juan Bautista with confidence. I looked at Einar, who shrugged. We rolled on.

The sea was a lot farther than it had looked from the ridge above the Hollywood Bowl site. It took us five hours, rumbling along in the wagon, though Einar informed me that Banning could do it in two and a half in one of his Concords.

"Bully for him," I snarled, retreating even farther into the shade of my hat. Juan Bautista had set his piece of plank on his head and made a little tent for himself by draping his towel over it. He sat in the relative cool, humming a little tune.

"Yeah, that's the way to go, if you don't have freight to pick up. Banning's got regular stagecoach service from L.A. to the coast. Another few years, and there'll even be a railroad," Einar said. "Not that that does us much good now, of course."

Ahead of us, the sun on the summer sea lit up the sky, and Catalina Island hovered out there like a lovely cool mirage, blue and eternally remote. Just when I thought I couldn't take another mile of this wasteland (I'd thought Porfirio was kidding when he said nothing grew down here), we rolled up a little hill and over the top, and there it was: San Pedro Harbor.

Except it wasn't a harbor, yet, of course. It was a vast expanse of tidal mudflat, stretching away to shallow water and a distant line of white breakers. Hell, there wasn't even any sand.

But there was sea air, at least, if a bit swampy, and there was a little stream flowing through willows, blessedly green after all those parched miles.

"Surf's up, dudes!" crooned Einar. "Check it out!"

Juan Bautista obediently scrambled about and sat up to stare. He gave a cry of disappointment. "Where's the *water*?"

"Hey, this is Los Angeles! No water in the rivers, no water in the sea. No, seriously, access your Richard Henry Dana. This is the worst harbor on the coast right now. Tide flats are so shallow, cargo ships have to anchor way the hell out there and send in longboats to unload. Amazingly inconvenient. But see that big house being built over there?" Einar pointed to a vast edifice being framed about a mile inland. "That's the place Phineas Banning's building for himself. See those wharves? They're the latest step in his big plan to make this the next world port for shipping. Way off there"—he swung his arm around—"is the old San Pedro landing. Nobody lives there now but some fishermen. And see that island? That's Dead Man's Island. First recorded murder mystery of L.A., or so I'm told. Dead guy buried there is supposed to have been a British ship's captain, poisoned by somebody when he put in here to pick up a cargo of hides. Who slipped him the fatal glass of sherry? Nobody knows."

"Where's Malibu?" asked Juan Bautista, craning his neck, as if that would make yellow sands and clean surf appear.

"North of here. Nothing much there now either, kid. Nobody even goes there, except when a cow slips down a ledge and has to be retrieved from the rocks. Honest, it's just a little trail between the cliffs and the sand, and when we get earthquakes, it isn't even that."

"Sight-seeing is the art of disappointment," I quoted.

"I want to go surfing," said Juan Bautista sadly.

So we drove down the hill and took him as far out across the mud flats as we could without getting the wagon bogged down, and left him to walk out to the waves while we went over to the shipping warehouses.

I got down and walked to stretch my legs while Einar negotiated with the warehouse foreman, one of our paid mortals, a fisherman named Souza. It turned out that we did actually have goods to pick up: a box of printed materials for Porfirio and two crates for Oscar from the Acme Manufacturing Company of Boston, Massachusetts.

When everything had been signed for and Señor Souza had helped us load it all into the wagon, we drove out again, edging along the tidal flats as far as we dared before proceeding the rest of the way on foot. The mud was heavy clay, hard to walk through.

"That *is* the sea out there; yes?" I said, shading my eyes with my hand, peering ahead. "Not a special effect?"

"Just a little farther now," said Einar, swatting at midges. And sure enough, after we'd clambered over some slimy rocks and past a wrecked whaleboat, there were bright combers and surf breaking on rocks and even clean brown sand. Juan Bautista seemed to have got some surfing in, to judge by his piled clothing and his wet hair. But he was sitting in his drawers on the sand as we approached, cradling something in his bare arms. A big unsightly something. As we neared, it struggled and flapped.

"Easy, come on, take it easy," said Juan; and at his voice the bird calmed and turned its big rocket-shaped head to watch us.

"What do you have there?" Einar asked, crouching down to stare at it.

"*Pelecanus occidentalis,*" Juan said. "Brown pelican. Old female. She's hurt. Look, I think that's fishing net cutting into her leg—I think her leg's broken—can you see? Can you get her leg free?"

"Sssh, ssh, let's see." Einar stretched out a careful hand. "You won't stab me, old lady, will you? No, you won't. Okay, that's fishing net, all right. I can try and cut it loose, but you'll have to hold her bill so she doesn't take a whack at me with it, okay, J. B.?"

"Okay," said Juan, his voice trembling.

I turned and walked away. I couldn't watch. It seemed to me the poor bird would have to be killed. I was profoundly grateful I was a botanist and free from the attachments people in other disciplines formed with the creatures they studied. Not that I didn't love plants. I walked up and down, looking out at the horizon where a couple of ships lay at anchor. I looked east, where Dead Man's Island raised its cone of mud. I looked at the ramshackle adobes and fishing boats beached at the old landing. I looked at the squared spaces where the new Union Army headquarters was being built, to save us all from joining a Confederacy in a distant and unreal world.

When I dared to look back, Einar was putting his knife away and talking in a soothing tone. "See how easy that was? Didn't hardly hurt the old lady at all. It's not a bad break, but it is broken, J. B. You need to make a decision now."

"We can't kill her!" the boy said in panic. "She's a brown pelican. They'll become endangered."

"I know. Okay, look. I can splint her leg now, and you can put it in a cast when you get her home, but what will happen then? How are you going to feed her? She eats fish, you know."

"There's trout in the stream," said Juan. "And I can give her food supplements, like I do with Erich. Please, Einar."

Einar was shaking his head, but he got a piece of driftwood and fashioned a splint for the bird's leg, cutting strands from the net to bind the leg securely.

I ventured close. "You have to remember, Juanito, she's an old bird," I felt obliged to say. "Even if this doesn't work, you've made what little time she has left more comfortable. So you mustn't feel bad if she doesn't make it. This happens to mortal things. Nature will make more of them."

"Not that many of *these,*" he said, and I couldn't argue with that, so I kept my other helpful remarks to myself.

We took her with us, across the sloughs to the wagon, and Juan Bautista climbed into the back with her and wrapped her in his towel so she'd feel more secure during the long rattling drive home. By the time we reached La Nopalera that evening, she was still alive, and he'd named her Marie Dressler.

At about the point where we passed the future Hollywood Bowl, we began to hear something, and it wasn't Symphonies under the Stars. "What is that?" I asked.

Juan Bautista, dozing in the back with his arms around Marie, sat up guiltily.

"That's Erich," he said.

"Uh-oh," said Einar, and uh-oh was right. When we finally came creaking up our canyon trail to the inn, the screams were sounding out once every two seconds and Porfirio was sitting out by the cook-fire, his hands over his ears.

Einar set the hand brake and jumped down. "Bird's upset, I guess."

"When did he start?" asked Juan Bautista, clambering out awkwardly, his arms full of Marie.

"Start? He never stopped," replied Porfirio through his teeth. "Not for ten seconds since you've been gone, muchacho. Please go in there *right now* and shut him up, okay?"

"Okay," said Juan Bautista, and ran for his room. As soon as he had gone inside and lit his lamp, the screams were replaced by happy little croodling sounds and a couple of dinosaur noises.

Porfirio's head sank to his knees. "Finally," he groaned. "Finally." Then he sat bolt upright. "Did he have *another* damn bird with him?"

"Another endangered rarity, chief," Einar said, getting the horses out of harness. "Just doing his job. California brown pelican with a busted leg. No big deal."

"We picked up some freight, too." I hastened to bring the box of periodicals. "Looks like you got your latest issue of *Punch*."

"How nice for me." Porfirio took the box with trembling hands. "Well, I think I'll go to bed now. I think I'll lie in bed and just read for a while. There's plenty to eat—Imarte and Oscar decided to dine out this evening. Help yourselves. Bye."

He got up and walked away, stiff-legged with controlled violence. I stared after him in frank admiration. I'd have wrung the bird's neck after the first hour.

*P*ORFIRIO EMERGED from his room looking rested next morning, as I was trying to figure out how much coffee to make.

"Eight scoops or six?" I asked, fumbling with the coffeepot.

He rolled his eyes and took the pot from me. "Here, let me. Will you do me a favor?"

"Sure."

"Go wake up Juan Bautista and tell him I want to talk to him."

I went to knock on Juan Bautista's door. Nobody answered, so after a moment I entered.

It smelled like birds in there, and no wonder; one whole wall was cages, in which several dozen little nondescript-looking birds hopped and twittered. There were a couple of big cages, and in one of them Marie Dressler was enthroned, staring at me dolefully. Her broken leg, fixed in a cast, stuck out at an awkward angle. There was also a large perch next to the bed, clearly Erich von Stroheim's night roost. All the cages were spotlessly clean, the perch too, and all the water cups were full of fresh water and all the food cups full of fresh food. But the bed was an unmade wreck, and anything that was Juan's was either lying in a heap on the floor or piled on his one chair. He might have been an immortal cyborg like the rest of us, but he was also a seventeen-year-old boy.

As I was reflecting on this, the door opened behind me and he came in. Erich von Stroheim was perched on both his shoulders, straddling his head like a bizarre hat. Juan Bautista was carrying a little trout in either hand.

"Oh. Hello," he said, and stepped past me to open Marie Dressler's cage. "Here's your fish, lady. Just caught, see? Look, breakfast!" She looked at him as though he were crazy, then tilted up her head to receive his offering. After a few tries she got them down.

"I didn't know you kept birds in here," I said by way of polite conversation.

"This way I know coyotes won't get them. That's a chaparral bunting, and those are white flickers, and this is a pink-faced parrotlet, and that's an oak flycatcher, and that's a rufous-chinned sparrow. There's a little Neele's owl in here too, but he's hiding. All these guys will go extinct in the next fifty years. Except not really, because I've saved them." There was quiet pride in his voice. I remembered the first time I found and saved a rarity, how excited I'd been. *Ilex tormentosum,* the last known specimen, growing in a garden in England.

I put England out of my mind. "So, you're shipping them off to the Company aviaries?"

"When I've finished studying them." He nodded at his processing credenza, which I hadn't noticed because his guitar was leaning against it. "Except for Erich, I guess. He's kind of bonded to me."

"Uh... that reminds me. Porfirio would like to speak with you."

"Oh," he said, and slunk out of the room. I followed, not that I wanted a seat at his dressing-down, but I really needed some coffee.

The coffee wasn't ready yet when I came to the cookfire where Juan was facing Porfirio, head lowered meekly. I kept walking past them, deciding to disappear into the oak trees for a while, but I could still hear their conversation.

"Okay, before you say anything, I just want you to know that I understand it was really irresponsible of me to go off and leave Erich like that, and I'm really sorry he screamed all the time I was gone, and

I hope it didn't bother the other operatives too much, and I promise it'll never happen again," recited Juan Bautista. He drew a deep breath.

Porfirio rubbed his unshaven chin. "You're never going swimming again, huh?"

"Well..."

"Never going to leave the bird alone for the night while you go out anywhere? Never going to go on field trips without him? How many endangered songbirds are you likely to catch with a condor perching on your head, kid?"

"Well..."

"Sit down, Juanito. We need to discuss your problem. It's not really that big a problem, as they go, but you need to understand a few things about life in the field."

"I thought I was doing a good job," said Juan, sounding stricken.

"You are. But you're going to be real unhappy, soon, and that's bad. It's especially bad for an immortal. We immortals need to avoid unhappiness at all costs, and do you know why? Because it's the only thing that can hurt us. Nothing else can get inside us and screw us up, not germs, not bullets, not poison—only unhappiness. And you can't do a good job when you're unhappy."

"Why am I going to be unhappy?"

Shit, the kid was so young.

"Because you have a pet. We don't have pets, Juan. Pets require time we haven't got, because we're operatives and all our time belongs to the Company. Pets require special housing and stuff we can't give them, because we never know when the Company is going to transfer us somewhere at a moment's notice. Pets require constant attention and love, and we can't afford to love them, because they're mortal and they'll die, which will make us unhappy, which will interfere with our doing a good job for the Company.

"See? Now, once in a while you people whose specialty is living things—ornithologists like you, or zoologists like Einar—will feel friendly toward something you've rescued. That's okay. Having friends is okay. Friends come and go, and it doesn't hurt much. But there's a different relationship involved here."

"Your problem is that this bird isn't a canary in a cage. It's a big, intelligent animal, and unfortunately its instinct is for complex social relations. It has bonded with you. That's bad, Juan, because when the time comes for you to go your way on your next mission, what do you do with Erich? You can't turn him loose. He doesn't know how to hunt. He doesn't know to be afraid of people. Access the whole history of the attempts to save his kind from extinction. Look at the problems condors have."

"I know."

"The only thing you're going to be able to do is ship him off with the rest of your collected specimens, because that's all he is: a specimen. That's all he can be to you. But it's going to hurt both of you, because he hasn't been a specimen, he's been your pet, your baby. You see what I'm saying here?"

"You're saying we shouldn't love the things we save from destruction." Juan's voice was muffled. He was crying. There was a long silence before Porfirio answered.

"Yeah," he said. "That's it, pretty much."

"I think it's crappy!"

"Yeah." Another long pause. "But it's the way things are."

A moment later, Porfirio continued: "This is not to say you can't love anything. Stuff that lasts forever, like your work or literature or cinema, that's safe. Look how happy Einar is. And look at those friends of Mendoza's who stayed here, they were actually in love with each other! Mortals, though...you want to avoid that. That can seriously screw you up. That'll make your present heartache look like a picnic. You just ask—" His voice broke off abruptly. I clenched my fists.

"So what do you want me to do?" Juan Bautista sniffed.

"No more pets. And start weaning yourself emotionally from the one you've got, all right? Better for you, better for him. Think how happy he'll be in the Company aviary. Once he has a mate, he'll forget all about you, and that's the way it should be."

"What about Marie?"

"She's a specimen. Once her leg has healed, she's off to the Company."

I put my face in my hands. Poor boy. I'd heard all this before, of course. Señors, when those clever twenty-fourth-century mortals devised us, they devised badly. Our fragile mortal bones are replaced with unbreakable ferroceramic; our weak mortal sinews are laced through with indestructible fiber, proof against any wrenching blow. Why not excise the wretched mortal heart too, give us a clean pump of steel, nothing that can weep at the appalling passage of the years? As I was weeping now, for the man I'd been unable to save.

I felt a hand touch my shoulder. But when I turned, there was nothing there but California, all sagebrush and red sand. What, was he going to start tormenting me in broad daylight? What had set him off now, the fact that it was an Englishman buried on Dead Man's Island? Was I never going to be free of England and dead Englishmen?

I ran down to the mouth of the canyon and out onto El Camino Real. I looked northward in longing for the forests of the coastal range. The road was free: it ran past me and kept going, skirting the dry hills, veering over to the coast, going on and on until it ended at what would one day be the Hyde Street Pier in San Francisco. If I stood there now, what cooler air I'd be breathing, what greener hills I'd see, and what a sound of the sea would be roaring in my ears!

As I stood there wishing myself anywhere but this flat-topped, sun-baked, bullet-ridden place, I picked up the approach of a mortal man, riding in from the city to the south. I scanned and dismissed him. It was the Yankee fellow who had come out to see Imarte, presumably back for another romantic interlude. To my dismay, he turned his horse's head in my direction and looked at me hopefully.

"Good morning, ma'am," he called out to me.

"Buenos días, señor," I said. Maybe if he thought I didn't speak English, he'd ride on.

"Ain't you the gal that works at the stagecoach stop, up there?" He pointed. "You know if Miss Marthy's at home to callers today?"

"No, señor, she is away," I said. "She is expected to arrive on the next stage, however."

"I reckon I'll wait for her, then," he said, but to my annoyance he continued to sit there on his horse and stare at me. "Uh...señorita? You know Miss Marthy very well?"

"Reasonably well, señor." What was this about? Had he caught something? It couldn't be from Imarte, not with the arsenal of amplified antibodies and God knew what else we Immortals carried in our systems.

"Well, would you know...? I'd like to get her something, something grand like what she ain't never had, but I don't know the lady's taste. She's got all them books in her room, and it's clear to me she ain't the common trashy kind of girl, you see what I'm saying? I never seen a lady so cultivated and refined that was so beautiful too, all on top of earning her living as she does. You reckon she'd like a Shakespeare book?" His eyes were big and pleading.

Oh, dear, the mortal fool was falling in love with Imarte. Twice as stupid as falling in love with an ordinary whore.

"I think, señor, that her tastes do not run to literature," I said, choosing my words carefully. "I think she likes history better. I know she enjoys the company of men who have lived interesting lives."

"Oh, I seen that right away," he said, leaning forward in the saddle. "She thought no end of the stories I had to tell her about me tellin' off General Vallejo. Real interested in what I did in Nicaragua. Seems to me she don't come by her profession from natural inclination, wouldn't you think, señorita?"

"Probably not," I agreed, and even if I disagreed, he'd hear what he wanted to hear. "But you know how difficult it is for a lady to make a living in these parts, señor."

"Why, sure," he said. "Poor beautiful thing, to be down on her luck the way she is. You can tell she weren't born to it. Why, by rights she ought to have servants waiting on her.... You know what she reminds me of? There was this storybook my Uncle Jack had when I was a kid. He used to read from it, all about this beautiful queen whose husband thought women were no good and he'd marry a new one every night and have her killed with a sword every morning. Only *this* queen kept her wits about her and told him a great big old story every night, and he let her live till next evening so's he could hear how it come out, only she kept the story going so he never did hear the end, and after three years he decided the hell with it and kept her. That's kind of what it's like seeing Miss Marthy." He sighed. "Except I'm the one doing all the talking."

"She enjoys tales of adventure, señor, especially if they're true," I said, in no mood to have a mortal pour out his heart to me.

"I been thinking I could tell her about when I was up in Frisco last year," he said. "Hell of a joke. Bunch of fellows up there had a plan going to sell out California to the secessionists. Young fellow went by the name of Asbury Harpending (and ain't that the worst silly-ass name you ever hear?) was trying to raise him an army. I nearly joined, too. Reckon Miss Marthy would like that?"

"It sounds fascinating, señor," I said. "But, is that not the stage-coach? Perhaps even now your beloved is speeding like the wind to your embrace."

He gulped and turned in the saddle, and thank God it was true: here came the northbound stage, throwing out a wake of dust cloud like a malevolent djinn. The Scheherazade of Cahuenga Pass had returned.

"Thanks for the talk, señorita," called the Yankee over his shoulder, and galloped away to be there when she dismounted. I hope she hadn't brought a customer home or there was likely to be lead flying under the oak trees.

No shots rang out, however, and after a while I sneaked back and managed to get my field kit and vanish into the bushes for a while, all by myself for a change.

I had a productive day, without the distraction of conversation. I got a good sample of genetic material from a specimen of *Quercus morehus* and, wandering into a neighboring canyon, I found a lone

Symphoricarpus mollis, which was on my priority (pharmaceuticals) list, as was *Ribes speciosum,* which I also bagged—several good specimens of that one. You never know when they're going to discover some miracle cure for something, up there in the twenty-fourth century. Three times now in my field career I've managed to win Favorable Mutation credits, earning me time out for private research. It occurred to me, that afternoon, that this might be a way to shake the dust of Los Diablos off my boots: find something so incredibly rare and useful that I'd win another holiday. I was in a great mood when I finally marched back to the inn that evening. Work always makes me happy. And I'd seen not one dour Protestant shade, not one reproachful phantom.

Porfirio, though, was glowering by the cookfire as I approached.

"No escort all day," he said sternly.

"Well, who was here to go with me?" I said. "The others have their jobs too. I need to be out every day, Porfirio, I have work to do. I'll take a Navy revolver, I promise."

"You didn't today," he said. "I'll issue you a holster. If you're going out alone, I want you to wear it at all times, understand?"

"When in Rome, et cetera," I grumbled. "Is this really necessary, though? Any trouble I ran into would be relayed simultaneously to the Company through the datafeed transmission. If I needed rescue—which I wouldn't anyway—Dr. Zeus would know immediately."

"Just because everything we see gets transmitted doesn't mean somebody's watching," Porfirio replied. "You think the Company's got enough personnel to watch every one of us around the clock? It may be months before somebody starts interpreting your signal, if ever."

"Why aren't you this restrictive on Imarte?" I complained, having no better argument.

"You think she doesn't carry a gun?" he said. "Beautiful little pearl-handled .22 in her reticule. Anyway her job is different, she's out in town most of the time, where she has some kind of law enforcement on her side if anything happens. If somebody tries to rape her or she goes to jail, no problem. She has a great time interviewing all the parties involved. You, you're out in the sagebrush, miles from where anybody can see. If you have a problem, you need to be able to solve it fast."

"Like Einar does." I shivered, remembering.

"Like Einar," Porfirio agreed. He looked as though he was about to say something else; but after an awkward moment he shrugged. "So, go put your stuff away. Dinner'll be ready in about fifteen minutes."

I went slowly, marveling at the gap between official policy and actual field procedure. We were always told that mortal life is incredibly precious and must never, ever be taken: they do enough of that themselves. We were warned that we would have to stand by and watch as mortals executed one another, or destroyed thousands of themselves in wars and riots. But *we* never take part in their primitive justice, never help them along their Malthusian path. Of course, there have always been rumors that the Company allows the occasional removal of a vile and evil mortal for the greater good. Sometimes, it's whispered, even an innocent mortal may die, if it's necessary for the success of a mission. I've even heard that tacitly admitted. Security techs like Porfirio would be the ones to take care of any unofficial assassinations; they're programmed for strong-arm work, the way facilitators are programmed to be devious and amoral.

But I didn't know what to make of how things were done in Los Angeles. Granted, most of the people sniping at travelers from the chaparral were murderers, either crazy or cold-blooded, whom any jury would hang in a second, so it made sense to kill them quickly and efficiently. But it was the speed and efficiency that had me unsettled. Got a problem? Bang, it's solved. No argument, no strategy, no getting to know your enemy.

I was still pondering this at dinner, over grilled beef and frijoles, and even Imarte's peculiar story didn't take my mind off it much.

"That man had the most *fascinating* account of rebel organizers in San Francisco," she said when she emerged for supper after a lengthy afternoon siesta.

"No kidding," said Porfirio, stirring the frijoles.

"You wouldn't believe the absurd and quixotic plans Southern sympathizers are forming up in the city. Even in places like Visalia. There is far more anti-Union sentiment in this region than I ever supposed." She sat, drawing a shawl about her. "This man was actually contacted by a cell trying to raise men for an army. Can you imagine what they could accomplish if they were able to recruit enough fighters? One of their plans was to intercept the gold shipments that provide Union funds for continuing the war, which I need hardly explain would cripple Lincoln's efforts."

I was surprised. I hadn't paid enough attention to the war to be concerned with such goings-on, but it seemed like a respectable plan. "Why didn't they go through with it?"

"I think it's because the majority of the organizers are young and hotheaded. My informant intimated that there was some sort of dissension among the members of the organizing cabal." Imarte accepted a plate of supper and frowned judiciously at it. "But the main reason, probably, was that the Comstock lode was discovered. Given the choice between resisting the tyrant's yoke and making a bundle, most of the nascent California Confederacy departed for Nevada."

"That figures," Porfirio said, and laughed. "I remember when all the Anglos deserted Los Angeles back in 1849, when the Gold Rush happened. Suddenly you couldn't get china, you couldn't get shoes—all the little stores were closed."

"Same thing in Monterey," I said, remembering the ghost town it had become. "Everybody went for the gold. That's so stupid, though, for the rebels! Just like the Japanese never getting around to bombing San Diego or Mare Island next century, which would win the Pacific war for them, but they never do it. Because, think about it. What would happen if the Confederates decided to play Sir Francis Drake and go privateering along the coast?"

"El Draque," said Porfirio, reminiscing as he rolled frijoles in a tortilla. "I saw him, once, for about ten minutes. Short little bastard."

"As it happens, that was part of the plan," Imarte told me. "The gold for the Union troops is shipped from San Francisco to Panama on the Pacific mail steamers. Seize those gold shipments, and you deal a serious blow to the Union. But apparently the logistical problems in obtaining a ship and ordnance for the enterprise were only just beginning to be dealt with when most of the conspirators left for Virginia City."

"This guy told all this top-secret stuff to a whore?" Porfirio shook his head. "No wonder the plot fell apart. Look at the blabbermouths they recruited."

"That must have been part of the problem," Imarte agreed. "Though I gather Mr. Jackson felt it safe to discuss the matter with me because the rebellion is pretty much a dead issue. Apparently the young man who was in charge of his cell departed for Veracruz."

"What's he gonna do down there? Fight with the ladrones to keep Maximilian out?" said Porfirio with disgust. "Shit, that's all they need, another Nicaragua."

Imarte shrugged. I washed down a tortilla with some lukewarm coffee. Who cared what the mortal monkeys did, anyway? We knew how it would turn out in the end. The Union would be saved, and poor old Abraham Lincoln would pick a bad night to go to the theater. France would get Mexico but wouldn't be able to keep it. I had work to do at my credenza.

"When did you see Sir Francis Drake?" Imarte asked Porfirio.

"Ha, gonna pick *my* brains, now? You anthropologist. It was in 1579. I was out with my brother's son. The kid was supposed to be delivering some silver on pack llamas from Tarapaca to Morro Morena, and I went with him to be sure he made it. Well, he didn't. About halfway there, who do we run into but this little stubby Englishman with a red beard, and—"

"Wait a minute!" I sat forward, staring. "Your brother's son? What are you talking about?"

"My brother's son," said Porfirio, looking down into his coffee as he stirred it. "I have family."

"But *none* of us have family," said Imarte. Even she was astonished. "It's Company policy to recruit orphaned children."

"Yes, it is," he said. "And I was orphaned. So was my brother... My mortal father was a soldier under Bernal Diaz. From Hispaniola. All those gentlemen adventurers decided they could make a fortune by going over to Mexico with Cortés to get gold and estates for themselves. They did it, too, though most of them didn't live long enough to enjoy them. My father was awarded some relative of Moctezuma's as a bride. People gave the Spanish lots of girls, every one of them princesses, supposedly, hoping the tie of blood would make the new conquerors part of the family. I guess they kept some self-respect that way. You know: He's not a white god, he's just my son-in-law. Well, some minor king gave his daughter to Cortez, and Cortez already had all the wives he wanted, so he passed her on to one of his officers, who wasn't interested in women so *he* passed her on to one of his subordinates, and to make a long story short, she wound up with my father, who kept her.

"I guess they loved each other. I remember her crying and crying over him when he died.... But before that happened they had children. Two, me and my little brother, Agustin. I was four. Agustin was only a baby. I don't know what happened and don't want to know. All I remember is fire and blood and my father dying and my mother weeping over him. She told me to wait, to take care of Agustin, and she dragged my father's body outside. She never came back.

"Then the lady came. She told me she was going to take me away somewhere safe, where I'd never die, that a kind doctor was going to take care of me from now on. You know, the story we all hear, when they find us. She tried to make me go with her and leave Agustin, but I wouldn't. I yelled and picked him up and wouldn't let go of him. In the end she had to take us both.

"Well, when we got to the nearest Company base, they had a problem on their hands, because here they were with two little mortal kids saved from certain death, but only one of them—me—fit the physical profile for the immortality process. What to do with baby Agustin?

"They were kind enough about it. They inoculated him against diseases, and they found foster parents for him, a good, loving couple who wanted a child, and one day, while I was undergoing the first cranial surgery for augmentation, they gave him away. I was so mad when I woke up and found out. What was Agustin going to do without me? I was supposed to look after him.

"But the nurse explained how they'd given him to these really nice people, and how he'd live a wonderful long life and never die of smallpox, and my poor mother and father would have wanted that, and didn't I want them to be happy up there in heaven? Anyway, what could I do about it?

"Well, I did something." He gazed into the fire. "When I was grown, after I graduated, I accessed Company records and got the name of the couple who adopted Agustin, and I went and looked him up. He didn't remember me, of course, and I couldn't tell him who I was; but I struck up an acquaintance with him all the same. His adoptive father had land and money, and spoiled the kid. Agustin had everything, but he was beginning to get into trouble when I found him. You know the kind of trouble rich kids get into. They're bored. Life has no point. They don't love anybody, and they don't think anybody loves them. So it's cards, whores, drink, and raising hell. I beat some sense into him, and we became sworn friends after that.

"His foster father approved of me as a good influence. My brother and I went places, did things together, just as though I were a mortal. He fell in love with a girl and married her; I was best man. They had kids, and I was godfather to half of them. He worked hard, he made good investments. I had to leave now and then when the Company sent me places, but I always came back to check on Agustin.

"The business with Drake happened when Agustin had to pay some rents to the bishop at Morro Morena. He sent Dieguito—his oldest boy—with the rent in silver on a pack train of llamas. Thank

God I went along. We were halfway there when out of nowhere we were surrounded by these lousy Englishmen, and I'm not using the term metaphorically. They were also armed to the teeth. They looked like they were starving. The leader was Francis Drake, a little short fat guy with a red beard. I wish I could tell you something memorable about him that would give you an invaluable insight into his character, but all he did was call us dogs and demand the llamas. He thought they were some kind of sheep. He was pretty happy when he found the silver.

"When his attention was distracted, I grabbed Dieguito, and we ran and got away. The English shot at us and called us filthy cowards— why they were sore about us running, I can't guess. Dieguito was humiliated and angry. He wanted to go back there and throw rocks at them or something. I grabbed him and asked him what he thought his father would rather have, a living son or a son killed by a bunch of pirates? Any father would like to know his son died bravely; but he'd much rather hear that there were going to be lots of grandchildren.

"When we got back, Dieguito saw that I was right, because Agustin wept and embraced his son, and embraced me, and said he would have given the boy's weight in silver to get him safe home again. Agustin said it was a lucky day for him when I insulted him in that tavern. Drake sailed on up the coast and out of our lives, and the Company sent me away on a mission, and I was plenty busy for a while.

"But then, one time I came back after being away a couple of years..."

"And Agustin had died?" I guessed.

"No, though it felt like it. He'd aged. Begun to age, anyway. The first gray in his beard, his face sagging a little. And his kids were growing up. While I still looked twenty." Porfirio reached around for a branch and thrust it into the fire, opening up a red cavern of coals that breathed heat at us.

"So what did you do?" Imarte said.

"Learned appliance makeup real fast. Pretended to get sick and hang by a thread for months. Agustin came to see me every day... and when I made my recovery, everyone said the illness had aged me, which was what they were supposed to say, so things were okay for a while. It was a pain getting made up every morning, but it was worth it to be able to keep an eye on Agustin.

"But time kept passing. You know what happened, eventually. Little Agustin the fat baby, with his dimple and his shock of hair, became Agustin the tremulous old skeleton, toothless, blind, unable to remember things. He'd had his years and years of long life, just as the nurse promised me; and this was what it had done to him. I sat by his bed, every day; I held his hand and listened to him mutter and twitch, or breathe with a sound like clothes being dragged over a washboard. I myself was so weighed down with the crap I wore to make me look old, I could barely move.

"I went weeping to his funeral—so many great-grandchildren there!—and Dieguito, old Diego now, comforted me by telling me his father would see me in paradise. I couldn't tell him there was just one little problem with that: you have to die to go to heaven, and I couldn't.

"I pretended to, of course. I made up a wax dummy with my horrible old features, then had a hot shower and stripped away all the appliances, all the latex and paint and white hair, and paid a servant to see to my funeral. I walked out of my own house young and free, and I got on a horse and rode north."

Out in the night a coyote howled, mocking.

"But I wasn't free," Porfirio said with a sigh. "Who was going to look after the great-grandchildren? I stayed away ten years. The Company sent me to Nicaragua, to Chile, to Mexico, to Texas. I did a lot of good work and had some free time, so I went back to visit Agustin's grave. They'd buried my wax dummy beside him, wasn't that nice of them? And Dieguito, who would have remembered me best, was blind now. Cataracts. His kids had no sense, they'd led soft lives and were letting the estates go to hell. *Their* kids were wild and living like Indians. Somebody had to take a hand. So I followed the oldest of the young boys around, watching him, and one night he left a cantina drunk and was set upon by thieves. I killed them and brought him home."

Just like that, he killed them. Well, he was a security tech.

"The family—none of them knew who I was, I looked twenty-five at most—welcomed me, thanked me, gave me a job as majordomo. I held it for a while, long enough to set things to rights again. Dieguito died, and the baby I'd held in a baptismal robe I saw as an ancient creature lying gaunt in his coffin. It didn't matter. The son had a son, and I was such a member of the family by that time that I was the god-father, and I held the little fat brown boy while the old priest anointed him and named him Agustin.

"It's gone on like that, you see? For centuries now, and the Company has been very understanding. I have a big family, and they need me. Their fortunes have changed—our estates were lost after the Grito—but the family has survived. There was nothing I could do about Agustin's dying, but his blood still runs in his descendants. I stay with them awhile, I watch them get old and pretend to get old for a while myself; then I ride away and stay away until they need me again. One night a stranger will come; and if any of the old people think he looks like Uncle Porfirio, who used to teach them how to ride, well, it can't be more than coincidence, can it? Because Uncle Porfirio would of course be a very, very old man now, if anybody knew where he was."

After a long silence he shrugged. "I'll have to be more careful, now that photography has been invented," he concluded.

Imarte was sitting with stars in her eyes. "That is so *beautiful!* What a unique chance you've been given! Think what a cultural thesis you could make of it, three centuries of history as experienced by one family!"

"You think so?" He looked sidelong at her. "How'd you like to have that responsibility? I'm never free. Three hundred years, and I'm still obeying my mortal mother's last request."

I thought privately that he'd been too hard on poor Juan Bautista about the birds. It's all very well to break the news to a young operative that love is a mistake, that attachments can't be formed because of what we are. But Porfirio had found a way around that, hadn't he? For him there was always a home fire burning somewhere, no matter how far he wandered on the dark plain, while the rest of us made do with ashes and ghosts.

Someone was standing on the other side of the fire, looking at me. The others didn't see him. I refused to lift my eyes.

"So, where are they now?" I asked. "Your family."

Porfirio shifted, uncomfortable. "Most of the direct line are working on a ranch in Durango. One of the girls married a man with some property, and all the brothers have moved in to work for them. They're doing all right, I guess. I haven't been down that way in ten years. I'll need to wait a few more years before I can go back there again."

I put his story out of my mind as I went to my room and set up my credenza for work, and I kept it out of my mind while I processed my specimens. In the end I had to shut it off and go to bed, though, and the second my head hit the pillow, the question leaped out at me like a thief from ambush: What had become of *my* family?

Long dead, their remains probably stacked in a charnel house beside some village church in Galicia. Had there been descendants? I'd had lots of brothers and sisters, so perhaps there were some distant relatives running around somewhere. There might be some woman even at this moment with my face, my hair, buying onions in the marketplace in Orense or Santiago de Compostela.

When I finally fell asleep, I had the nightmare again, the old nightmare that I always forget until I'm actually inside it once more, where I'm in my parents' house in the middle of the night. It's dead-black night, but the moon shines like an arc lamp, and I can see them all lying together in the one big bed. There is my skinny father and my ever-pregnant mother, and there are all the little children I used to fight with so bitterly for our shared toys, or a scrap of food, or our mother's attention. I know all their names, but I always forget them when I wake up.

My family is asleep, as silent as though they were underwater, and nothing will wake them. I'm the only one awake. I try my best, but I can't get anyone to wake up and be company for me. The moonlight is so white, the night is so still. I wander around the room disconsolately, but they never wake up to notice I'm there. They will sleep forever. Only I am awake; only I can never sleep.

This time, I couldn't bear it and ran outside into the moonlight. It was a mistake. Apple trees stretched in every direction, white with blossom, and the air was full of perfume. He was standing there under the trees, tall in his black robe, waiting for me. As I halted and stared, he extended his arm in its long sleeve, that graceful gesture that was one of the first things I'd ever noticed and loved in him. Inviting me, beckoning me, summoning me.

I struggled upright on my narrow cot, gasping like a fish out of water, soaked with chill sweat, and for one terrifying moment I thought the spectral moon was shining in here too, because it seemed to me there was a flash of eerie blue that faded and flickered away. I sagged against the wall and wept, not bothering to wipe away my tears. Here came the footsteps again, Porfirio running out to see what the disturbance was; but he stopped, and after a long while turned and went away without speaking.

I lay down again, shaking, pulled up the blanket, and curled on my side. I was so cold.

I WISH WE HAD SOME TOAST," Oscar was complaining at breakfast. "Oatmeal. Soft-boiled eggs. Real food."

"This isn't a civilized country yet, remember?" Porfirio said to him with a grin. "You'll get your oatmeal eventually."

"Anything would be preferable to this monotony of leftovers." Oscar rested his chin on his fist, staring glumly at the beef in the skillet.

"You want to talk to Dr. Zeus about allocating me a bigger budget to run this place?" Porfirio flipped the steaks adroitly. "So, hombre, how's that pie safe? Got a buyer for it yet? Should I start peeling those parsnips?"

Oscar pursed his lips. "I feel lucky today," he said. "Mendoza, will you come with me and bear witness?"

"To what?" I looked up groggily from my coffee. I hadn't been sleeping well lately, to put it mildly.

"I want someone present who can testify to my triumph."

"Oh. Actually I was going out into the temperate belt today, Oscar."

"We can go that way. There are houses out there. Why, I haven't even visited that area yet. Those people are probably desperate for good-quality merchandise at affordable prices." His eyes grew wide and reverent.

"Okay," I said, getting up to fetch my field gear. It'd save me a long walk; why not? When I came out, he'd already hitched up Amelia and was pacing back and forth, energized.

"Your chariot awaits, ma'am." He bowed me to my seat. "Where shall we go?"

"Take Franklin to Hollywood to Sunset," I said. We had all adopted Einar's use of future street names, and that was the route that followed the foothills through the temperate belt. He gee-hawed to Amelia, and away we rolled.

This was a much prettier drive than the road that cut across the plain, with inviting green canyons that opened up to the north; unfortunately it was also a lot more dangerous, as bullets sang out of the thickets at regular intervals. We dodged them and shot back if they seemed too persistent; I scarcely wasted a thought on it now. I was able to get good specimens of *Vitis girdiana* near the future intersection of Laurel Canyon and Sunset Boulevard; I found an interesting mutation of *Chrysothamnus,* with possible commercially valuable properties, at Sunset and Queens Road. Oscar bore with my frequent stops patiently, but kept his eyes trained on a thin column of smoke that rose ahead.

When we finally came around a foothill and saw its source, he sighed in disappointment. The house was old, built of tules in the local Indian style, and in fact there was an Indian lady in the yard, standing on a rock to load acorns into a kind of basketwork silo. If not for the fact that she was wearing European clothing, we might be back in pre-Columbian days. She turned to stare at us as we pulled up before her yard.

"Good morning, señora," I called to her in Spanish.

"And to you," she said, getting down and wiping her hands on her apron.

"Look at that!" gasped Oscar. I thought he was enchanted by the primitiveness of it all, but it was the silo that had his attention. He was out of the wagon and into the yard much too fast for the dogs who lived there, for they surrounded him in a snarling mob before he could reach the lady.

"Please excuse him, señora, he means no harm," I said from my seat in the cart. She nodded and called the dogs off. Oscar had his hat in his hands at once.

"My apologies, a thousand pardons, señora, but I couldn't help seeing that you are in dire need of superior food-storage facilities!"

She just nodded and looked at him. Probably she was deciding that the white man was up to no good if he apologized to her this abjectly, but her face was blank, her expression mild.

Oscar gestured with his hat at the acorn silo. "This structure, señora, it's very ingenious and well made, but it's nothing more than *natural materials*. Are you not at the mercy of the ground squirrel, the raccoon, the scrub jay, and a host of other pests? Do they not voraciously deplete your larder?"

"Sometimes," she said.

"Well, allow me, señora, to offer you a solution to these depredations, a way of ensuring that your hours of backbreaking labor gathering the fruits of Jove's tree are not for naught!" He bowed her toward the cart. She went with him, placidly folding her hands, no doubt wondering who Jove was. The dogs snarled and followed, but kept their menace low-key.

"What you need," Oscar said, unfastening the side of the cart, "is a modern, sanitary method of preserving food. Now I think, señora, I *think* you'll agree that what I have here just fits the bill. Behold!" He flung back the side, displaying the pie safe gleaming among his wares like the central diamond in a crown. "The Criterion Patented Brassbound Pie Safe!"

Her face remained perfectly still, but a light flickered in her eyes. Then they grew a little bleak.

"It's very beautiful, señor," she said.

"Oscar—" I said. He ignored me.

"Regard the metal fittings. This is a first-rate device guaranteed to be impervious to pests, whether of the gnawing, crawling, or pecking variety. No less than eight separate compartments for the storage of your acorns and, er, whatever other fine foods you wish to keep pure, fresh, and unsullied. Now, I've a talent, if I may say so, señora, for supplying needs, and I can see plainly that *you need this*. It may have been designed for other forms of edible goods, but such is the versatility of its design that it will admirably preserve foodstuffs from any ethnic cuisine whatsoever."

"I'm sure it would, señor."

"Oscar—"

"Now, it may be," he said, raising a hand, "that you've put aside hard-won savings, in the anticipation that Necessity may call at your, uh, door. I might suggest that you could make no better investment against Want than this splendid item, which will safely reserve your stores against all possible losses. Ordinarily the Criterion Patented Brassbound Pie Safe is sold for no less than thirty dollars; but for you, señora, in your most obvious need, I will offer it for the special low price of *ten* dollars. Only say the word, señora, and you need never fear the loss of your acorns again."

I buried my face in my hands. She was taking them all in in a long bitter stare, all those pretty and improbable things she'd never thought of having and shouldn't have thought of having, because she'd never have them.

"It is certainly a beautiful thing, señor," she said meekly. "I am afraid, though, that I have no money."

Oscar gaped. "Well—why, I'll tell you what, then. You can pay for it on the hire-purchase plan! Twenty easy installments of fifty cents each, how about that? With the first payment deferred six months. You can't afford not to take advantage of this once-only offer."

"Yes, I can," she said. "I have no money at all, señor. My husband works on the big rancho, and the man who owns it lets us stay here in return. We never have any money."

"But—but my good woman, how do you live?" he said.

She waved a hand at the acorns, at the venison jerky drying on the fence, at the neatly woven baskets of pinole meal.

"Come on, Oscar," I said.

"Uh, well. If you ever *should* obtain hard currency, I'm sure a thrifty housewife such as yourself will invest it in the wisest possible way," Oscar gabbled. "And may I present you with a complimentary volume of the poetry of Percy Bysshe Shelley? I trust you'll remember me, señora, when you require the finest in home furnishings. Good day."

"Thank you. Good day," she said, staring at the little book in its bright pasteboard binding. Oscar leaped into the seat, and we rocketed off.

"*Shelley?*" I asked.

"That was my low point, my absolute nadir," Oscar groaned. "Dear Lord, what possessed me? It was her need, you know, her utter need. It seduced me. I must supply where I see demand. It's a compulsion. Other operatives would be content with simply gathering valuable anthropological data or ferreting out hitherto unrecorded ethnographical statistics. I must be *more*. I must be the genuine article. That's my problem: my standards are too high."

"Well, it's not like you're a failure," I said helpfully. "You're doing great work for the Company."

"For Dr. Zeus, I'll grant you. But what about the worthy gentlemen at the Acme and Criterion Companies? Mere mortal merchants, say you; yet I believe in complete commitment, absolute fulfillment of all responsibilities, be they ever so trivial." He shook the reins with noble determination. "Giddap, Amelia! To the next customer."

But worse was yet to come.

Farther down the road, in a green clearing beside a still-bubbling spring, we saw a fine adobe and garden. The walls were freshly plastered, the window frames painted, and a tall paling fence warned trespassers away from the yard, where cabbages were growing in precise lines and peach and plum trees stood to attention.

"Now, look at that," said Oscar, laying down the reins in admiration. "Look at the industry and thrift evident in that pleasant scene. Surely this is the residence of a wage-earning individual. And his spouse. Prudent housewifery is in every line of that garden plot. I can taste that New England boiled dinner now."

"Those are awfully big dogs," I observed. They sat alert, one on either side of the door, watching us silently. I hadn't the slightest doubt that if Oscar so much as put his foot inside the gate, they'd tear it off.

"Hem, you're right. Well, let's not repeat my previous error." Oscar got down and went around to the back, where he drew out a pan and a long wooden spoon. He commenced to beat out a brisk tattoo on the pan, looking hopefully at the house. The dogs pricked up their ears but made no move.

"Good day! Hello there! Is there anyone at home?" he called. The door opened, and a woman looked out.

Whoops. I transmitted to Oscar. *She's an Anglo. Off-limits for your pie safe.*

He faltered only a moment in his disappointment. "Well, good morning, there, ma'am!" he said in English. "I wonder if you'd be interested in any of the superior merchandise I have to offer?"

"*Nein,*" she said, and he shot me a look of triumph.

"You are German, madam?" he said in a close approximation of her regional accent. "From Bavaria, yes?"

"You, too?" Wonderingly she emerged from the house and came a little way toward him. "In this foreign land?"

"Many years now, but I assure you it is so. How pleasant it is to hear a cultivated voice again! Come now, my dear, I have many things here that you may need, though you may never have considered that in such a lawless and unimproved country they could be obtained. Come, see what I have to offer to you." Oscar put his hand on the latch, and the two dogs instantly sprang to their feet, growling. She shushed them and came a little closer, peering at us. He might have been a countryman, but he was still a peddler.

"Have you the polish with which to clean silver?" she said.

"Yes, *natürlich!* And I have additionally stove blacking, laundry bluing, wash powders, and these very fine clothespins that have a patent pending for the superior spring mechanism that they employ. Consider, here, the little figures of china bisque, very sweet, the little doves billing and cooing and the little shepherd boy playing love songs with his flute. And this pan for the baking of cakes, with the hearts printed in the bottom so as to make the design upon the finished cake, wouldn't you like to have this?"

"No," she said. "Just the polish for silver, thank you."

"Ah, but, my dear! Here is your silver polish, to be sure, but behold! Printed music for performance on the piano, the spinet, or the organ. And confections also, barley-sugar sticks in the flavors of apple, blackcurrant, or strawberry. And see what fine things I have for sewing."

"Thank you, no. How much for the silver polish?"

"Five cents American."

She raised her eyebrows slightly but fished in her apron pocket and paid him. He handed her the silver polish, and she turned to go. He nearly made a desperate lunge over the fence, which the dogs were only too happy to have him do.

"But, dear lady!" he screamed at her back. "See, here, this thing which you will find is an absolute necessity in this wild and dirty country. It is the Pie Safe Patented Criterion Brassbound." He flung wide the panel, revealing it in all its glory. "It keeps the bread loaves and the rolls from going stale. It keeps the mice, the rats, the insects from invading the pastries. You of all people would want such furniture for the kitchen that you bake in."

The woman turned and followed his gesture with her eyes. For a moment they were warm and approving. "Ah, yes," she agreed, nodding her head. "I do not know what I would do without the one I have."

"You have such a one?" Oscar asked, going pale.

"*Natürlich*, there in my kitchen inside the house. But mine is bigger than that, and bound not in brass but in nickel that is plated with silver. And it has not pineapples upon it but the design of pheasants."

She looked closer, critically. "Also, yours does not have the egg timer or the barometer built into the cabinet, as mine has."

Immortal or not, I thought he'd keel over dead right there on the spot. She realized she'd dealt him some sort of near-fatal blow, though, because she hastened with a kindly word: "All the same, it is a very good pie safe, and you will certainly sell it to somebody. I have no need of it, however. Good day, my dear sir."

Well, I couldn't laugh, he looked so stricken when he crawled up on the seat beside me. We drove away in silence. About halfway back to La Nopalera, he drew a deep breath and said, "I'd be obliged to you, Mendoza, if you wouldn't mention this mortifying occasion to the others."

"Don't worry," I said. I had no wish to gloat. The day's outing had been successful for me; I had got a couple of good specimens not only on the drive out but also on the way back, I scored a previously unclassified member of the *Celastraceae,* some exotic low-elevation form of *Euonymus* by the look of it. Happy me.

I COULDN'T GET THOSE green canyons out of my mind. Accessing topographical data, I decided that Laurel Canyon, with its drastic range in elevations, had the best chance of mutation-yielding microclimates and diversified habitats. I was intrigued, also, by the blue-hazard notations on every reference to the area I encountered.

"I thought I'd stroll over to Laurel Canyon today," I said, one morning at breakfast, casually.

Porfirio choked on his coffee and glared at me.

"Are you nuts?" he said. "That's a blue-hazard precinct, dummy."

"So my files tell me, but I've never encountered one before. It's just a kind of energy sink, right? A locus of natural unnaturalness in the landscape?" I was a little taken aback by his reaction.

"You could say that," he growled, mopping spilled coffee from his chin with one hand. "It's just the biggest damn one on the continent, that's all."

"Oh," I said. "Does that mean I can't go there?"

"Not alone, you can't, you of all people, and not without the right field gear. What the hell do you want there, anyway?"

"Well...it has all those steep isolated canyons and drastic heights and depths. There are probably a lot of rare endemic species of plants growing there. I'd be stupid not to look for them. And what do you mean, me of all people?"

He looked over uneasily at Einar, who was grooming Marcus, and at Juan Bautista, who was watching him. "Okay," he said in a lower voice, not answering my question. "I guess there's stuff back up in there worth collecting at that. But you're going to take the following precautions, understand? Now listen carefully..."

Two hours later:

"God, I feel stupid," I moaned to Einar as we approached the canyon on horseback. "What if mortals see us?"

"We shoot 'em," he said glumly. I hoped he was joking. We were wearing absurd-looking helmets with Crome filter lenses and a lot of other cunning little mechanisms built into them with no consideration for style or convenience. We wore gauntlets full of wiring and large, ugly, and ill-fitting boots with circuitry patterns on the outside. Things like Batman's utility belt were cinched about our waists. To make matters worse, we were tethered each to the other by a long silver line. If one of our horses startled and bolted, somebody would be dragged.

"We look like extras in a cheap science-fiction film," I complained.

"In a damned expensive science-fiction film," Einar retorted. "You know how much it cost to make this stuff, here in 1862? And these are the only sets of this gear in the continental U.S. at this time. They were made just so we could go into Laurel Canyon, if we had to. So enjoy the fantasy. Tell yourself we're explorers on a forbidden planet or something."

"It can't be *that* weird, no matter what Porfirio says," I muttered. But as we came to the entrance of the canyon, I fell silent.

I saw a narrow passage between soaring walls of granite, thinly grown with whatever little plants could cling to their vertical surfaces. The way in followed a creek bed through which water was still cascading down. From the wreckage of broken trees and from the high-water mark on the cliff faces, you knew that this was no place to stand during the winter floods. Water must come thundering down that channel like cannon fire. A dramatic scene, with the leaning dead cottonwoods and the majestic atmosphere, the mountains impossibly high on either side. A little trail led into the canyon, a sandy embankment on the left-hand side above the water, and disappeared into dark trees.

Einar unslung his shotgun and cocked it. Cautiously we rode in.

"Now, remember," said Einar, "don't scan. Every conditioned reflex and instinct you've got is telling you to, but don't. Let the helmet do it for you. If you try, yourself, you're going to pick up data you won't believe."

"This is nuts," I said, as my horse picked its way timidly. "How are mortals going to live here? But they are, aren't they? And this is right in the heart of Hollywood."

"I know," he said. "They just...become part of the strangeness. Raymond Chandler wrote about it in his Philip Marlowe stories, but he didn't tell half of what he knew. There'll be a murder that happens right up *there*"—he pointed up a nearly vertical slope—"that he writes about in *The Big Sleep*. But it doesn't happen the way he says, it never makes the papers, and it's never solved, either. The guy isn't a pornography dealer, he's a high-ranking member of a hermetic brotherhood. There's a brilliant flash and a scream, all right, and a naked girl and some ancient earrings with a curse on them. The curse doesn't make it into the book, but a lot of the other details do."

"How lurid," I said, and then started, because I heard a sound I shouldn't have heard in that place, not for another half century at least. I turned my head to stare down the trail behind us. I knew that sound from cinema: the rattle of an internal combustion engine, the rush of displaced air as something sped toward us, but I had no visual input at all. Forgetting myself, I scanned, and *knew* there was something approaching. In my desperation I yanked up the Crome screen visor so I could see with my eyes.

"Mistake," Einar gasped. He was right. Without my visor the place lit up, every tree, rock, shrub, and blade of grass outlined in blue neon. The automobile was lit up like that too, a 1923 Avions Voisin, a lovely, elegant thing except for being glowing blue, slightly transparent, and a little out of place in 1862. Einar leaned over and got a firm grip on my horse's reins, or I'd have been away from there in an instant. The car zoomed up, till I was right between its bug-eyed headlights, and I got a clear glimpse of the hood ornament in the shape of a rearing cobra.

With a crackle of static the car whooshed through me and on, up the canyon. My mouth was open. Einar managed to reach out and click my visor down. Visual references were once again normal.

"Told you not to scan," he said reprovingly.

"Was that a ghost?" I asked at last. At least it hadn't been a sixteenth-century Protestant martyr.

"Or a temporal anomaly, or a hallucination, or—anything. Keep the visor down, don't scan, and start looking for rare plants *now*. The sooner you get what you're after, the sooner we get out of here."

"Okay," I said, and we rode on.

The road continued up, clinging to the hillside above the creek bed, and I saw condors wheeling in the sky and deer leaping away from us, and they were really there. I saw a coyote loping along in broad daylight across the canyon, and he was really there too. It was the sounds that dismayed. There were gunshots (which may or may not have been real), and there were more whizzing automobiles, and there was singing and chanting. How was I supposed to look for rare endemic plants with all that going on?

"All right," I said at last. "I give up. What's the deal here? And does it get any better, do we ride out of it?"

"No, it gets worse," Einar said. "We're still on the edge. We haven't come to Lookout Mountain Drive yet."

I frowned. "Lookout Mountain Drive? That sounds familiar."

"Here's the explanation as I understand it: weird geology around here. Look at all this decomposing granite. It's quartz-bearing, crystals all through the rock if you know where to look. There's another outcropping of high quartz concentration over in what'll be Griffith Park, and that place has some bizarre happenings of its own, but this place is the mother lode." Einar turned uneasily in his saddle, starting to scan, and stopped himself with visible effort. Something enormous went snorting and blowing past us, and we heard small trees snapping and big trees being pushed aside.

"I knew it would be bad, but not like this. The local Indians say the canyon was cut through by the God Himself, that He was chasing Coyote who'd stolen the moon, and Coyote had burrowed down under these mountains with it, and God grabbed the mountaintops and ripped them apart, made this long fissure, to get to where the moon was hidden. It was down so deep, though, that God gave up and threw a buffalo gourd up in the sky to be the moon instead, and the old moon's still buried here somewhere.

"An interesting story, in light of the fact that the biggest damn quartz deposit in the known universe lies about a thousand feet below the intersection of Laurel Canyon Drive and Lookout Mountain Drive. We know it's there; the Company did radar imaging of the whole area, once they noticed this place is so full of Crome's radiation, it can wipe out our sensory displays. Apparently there's a single crystal down there the size of—of that thing that just went stomping by us. And that's just some of what they found. Nothing supernatural or extraterrestrial, you understand, just the biggest naturally occurring Crome spectral sponge in the world. As near as Dr. Zeus can figure out, it stores Crome's radiation generated by anything passing over it that has a nervous system. Animals, Indians, and bandits is about all there is now; but as people begin moving in here, there will be a lot more energy absorbed.

"And every so often it discharges, and then all hell breaks loose, and that's what we're seeing now," Einar concluded.

"It figures, that this is supposed to be Coyote's fault," I said disgustedly. I saw a bush I didn't recognize and stopped. Handing the reins to Einar, I slid down and bent to examine it. Yes, it was really there. "But why are we seeing it now? There's nobody living up here yet to generate all this stuff," I argued, groping for my collecting gear. Damn this visor anyway. How was I supposed to take readings? "What's causing the blue lights and the auditory illusions?"

"It could be picking up Crome from us. One theory is that every time it discharges, it sets up a shock wave that puts stress on the temporal field, and the whole fabric of time ripples. My guess is, they're afraid we might slip through a hole or something, and that's why the connecting cable. If one of us goes through, the other can pull him out." Einar lifted his gun to his shoulder involuntarily, then lowered it. "We're also recording and broadcasting data to Central HQ, I'm sure. So, is that a rare plant?"

"Looks like a mutation of *Myrica californica*," I said in satisfaction. "Jackpot, on the first try. Not that I can tell much about it in all this armor."

"Cut a couple of branches and let's go, okay?"

"Are you scared?" I looked up at him. My own fear had evaporated the second the bush read positive for mutation. What else might I find up here?

"Me? Hell no, I'd love nothing better than to get myself sucked through a temporal rift into Jurassic times or something." Einar turned his head, sweeping the area visually. "Let's move on. Want to see where the Haunted Tavern will be? It's just up ahead."

"Neat," I replied, tucking the specimens into my collecting bag and climbing into the saddle again. We rode on, though unseen sirens screamed past us.

A few hundred feet ahead, the gorge widened to a sort of clearing, with another steep canyon opening to the left. Immense sycamores darkened the way ahead of us. We rode to the center of the clearing. For the moment, all we heard were natural sounds, the creek bubbling to our right, the wind in the leaves.

"Nice spot, isn't it?" said Einar, actually relaxing a little. "Someone will build a brick commercial building here. The top part will be the Canyon Store, eventually, and a lot of famous rock stars will buy their groceries here. Around the corner and downstairs, though"—he pointed over his horse's tail—"is where the Haunted Tavern will be. The earliest record of it is as a speakeasy, then later it's a cozy bar. Nice little watering hole for thirsty movie people going home to Encino after a day at RKO, or going home to Beverly Hills after a day at

Universal or Republic. They'll shortcut through Laurel Canyon with a stop right here. It's private, it's unfashionable, it's hard for wives or reporters or detectives to find them in the little dark basement bar." He leaned forward in the saddle, and his crazy smile looked crazier than usual under the visor of the absurd helmet.

"Now, you've heard the story about John Barrymore's wake? How, after he dies, a bunch of his drinking buddies steal his body from the funeral parlor and take it with them for one last night on the town? He's supposed to be carried all over Hollywood during this one long wild night before his funeral. That much is legendary.

"What didn't make it into the legend was how the party finished up. This part of the story is supposed to have been told to a male nurse at the hospital where W. C. Fields died. According to the nurse, the last stop on the route was this basement bar. The place was locked for the night, but Gene Fowler picked the lock, and they got in. Laid out cash on the bar and mixed themselves drinks. At this point, Barrymore is supposed to have sat up in his coffin and demanded to know where *his* drink was. They were in a pretty philosophical mood by that time, so they just poured him a martini. I don't know what's supposed to have happened after that, but people say..."

"What?" I shivered, hearing an invisible glass break.

"Well, the place operates on and off after that. Sometimes it's a bar, sometimes it's a restaurant, sometimes it closes down for years at a time. But whenever it's a bar, sooner or later, *John Barrymore comes in for a drink.* And once he's seen, the new owners know they might just as well give notice to the Realtor and move on; because before long the place is packed after hours with the thirsty dead, W. C. Fields and Victor McLaglen and Erroll Flynn, to name but a few. They drink the booze, they break the glasses, they have loud conversations in the parking lot at four A.M. Local residents get mad as hell and call the cops. What can the cops do? No use for the bar's owners to swear that they close at midnight, either. The place gets shut down again, until the next hapless guy comes along and decides it's a great place to open a cozy little bar."

Smash! This time it was a bottle breaking, and my horse shied and started forward.

"Let's go on," I said.

We rode up the canyon, with me stopping at frequent intervals to investigate the truly amazing number of unusual endemics that began to occur as we drew closer to Lookout Mountain Drive. I found a purple form of *Marah macrocarpus,* a variant of *Lonicera subspicata* with scarlet flowers, and the strangest-looking *Baccharis glutinosa* I'd ever encountered. I was so absorbed in my discoveries that I paid little attention to the trumpeting mammoths, trolley cars, and bagpipers that passed me on the way. Einar had to reach into his saddlebags, though, where he'd stashed a whole box of Theobromos, the Mexican kind that comes in six round cakes in an octagonal box. He just kept unwrapping them and wolfing them down, working his way through them as though they were rice cakes. As a result, he was mellower than usual by the time we got to Lookout Mountain Drive, and swaying gently in the saddle.

"An' here it is," he said, swinging an arm in a half circle. "The strange heart of all strangeness anyplace. Look normal to you? Ah, but we know better."

Actually it didn't look normal to me, even through the visor, though it was just a sunny clearing opening up to the sky. There was something a little skewed in the perspective. I couldn't quite tell how wide the clearing was.

"So this is the mystery spot?" I tried to sound nonchalant.

"Yes, but not some lousy little carney mystery spot with trick angles and optical illusions," said Einar. "If you took that visor off, this place would light up like Times Square. All kinds of unusual mortals will be drawn here. One guy, he'll be a naval officer and engineer with a wife who's a practicing witch. They'll settle here for a while, and he'll actually write an exposé of the place. Then he'll think things over and rewrite it as a piece of science fiction. Did you ever hear of Dr. Montgomery Sherrinford?"

I did a fast access on the name. All that turned up was a footnote in a biography of Aleister Crowley and a half paragraph in a work on theosophy.

"Some kind of Freemason?" I asked.

"Starts out as one. They eject him. He becomes a Rosicrucian, and they throw him out too. Same thing with the Order of the Golden Dawn. Madame Blavatsky gives him the heave-ho, and so do those people up at Summerland. He travels all over the place before he finds Lookout Mountain Drive, but *then,* man, his luck changes. He builds a kind of temple right there"—Einar pointed to our left—"and he builds a mansion up there on the hill. In later years people will call it Houdini's mansion, but no—it was built by Dr. Sherrinford. He *knows* the vibrations on this spot are like nothing else anywhere. Gets himself a cult going, becomes its high priest, lots of spooky goings-on all around this very intersection. A lot of famous players and their bosses too, from the early days of movies, come to 'services' here. Not because of the guy's charisma, but because he has real powers—also he knows where a lot of bodies are buried, metaphorically and otherwise."

"I never heard about any of this," I said doubtfully.

"You have to know where to look, but the references are there. In this correspondence, in that library collection. Anyway, Dr. Sherrinford has this big thing going. Silent-film stars at his beck and call. Blackmail money. Devoted followers who set about the task he sets them, which seems to be tunneling into Laurel Canyon. He gets them looking for the source of the power. He's never too clear on what it is, but he's got a good idea *where* it is. He'll completely undermine his temple with tunnels. And it seems he gets all the way down to the big crystal, too, because all these rumors start flying around of an incredible discovery and miracles and contact with the other world.

"Now, *we* know you can't do anything with Crome's radiation, not anything useful anyway. Dr. Sherrinford won't know that. He'll think it'll give him power. He builds an underground chapel a thousand feet below, reached by a little elevator going down a shaft, and he takes his disciples down there, and they hold chanting services.

"You know what happens when you have a lot of people generating a Crome-effect field around a spectral sponge. Just like electricity, it absorbs the charge, absorbs the charge, until finally it discharges, boom! And all hell breaks loose, ripples in the temporal field, ghosts, visions, apports, you name it. It happens, or seems to.

"That's what Dr. Sherrinford's disciples keep praying for. It's like a bunch of monkeys in a cage, hitting the same lever over and over again until the bell rings and a bucket of monkey treats are dumped on them. Or it's like somebody with a cup of nickels playing a slot machine. Mostly Dr. Sherrinford's crystal spirit ignores its worshipers, but every so often it blasts them with a miracle and a lot of stimulation of the hippocampal region of their brains.

"Harry Houdini is in California making a movie for Lasky, it's called *Terror Island,* and he's doing location shooting over on Catalina. And this guy comes up to him in the restaurant at the Hotel Metropole and tells him about the goings-on at Dr. Sherrinford's temple and asks if he wants to come attend a service there. It's implied that the dead speak at these parties.

"Well, that's just the right thing to say to Houdini—or the wrong thing, depending on your point of view. His mother died a few years previous, and he has this strong attachment to her, kind of a Freudian thing, you know? He's been positive she'll send him a message from the beyond, only years have gone by now and she hasn't, though he's paid plenty of bucks to spiritualists and mediums. Not that they don't claim she's trying to talk to him, but the messages are all obvious fakes.

"Finally he decides it's all a lot of bull and becomes an obsessive debunker. Inside, though, *he wants to believe.* So he flies back from Catalina with this guy, and they go to Laurel Canyon. They meet Dr. Sherrinford. What happens next?

"Nobody ever gives complete testimony; but again, if you know where to look, you can piece it together, what happens down in the crystal chamber. Houdini goes there, all right, with Dr. Sherrinford and his disciples, and they hold a big ceremony with chanting and pull out all the stops, they're levitating and speaking in tongues. It sets off the crystal. And when it discharges, apparently a *lot* of dead guys want to speak with Houdini. Only problem is, some of them are ordinary dead and some of them claim to be dead guys from the future, from a time when there isn't time. And they aren't all agreed on the usual spirit patter about being happy on the other side and telling everyone that it's all niceness and harmony over there. In fact, they start to fight.

"They fight so violently, they cause something like a small earthquake. The tunnel collapses, or becomes blocked. What happens to Dr. Sherrinford and his gang is never known, but Houdini manages to escape by getting to the jammed elevator and worming his way through an air vent, after which he climbs the cable. He takes off down the canyon into the night.

"Why doesn't he call the cops? Why doesn't he make any attempt to rescue Dr. Sherrinford's people? We'll never know. Whatever took place, it scares Houdini half to death. He opens negotiations to buy that property, though, which shows that something about it has a hold on him. History's a little vague about whether he ever closes the deal, but there's an account that he's visited in his hotel room by one of the disciples, who may or may not be a survivor of the crystal chamber. Houdini leaves on the train for New York the same day, and never stays in Los Angeles again. In fact he leaves America a month later and goes on an extended tour abroad. Spends the rest of his life trying to prove that there *is* no other side and that the dead can't talk."

"So there'll be an earthquake," I said, shrugging. "It buries the cultists, and Houdini gets out because of his special abilities. Afterward somebody blackmails him about running off and leaving the others to die. Creepy, but not inexplicable."

"I'd agree," Einar said, grinning at me, "except for the fact that in 2072 a bunch of people in white robes come wading out of the surf off Bermuda claiming to be Montgomery Sherrinford and his disciples. They disappear into an asylum and out of the historical record pretty fast, though."

"Hoaxers," I said firmly, shaking my head. I caught sight of a weird-looking thing poking through the dead leaves at the base of a *Rhus laurina*. A kind of fungus? Root parasite? Urn-shaped flowers bright green—some member of the heath family? At *this* elevation? And what were those curling scales? I accessed at top speed and found not a single identification. If it were possible for my immortal heart to skip a beat, it would have done so then. Visions of Favorable Mutation bonuses for *Sarcodes mendozai* danced before my eyes.

"I'm going to dismount now," I informed Einar. "I think there's something really remarkable here."

"You can say that again," said Einar, taking firm hold of the cord that connected us. He watched as I slid down—and I could feel something through the soles of my boots, a pulsing. There was a cracking sound and a flash of bluest light. I grabbed at my saddle in panic, but that was no good either, the horse just swayed away from me. Einar seemed a long distance off. And where was the damned plant?

I looked around, expecting to see a landscape festooned with melting clocks. What I saw was no less strange. Immediately beside me, and stretching up and down the canyon, was a long river of gleaming rounded things, inching slowly forward in a stinking miasma of chemical smoke like so many mechanical turtles. They weren't blue. They weren't transparent. Behind smoked glass, open-mouthed faces stared at me.

"Einar." I felt blindly for the cord. "There are unborn here."

"I know." His voice was faint. I looked over at him, and he was staring at me in horror, just as solidly there as I was, as the vehicles were. "So much for the cord, huh? I guess it just pulled me after you."

"These are late-twentieth-century automobiles."

"Yes."

I found myself hyperventilating. It was a mistake among the gasoline fumes. I looked around wildly. Everywhere were strange Japanese names in chrome. To hell with *Sarcodes mendozai*. I scrambled back up on my horse. The cars didn't go away. People were pointing at us.

"They're pointing at us," I said. "What do we do, for God's sake? Will they shoot at us, will they start rioting?"

"Let's stay calm," Einar said, though his knuckles were white where he gripped the reins. "Let's ride straight up that ridge and out of here. Maybe we'll, like, snap back to 1862 painlessly. Okay?"

We didn't. From the ridge above, we looked out on a clutter of houses. And what was the matter with the distant plain? Had the sea level risen? No; that roaring, gleaming gridwork was a city, stretching away to the horizon. We stared at it in shock. It was a city in the future, which I had always thought would be beautiful, but it wasn't beautiful at all. The air was brown. The sunlight looked red through it, sunset color at midday.

"Now...this *isn't* possible," I said to Einar. "Right? You can't go forward past your own time. Everybody knows that."

He nodded mutely.

"So it's just an illusion. No transcendence field, no stasis gas, so we can't even have gone back in time, let alone forward."

He nodded again. "Except," he said reluctantly, "that there are some recorded instances of people doing it. People in old-fashioned clothes suddenly turning up in future traffic and getting hit by cars, for instance."

"And of course those have to be unsubstantiated fictions, because it can't really happen. Dr. Zeus says so." I drew in a lungful of the acrid air and coughed. "Is this *smog*? How can people live like this?"

"Come on." Einar turned his horse's head. "There's supposed to be a relay station in Hollywood in this time period. Jumping ahead through time may be impossible for Dr. Zeus, but it obviously ain't impossible for Lookout Mountain Drive."

We rode down the ridge, accessing coordinates as we went. Immediately to the south of us rose a gated wall topped by what would have been Ionic columns if they were ten times bigger. As it was, they looked cheesy. Beyond them was a sprawling community of flat-topped mansions in ghastly mid-twentieth-century style, roofs covered with white gravel, walls faced with Hawaiian lava, everything deliberately off-center and out of balance, from the winding front walks to the kidney-shaped pools in each backyard. Black letters on the wall told us this was MOUNT OLYMPUS.

We found our way in, past the corner of Vulcan Drive, and proceeded down Olympus Drive. "Oh, they *didn't*." I said. "Did they?"

Einar smiled wryly and pointed at a little cul-de-sac with the grand name of Zeus Drive. The architecture there was just as crappy, even on the house that was obviously our relay station, the one with the Dr. Zeus logo picked out in green pebbles on the red-pebble tessellation of the front walk. There wasn't a living soul in sight, which was a good thing, under the circumstances.

We rode up the concrete driveway and sat there looking uncertainly at the very ugly house. There were no stables anywhere that I could see, though there was a sensor array on the roof, disguised to look like satellite television equipment.

Uh... Operatives Einar and Mendoza reporting. Please provide codes, transmitted Einar. As we watched, the broad garage door swung open of its own accord to reveal a couple of frightened-looking techs in coveralls.

"Come inside. Hurry!" hissed one of them. We urged our horses forward, and as soon as we were inside, the garage door clanked down after us. Our horses, who had been patient and unflappable until then, spooked; I just scrambled off mine and dodged its panicky dance, but Einar controlled his with an iron hand and caught my mount's reins. The techs cowered in a corner.

"Whoa, whoa," said Einar. He dismounted and caught his horse's head, stroking its muzzle and looking into its eyes. "You don't want to step on anybody, do you? Of course you don't. That's a good boy. And how about you, sweetie, you want to calm down too? Pretty girl. Good girl."

"You're talking to the *horses*," said one of the techs in disbelief.

"Yeah," he said, and I don't think he noticed that they found it distasteful. I noticed, though. I knew who they were at once: operatives from the future, doing time on a mission in what was *their* past, though their past was more than a hundred years ahead of us. I've worked with that kind before. They're stuck-up.

"I guess you're wondering what we're doing here," Einar said, but the tech who had more buttons on his coveralls than the other snapped:

"No, we're not. There was a distortion in the temporal field. We monitored it. You're an anomaly. You'll have to report immediately to the temporal transference chamber for return to your point of origin. This way!" He pointed, and the other one opened a door in the wall beside what appeared to be late-twentieth-century laundry appliances.

"What about the horses?" I said.

The tech got a look of horror on his face. He wrung his hands. At last he replied, "They'll have to come too. Just hurry!"

They scuttled ahead of us through the door. Einar and I exchanged bemused glances, but led our respective mounts through the doorway.

Horses look *big* in houses. Ours clopped after us through what was apparently a kitchen, across a smooth substance that must have been linoleum tile—I didn't think it looked all that bad—but the sound of their hooves was muffled when we emerged into a much larger room, because it was carpeted in synthetic fiber of a sickly beige color.

I was disoriented at once. The floor was on a couple of different levels, for no reason I could understand, and one whole wall slanted inward. Across the room was another rise to the floor, and there was a fireplace with no mantelpiece, only flagstones set *around* it, flush into the wall instead of on the floor, where flagstones belonged. In front of the hearth, where the flagstones should have been, the beige carpet went right up to the andirons. Stranger still, the entire west wall of the room was made of glass: four enormous panes gave a breathtaking view of the roofs of other houses across the canyon but robbed the room of any warmth or privacy.

The horses were disoriented too. Einar's gave its opinion of the decor with one good lift of its tail.

The tech leader jumped three feet, clapping his hands over his nose and mouth. "Aaagh! You *filthy*—oh, you *filthy*—"

Someone in the room burst out laughing. An immortal rose from a shapeless piece of furniture and surveyed the mess. She wore the unisex clothing of that era, ordinary jeans like Einar's and a plain white cotton shirt. She turned to us.

"You must be the two unfortunates who surfed the temporal wave. How do you feel?" she said pleasantly, as though what had happened was no big deal.

"There is excrement on the floor. The carpet will have to be disinfected," said the tech.

"Oh, shut up and go get a shovel. If we've got one around here. You'd have to be Zoologist Einar and, let's see, Botanist Mendoza, wasn't it? Maire, regional facilitator." The immortal shook our hands, for some reason pausing with me, but only a fraction of a second. "Don't worry. We can deal with the Lookout Mountain anomaly a lot better in this era; we've been studying it from this station for years now. You'll be all right. I'd love to let you stay a couple of days and show you around, but—"

"Those *things* have got to get out of here," said the tech. "What if one of them does number one?"

"—as you see, we have a crisis on our hands," Maire said, indicating the tech with a grimace. "So if you don't mind, we'll just whisk you back to 1862. Sorry we couldn't be more hospitable." With a wave she directed us into a space beyond the room—there wasn't exactly a doorway, and I couldn't quite figure the geometry of the house, but it seemed to be an entry hall. One wall was covered with beige drapery. She pulled a cord, and the draperies drew to one side, revealing not a window but a glass chamber, smooth and featureless inside. It looked like one of those streamlined aluminum travel trailers mortals will tow around behind their automobiles in that century, but it seemed to have been built into the house.

Maire pressed a series of buttons, and a door slid open. She gestured for us to enter. The horses didn't want to go, but Einar managed to sweet-talk them over the silver threshold. As he was doing so, I heard the roar of an automobile outside approaching the house, stopping abruptly as it pulled into the driveway. Once the horses were in with us, the door slid shut, and we felt the cabin pressurizing.

"Nobody seems very surprised to see us," I murmured to Einar.

"Well, but they had to have known we were coming. The Temporal Concordance would have told them." Einar soothed and stroked my mount, which was more panicked than his.

"But if what we just did is impossible, you'd think they'd want to study us—" I broke off as Maire stepped forward to the control console.

She tapped in a combination on the buttons and stood back, looking at us through the window. She took a small cylinder from her pocket and spoke into it. Her voice came hollowly from the air above our heads. "It's warming up. Transcendence in approximately thirty seconds. Brace yourselves."

Yellow vapor began to curl into the air from no source I could see. I inhaled deeply; stasis gas is a lot easier on the lungs than smog. Beyond our window, the door opened, and a man entered the house, setting down a leather case and tossing his keys on the hall table. He was an immortal, in an expensive-looking twentieth-century suit that must have been tailored but somehow seemed too big on him. He looked familiar. As he turned his head to stare at us, I recognized him: Lewis, with whom I'd been stationed at New World One for years and years. Strange, I thought, two old friends in a matter of months. Lewis had been the last person I hugged back in 1700, when I said good-bye at the transport lounge before I came to California. Hadn't he been going to England? But that was three hundred years ago by this time. I smiled and waved. I could see Maire smiling too, pointing at us and explaining something to him, but of course I couldn't hear behind the glass.

He didn't hear her either, I don't think. He was staring at me with the most incredulous expression on his face, which had gone perfectly white. Suddenly he flung himself at the window, pounding on it, shouting silently at me. What on earth? And why the urgency? The air in the room grew suddenly icy, the yellow gas boiled around me and obscured his desperate face. I was growing numb with the transcendence, but I managed to read his lips.

Mendoza, for God's sake! Don't go with him!

I turned my head slowly to Einar. He was looking confused. He met my eyes and shrugged. I looked back at Lewis, shaking my head and holding out my hands. Were those tears in his eyes? He was mouthing *no* over and over, both palms pressed flat against the glass as if trying to push it in. The yellow gas was almost opaque now. I reached out my hand in slow motion and set it on the window, palm to palm with him through the glass, though I could no longer see his face. Then the transcendence came, and it was a lovely thing, pleasurable even with the feeling of infinite violence being done to one, as if you were picked up and thrown into the void forever, or flying...

Then there was a strong wind blowing the fog away, and I stumbled and fell to my knees, choking. I was groping in red sand, trying to rise in a thicket of sagebrush and spurge laurel. There were the horses, flailing and struggling, and there was Einar, doubled up on hands and knees, gasping out yellow smoke.

I scanned blearily. No houses, no deadly city on the plain. We were on the ridge above Laurel Canyon, in the same space we'd occupied 134 years earlier. Later? Whatever. I sank down as Einar was doing and panted, clearing my lungs. Neither one of us said anything for a few minutes. Even the horses gave up and lay still while their mortal nervous systems recovered.

Finally Einar turned over and sat up, resting his head in his hands. "What was up with that guy?" he asked. "Why didn't he want you to go with me?"

"No idea." I shook my head. "We used to be good friends, back before I came to California. I haven't seen him in ages."

I couldn't remember ever having seen Lewis that upset, even when his lady friends dumped him, as sometimes happened. He was one of those genuinely nice guys who somehow always wind up alone. I was always alone, myself. It had been what made us friends.

Einar and I both shrugged.

Once the horses were able to get up, we left that place, walking and leading them, because the trail down from the ridge was steep and tricky. Halfway back, my horse began to cough and shudder, then abruptly fell. Blood gushed from its wide nostrils as it gave one last convulsive twitch. The stress of the time journey, I guess. Einar sank down on his knees and cried.

It was hours before we stumbled into our own canyon, to the welcome smell of beef being grilled over a mesquite fire. There was blessed silence: no cars, no phantoms, only the oak trees and chaparral and one or two stars winking in the twilight sky. Porfirio was crouched over the fire, turning the steaks. He looked up as we approached.

"There you are. What happened to the mare?"

"She had an accident," said Einar sullenly, and led his mount away to the stable.

Porfirio winced, and I thought he was recalculating his operating budget. He looked at me. "And you? Any problems?"

"Not really," I said. Well, we'd come home in one piece, hadn't we? I sank down beside the fire.

Porfirio still stood, considering me for a long moment. "Mendoza," he said, "I'm a security tech. I can tell when people are lying."

I glared at him, señors, feeling very Spanish. How dare he say I was lying? Even if I was. "All right, something happened," I admitted, pulling off the stupid high-tech armor that hadn't worked. He swore. I snapped at him, "I don't know why you bothered to make us carry all this garbage. I suppose you had some communiqué from the Company about what was going to happen today? Did everybody but *me* know? One of those rules you're not supposed to break, about telling people what's in their future?"

"Something like that," Porfirio said.

"Why did you ask me, then, if you knew?"

"Because they didn't tell me much," he said bitterly. "They never do. Never enough to be of any use."

"That figures." I sighed and slumped forward. I was so tired. I

was about to tell him about the accident when he took my breath
away by asking:

"How long have you been a Crome generator?"

I began to shake. "I'm not! There was just one time, when I was
young—only that once. My case officer thought—he said it was probably nothing. Never since then, I swear!"

"Mendoza," he said, "since you've been here, not one week has
gone by that there hasn't been an incident. I've looked out and seen
the blue light pouring through the cracks in the boards, as if you had
lightning in there with you. You didn't know? You slept through it
every time? What's been happening to you?"

I shook my head. How could I tell him, when I didn't know myself? Bad dreams? I debated telling him about my dead lover who had
risen from his grave to follow me across three centuries, an ocean, and
a continent to make my life intolerable in this already intolerable
place. What I said instead was, "I appear to be malfunctioning."

We regarded each other in silence.

"Are you going to ship me out and send for a replacement
botanist?" I asked. That was according to regulations. Ironic, isn't it,
señors? I was holding my breath, petrified at the thought that my field
career was over. If only he *had* shipped me out.

Porfirio shook his head grimly. "I don't do that to my people.
You've done a lot of good work, Mendoza. If you throw enough
Crome to read by, so what? It doesn't seem to be hurting anybody but
you. I know you have some bad memories, but you never let them interfere with your work. Look...the rules are different down here.
Don't give me a reason to have you replaced, and I won't. Okay? But
don't ever lie to me, because I'll know. So what happened today?"

I told him, as he took the steaks off the fire with greatest care and
arranged them on an iron platter. He listened without a word, going
about the business of setting out the evening meal as though I were
telling him the plot of a film I'd seen. At last I finished, and he handed
me a plate of supper and sat down across from me as I ate.

"Mendoza," he said finally, "watch your back."

That was all he'd say on the subject.

Obviously he had an idea of what was coming. And on that day in 1996, Lewis *knew,* señors, what would happen, knew that I'd sit before you in this place now, telling you this story. He was trying to warn me. It was kind of him, though it did no good in the end, and I hope it didn't get him into trouble. This just proves once again the only unbreakable law I know: that history cannot be changed.

*T*HE SUMMER WORE ON; it grew hotter and browner and dustier, and
then in the evenings the wind began to change. Big purple rifts of fog
would come blowing in from the coast. In the brown canyons the big
leaves of sycamores began to drift down, smelling spicy and sweet
when one crunched through them. Deer began to descend from the
brown hills, looking around hopefully for garden produce, which
they didn't find; but we did get venison for a change. The moon got
very big, very silver, and the coyotes rejoiced.

Porfirio began to stock up our supplies for the winter. Not that
there was ever any snow, and we knew, as the mortals didn't, that this
year there wouldn't even be winter rains to flood out the roads. But it
was a safe bet that some disaster or other was going to strike, this
being southern California, so it was just as well to be prepared.

So Einar was sent out time and again, to Los Angeles with lowing
longhorns for Dr. Zeus, and he came back with wagonload after wagonload of crates, barrels, and sacks. Porfirio and Einar would haul
them into the storeroom, where Juan Bautista and I (and Erich and
Marie) would uncrate stuff and check it against the order list. Dozens
of sacks of pink beans, dozens more of masa, enough coffee beans to
wake the dead, jars of pickles and preserves, cones of brown sugar,
boxes of salt... and seven cases of canned sardines.

"Jesus, why'd he order all the sardines?" I said, staring astonished into an opened crate. "They're not even on his list. Hey, Porfirio?" Juan Bautista got a funny look on his face and put up his hands to shush me, but Porfirio had already backed in, carrying one end of a barrel.

"What?" he grunted, backing in the rest of the way so Einar could ease his end down.

"Never mind, I figured it out," I said, but he turned frowning and noticed the funny-looking cans in the opened crate.

"What the hell are those?" He picked up one of the cans. "These are sardines! I didn't order these. None of you guys even like them."

"I like them," said Juan Bautista in a doomed voice.

There was a frozen moment, which unfortunately was broken by Marie Dressler limping across the room and looking up at Juan Bautista expectantly.

Porfirio blew his top, and then blew it louder when he found out that that opened case was one of seven, but I really thought the roof was going to come off the adobe when he discovered that Juan Bautista had added them to the station's order list, which meant that they'd been paid for out of the station's operating budget.

"Didn't I order the damn bird a sack of pelican chow?" shouted Porfirio.

Juan Bautista hung his head. "She's too old for it. It makes her droppings runny."

I left then and at some speed, not wishing to be there when Porfirio came down off the ceiling. Einar was already gone.

I was up in my favorite retreat by the creek, gloomily contemplating my future, when Juan Bautista came wandering along the creek bed half an hour later. Erich was perching on him and Marie was cradled in his arms. He was sniffling a little.

I cleared my throat, so he wouldn't think he was alone and go into some soliloquy of teenage despair.

"Oh," he said. "Hi." He came over and sat down beside me. I edged away slightly, not caring to be that close to Marie's beak.

She had a wicked kind of hook on the end of it, like a mandarin's thumbnail.

"Is Porfirio through screaming?"

"I guess so," he said. "I guess I shouldn't have ordered seven cases. And it was wrong not to tell him about adding to his order. But what am I supposed to do? She's old. She's an endangered species. Fish is what she's supposed to eat. We can't take any more out of the creek, or the breeding population will go below sustainable levels. *He* ought to try that lousy pelican chow, see how *he* likes it."

This implied that Juan Bautista had sampled it himself, which I didn't want to think about. "Well, don't worry," I said. "If Imarte peddles her papayas vigorously enough, she'll earn back the budget deficit." But he wasn't amused, he was sunk in the self-righteous bitterness that only the very young can feel.

"Darned grandfather," he muttered.

We sat there a moment in silence. "What," I asked cautiously, "was that supposed to mean?"

"It was my grandfather got me into this."

"You mean, a real grandfather? Your mortal father's father?"

He nodded. After a moment, he drew a deep breath and began.

"We lived on one of the islands. I don't even know which one, San Miguel or Santa Rosa. All our people had left to go live at the mission, but Grandfather took us back—my father and mother, I mean. He wouldn't leave his holy place. He was the...I guess he was the priest. The word for it sounded like *sishwin*. Anyhow, his god told him he wasn't supposed to leave the island, so he had to go back. That meant my father had to go back, too, because he was supposed to be the sishwin after Grandfather died, and my mother went too, because she was going to have me. They went by canoe. My mother was sick the whole way. I remember she used to talk about it.

"She and my father had a lot of fights. I was born over there, and there weren't any medicine women to help when I was born, just my father, and she was always talking about that. She wanted to go back to the mission, she didn't mind being a Christian, and she talked about that a lot too. And she was always afraid I would fall off a cliff into the sea.

"My father didn't want to be there either. When they were speaking to each other, he'd tell her how mad he was at my grandfather, how our old god was fake nowadays and Grandfather was just being stubborn about staying on the island. I remember he said he could never be a sishwin, because even if the old god cared, Grandfather would never think my father was good enough.

"But they never said anything when Grandfather came into the house. They were scared of him. He was scary-looking. He looked at Daddy like he was dirt, and at Mommy the same way.

"He liked me. He used to take me out to his holy place. There was a big wooden statue of the god there with the sun and the moon on his head. There were big black ravens, and I guess they were bigger than the ones here on the mainland, because I've never seen them that big since I came back. Grandfather used to show me how to feed them. Some were tame and would hop on my hand and let me scratch their necks. Some could talk. I used to think that was magic, because back then I didn't know how smart the *corvidae* are.

"Grandfather told me a lot of stuff about how I belonged to his god, and how if Mommy and Daddy were bad weak people, *I* wasn't, and I was going to be a powerful sishwin just like him, and someday our god was going to send the bears to get all the bad weak people who stopped paying attention to him.

"I just kept quiet and played with the ravens. I liked to stroke their feathers. They were so shiny black, they were blue and reflected the sky. I thought they were the prettiest things.

"Then something bad happened. I don't know what it was. Daddy and Mommy were yelling at each other, and I sneaked away to play with the ravens. There was one that liked to have his neck scratched, behind the feathers, and he just wanted you to go on and on and he'd close his eyes like saying, I can't stand this, it's so good.

"Grandfather came and got me and put me in the canoe. He said a lot of scary things. We went across the sea, and sometimes he'd stand up in the canoe and shout at the sky. I curled up in the bottom of the canoe and closed my eyes.

"We came to the mainland, and Grandfather hid the canoe in a cave. We sneaked across the hills, so the soldiers wouldn't see us, and we came to the big mission. It was the biggest place I'd ever seen. There was a Christian priest sitting on the steps. I don't know why he was sitting out there in the middle of the night."

"I do," I said tensely. "Short man, was he, in a brown robe? Stocky? Little black eyes?"

"Uh-huh. Grandfather carried me up to him and said, Here, you take children, take this one. And he turned and walked away. He left me there. I never saw him again." Juan Bautista's eyes were red, but he didn't start blubbering, thank God.

"Well, the Christian was really surprised. He sat up and asked me what had happened. I told him everything I knew, which wasn't much. He was nice. He asked me a lot of questions and told me everything would be all right now. We went into the big kitchen in the dark, but the Christian could see in the dark, and he got me some food. Then he took me to his room and put me in his bed and told me to sleep. I asked him where he was going to sleep, and he said he didn't sleep."

"He doesn't," I said. "Not much, anyway."

"He hid me in his room a couple of days. He shaved my head, because of bugs, he said. He measured me and looked in my eyes. He let me play with a glass. I'd never seen glass before. It broke, and I cut my finger, and he took some of the blood and put it in something that was probably a machine, but it didn't look like one."

"And let me guess," I said, clenching my fists. "He sat you down and gave you a talk about how sad it was to get old and crazy like your grandfather, but *you* didn't ever have to get old or die."

"That's right."

"And I'll bet he told you that it was sad you'd lost your family, but you could have a wonderful new family who would help you become smart and live forever."

Juan Bautista looked at me. "I guess that's what we say to all the kids we rescue, huh? The next day, he brought me out and told the other Christians that I was a little orphan who'd been left at the mission, but that he'd discovered I had family at a rancheria up the coast, so he was going to take me there, because the mission couldn't provide for orphans anymore.

"We walked and walked, and after a couple of days we came to a big hill above the sea. You could see the islands from there. We stopped and built a fire and waited until dark. In the middle of the night the ship came, a big silver ship. It scared me half to death, but the Christian explained what it was.

"It landed, and the door opened, and nice people came out and took me inside. I was happy, for the first time I could remember except when I was with the ravens. Nobody ever fought or yelled. There was lots of food. And when they found out I liked birds, they made me an ornithologist." Juan Bautista sighed. "So I guess I'm better off now. I really shouldn't blame my grandfather. Because if he hadn't taken me to the Christian, I'd probably be dead or a slave. And it isn't Porfirio's fault that Marie is old and can't eat the pelican chow."

"No, it isn't." I gazed into the brown water of the creek.

"You want to go eat some sardines, old lady?" said Juan Bautista, burying his face in the spiky feathers on Marie's neck. "They're good for you. We'll go get some treats, and I'll play for you, how about that? I'm learning Nunuz's *Sinfonia Asturias*. She really likes the slow movement."

Erich von Stroheim reached down and groomed behind Juan's ears, tugging a long tail of silver hair and pulling it slowly through his beak until it stood out at an angle. He cocked his head, studying the results.

PART TWO

"THIS IS THE BIG ONE!" Einar said, leaping down from the wagon.

"What big one?" Porfirio asked uneasily, looking around at the hills as though he expected them to rock and roll.

"The epic. David Wark Griffith's *Intolerance*." Einar flourished a big silver film can at us. "It just came in. Polish up your rhinestones and press those tuxedos, ladies and gentlemen, 'cause we're going to Babylon tonight!"

There's nothing like a sense of occasion to lift your spirits. Imarte was delighted when she heard what was on the evening's bill, and prepared a special treat; in addition to our popcorn and non-bathtub gin we had little rose-flavored chunks of gummy candy, prepared (she assured us) exactly as it was served at Belshazzar's feast. She would know, I guess. Nor was that all; she and Einar made a last-minute trip over to Sherman and managed to get roses from somebody's garden, big trailing fronds of yellow rambler, and spent most of the afternoon picking off thorns and weaving them into serviceable crowns. We settled down amid the cushions wearing chaplets of roses, and a big yellow rose waved above Einar's right ear as he stood up and pretended to talk into a microphone.

"And welcome once again, my fellow immortals, to this evening's edition of the Cahuenga Pass Film Festival. Tonight's offering is maybe the quintessential Hollywood film, the first cinema epic, and has been hailed as one of the greatest films ever made *and* one of the worst. How did the inimitable D. W. manage to grab the brass ring while simultaneously falling off the painted pony and landing on his head?

"Budget and bad timing, folks, combined with the same wholesome naïveté that left him astonished when black audiences failed to enjoy his film glorifying the Ku Klux Klan. Nobody could ever say Griffith was a slow learner, though, and so for his next film he singled out a slightly safer group to pick on: prissy old ladies of both genders. You may not agree with his unique insights on psychology or his scholarly footnotes as the evening progresses, but I can promise you this much: the visuals are killer.

"Now, this print will not be accompanied by the original score, but we are fortunate enough to have in our audience an expert who will provide us with fascinating commentary and insights of her own." He bowed at Imarte, and we all applauded politely. She waved a gracious hand. "On matters Babylonian, Persian, and prostitutional we defer to thee, O scarlet one. So, everybody, breathe a silent prayer to Ishtar, the goddess at Heaven's Gate, and hold on to your cushions, because it's gonna be a truly bumpy ride!"

He clambered over Juan Bautista and Erich (Marie was more obliging about being left in her cage) and started the projector. We were briefly treated to his black shadow on the screen while he blew out the lamps; then we were silently told that we were watching INTOLERANCE, *a Sun-Play of the Ages.*

"What's a sun-play?" Juan Bautista asked.

"Photoplay, get it?" Porfirio explained.

"Oh."

The screen advised us that we were going to watch a story of the battle of the forces of Hatred and Intolerance versus Love and Charity. Great, I thought, as though a roomful of immortals hadn't seen *that* plotline a few hundred times already. But this was supposed to be a great classic, so I opened my mouth only to stuff in some popcorn.

"Okay, here's the great leitmotif," said Einar. OUT OF THE CRADLE

ENDLESSLY ROCKING, the screen told us, and there was Lillian Gish rocking the biggest cradle I'd ever seen, while the Three Fates looked on from upstage. There followed something incoherent and vaguely poetical about eternal hopes and fears, eternal joys and sorrows, and then we were watching a grand ball for a wealthy modern (early-twentieth-century) industrialist and his spinster sister.

"What is that woman wearing on her head?" Oscar inquired, frowning at the screen. "She looks like a circus horse."

She did, too; she was aging and plain, which made her easy prey for the Uplifters, a villainous society of ladies who wanted her money so they could ruin everybody else's fun. Now that she was no longer attracting the boys, she just naturally fell into their clutches, and was persuaded to hand over her brother's millions to the cause of Reform.

"Notice the subtle misogyny in Griffith's depiction of older women," said Imarte with a sniff.

"Subtle!" I scoffed through my popcorn.

Now we got to meet the Little Dear One, portrayed by Mae Marsh, a teen miss given to hysterical displays of affection, living happily with her aged father (a mill worker for the wealthy industrialist) and a host of small barnyard animals. Next we met our hero, Bobby Herron, as the Boy, who sported a black mustache in defiance of all heroic convention.

"He looks like Gomez Addams," said Juan Bautista. Our giggles died as the scene advanced and Griffith showed us the gray laboring masses shuffling in lockstep through the gates of the mill. This was the Future, this was the Metropolis, this was the century that would bring us to 1984. Where would I be in 1984? Or 1996? I reached for my martini and had a bracing gulp.

The scene changed. There was Lillian Gish with the cradle again and then the two tablets of Mosaic law, and we were at the Jaffa Gate watching camels and old bearded men in striped headdresses. Griffith explained what a Pharisee was, making sure we didn't miss the parallel with the Uplifters, and then showed us some of the Judean variety praying ostentatiously.

Wham! Scene change to France, A.D. 1572, where problems between the Catholics and the Huguenots were about to come to the boil.

"Hey! Really good clothes," I said in surprise. Everyone nodded except Juan Bautista and Oscar, who hadn't lived through that century. Then we were shown Catherine de Medici, the villainous queen mother ("*That* meddling old hag!" snarled Imarte, with such venom, we all turned to look at her) and her two sons: the king, a slender fellow with a tendency to curl up sideways on his throne, and his brother the prince, an effeminate who kept puppies in his codpiece. We were shown the French court milling around in a large room; then we met our Huguenot heroine Brown Eyes (with a tight close-up on her face, so we got the idea) and her nonentity boyfriend, Prosper Latour. We also met an obviously villainous soldier who was smitten with lust for Brown Eyes.

"I bet I know what's going to happen," said Juan Bautista, sitting forward.

But before we could guess, we were whisked back to the twentieth century, where the poor mill workers were innocently dancing at an ice-cream social. The Little Dear One was there, gleeful as usual, and so was the industrialist oppressor, snooping on his workers and scavenging dropped change from the sidewalk. This was straight out of Dickens, only grayer and more banal.

"When do we get to Babylon?" I complained.

"Right about now," Einar said, and lo, we beheld the Imgur Bel Gate of Babylon! Intricate, massive, worked by twin capstans carven with lions rampant, manned by dozens of slaves. Elephants plodding through the streets, looking small as cows before the vast walls. Enormous winged bulls with the heads of bearded kings. Now *this* was imagery. We cheered and applauded.

"Shot right here, folks, on Griffith's lot off Hollywood Boulevard," said Einar.

"Actually it didn't look at all like that," Imarte said.

"Well, it ought to have," Porfirio said.

In the midst of the gorgeously costumed bustle there were a few people just sort of sitting around in the street as though they were waiting for the next bus, and Griffith made sure we noticed one of them, she whom the title card declared to be the Mountain Girl.

"So, is there some reason he never gives these people names?" Porfirio asked.

Einar shrugged. "It's poetical or something. The actress is Constance Talmadge."

"Good Lord, what does she have on her head?" Oscar exclaimed. We all looked intently. No gorgeous robes for this chick; she appeared to have a couple of fur rugs tied around her boyish figure, and on her head were eucalyptus nuts sewn to a felt beanie.

"Needless to say, this is *not* an accurate historical costume," Imarte remarked.

The Mountain Girl was no drooping harem lily; she was a tomboy, as cute and spunky as Mary Pickford. And here was somebody else waiting for the same bus: Griffith explained that this handsome bare-armed guy with flowers in his hair was the Rhapsode, a warrior-singer-poet. He made eyes at the Mountain Girl, who of course—the little spitfire—rejected him indignantly.

"Now, get a load of his seduction line," said Einar.

"Dearest one—in the ash heaps of my backyard there will be small flowers; seven lilies—if thou wilt love me—but a little," read Juan Bautista uncomprehendingly, and we fell about laughing. The Mountain Girl wasn't impressed either. The scene changed, and we met the High Priest of Bel-Marduk and his god, both of them pretty sore that all the people were worshiping Ishtar these days. Another scene shift, and Griffith advised us that we were about to meet the ruling Prince of Babylon, Belshazzar, riding in his chariot along the top of his city walls, which were careful historical reconstructions of the real ones.

"Really?" we all wanted to know.

"They weren't quite that high," admitted Imarte. "But when you were arriving from a three-hut village and seeing them for the first time, the effect was very nearly the same."

Belshazzar, a slender creature in a tall hat, was the Apostle of Tolerance and Religious Freedom; and here was his bodyguard, the burly Two-Sword Man; and here were the Handmaidens from Ishtar's Temple of Love and Laughter. They came dancing crazily out through the gate before the big parade float that bore the statue of Ishtar. Next we met the Princess Beloved, much more the conventional harem-lily type, and she and Belshazzar made a lot of pseudo-Biblical protestations of love for each other. Yes, all was happiness in old Babylon. But now, Griffith told us, the Mountain Girl's Brother (he had no name either) was having trouble keeping her in line, so he was going to drag her off to "the First Known Court of Justice in the World" to make her behave. A scholarly title card explained how Babylon's ancient laws were the first to protect the weak from the strong.

"Occasionally," Imarte said. "And of course you're all aware that the Babylonians were not the inventors of law." We all nodded, watching the antics of the Mountain Girl before the judges. We knew about the Neanderthal Code of Punishable Acts. Of course, there'd always been the rumor that the Company had been involved in that, somehow...Whoops! The judges sentenced the Mountain Girl to be dragged off to the marriage market. We all leaned forward in anticipation.

"Damn," said Porfirio, as we jumped forward through time over the Cradle Endlessly Rocking and found ourselves back in the twentieth century, where the nasty old Uplifters had spent so much of the wealthy industrialist's money that he was obliged to cut wages at the mill by ten percent. So we got to see one of the dreary labor strikes of the twentieth century, complete with soldiers—or were they Pinkerton men?—firing on the protesters. THE SAME TODAY AS YESTERDAY read a sign painted on a fence; and we immortals silently acknowledged that bitter truth. The Loom of Fate wove death for the Boy's Father when he took a bullet, and in the aftermath everybody went off to the big city to look for other work: the Boy, the Little Dear One and *her* father, and another girl, the Friendless One.

"I want to see Babylon again," Oscar complained.

Instead, we got to watch as our nameless ones suffered the inevitable consequences of urban relocation: the Boy rolled a drunk and turned to a life of crime, the Friendless One met a pimp called, for no reason any of us could figure out, the Musketeer of the Slums, and the Little Dear One's hysteria grew more pronounced.

"This is depressing," said Juan Bautista, and then: "All right!" because there was Ms. Gish and her Cradle again, and we were back in Babylon at the marriage mart.

Griffith explained that in the ancient Babylonian marriage market, the money spent to purchase pretty girls was given to plain girls for dowries, so that all might be happily married, and that "Women Corresponding to Our Outcasts of the Street" became wards of church and state for life. Imarte shook her head sadly when I looked to her for commentary. The men in the room were keeping their eyes on the screen, however, as Griffith's camera moved slowly past pretty girls in various states of undress. And here was the Mountain Girl, swaggering little hoyden, chewing on a couple of scallions as she awaited her turn and sticking them sullenly in her bodice when told to stop.

"This episode is pure fabrication," Imarte said. "I find the scene noteworthy for what it reveals to us about the sexual repression of the early twentieth century, however. Of course, you're all aware that white slavery will be a popular motif of escapist cinema during that period, and it's interesting to regard the paradox of sexual bondage viewed as a liberating experience. In *The Sheik,* for example..."

I tuned her out. Of course the Mountain Girl was a failure in the marriage market, winsomely scowling and threatening her prospective husbands, and then raging when they laughed and refused to buy her. But, out of nowhere, Belshazzar appeared with his attendants and wanted to know what all the fuss was about. When her plight was explained to him, Belshazzar granted her the right to marry or not as she wished, with a nifty bit of stage business involving a cylinder seal rolled over a clay tablet, shown in tight close-up (Imarte interrupted her lecture long enough to remark approvingly on its verisimilitude). Exit Belshazzar, followed by moony stares from the Mountain Girl, clearly smitten with him.

But what was this? Now we had the Rhapsode, working in the tenements to convert backsliders to the true worship of Bel.

"So he's a missionary?" Oscar said with a frown. "I thought he was a poet-warrior-singer or something."

"He's an utterly imaginary creature," said Imarte dismissively, but I was intrigued. He was a potentially interesting character, this Rhapsode. Was Griffith going to develop his warrior and zealot sides? Was he a hero as well as pleasure-loving esthete? Was he going to have some kind of relationship with the spirited if somewhat gauche Mountain Girl? Maybe so, because here she came, and again he was making protestations of love to her. But the Mountain Girl drew back from him, declaring:

"Put away thy perfumes, thy garments of Assinu, the Female Man," read Oscar. "I shall love none but a soldier."

"I guess she told *him*," Porfirio said. But then the scene changed to the interior of the Temple of Ishtar, and the attention of all gentlemen present was riveted on the screen, as Griffith treated them to a nicely detailed study of the Virgins of Ishtar frolicking in various pools and fountains, or lounging around in—well, in no clothing at all, one or two of them.

"Wow," gasped Juan Bautista.

"Pre–Hays Code, guys," said Einar. "Cool, huh?"

"Now, this, actually, is fairly accurate," Imarte said. "Though there would have been rather more nudity. The ancients were considerably more realistic about sexual needs, to say nothing of the issues of climate and comfort. Notice the continual depiction of Babylon by Griffith as a model of humane and sensible government, which will be really rather daring of him, considering that American audiences of that era are inclined to take the Old Testament view of Babylon as depraved and vice-ridden."

Here was Belshazzar again, with the Princess Beloved, billing and cooing in the Temple, and he was promising to build her a city of her very own, because:

"The fragrant mystery of your body is greater than the mystery of life," read Juan Bautista.

"Roughly translated as, Gee, did you step in something one of the elephants left?" I jeered. But Griffith just kept piling on the splendors, the Virgins of the Sacred Fire of Life dancing in the Love Temple, the harpists and yawning harem guards, Belshazzar and the Princess Beloved standing at a high window viewing the magnificence of Babylon spread out below them. When he stuck to the images, the phenomenal images, you were caught up in this silly thing in spite of yourself.

"The Cradle again," said Juan Bautista, and here was the Little Dear One in her tenement, trying to get a Hopeful Geranium (actually a pelargonium) to thrive. When she wasn't doing that, the innocent creature was watching whores from her tenement window, practicing their walk so she'd be popular too. Griffith was inviting us to smile in fond amusement here, but you could see where it was leading, and, sure enough, the next scene took us to the Friendless One in her new job: sitting in a bar in her negligee, drinking gin. She got up to go solace herself with the Musketeer of the Slums, but their passionate moment was interrupted by the Boy, who was now a Barbarian of the Streets. You could tell, because he'd taken to wearing a derby and smoking.

Next scene, the Little Dear One and the Boy encountered each other at his newsstand (a blind for his more criminal activities, we were told) and she did her prostitute walk for him. It worked! The next thing we saw was the two of them in her hallway with him vowing eternal love, a little less poetically than Belshazzar. ("Say, kid, you're going to be my chicken," read out Juan Bautista.) But the Little Dear One's old father broke it up, dragging her upstairs to pray for forgiveness before a little plaster statue of the Holy Mother and Child. ("Notice the recurring goddess images here," instructed Imarte.) After a brief Cradle shot, we saw the old man lying stiff in his winding-sheet and the Little Dear One weeping by his corpse.

"We want Babylon, we want Babylon," chanted Einar. Instead we got the Wedding at Cana, with a very bouncy and giggly young couple being fed the first mouthful of chickpeas at their reception. Whether or not the bride was expected to smear the next handful on the groom's face we never got to see, because the scene shifted to a shot of some white doves and then the entry of Jesus. He looked just like Belshazzar, except he didn't have a hat. But here were those mean old Pharisees again, snooping around and remarking that there was Too Much Revelry and Pleasure-Seeking among the People. Not for long, though—the wedding party ran out of wine!

I set aside my popcorn and leaned forward, wondering what special effect Griffith had to wow us with the water-into-wine miracle. But all we saw was a long shot of Jesus praying over some jars, only you couldn't quite make him out. At first I thought it was some defect in the print, but then I got the trick: Jesus was nearly obscured by a cross-shaped shadow. "Notice the metaphor," Imarte said, "Divine Love being blotted out by the instrument of torture and execution."

"We noticed, thank you," I said. A thought occurred to me. "Hey, did *you* ever meet Jesus of Nazareth?"

"No." She took a sip of her martini. "I was stationed in Turkey at the time."

"But somebody must have. Surely the Company was in on that moment in history too, right?" I wondered aloud. "Is there footage in a Company archive somewhere of Jesus trashing the temple vendors, Jesus on his bloody cross, Jesus giving the Sermon on the Mount?"

"Yes," Einar said, as we watched the wedding guests celebrate the miracle. "A fundamentalist group paid the Company big bucks to catch the man's act on film. They didn't like what they saw, so they paid more big bucks to have it suppressed."

"You're kidding!" I leaned forward. "So he was real? So he worked miracles?"

"Oh, yeah," said Einar, nodding. "That wasn't the problem."

"What *was* the problem?" Had he been a Crome generator too?

"Sorry, guys, that's classified information," he said, and we booed him and threw popcorn until Juan Bautista cried:

"Whoa, how did we get to France again?" Because we were back in France, no question, and Brown Eyes and her family were having a cozy evening at home with visiting swain Prosper Latour. ("How come he gets a name when nobody else does?" asked Porfirio.) Prosper left to go home, and Brown Eyes saw him to the door, where the same mercenary soldier spotted her again. He made his moves, but she was a nice Protestant girl and declined his advances.

I took my eyes off the screen long enough to quaff some martini. When I looked up again, we were back in the twentieth century, and the Boy and Little Dear One were having an outing in the Good Old Summertime.

"Notice San Pedro standing in for Coney Island," Einar said.

They went back to the tenement, and the Boy tried to muscle his way into the Little Dear One's room, but she shut him out and prayed tearfully to the Holy Mother to help her be a Strong-Jawed Jane. I accessed my historical idiom file for a definition of this colorful phrase, without results.

Fate was smiling on the Little Dear One, because the Boy proposed marriage. We were shown briefly how the insidious Uplifters were gaining more and more power, and then—

"This is almost as disorienting as real time travel," I said, as we found ourselves watching the Pharisees spying on Jesus.

"Behold a man gluttonous and a winebibber, a friend of publicans and sinners," read Juan Bautista. There was Jesus sitting in what appeared to be a cafe, chatting pleasantly with a fellow customer. But wait! Here was the Woman Taken in Adultery, and the Pharisees all ready to stone her, rocks in hand like extras from a Monty Python sketch. Unbelievable overacting from the Pharisees when Jesus zinged them with his ruling, and unbelievably strange dancing when the Adulteress made her grateful exit. Jesus just sat there and looked benign, apparently the only good actor in Galilee.

We all groaned to find ourselves back in the twentieth century again, viewing more of the Uplifters' nasty handiwork. Griffith came right out and said it this time, that When Women Cease to Attract Men, They Often Turn to Reform as a Second Choice. We booed and threw popcorn as he showed how these villainous spinsters were responsible for bootlegging, secret poker games, and flirting in alleyways. Meanwhile, the Little Dear One was working her own reformation on the Boy, extracting his promise to quit his criminal gang, and her victory dance was truly savage and bizarre. And premature: for no sooner had the Boy quit his gang than the Musketeer of the Slums got him framed for theft, and the Boy was whisked off to prison.

Babylon again! We cheered, but there was trouble brewing; the wicked High Priest was still interminably plotting, prophesying doom if people didn't leave off this Ishtar nonsense and return to Bel-Marduk. Enter Nabonidus, Belshazzar's crazy old father, excitedly showing off his latest archaeological discovery and remembering to mention that Oh by the way, Cyrus the Persian is massing with his armies to destroy us.

"Notice the subtext of implicit condemnation of intellectual pursuits," observed Imarte.

"Whatever," I said. "Wow, these must be the Persians!" It was the war camp of Cyrus. Griffith showed us milling soldiers, engines of war, and chariots of fire. The exotic hordes of Cyrus, the Medes, the Persians, the Ethiopians. ("Look, *real* black guys this time!" Einar said. "Most of the Negroes in *Birth of a Nation* were white guys in blackface.") There were some bone-gnawing white European males designated merely as Barbarians, then Cyrus himself, shouting orders from his war chariot, turning sharply right, left, right, a big martial profile from a wall painting. He looked like a Klingon member of Sergeant Pepper's Lonely Hearts Club Band.

"Damn," yelled Porfirio, because in mid-spectacle we were hauled back to the twentieth century, where the Little Dear One was now the Little Mother. There was some touching footage of her playing with her baby, but we knew tragedy was in the offing, and, sure enough, the evil Uplifters were at it again: Griffith showed them descending on slum neighborhoods like stiff harpies, and nailing the Little Mother when they caught her with some whiskey she was taking as a cold remedy. When they came for her baby, the Little Mother fought back with such frenzy that they smashed her to the ground senseless, hefty muscular broads as they were. We saw her clutching feebly at one baby sock, dropped in the struggle, all she had left of her child.

"Emotionally involving," admitted Imarte, "though overall I *think* Chaplin handled the same theme more effectively." I resisted an urge to shush her, because it was an upsetting scene after all, but then Griffith went and threw in the kitchen sink by showing us a Suffer Little Children to Come unto Me tableau, with Jesus and what must have been half the child population of Hollywood, happy little extras earning a day's wage.

Then, thankfully, we were back in France, watching the Catholics cower as the Huguenots ran around wild in the streets and smashed a perfectly good plaster statue. We can't have this kind of thing going on! announced Catherine de' Medici. Time to do something about those pesky Protestants.

But we escaped to Babylon again, and Cyrus jumped athletically into his chariot and ordered his armies to march on Belshazzar's city. And here was Belshazzar, mustering up the city guard, pausing only to bid a fond adieu to his Princess Beloved. She bid him one heck of a fond adieu herself:

"My Lord, like white pearls I shall keep my tears in an ark of silver for your return. I bite my thumb! I strike my girdle!" Juan Bautista read, and began to giggle helplessly. "If you return not, I go to the death halls of Aflat!"

"That's Allat," Imarte corrected him primly, which only made the rest of us snicker more. We watched as the Mountain Girl decked herself out in her brother's second-best armor and rushed out to help defend her city, just like Xena.

"Get ready, guys," said Einar, "this is one of *the* great cinema battles of all time."

He wasn't kidding. Thousands of costumed extras stormed those magnificent walls, battered those glorious gates, and, by God, life-sized siege towers were actually pushed into place by real elephants, because Griffith hadn't had any other way to move them. The Priests of Ishtar assumed odd positions and prayed to their goddess for deliverance. They made burnt offerings, the flame and smoke of their sacrifices flowing up with the flame and smoke of the battle. The Mountain Girl sent a rain of arrows down on the attacking hordes. The burly Two-Sword Man, fighting with (surprise) two swords, swopped off a Persian head as neatly as I've ever seen it done on film. More shots of the Mountain Girl fighting valiantly for her Prince, intercut with the Princess Beloved peering fearfully out the window at the battle, posturing dismay and terror with palms angled stiffly, and you knew she didn't deserve Belshazzar the way our plucky heroine did. The catapults of the attacking host launched rocks on the defenders, and the defenders pushed one of the siege towers outward, outward, until it tilted and fell, all eight stories, with a crash they must have heard in San Pedro. And now the battle was going on into the night, with flames along the battlements to rival the burning of Atlanta in *Gone with the Wind*.

"Look at that!" said Oscar. We stared at the secret weapon of Babylon, an armored tank that Jules Verne might have designed if he'd been around in Belshazzar's day. It was huge, with spiked wheels that rolled it implacably forward and long nozzles that shot out jets of flame. How absurd, how improbable, how *marvelous!* We all applauded.

"A blatant anachronism," Imarte said, but we ignored her. Who were we, cyborgs in the Old West, to talk about anachronisms? We cheered as the engine of destruction laid waste to the Persians, burning and bringing down more siege towers in flaming ruin. The forces of Cyrus were routed! Wild celebration in Babylon! Dances of joy and bliss! What a spectacle!

Intermission.

"Rats," I said, as Einar crawled over to the projector to change reels.

"Stay cool," he said, groping for the film can. "The best is yet to be."

But when the silver world returned, we were in the twentieth century again, with more tragedy building: the Musketeer of the Slums now had his lustful eye on the forlorn Little Mother, intimating he might be able to rescue her baby from the clutches of the Uplifters. He was jealously shadowed by the Friendless One, however. The Boy got out of prison, but this did not discourage the Musketeer from his dastardly plan—

"Thank God," said Porfirio, because the Cradle appeared again, and Griffith told us we were about to behold the Feast of Belshazzar, "Imaged after the Splendor of an Olden Day."

Einar gave a whoop of excitement. "This is it, Babylon the Great! For those of you who were wondering what could possibly top the magnificence of that battle scene..."

But he didn't need to say anything more, because there before us was the first long shot of Hollywood Babylon in all her glory, and it took my immortal breath away. A central court so huge, it beggared all comprehension of scale, with gods and goddesses stories high, rearing elephants in stone, and thousands of tiny figures there below us on the wide stairs as the camera moved slowly in on the scene. How had he done it? And still the camera moved in, and yes, there were real people on those painted stairs, and your eye had to believe that this was no matte shot, no miniature, this truly was the ancient and massive splendor that had died away from the world, caught on silver nitrate by giants who were in the earth in those days.

The camera took us up the great stairs through the mad bacchanal, with all the little incidents to catch attention: the grim Two-Sword Man fondly stroking a white dove, the temple priestesses dancing stiff like wall paintings come to life, the Priests of Ishtar chanting praise to Her. I heard Imarte sniffling: was she crying? And here were Belshazzar and the Princess Beloved in all their glory, scarlet and purple, emerald and gold, glowing through the austere silver print.

Now we saw the Mountain Girl confidently expecting to walk into the banquet hall, but of course she was turned away, the little ragamuffin. Next we saw the High Priest of Bel, scheming to make his defeat a temporary one, summoning the Rhapsode and ordering him to ready the chariots for a secret visit to the camp of Cyrus. But what was this? Did the warrior-poet-singer-missionary balk at this base treachery? No! He looked confused, he abased himself, he ran off to do the High Priest's bidding. He wasn't really going to be a dupe and betray Babylon, was he? Surely he would form some clever plan to thwart Cyrus, the High Priest, and the rest of them. It wouldn't work out, of course, unless Griffith had decided to change history...but, having created such a potentially interesting hero, was Griffith really going to waste him? I drained my martini and fumbled around in the dark for the cocktail shaker. I had to pry it loose from Imarte's grip: she was staring at the screen as if mortally hurt, and she *was* crying. Son of a gun.

The Mountain Girl was thirsty, too; she was purchasing a drink of goat milk to celebrate, squatting down and milking the goat herself. Something about the motion must have reminded her of Belshazzar, for she promptly got that moony unrequited-love look on her face, with intercut shots of Belshazzar at his feast, and back to her tugging on the pendulous squirting udders. Einar and Porfirio were rolling on the floor, choking with laughter, and Oscar had his handkerchief up in front of his face.

More revelry, more splendor. We reclined at the table of a Babylonian noble crowned with flowers; we were invited to partake of spiced wine cooled with snow brought down from the mountains. We watched a Babylonian gallant idly stroking the head of a leopard, which lay bound and snarling through the roses in its jaws. We watched a tame bear being fed party delicacies. We watched a swaying-drunk soldier telling the cameraman about the little monkey that clung to his helmet. And here was the Mountain Girl again, and the Rhapsode coming around a corner to catch sight of her. Still smitten with her boyish charms, he made another pitch for her and was indignantly spurned. But he kept following her around and then—

I groaned and downed my martini in a gulp. So much for the potentially interesting hero. In his efforts to impress the Mountain Girl, the Rhapsode did it, he blabbed about the secret mission to Cyrus's camp.

What was Catherine de' Medici doing here? Oh, we were back in France. Pressure was being put on the King to sign the order allowing the Catholics to massacre the Huguenots. Would he do it? No, no, a thousand times no! He ran around the room screaming, he tore his hair, he stamped his feet, he curled up in his throne and kicked his legs. He signed it, though, as his nasty and effeminate brother played with a ball-and-paddle game. Next we saw sedate Protestant joy at the Brown Eyes residence as she and Prosper Latour were betrothed. Ominous foreshadowings as the happy family snuffed their candles before retiring for the night, and Prosper walking back to his lodgings and noticing those groups of soldiers going around chalking X's on the doors of the Protestants. Did he have a clue? Nope.

"In the Temple of Loooooove!" yodeled Einar, and we were back in Babylon again. Apparently an orgy was in progress. More harem hijinks, more voluptuaries rolling around in perfectly astonishing attitudes of invitation, more dancers on the grand stairway performing some kind of goose-stepping polka, another seminaked girl—

"Watch," Einar announced. "Long-distance gynecology. You won't see a shot like this one until *Basic Instinct* with Sharon Stone, 1992."

"Dear Lord!" Oscar went into a coughing fit, his eyes bugging out of his head.

Juan Bautista blushed furiously. "Could they *do* that back then?" he asked.

Einar grinned. "No Hays Code yet, like I said." Now we saw the

Princess Beloved coyly sending a white rose in a little chariot drawn by two white doves across the banquet table to Belshazzar. But not everyone was celebrating: the evil High Priest and other objectionable members of the clergy climbed into their chariots and sneaked away to Cyrus's camp. Not unobserved. The clever Mountain Girl stole a chariot to follow them, riding like the wind past the Three Fates and Lillian Gish, to—

New York? What were we doing in this cramped tenement, with the Musketeer of the Slums attempting to rape the Little Mother? The Boy burst in and struggled with the Musketeer, while the Friendless One clung precariously to the window ledge outside, trying to get a clear shot. Bang! Huge clouds of smoke, the Musketeer staggered into the corridor to die, the Friendless One dropped the gun into the room and took to her heels, and in no time at all the Boy was on trial for his life in a huge courtroom. The Prosecution was clever—you could tell, because he wore pince-nez—while the Defense Attorney was a stammering novice, so we weren't left in much suspense about the outcome. Not so the Little Mother, who giggled encouragement across the courtroom at the Boy, at least until the brutal sentence was read, when she screamed and fainted. Somewhere in this scene we went to Jerusalem, briefly, where poor Jesus was struggling with his cross through the howling mob, and then we were back in the twentieth century again, where the Friendless One was trying to get up nerve to confess to her crime.

I had another martini, and it seemed to help. We went back to where Cyrus was greeting the High Priest and his cronies while the Mountain Girl listened in on the conspirators, but then we were interrupted by scenes of various efforts to save the Boy, and there were Model Ts racing back and forth, which inexplicably became chariots racing along the Euphrates, only Einar was explaining that it was really a slough down near Long Beach with some palm trees planted to make it look like the Euphrates, and there was Catherine de' Medici again!

"What the hell is she doing here?" I heard Porfirio inquire, but it soon became obvious, because Brown Eyes and her family were having a Terrible Awakening as the Catholic forces battered down their door.

Were those automobiles coming to the Huguenots' rescue? No, we were back in New York, and then we were racing along beside the Euphrates, and—hey! the Friendless One finally confessed! The Mountain Girl was racing ahead of the army advancing on poor Babylon, and the damn Cradle was rocking faster and faster. Two Model Ts chased each other, then it was a race car chasing a train, then the Boy was receiving last rites from a priest, then a priest was hiding a terrified Huguenot child under his cloak, then Belshazzar and the Princess Beloved were pitching woo all unmindful of the train bearing down on them or the Huguenots being slaughtered in the next room. Here came Jesus wearing a signboard, narrowly missed by the race car bearing the last-minute testimony that would reprieve the Boy, who was fainting in the priest's arms, no doubt at the graphic rape and murder of Brown Eyes by that darned mercenary ("I *knew* he was gonna do that!" said Juan Bautista). Prosper could have saved her, but he couldn't get through the crowds of soldiers massacring Protestants, and the same crowd was slowing down the Mountain Girl too, because it took her forever to make her way to Belshazzar's party to let him know what was going on, by which time it was too late to save Brown Eyes, but at least the governor was willing to reprieve the Boy! And now it was the train racing to get to the prison before the execution, but Belshazzar could get only twelve men to help him defend Babylon, and the Princess Beloved couldn't get *anybody* to go with her to the Death Halls of Allat. Oh hell, oh spite!

Prosper was killed, the Mountain Girl was killed, Belshazzar and the Princess Beloved killed themselves, and there was a close-up of the Mountain Girl lying killed, which irised out to show that the forlorn little doves had pulled the rose-chariot up to her lifeless body. Juan Bautista burst into tears, but Catherine de' Medici was pleased with herself and so was Cyrus, who guffawed crudely right in the camera's face, as meanwhile everybody piled out of the train and into another car, which raced on to save—gee, who else was left alive?

Not Jesus. A confusing mass with a lot of smoke resolved itself into Golgotha, with the three crosses dimly visible on a dark skyline. So the car raced on, but the Boy was already mounting the scaffold, they were binding his hands, they were binding his legs, they were putting the black hood on him, and men with razors were standing by to cut the cord that would drop the trap. *Would rescuers get there in time?*

Surprise! They did. Dazed Boy being embraced by passionately twitching Little Mother. General expressions of joy and satisfaction. "Here comes the summation," Einar told us.

WHEN CANNON AND PRISON BARS WROUGHT IN THE FIRES OF INTOLERANCE, read the titles, over scenes of battlefield and prison. A lot of angels appeared, dangling in a rather crowded sky, and all the fighting stopped.

AND PERFECT LOVE SHALL BRING PEACE FOREVERMORE. More people staring up in confusion at the angels.

INSTEAD OF PRISON WALLS, BLOOM FLOWERY FIELDS. A scene showing convicts in their striped uniforms walking through the walls like ghosts and disappearing. Then an exterior shot of a prison doing a vanishing act too, leaving the Hollywood Hills in the distance. Now we saw little children disporting themselves at a church picnic. One bold toddler grabbed a tiny playmate and gave her a big kiss.

"If he tried that in the twenty-first century, he'd be arrested and put in therapy the rest of his life," said Porfirio gloomily. I was waiting for a final title card that would finish Griffith's sentence, but instead we saw a lot of people yelling glory hallelujah at the angels and then one last shot of Lillian Gish and her Cradle, endlessly, endlessly rocking.

White light, flickering on a blank screen.

Einar moaned, stretching sensually.

"So, what happened to the Baby?" Porfirio asked.

"What happened to the goddamn Rhapsode?" I asked.

Before either of our questions could be answered, Imarte leaped to her feet, scattering popcorn in all directions.

"I must go there," she announced. "Now."

"Where?" Oscar stared at her in bewilderment. We were bewildered too; there hadn't been a peep out of her in the last few minutes, but now she turned on him with a snarl.

"I must go to Babylon!"

"Imarte, what'd you put in that rahat locum?" said Porfirio, but she pushed her chaplet of roses back from where it had slipped over one eye and fixed him with one of the scariest expressions I'd ever seen.

"I *will* go to Babylon, fairest of cities, beloved of Ishtar," she said. "I will not lose it again!"

"Cool," said Einar, scrambling unsteadily to his feet. "Let's go now. Come on, you guys, it's just over on Sunset. God knows there's no traffic. We can get there in no time."

I remember that Porfirio did some protesting, and so did Oscar, but one way or another we found ourselves galloping through the night. That is, Einar and Imarte galloped; the rest of us rode in the wagon, driven by Porfirio at a rattling clip as he tried to catch up with those two. I clutched at my chaplet of roses and wondered what I was doing as we thundered along through the damp night air under a very amused moon.

It was a wide sloping piece of ground where we stopped, an old floodplain with a view of the distant lights of Los Angeles and the more distant sea, pale and obscure under the moon. Was that Catalina Island out there?

Einar and Imarte had dismounted. She was standing motionless; he was striding with arms outstretched through the sagebrush and chamise.

"Right here," he was saying. "This will be the lot adjacent to the Fine Arts studio complex. Can you see it? And where I'm standing, babe, we're on that Grand Staircase! Look up there behind us in the moonlight, there are the elephants! There are the winged bulls bright as day. They're here, and more real than this empty place or the asphalt that covers it later. Silver nitrate's made Babylon eternal for all time, and the prophets can't do a thing about it. This is Ishtar's city of love and tolerance. Can you smell the incense? Can you hear the music?"

I very nearly could. I found I was still clutching the cocktail shaker and took a fortifying gulp. Imarte stretched out her arms to the moon and gave a plaintive cry. She began to dance, there in the moonlight, over the stones and red sand, through the yucca and the cactus and other herbs that never lifted bud or branch in Belshazzar's city so long fallen. It was no stiff absurd dance either, no attempt to choreograph a flat wall painting; it was lithe and savage, a little unsteady, something you'd really dance at a bacchanal.

"Is she nuts?" asked Juan Bautista, who cowered shivering beside me. "What's she doing?"

"She's just had enough gin, that's all," Porfirio told him.

"You think that's all it is?" I had another belt from the cocktail shaker. "She's crazy with pain. She's so much older than the rest of us, and she was really there, wasn't she, when Cyrus came crashing down on Babylon. What if you'd loved a place like that, and seen it go down in flames? What if you'd buried it in your heart for centuries, all that lost glory safely forgotten, and then one night, when you least expected it, something brought it to life for you again? How do you think you'd feel? How *will* you feel, kid, a hundred centuries from now, when you're as old as she is?"

"I won't be like that," said Juan Bautista. "That's not supposed to happen to us. We don't go crazy, we can't, we're perfect! Aren't we?"

"Shut up, Mendoza," said Porfirio quietly, and Oscar fumbled the cocktail shaker from my icy grasp.

"Of course we are, son, we're positively the last word in cybertechnology," he assured Juan Bautista.

I staggered to my feet and flung my chaplet of roses out into the middle of what would be Sunset Boulevard one day, when all this sweet wild land would be buried under an urban nightmare. And what would *I* be feeling, when I was as old as Imarte? What would have become of the places *I'd* loved? What if there were no more oak trees or redwoods, what if California itself slipped under the Pacific, drowned and broken up, as lost as Atlantis?

And I was going to lose it all, when that steel cancer of a future city was built. It wouldn't even take a global calamity: just millions of mortals moving west. I would lose my wilderness just as I'd lost Nicholas, and how would I live then?

I drew in my breath to howl at the moon, but Einar came bounding up to the wagon. He held up his pistol by its barrel, pretending it was a microphone again. "Let's hear what our studio audience has to say! Sir, can you tell the wonderful people out there in the dark what personal revelations *you* had tonight?" He thrust it under Oscar's nose.

"Oh, this is silly," Oscar said. "But—very well." He took the gun and held it up. "If you really want to know, why, I think there's a brilliant message in that film, and Griffith really was a genius born too soon. He's telling us loud and clear just what's going to bring on that earthly paradise he envisions at the end, and you know what it is?

"Technology. Yes, sir, ladies and gentlemen, consider for a moment. What turns the tide of battle (albeit temporarily) against the Persians? None other than the superior technology of the Babylonians, as exemplified by their marvelous machine of war. And consider! Don't the other tragedies occur because prospective rescuers are delayed in their efforts by inferior means of transportation? Reflect upon the fact that, of all the stories presented, the one story that ends happily does so solely because of modern and efficient means of locomotion. Yes! The automobile brings the Boy's pardon! Now, just what would have happened if that Mountain Girl or the French fellow had had Fords with which to speed to the rescue of *their* loved ones?"

"What would have happened if Christ's apostles had had grenades and rocket launchers?" I said, dropping into the bed of the wagon.

"Precisely! That is, er, anyhow, it seems mighty clear to me that what the great David Wark Griffith was foreseeing was nothing less than us. For are we not the veritable saviors of Earth, the ultimate marriage of man's mechanical genius with his biological possibilities? Why should any cyborg feel shame? Is it not an honor to be descended from the noble Model T no less than from Adam? I don't know about you folks, but I'm proud, *proud* of my mingled heritage." Oscar flung his chaplet out into what would one day be the roof of the Kinema-color lab. He handed the gun back to Einar, who was applauding.

"Bravo, Mr. O! And what about you, sir, do you have an epiphany you'd like to share with the folks listening at home?" He thrust the gun at Porfirio.

"What home?" I said. "We have no homes, none of us."

"Shut up." Porfirio put his hand on my shoulder. "You want to know what I think, pal? I think it's time to rein in this party. Maybe you should go catch Salome of the Seven Veils and get her back on her horse."

"No, man, she's okay," Einar's eyes were glowing. "Don't you see? She knows how to deal with this time thing. She understands. That's why she's dancing. She can *see* Babylon. It exists for her outside of time, it's neither past nor future but right now. Always.

"Haven't you guys figured it out yet? Don't you know what it really means to be immortals? We transcend time, it has no meaning for us, it ceases to exist, because it's all simultaneous. We're here *now,* and we're on Griffith's set *now,* and we're in 2355 *now! We're the ones controlling reality, from in here.*" He struck his fist against his indestructible skull.

"We are time machines! The truth's been right in front of our noses since cinema was invented. Hell, since photography was invented. Hell, since *writing* was invented. Make an image of something, and it escapes the flow of time. That's why it's forbidden! Dickens had a grasp on it with his ghosts, Mary Wollstonecraft Shelley almost got it, and Einstein came so close to the truth. The dead heroes are brought in to Odin, and they rise again, they feast all night and fight all day again, and their deaths mean nothing, because they've escaped time. That's the whole point of the metaphor with Dr.

Zeus, you guys! He's the liberator. *Zeus defeats Chronos.* Everything's happening at once! We can perceive time in a way mortals can't, we can make it irrelevant. Don't you see?

"All you have to do is understand, and you're free! You're out of here!" With an ear-piercing whoop he snatched off his chaplet of roses and whirled it up, up, black against the moon for a second before it bounced down and rolled away in the direction of L. Frank Baum's house.

I did understand: Einar was mad as a hatter. There were rumors that some of the really Old Ones weren't too stable. I knew Imarte was several millennia old, and she'd lost a screw tonight. How old was Einar? That mention of Odin was probably a clue. He wasn't so crazy, he couldn't do his job; just crazy enough to be happy on this black plain, under this cold moon. Wasn't he the lucky guy?

Shuddering, I pulled my shawl around myself. I needed Theobromos. I'd have some as soon as I got back to the inn. No, I couldn't; I'd been drinking gin. Where had I heard that Theobromos and gin didn't combine well?

It's hell to be a cyborg and have immediate access to any stray memory that one rashly summons up. There I was at a New Year's ball, at a table with three other immortals. There was the little neophyte Latif, there was my damned demon godfather Joseph, and there was poor Lewis, who was feeling ill after overindulging. Precocious Latif had explained about the toxic effect of Theobromos combined with martinis.

Lewis. Somewhere my friend Lewis was weeping for me.

Juan Bautista's teeth were chattering in his head, and Imarte's dance had become so frenzied, she was a blur in the moonlight. Einar was dancing too, kicking up his boots and waving his long arms as he chanted a song, something in third-century Norwegian about hauling on the oars and steering for the land where palm trees grow.

Porfirio pitched his chaplet over the side of the wagon and drew his six-shooter.

"Our revels now are ended," he announced, and fired three shots into the air. Instantly we were all sober, converting the alcohol in our bloodstreams into water and sugar, as we were programmed to do when confronted by hazard.

"What on Earth—?" said Imarte. "How embarrassing." She got up from where she'd been rolling in the dust, near what would one day be the statue of Ishtar, and hastily brushed herself off. "Was I indulging in grief accommodation again?"

Einar was crawling out from under the wagon, where he'd vanished when the shots went off. He got to his feet and looked around sheepishly.

"Cold out here, isn't it?" was all he said.

"Well—we were only having a bit of fun, weren't we?" said Oscar.

"Speak for yourself," I said. Juan Bautista had his eyes closed; he was huddled up with his cheek pressed into Erich von Stroheim's feathers.

"Let's go, guys," Porfirio ordered. He took the reins and swung us back around for La Nopalera. Einar and Imarte climbed into their saddles and followed, all along the empty road, and the lights of Los Angeles grew fainter behind us, until they vanished like a dream.

*I*T HAD BEEN A great movie, all the same.

Thinking about it all, about Babylon and France and Jerusalem and that cold urban future, one tended to forget one was living in the midst of a historical upheaval just as impressive. France was finding that it was a great deal harder for the Second Empire to crush a bunch of ignorant mestizos than had ever been expected, while England and Spain sat back and watched in disgust. The North Americans were busy filling up the history books too: the Emancipation Proclamation was issued, for example. In future cinema it would be depicted by black hands stretching up toward beams of sunlight, broken manacles dangling from the wrists, to the accompaniment of a swelling chorus of this or that hymn, usually fading into a long shot of the Lincoln Memorial.

So sentimentally is the birth of a baby presented. The reality is far more an occasion of blood, of fear and uncertainty, of shock that displaces the joy that should be felt on such an occasion. While not one of those people to whom that piece of paper meant so much would ever have gone back to being slaves again, they must have known that the chains would be ten times as hard to break now that they were invisible and intangible.

But how could any of it matter to us? We went on about our daily life in a world where Watts and South Central were still Spanish land grants where vaqueros roped steers, and the longhorns herded down from the Tejon Ranch bore a brand of Cross above Crescent, commemorating the ancient victories of the Spanish Crusaders over the Moors, and I still thought of black men as turbaned kings with scimitars. What did this Civil War have to do with me?

You see? I had no sense of Realpolitik at all. Not that I wasn't warned.

I WAS RETURNING FROM a profitable day in the less surreal regions of the temperate belt when I picked up the warning signal being broadcast by Porfirio. It told me to approach with caution, so I left the road and came overland through the sagebrush, straining to pick up more of the transmission. All I could hear was Porfirio's end of it, at first.

But why would I lie to you, señor? Señora Marta comes and goes as she pleases. You must know this. She pays rent on her room, and I don't ask her what she does in there and she doesn't tell me. Come and have some coffee.

Of course I would tell you if I knew, señor.

No, señor, I'm not in love with her. No.

She didn't tell me, señor. What about some coffee?

I don't love her, señor.

Yes, I would tell you. Would you like a cup of coffee, señor?

No, señor, I never said that. Señor, please, put the gun away. There's no need for that. Listen to me, señor, you know what? If he's with her when she comes home, I'll help you shoot him. Please stop waving the gun in the air and sit down and have some coffee—

There followed a salvo of shots.

Now, you see, señor? You're not at your best, or you'd have hit something for sure. And you don't want to hang, señor. Señora Marta would cry if you were to hang, eh? No, señor, she didn't tell me.

No, señor, I'm not in love with her.

Señor, you really would feel better with some coffee in you.

Mental note: no torturer in a dungeon cell ever devised anything as frustrating, as inescapable, as terrifyingly pointless as a conversation with a drunk.

Yes, señor, that's a good idea. Yes, by all means.

All right, señor, that's a very, very good idea. There is your horse.

No, she didn't tell me, señor. Maybe if you get on your horse and ride out now, you'll catch them.

Very good! Buenos noches, señor. That way. The road is that way.

What would you want to shoot the horse for, señor?

Yes, you're right, that would show her. Yes, I'm sure she'd weep over your grave. I think you want to put it in your mouth, though, señor, not against the temple like that. There! You see how easy it is to miss?

Very well, señor, if you say so. Yes, that way. That way, señor. Buenos noches, señor. Vaya con sathanas.

When the all clear was finally broadcast, I came slinking down out of the hills to find Porfirio sitting beside the fire, mixing himself a double mocha by dissolving most of a cake of Theobromos in a pot of black coffee.

"Who was that?" I asked, shrugging off my pack.

"Mr. Cyrus Jackson," Porfirio said, baring his teeth. "Some knight chivalrous, huh? Good thing the 1600-hours stage is late, or there'd have been a nasty scene."

"Where is Imarte, anyway? I haven't seen her for a few days," I said, reaching for a tin plate and digging a spoon into the frijole pot.

"She went up north for something," Porfirio said. "Christ knows what. She didn't tell me." I joined with him on the last sentence.

Juan Bautista emerged from his lean-to, looking perturbed. "Is that drunk guy gone? I was scared he'd shoot at my birds."

"Gone but not forgotten, unfortunately," said Porfirio. He raised his head, listening. "And there's the stage. I think I'll just go dump this whole mess in Ms. Imarte's ever-ready lap." He took a terrific slug of Theobromos-adulterated java straight from the coffeepot and stalked off down the canyon, carrying the pot with him.

After a few minutes we heard the driver's whip crack as the stage continued its journey to Los Angeles, and Porfirio and Imarte came slowly up the canyon.

"I told you I was sorry. What on earth can I do?" Imarte was saying.

"You can deal with the guy, that's what you can do. You led him on, and now he's got a fit of killer jealousy. Why did you give him the idea he was anything but a customer to you, anyway?"

"He was a good source of data," Imarte said, drawing her feathered shawl around her against the twilight chill. "He provided me with no end of fascinating material that has, in fact, led me to an astonishing discovery. You wouldn't believe it, but the evidence is overwhelming, that not only is there an active Confederate plot—"

"He wants to kill you for being unfaithful to him," Porfirio said.

"Oh." She knitted her brows. "I'll have to do something, I suppose. Don't worry. We'll deal with the inconvenience somehow. Believe me, it's worth it. Have you any idea what his simple anecdotes have revealed?"

"Why don't you tell us?" I said, soaking a tortilla in steak juice.

She was so enthralled with her big news, she actually sat down beside me. "There is a conspiracy," she uttered in thrilled tones, "that may involve the highest-ranking members of Parliament, to take California for the *British*."

"The British? Why would they want California?"

Imarte gave me an arch look and paused dramatically, during which time the answer became obvious. Gold, vast natural resources, most of the Pacific coastline... Okay, any government in its right collective mind would covet California. But the British?

"I thought it was an odd series of coincidences at first," Imarte said, gazing pensively into the fire. "All those British nationals passing through, filing claims to search for gold on Catalina. Why Catalina,

where no appreciable gold has ever been found? Why are they shipping engineering equipment over there? Why are they taking such
pains to determine who actually owns title to the island? Because they
are, you know. I slept with a man who informed me that a fortified
base is being constructed by the Albion Mining Syndicate, to be called
Queen City. Of course he didn't call it a fortified base, but by asking
certain questions about this so-called mining town, I was able to determine that the site it occupies has considerable strategic importance
and is, in fact, being prepared for ordnance emplacements. Moreover,
no attempts whatsoever are being made to prospect for gold."

"Wow," said Juan Bautista. "What would happen if the English
took over California?"

I rolled up frijoles in a tortilla and bit into it. "They won't, we
know that, so what's the point of wondering? They gave up Oregon
without a fight, didn't they? Why should they try to take the West
Coast now, even if they want it?"

"Ah, but you see," Imarte said, holding up a forefinger, "the political situation has changed. The Americans, who might once have
prevented them, are locked in a devastating civil war whose outcome
is still unknown. Europe is making a play to regain lost empires in
South America. If the continental royalty manages to conquer Mexico, if the American nation falls apart—and these mortals haven't our
advantage of knowing how it all turns out in the end—why, then,
Manifest Destiny comes undone and the whole of the New World is
up for grabs again. There have even been rumors that the Russians are
beginning to regret pulling out of California. Can anyone wonder if
Queen Victoria's ministers"—she searched for a metaphor—"want to
be first in line, shopping bags in hand, when the doors are flung open
on the Great American Fire Sale?"

"What does it matter, anyway?" I said crossly.

"Don't you think it's fascinating? This is secret history. It lends so
much more understanding, so much fire and color to the dramatic
pageant unfolding before our eyes. Imagine all those British diplomats
playing the Union and Confederate governments off against each

other, deploring slavery while covertly aiding the rebels, yet planning
still another layer of double cross by preparing to step in and seize territories from the survivors should the Confederacy win!" Her eyes
were gleaming. "Given the size of the empire they control already,
why should the British think it unreasonable to go on playing the
Great Game here?"

"You're sure about this?" Porfirio asked, taking another swig
from the coffeepot. "God knows they were eager enough to stick their
fingers in the pie of Texas."

"I've been collecting information. Even now there's a plot brewing in San Francisco. The nephew of a British statesman has persuaded a stupid young American to join him in a privateering
expedition—supposedly to aid the Confederacy by raiding the Pacific
Mail and diverting the gold shipments from the San Francisco Mint to
the Confederate cause. I don't yet know how they plan to do it, but
I'm fairly sure the Albion Mining Syndicate is involved, from their
base on Catalina Island. Are you aware that any maritime power po-
sitioned there with even minimal ordnance could effectively control
the entire coastline of California at this point in time?"

"Pirates!" Porfirio slapped his knee. "Goddamn Francis Drake is
at it again!"

"But that's awful!" said Juan Bautista. His eyes were big and
worried.

"It's not going to happen, dummy," I said. "Access your files. If
there actually ever is such a plot, somebody screws it up, because it
never makes the history books."

"It might not be so bad if the British took over," said Porfirio with
a grin. "Have we fared all that well under the Yankees? I'll bet General Vallejo kicks himself every day for not shooting John C. Fremont
when he had the chance. And think about a colonial governor and the
Union Jack flying over the Plaza. All those damn cowboys and their
guns expelled. Think how the future of California would change. No
Prohibition, so no bootleggers, so no Mob. No cops with guns. No
movie people either. Just lots of plantations run by old aristocratic

families. It'd be Lower Canada, man! Nothing would *ever* happen here."

No freeways, no smog, low population density. That horrifying city on the plain I'd glimpsed would never exist. Would that be such a bad thing? But of course it was never going to happen. Catalina Island had a strange enough future ahead of it, but being the Californian Hong Kong wasn't part of the package.

I shrugged. "So what are you planning to do with all this fascinating secret knowledge?" I asked Imarte.

"Take notes. And so should all of you," she admonished us. "This is the life, the hidden motivation of mortal history. It concerns every one of us."

"It concerns *you*," I said. "I have more important things to occupy my time."

"Oh, yes, finding seventeen different mutations of mugwort *would* take precedence over the destinies of nations any day." She tossed her head.

"Can it, ladies," Porfirio said.

We heard the rattle and creak of Oscar's wagon approaching. He was leaning backward in the seat, peering down the canyon behind him. He was concerned. "Er, there appears to be a mortal fellow lying dead drunk in a ditch back there by the grade," he said. "His horse is unharmed, however."

Porfirio sighed.

I was afraid all this talk of the damned Brits would set the dreams off again, and I was right. It was a surprisingly quiet dream, though; at least it wasn't more endless replay of the past.

I was on a ship, not a miserable little dark galleon like the one I'd left La Coruña in so long ago, but a modern ship, one of those beautiful three-masted clippers the English were making nowadays, with iron-framed hulls, so much safer than the Yankee variety. Every detail exact. Salt spray, brisk chilly breeze, white clouds of canvas taking up miles of sky, nimble sailors mounting through the shrouds and ratlines. This ship was taking somebody somewhere fast. I seemed to be having a *nice* dream for a change. I'd never been on a modern ship before. I wandered around, looking at things with great interest, observing Jack-Tars holystoning the deck and doing other terribly nautical things.

"Here now, girlie," croaked a voice in my ear, and I turned in astonishment to behold a black-bearded sailor grinning evilly at me. "Ain't you been in to see him yet?"

"Excuse me?" I said.

"He's aft there," said the seaman, "in the deckhouse. He's comin' through, ye know."

"Oh," I said.

Then the dream faded away into something else, something less vivid, and I thought that he wasn't coming after all, because I'd turned out to be a Crome generator. I woke crying, pitying myself.

OUR IMMORTAL LIVES went on. The hills went from brown to a more weathered shade of brown. The leaves of the black walnut trees turned bright yellow, and so did the few cottonwoods; they were the only ones to make any ostentatious display of color. There were also bright scarlet berries on the toyon holly bushes, and they were pretty hanging in clumps among the dark serrate leaves; but the rest of southern California was unrelievedly drab.

The days dawned gray, which burned off to a glaring white sky around noon, hazy and painful to the eyes. Smoke from the cookfire hung in the cold, still air and did not dissipate. Small wonder smog would become a local institution. There was no rain to wash it away, either, though the dewfall was heavy and our adobe rooms became chill and dank unless lit braziers were kept in them half the day, which increased the smokiness. Oscar made a few wistful remarks about how good New England food would be now that the weather was getting nippy, but there were still no takers for his Criterion Patented Brassbound Pie Safe.

If I were home in the Santa Lucia Range, what a dark green the mountains would be, what a dark blue the sky, with cold winds that drove out the summer fog. And the redwoods and the cypresses would stand like dark gods, offering up their own aromatic blood. The broadleaf maples would blaze like flame, the stars glitter like broken glass. I could travel my secret ridge routes all day with no company but the sea hundreds of meters below me, and the occasional white sail on the far horizon to prove I wasn't the only living soul in the world.

And if I wanted company, or at least civilized food, I could always hike north to Monterey, or stop in at the Post's little rancho at Soberanes Creek; though I didn't do that often, because I unnerved the settlers, and in any case I seldom wanted company. The trees and the sea were enough. Not even *he* could find me there, my wraith, unable to summon me from my restless bed when I didn't have one, unable to break my human heart when I'd transmuted it into green leaves and stars.

But here I was in this glaring purgatory of a cow town. Winter was decidedly not its best season. The weather wasn't our only problem; Imarte had given Cyrus Jackson the brush-off somehow, more or less tactfully, but he hadn't accepted it. Several times we spotted him by infrared, sitting off on the hills at night, watching our little canyon. As long as he did nothing but lurk, he was welcome to his miserable vigil; but you never know when mortals are going to decide to go out in a blaze of glory and try to take you with them, so we monitored him closely.

Imarte didn't care. She had her fascinating theories, her invaluable first-person narratives, and her wealth of irreplaceable historical detail. When she wrang a source dry, she dropped the source. I am afraid that, although an anthropologist, she lacked a certain love for her subject, or perhaps its immediate and particular personification: the human heart.

I should talk, eh, señors?

Anyway, we were all a little nervous, as the cold weather set in, scanning the dull hills for desperate mortals with guns. They were everywhere down here anyway, but now we had our own special desperate mortal with a gun.

One day, when the northbound stage stopped by, I went down to watch Porfirio change a shoe on the lead horse. I had seen him shoe horses before; but Einar was the only other person around, and he and I had taken to avoiding conversation with each other since our visit to 1996.

It wasn't a long stop; no passengers had to get on or off; they wouldn't have stopped except for the loose shoe. During the whole time, though, one of the passengers had his attention riveted on Porfirio. He was a young kid, maybe Juan Bautista's age, Mexican from the look of him and very well dressed, with a high shirt collar and the old-fashioned silk tie that stuck out like paddles from either side of the central knot. Leading the horse back to its place, Porfirio noticed the boy's intense regard and glanced up at him once, curious. The boy looked away immediately.

"What was with the kid who kept staring at you?" I asked as the stage went bounding and creaking away and we closed up the smithy shed.

"Beats me," Porfirio said. "I think I'll make some tamales dulces tomorrow, what do you say? It's early for Christmas, but I've really got a craving for something sweet."

He made hot chocolate that night instead of coffee, and we got into quite an elevated mood, sipping it around the fire and laughing. We all sobered up, though, the instant we picked up the mortal coming over the ridge to our immediate north.

"Chief?" Einar was on his feet at once, shotgun unslung and cocked.

"I read him." Porfirio was in the shadow of an oak tree faster than mortal eye could have followed, his Navy revolver out. Einar faded into the gloom behind the house.

"'Scuse me," murmured Juan Bautista, grabbing up Marie Dressler, who clacked her beak at him in protest. He sprinted for his room clutching her in his arms, while Erich rode his head, balancing expertly.

I remained where I was, warming my hands on my mug and peering doubtfully up at the ridge. Yes, there he was on infrared, making his stealthy way down the hill in our direction. Carrying a gun, too.

But it wasn't our lovelorn filibuster... Who the hell was this, creeping along like a thief, his heart thudding painfully? He raised the gun to sight on our circle of firelight, and I winked out on him, to continue my scan from the shadows under a spurge laurel. He lowered the gun, staring in disbelief at the deserted fire. This was a young male mortal, no intoxicants in his bloodstream but with a number of the toxins produced by fear and exhaustion. No disease signatures... some healed fractures, very old. Unhappiness. He didn't want to be here, he didn't want to be doing this. He was tired and cold. Where had the person gone, who'd been there a minute ago? he was thinking in Mexican Spanish.

I saw Porfirio and Einar working their way uphill toward him. Porfirio stopped about twenty feet below, and Einar circled around until he was just above him, only about ten feet away in the sagebrush, moving without a sound until he suddenly stood up black against the stars and said loudly:

"*¿Qué pasa, amigo?*"

The kid whirled, swinging his gun around, but Porfirio nailed him from behind before he could get off a single shot. That was that. He pitched forward, and I saw Porfirio and Einar closing in on him cautiously. I remembered my hot chocolate and took a sip. No reason to come out until they'd brought the body down. He wasn't dead yet, anyway, just unconscious and bleeding a lot.

Then what a howl of agony. Not out loud, I don't think it would have shaken the Earth that way if he'd been using only his voice: it was Porfirio's heart that was screaming, cutting through the subvocal ether like the sound of all possible things malfunctioning at once. My hair stood on end. I came blundering out through the bushes to see him crashing down the hillside, bearing the young mortal in his arms, and you couldn't have told who looked more deathlike, gray-faced Porfirio or the mortal. Einar was bounding along after him.

"Chief! Chief, what is it? What's wrong?"

"Code blue!" snarled Porfirio. "Equipment! Three pints Hemosynth!"

Nobody can say we don't move fast in an emergency. The boy was restarted and stable in no time, bleeding stopped and wounds bound, all kinds of stuff pumping through him that wouldn't be discovered by mortals for decades. His nice clothes were ruined, of course, including the silk tie, which had come undone and was covered with blood. He was one lucky kid for all that. Porfirio's shot had missed his heart. We stretchered him into Porfirio's room, and Porfirio sat down beside him and told us all to get the hell out of there, which we did.

What to do after that but go to bed? Nobody was going to answer our questions; nobody was going to explain why the little creep had come sneaking back to gun for us, or why Porfirio had been so suddenly horrified, after plugging him with as neat a piece of cold-blooded shooting as I've ever seen, or why such pains had been taken to save his young life.

I was awakened at dawn by Porfirio coming into my room. He still hadn't washed the blood from his hands. "He's starting to come around," he said hoarsely. "He can't see me. Go to him, please."

"You want to tell me what's going on?" I said, swinging my legs over the side of the cot and groping for my boots.

Porfirio leaned against the doorway. "He's one of my family. I didn't recognize him. Haven't seen him since he was seven years old."

"So why was he shooting at you?" I stood up and pulled my shawl around my shoulders.

"I shot his father."

"You shot his father," I said, looking at him.

He was looking down at the dirt floor. "Yeah. You know how I recognized him? His father broke all the fingers on his hand that day. Just held his little hand down on the table and pounded it with a bottle. The fingers healed crooked. That was how I recognized him."

"Oh," I said.

The boy didn't wake much. I gave him water and spoke to him soothingly in Spanish, telling him he was all right. Most of the time he was passed out, sedated while the miracle cures Porfirio had filled him with did their work. I examined his hand and found the evidence of old multiple injuries. It must have been a very little hand when it was hurt so badly. Whether or not Paradise exists, señors, there must be a hell. People who do such things to their children belong there, and for all eternity too.

Einar came in to take my place at noon, and I went out into the ghastly white day. Porfirio was nowhere in evidence, but Imarte was standing by the cookfire with an apron tied on over her whore's finery. Of all things, she appeared to be making lunch; she was tossing handfuls of barley into what smelled like goat stew.

"What's that supposed to be?" I asked, squinting at it through the glare.

"It's the only thing I know how to make," she said defensively. "It's a *very* old recipe."

"Where's Porfirio?"

"Asleep in my room, poor dear. Goddess, what a tragedy." She sighed. The subtext here was that she knew more about it than I did, so I just sat down and refrained from asking anything else until she couldn't stand not telling me a second longer.

"You know what happened, of course."

I shook my head. "Only that the kid is one of that family of his. There seems to be revenge mixed up in it somehow. And child abuse."

"If that were all! Remember when we asked Porfirio where his family is now? Remember he told us that a great-niece had married a ranchero, and her brothers had come to work on the rancho for him? Well, it seems this young man is her son, hers and the ranchero. The boy's father appears to have been one of those unfortunates with two personalities, a fairly decent one when he was sober and entirely another kind when he drank. A lot of unresolved rage there, apparently." She tossed in the last of the barley and looked around. She found the raisins she wanted and sprinkled them in too.

"In any case, after the child was born, the father's dark side came more into control. He was sober less of the time. Fortunately Porfirio (who was there) and the girl's brothers looked after the man's business affairs, but, as so often happens with this type of personality disorder, he was anything but grateful. More and more, his rage manifested itself in violence against his wife and, in time, no doubt as he perceived himself being displaced in her affections, against the child."

"So he showed them all by crippling the baby's hand." I rubbed my eyes wearily. I hated mortals.

"Ah, but that's not the whole story. The wife, for her part, had a classically codependent personality. She manifested her own feelings of low self-esteem by remaining with her husband in spite of their abusive relationship and, from what I understand, transferring *her* anger to her brothers and to her 'Uncle' Porfirio."

"It figures."

"Quite a standard pathology, actually," said Imarte, stirring the pot busily and frowning as she considered the seasoning. "And of course it broke Porfirio's heart. He seems to have loved the child and assumed the role of father in his life. He taught the boy to ride, he remembered his birthday with presents, he read to him from Cervantes. This, however, only brought about greater feelings of resentment and alienation from the actual father, and in time precipitated the final crisis. The tragedy occurred on one of their colorful fiesta days, the one with all the skeletons."

"The Day of the Dead."

"The family had made some attempt to celebrate, with decorations and candy for the little boy. The father, driven by his usual compulsion on festive occasions, began to drink early in the afternoon. Once again he was unable to deal with his rage, and by twilight he was fairly violent. The incident with the child's hand was apparently provoked when the child hid from his father behind a chair."

"I'm glad Porfirio shot the son of a bitch."

"Oh, he didn't shoot him in retaliation for the boy," Imarte said, sorting through the little cans of spices she'd set out. She found one she liked and dealt out a few dashes into the stew. "The wife was able to emerge from her passive role long enough to take the liquor bottle from her husband. He turned on her, accusing her of betrayal. He said he'd kill all three of them, then thrust the muzzle of his pistol in her mouth. At this point Porfirio and the brothers, who had just ridden up, intervened. As they burst through the door, the husband turned and shot at them. He wounded one of the brothers mortally. That was when Porfirio drew his own gun and shot the husband dead."

I drew my shawl over my head.

"As is usual in these cases, the woman blamed everyone but her abuser. She threw herself on her husband's body, shrieking incoherent lamentations and protestations of eternal love. The surviving brothers found Porfirio a horse and helped him to escape. The Company was obliging about stationing him as far away as possible. That was ten years ago. Last night, the young man made his attempt on Porfirio's life."

"He can't blame Porfirio for what happened!"

"You think not?" She gave me a sadly tolerant smile. "But you yourself are a product of Hispanic culture, you ought to understand. These male-dominated societies all follow the same code of honor. Porfirio killed the father, therefore the son must kill Porfirio. It's depressingly simple."

The immortal uncle was accustomed to solving the problems of this classic dysfunctional family, but he hadn't quite brought it off this time, had he? Poor man. Briefly I thanked God that my blood were strangers to me, if indeed the line hadn't died out.

"How do we explain to this kid that he can't finish his vendetta, because his target's an immortal?" I asked. Imarte shrugged gracefully.

Just then Porfirio emerged from the inn, carrying a blanket and a bag, and went straight to the stable without a word. A few minutes later, he came out, leading a saddled horse, and approached us. His face was blank, curtains drawn and shutters closed.

"I'm taking off," he said. "I'll be camping up the pass, if you need me. What you're going to tell Tomas is, I was just the blacksmith here, and you didn't know I was wanted for murder in Durango or anything else about my past. Tell him Einar runs the place, and when Einar found out what happened, he went for the sheriff in Los Angeles, but I ran away before I could be arrested. You have no idea where I've gone. Help him get well again and then put him on a stagecoach and send him back to Durango. Okay? I'll send you my location coordinates so you can let me know how he's doing."

"You want us to bring you supplies?" I asked. "Food, aguardiente, anything?"

He just shook his head and swung up into the saddle. We watched him urge his horse to a swift canter, and away he went down the canyon.

Imarte sighed deeply. "The grim history unfolds," she intoned. "How thoroughly characteristic of the American West, yet analogous to clan feuds in Corsica or Scotland. How unfortunate, but how fascinating, don't you think?"

"Unfortunate," I replied.

Tomas was out of danger pretty quickly, with no infections to complicate things; no fever, no ravings, only a pale polite boy with enormous dark eyes asking us if we knew where the blacksmith went. We told him what Porfirio told us to tell him, and he accepted that quietly enough, and was unconscious again. His body needed the sleep. Young mortals heal almost as fast as we do.

After a few days he was able to ask Einar to go recover his trunk, which he'd hidden in a bush in Encino after leaving the stagecoach at Garnier's. It contained two other suits of clothes, a shaving kit, and several small personal items, including a daguerreotype of a woman and child. His mother, no doubt, because the child standing stiffly beside her chair was certainly Tomas. He had a wistful little smile for the camera. She was dressed in black, and her eyes were black too, cold and angry. Was there maybe a resemblance to Porfirio in the shape of her face, the chill in her eyes?

Tomas asked for his gun back. We checked with Porfirio, who was hiding out in a high narrow canyon on Mount Hollywood; he sighed and then transmitted his okay to give it back to the boy, cleaned and loaded. This was Los Angeles, after all. We hung his gun belt over the bedpost. He woke up long enough to see it there and gave us his little grateful smile, just like the child in the picture. Then he slept again.

So there was this kid, in Porfirio's room, with his luggage and his weapon and his mystery. Imarte hovered over Tomas, attending to the tiniest details of nursing with perfection, hoping he'd murmur some part of his story in a delirium or gasp confidences into her motherly bosom. He didn't. He barely spoke at all, to any of us, and when he did finally speak, it was to Juan Bautista.

I was sitting by the bed, reading a back issue of *La Estrella* and waiting for Imarte to take her turn at vigil, when Juan Bautista entered the room. Tomas opened his eyes at the noise, and then opened them wider. It's not every day you see silver-haired Indian kids with condors perched on their heads.

"That guy came and wanted to talk to Imarte again, so I said I'd take over for you," Juan Bautista told me in Cinema Standard.

"Fine," I said, and rose from the chair. I was starving. As Juan Bautista sat down and I left the room, I heard Tomas asking shakily, in Spanish:

"Why do you have a bird standing on your head?"

I fixed myself a plate of Imarte's goat stew, that's how hungry I was, and sat down with my back against the wall to eat it. As I ate, I became aware that there was a conversation in Spanish going on in the room on the other side of the wall. Sharpening my reception, I was able to pick it up.

"...and I feed her fish when I can get them," Juan Bautista was saying. "Mostly sardines, you know, in those little square cans with the funny openers?"

"That's really neat," I heard Tomas reply.

"Yeah. I thought about getting her some canned oysters, but they're *way* expensive."

"I had some oysters in Santa Fe one time. I didn't think much of them. What do you feed the other ones?"

"Just seeds and stuff. You know. Except for the little owls—I catch crickets for them. Watch out. He's telling you he needs to go to the bathroom. Here, give him back a minute. Good boy! See, I've trained him to let me know. Now you can hold him again."

"He's, like, the biggest parrot in the world or something," Tomas said, giggling weakly. "Boy, I'd love to have one of these guys to wear on my shoulder when I walk around the ranch. Condors don't talk, huh?"

"No. Only the *Psittacidae, Corvidae,* and *Sturnidae* talk. The *Sturnidae* are just mimics, though, they don't understand speech like parrots."

"We used to have a parrot when I was a kid." Tomas's voice was a little sad. "My father bought him for my mother. He was...a real man, my father."

"And he was killed by that blacksmith who worked here?" Juan Bautista said, cautiously. I frowned at my empty plate and wondered if he was going to let slip any details he shouldn't know.

"The same man who shot me."

"You came looking for him?" Juan Bautista asked.

"I didn't think I'd find him, I didn't think he would still be alive, not the kind of guy he was. I thought...if I could just find his grave or something, I could spit on it and go home and tell my mother I'd done that, at least. I was going up to San Francisco to look for the grave, because I'd heard they had a lot of criminals up there. But then the stagecoach stopped here, and there he was, and I knew I had to kill him. For my father."

"You loved your father?"

"I was only a kid when that son of a bitch killed him, but I remember we used to do stuff. He taught me how to ride. His favorite book was *Don Quixote,* and he used to read to me from it, and one year for my birthday, you know what he did? He made me a whole set of wooden figures from the book, he carved them himself. There was a Don Quixote with these long jointed legs, you could sit him on Rocinante or you could make him dance or turn somersaults. He had a lance and shield and helmet. There was a windmill with vanes that really turned, and there was a giant's face carved on it. There was a Sancho too, but he didn't do anything, he just sat on his mule. They were the best toys....My father loved me better than anybody else ever did." Tomas's voice grew a little muffled.

"But...what happened to your fingers?" asked Juan Bautista, bewildered. He didn't get it.

"That was the other guy, the one who murdered my father. I don't remember what happened, I was too little, but my mother said he'd been drinking. He was this lowlife friend of my uncles'. They used to work on our ranch, and they brought this friend of theirs. He was our majordomo for a while. But he was a drunk, always getting into trouble. I remember he'd yell and break things, and I'd be scared. I don't know why my mother let him yell at her that way, she was so stupid. Wouldn't you think she'd just have told my father? *He* wouldn't have let anybody talk to his woman that way, if he'd known. But I guess he never found out about it, until that night."

Had the mother twisted the story for her son? Or had she simply never answered his questions? What was wrong with the mortal woman, anyway?

"You want some of this tea?" Juan Bautista's voice was a little shaky. "It's good for you."

"Thanks." There was a pause as Tomas drank, and then he continued:

"Sometimes I can remember a little. We were having a party. I was scared. I remember the yelling. There was a fight. That guy was drunk, and he hurt my hand and killed my father and one of my uncles when they came in. He ran away, and nobody ever caught him.

"After the funeral, my mother sent the rest of her brothers away, because it was their fault that guy came to the ranch. She said she'd rather have me be the man of the family than any of them. Sometimes, I wish she hadn't done that, because it's hard running the ranch without help. She's still angry after all these years."

Poor boy. What a weight on his shoulders.

"Still angry?" asked Juan Bautista.

"Oh, yeah. She told me I had to find that guy as soon as I was old enough and avenge my father's murder."

"Well..." I could hear Juan Bautista shifting around uncomfortably. "You know what? You could go back and tell her you got him. He shot you, but you shot him first, see? And I'd be a witness for you. We could write a letter. You know, like a deposition? Everybody here would sign it, telling her how you killed him. Then you could go home with proof, and it would be all over."

"I can't lie to her," Tomas said. "She always knows.... Anyhow, I don't want to go home until I've killed him. It wasn't until I saw his face that afternoon that I remembered how scary it used to be, how my mother cried. I have to kill him for her, but I also have to kill him for me, for taking away my father. I hadn't even remembered how much my father loved me until I saw that man."

"But he almost got you," Juan Bautista said. "He's a real good shot, and now he knows you're after him. You'll get killed next time."

"Maybe I'll kill him instead." Tomas didn't sound certain. "Or he'll kill me, and then I'll be in Paradise with my father. I don't care which. What would you do, if you were me?"

"I don't know," Juan Bautista said. "I'm an orphan." He sounded as though he was grateful for that. "But I wouldn't want to die for no reason. I mean...what if your mother got some of the details wrong?"

"She never gets details wrong."

"Have you asked your uncles about what happened?"

"How could I?" Tomas sounded tired. "She sent them away, and they never came back. I don't know where they went or if they're even still alive."

"You need to sleep some more," Juan Bautista said. "Your blood

pressure's too low." I winced; this was the kind of cover-blowing remark young operatives make. He might as well tell the mortal boy he
could scan him. "You can't do anything anyway until you get well. So
you should rest and drink a lot of tea, okay?"

"Okay," said Tomas in a fading voice.

He rested and drank a lot of tea, and the color began to come
back into his face as the days passed. Soon he was able to get out of
bed and totter around the room, and then to put on his clothes and sit
outside in the chilly November sunlight.

Tomas was a nice boy. He was quiet and courteous, for a
seventeen-year-old; he didn't brag or try to impress us with how
tough he was. He spoke respectfully to ladies and deferred to Einar
and Oscar. He was really taken with Juan Bautista's aviary, and the
two of them spent hours in there cleaning the cages and talking about
birds. And wasn't he a good son? Ready to roam the face of the earth
to deliver blazing death to a stranger, or suffer blazing death himself,
for his mother's sake.

"What are we going to do?" said Juan Bautista, late one evening
when Tomas was safely asleep in Porfirio's bed. "I never knew mortals
were crazy like this. They look so normal. How are we going to stop
him from going off to hunt for Porfirio, when he's better?"

You can't, transmitted Porfirio from the mountain. He sounded
glum. *He won't go home looking like a fool or a coward. If I could
take my head off and send it home with him as a trophy, I'd do it.*

"Why not simply let the lad continue with his search indefinitely?"
said Oscar. "It doesn't sound to me as though his home is a terribly
pleasant place. Perhaps he's better off wandering the world and having
adventures. Certainly he won't expect you to come back here. We
might see him on his way, and then you could come out of hiding."

*What kind of adventures is he likely to have, poking his nose into
every den of thieves he comes across, looking for me? Because that's
what he'll do, you know that, and the next time he gets shot, I won't
be there to hook him up to a life-support system.*

"He's stubborn," Imarte said. "I've done my best to explain to him how this kind of primitive revenge ritual invariably results in the destruction of all parties. Regrettably, he comes from a society where a greater value is placed on abstract cultural values than individual human life. One is reminded of the Japanese custom of—"

"I don't suppose there's any way you could tell him the truth?" I asked Porfirio. "That his memories are all screwed up, that his father was the real bastard and you were the good guy?"

Can you think of any way I could get him to listen to me? transmitted Porfirio bitterly. *And even if I could, what then? He thinks he had a father who loved him and died in his mother's defense. Her version of the story's a lot more palatable, isn't it? What happens when the pretty paper is stripped off my ugly present of truth? His mother becomes a liar, at the very least.*

"She sounds like a crazy bitch anyway. Why should she hate you?" I said.

I killed the man she loved. She would have forgiven him anything, but she'll never forgive me. And I shouldn't be forgiven! I could have prevented this. If I'd been quicker, I might have stopped the bullet that killed Bartolo. I might have disabled Jaime without killing him. I might have been there for the boy all these years. God in heaven, see what she's done. The family is broken, scattered, when I'd fought so hard to keep them together where I could look out for them. How will I ever find Juan and Agustin again? Are they even alive? And she, look at what she's become, look at what she's done to that boy. If I had only stayed . . .

"You couldn't have, man," Einar said. "You know that. You belong to the Company. First time Dr. Zeus had a job for you somewhere else, you'd have had to go. And even if you'd stuck around, do you think you could have kept on micromanaging their lives forever? We may be immortals, but we can't control mortal destinies. We can help them when they want help, but that's it. When they want to destroy themselves, not even God can stop them."

"That is so true," I said, with all my weary heart. "It's that lousy rotten free will of theirs. All we do is run around cleaning up after it."

"We're the everlasting janitors in the Big Bathroom," Einar agreed. "Our only consolation is knowing how much worse things would be if we weren't part of the equation. Anyway, kids: here's an idea, culled from my centuries of wisdom and cinema expertise: We've all seen films where a guy fakes his own murder."

"I can think of several," Imarte said. And then, "Oh."

Let him shoot me?

"We'll load his gun with blanks and fix you up ahead of time with a full suit of charges and stage-blood bags. He'll think he's blown you away and go home with the revenge thing all finished." Einar jumped up in his excitement and began to pace. "Six Cawelti squibs, a sheet of body armor, some red dye and corn syrup—man, we can make you look like you had breakfast at the OK Corral!"

*I*T TOOK NO MORE THAN a week to prepare, during which time Tomas was getting stronger. Against Imarte's entreaties, he set up a target on a tree and practiced shooting at it. Juan Bautista tried to talk him into going home, but there was no arguing with the boy: as soon as he was well enough, he planned to take the stagecoach out to Calabasas, famed locally for its bandit population, to see if Porfirio had gone there to hide from justice. On the day he was finally strong enough to ride, however, Einar came riding up from the bottom of the canyon at a dusty gallop.

"Hey! Amigo!" he called out in crude Texan Spanish. Tomas turned. He'd been target shooting. "Yeah, you. I think I finally got a line on that no-good murdering hombre that killed your pa. Looks like he's holed up not five miles from here. You want to go see if you can get him?"

I looked up from the cookfire to watch the boy's reaction. He stood frozen, staring with those enormous dark eyes. Slowly and deliberately he holstered the pistol. "Will you have the kindness to loan me a horse, señor?"

"Get him a horse, Juanito," Einar said.

Juan Bautista gulped. "You don't want to do this," he told Tomas. "Think how bad you'll feel afterward."

"No. If I get it over with, I can be my own man," said Tomas.

So Juan Bautista brought out a horse, saddled and bridled, and Tomas climbed awkwardly into the saddle. He looked sick and dizzy up there.

Einar reached over and took his pistol out of its holster. He spun the empty chambers. "Won't do you any good unless you reload, son. Here, take mine." He handed off the gun full of blanks, and I looked meaningfully at Juan Bautista. First bit of stage business in our play accomplished.

Tomas stuck the gun in his belt and drew a deep breath. "Let's go, señor. Take me to that murdering son of a whore."

They rode away down the canyon, dust clouds spiraling up. Juan Bautista stood looking after them, wringing his hands. "I have to see," he said, and ran for the stable, from which he emerged a moment later leading another horse.

I ran to him as he got into the saddle. "Take me along. This ought to be some show."

He put out a hand, and I leaped up behind him, just as Imarte came running out of the inn. "What is it? Is it time? Don't tell me they've left—"

"We'll let you know how it went," I said, and we galloped away.

We followed the dust clouds north through the pass, up the grade to Dark Canyon, and over the flank of Cahuenga Peak. We were coming to the high ground behind Mount Hollywood, which sloped gently down toward the river, and I wondered if Einar had chosen the spot deliberately. You could call it an appropriate location for a shoot-out; this was the site of an immense graveyard in the distant future. Nearer our time, Griffith would shoot the battle sequence from *Birth of a Nation* here, and for all I knew the battle scene that ended *Intolerance* too. Einar had told us about it enough times, in his babbling enthusiasm. Now, before it became that famous place, it would serve as a small and private theater for a grim farce.

But where were the actors?

We saw the two horses tethered in a stand of oak trees. And, just creeping over a ridge and peering into the hollow beyond, there were Einar and Tomas. Juan Bautista urged our mount forward.

Porfirio was advertising his presence. A plume of smoke rose thinly. He'd made a cookfire.

"Up there," I said, pointing to our right. We could climb a winding trail for a better view. Juan Bautista hesitated, then swung the horse's head uphill, and we ascended hurriedly, peering through the oak trees.

Porfirio was sitting by his fire, warming his hands. He looked tired. He glanced up as Einar broadcast, *We're here, man. Is it a good day to die?*

Always. Porfirio looked down at the embers again, deliberately ignoring the mortal boy's clumsy approach through the weeds. Oh, God, the kid slipped, was tumbling down to land in a crouch not ten yards from where Porfirio sat. Did he really want to do this? Up on the ridge, Einar pulled out the little electronic control and waited.

Porfirio raised his face. Tomas made a stifled sound and staggered backward. We couldn't see his face, but we had a fine view of Porfirio as he got to his feet and held out his hands, his empty hands.

"Very good, *mi hijo.* It's my turn. Blood for blood, so you can be a man."

Then the boy was firing wildly, *bang bang bang,* and the charges detonated in perfect time with his shots. The blood bags exploded outward, and Porfirio spun and fell. The noise of the shots echoed; it hit the face of the ridge like a wave breaking and rolled back down the slope, prolonging the moment, washing us in the sound. Out on the valley floor beyond the river, a dog began to bark.

It's a wrap. Beautiful, Einar transmitted. *You all right?* He came jumping down the slope, stuffing the detonator remote into the pocket of his jeans.

Damn things hurt came the answering transmission. I confess I was relieved to hear Porfirio reply; that had been a truly convincing death scene. Look at him now, the way he lay there ashen and motionless, his lean villainous face frozen in a snarl like a dead animal's. But then, who could counterfeit death better than an Immortal? We see so much of the real thing.

Tomas had dropped the gun and was doubled up, retching. Einar caught him and steadied him. "Come on, boy. We have to get out of here. No sense getting yourself hanged. Let's go, let's go." He practically carried him up the slope and down the other side, to the place where their mounts were waiting. Juan Bautista spurred our horse through the sagebrush toward them.

"Did you get him?" I asked, playing my part.

"Got him, all right," Einar said, boosting Tomas into the saddle. "Now this boy's satisfied his debt of honor and he can go home to his ma with a clear conscience. Isn't that right, son?"

Juan Bautista rode up to Tomas and peered into his face worriedly. Tomas looked deathly ill again, as bad as on the night he'd been shot.

Then we all thundered away through the November evening, and the sun was setting red as blood, and the shadows were long. Tomas wept the whole way, and when we walked our horses into the innyard, he tumbled off his horse and into Imarte's waiting arms.

She folded him into her bosom.

"You poor brave boy. You come with me, tell Marta all about it," she cooed. *I trust everything went off as planned?*

You shoulda seen, Einar transmitted.

If anyone had bothered to tell me in time, I might have, she replied, giving me a nasty look. She turned and pulled Tomas away with her into the inn, doubtless to obtain a first-person narrative from him and gain valuable insights into the culture of machismo. The damned harpy.

She nursed him through the hysterics, and I think she rewarded him the way a man wants to be rewarded, and as the evening wore on it, she gave him aguardiente too to bolster his sense of worth. He cheered up tremendously and began to swagger and sing, as I'd never heard him do before. We all assumed it was the relief of being out from under this burden he'd carried his whole young life. But Juan Bautista listened for a while and then vanished silently up the canyon, taking Marie and Erich with him. I busied myself with making some plain beef stew—I'd had all the Chaldean Surprise I could stand—and Einar bounced around taking care of his innkeeper duties, still pleased with himself at the way his special effects had turned out. Even he began to look a little concerned, though, as the noise level in Imarte's room rose.

I was trying not to listen to what seemed to be an argument developing, when I picked up Porfirio on the ridge behind us, just arriving.

Mendoza?

Yes.

I could use some hot food.

Hang on.

I ran and got a blanket from my room, and half a case bottle of aguardiente, wrapping them together. I got a bowl of stew and a spoon and hurried up the canyon. As I ran, I could hear Tomas emerging from the inn, shouting to Imarte to leave him the hell alone.

"Whoa, son, where are you going?" Einar said, getting up.

"Set up the bottles!" the boy shouted. "Set up the bottles and give me that gun!"

Target shooting again? I shrugged and kept climbing.

Porfirio was sitting quietly in the darkness, gray as a ghost, which he looked like in his serape with the holes and bloodstains all over it. I put the bowl of stew into his hands and threw the blanket around his shoulders.

"Thanks." He turned the bowl in his hands, savoring the warmth. I sat down beside him and uncorked the aguardiente bottle.

"How is he?"

"I think he's having some kind of hysterical reaction," I answered delicately. "But I guess that's normal if you think you've just killed somebody. It looked great, by the way."

"The kid's drunk," Porfirio said with a scowl, gazing at the circle of light around our cookfire. "Listen to him."

Gunfire, followed by Tomas's shrill laughter. He was telling Einar to bring more bottles to shoot at. I had a gulp of aguardiente myself. Porfirio spooned stew into his mouth, but he never took his eyes from the fire. They were dark and cold.

"Listen to him, down there," he said. "He thinks he's some killer, he thinks he's one hell of a man."

"You did your best," I said. "What else could you do, Porfirio? At least this way he can go home and make his mother happy."

"She'll never be happy," he said, emptying the bottle and throwing it away. "My fault, I guess."

More shots. We could hear Einar making a very tactful suggestion and being refused indignantly. Porfirio exhaled hard.

"I was so relieved when she married Jaime. At last, I thought, somebody who'll take care of her, and he's even got money. But see how that turned out. I could go looking for Juan and Agustin, I guess, when this job is over; I could try to track them down and see if they've married, if they've kept the family going. But what am I going to do about her? And what am I going to do about that kid?

"Look at him down there, strutting around with his gun. He's bought into the whole damned lie about blood and honor and revenge. He was made to feel like a little nobody all his life, but now it's payback time. Nobody's ever going to tell *him* what to do again, not now that he's killed somebody. Ay, ay, ay."

Porfirio buried his head in his arms. "Who will take this curse off my family?" he asked the night.

The party didn't last much longer. Tomas got cold and ran out of things to shoot at, and Einar got tired of dodging bullets and vanished into the bushes, so Imarte came out and tried to get the boy to come to bed before he caught pneumonia or fell into the fire. He tried to hit her. You don't do that to an Immortal. She swiftly knocked him out and carried him indoors like a sack of flour.

Some time in the afternoon next day, Einar roused him and got him into a change of clothes. When the 1600-hours stage came rolling up, Tomas was bundled into a seat, still groggy, and Einar loaded on his trunk and paid for his passage southbound.

Porfirio came out of the hills, and our lives resumed their courses. I don't suppose I'll ever see that young man again; but I can imagine how he'll turn out.

Can't you, señors?

WELL, IT JUST GOT DARKER and crazier in bad old Los Diablos. Bad things come in by the armful and leave by inches, it's said. Winter came, but no rain; smallpox instead. It began in the old shacks on the hill where the poorer citizens lived, Sonoratown, the locals called it. The few remaining Indians were dying like flies, and then the Mexicans were being wiped out, and pretty soon there were even rows of coffins being carried to the Protestant cemetery. Stagecoach service became irregular, to say the least, in the dry and bitter cold.

Dry. There wasn't a creek or a freshet running. Our little stream became pools of standing water, shrinking perceptibly day by day. I don't know where the trout went. Our well hadn't given out, but we were taking serious measures to conserve water. Whatever water we used to wash I took to carrying out to the oak trees, to pour over their roots. Within hours after emptying a pail, you could see tiny blades of grass emerging where the water had been splashed. The land was desperate to cover itself with green; but the rain never fell, and next morning there would be deer slot everywhere, and the grass would all be gone.

There was water in the sky, all right; there was water vapor holding the haze together, which stung the eyes at midday and kept the adobe rooms cold as death. There was water in the slate clouds that rolled over us and kept going without releasing so much as a drop.

The longhorns began to rove into people's vegetable patches, and the last of the old rancheros looked at the brown hills and wondered if they oughtn't borrow some more from the Yankee moneylenders to tide them over what might be an unprofitable year.

We froze, but we got no rain. San Francisco got rain; but, then, San Francisco never doesn't get rain. It rained back east in Vicksburg, where another battle was fought, and we read rumors of soldiers drowning in their tents. It rained in Mexico, where Juárez sat in his room and calmly considered what he ought to do about Europe. Everybody else got rain, but we were dying of thirst.

And smallpox.

Oscar stayed home a lot, driving the rest of us crazy; but how was he going to sell anything with people hiding behind their doors, more afraid of the disease than they'd ever been of stray bullets? We saw almost nothing of Imarte, though, so it was a fair trade. She was having a field day, moving among the dying like a scarlet angel, easing their journey out of the world in exchange for life stories gasped out to the sympathetic stranger. To be fair, I believe she nursed a few back to health. When she wasn't busy compiling statistics on mortality, she found time to get some suspiciously British mining engineer to buy her a Peach and Honey at the bar of the Bella Union, and one or two spilled a few more details to support her pet conspiracy theory. The whole thing was so ludicrous, we actually encouraged her to talk about it, on the few occasions she came home; we needed the laughs.

And who wanted to celebrate Christmas, on the underside of hell? Time was when I enjoyed walking to a town and slipping into a pew to watch a *pastorela,* with the earnest mission Indians trying so hard to get to Bethlehem and all the teenaged boys in the parish portraying the devils who tried so hard to prevent them (a role so natural for any teenaged boy). I loved the way the spoken verses would echo in the old church, and the way the flames of the candles winked in their glass cups, and the way the sleepy mortals observed a reverent hush all around me. It was all so charming. And when the Indian pastores finally made it to the stable, after vanquishing Señor Satan (who always bore a close resemblance to a gentleman of Old Spain), and the central Mystery unfolded, how lovely to see the black-eyed Mother with her Indian cheekbones and serene smile as she displayed the tiny red Child with his shock of black hair. One could almost come to love mortals again.

Or not. Other years, I'd been alone in the night, where the great trees towered black against the stars, so many white stars, and the air was cold and full of the smell of evergreens. I'd been in the heart of the Mystery then, too. The stars rang like little bells at midnight, and one moment the air would be dead calm on the forest floor, and then a wind would spring up, just on that stroke of midnight, a wind magically warm and full of perfume, and you knew that the Light had begun to fight his way out of his grave, and winter would not last forever.

But this winter of 1862, that promise seemed to have failed. So many coffins, and not a drop of rain.

I DON'T SUPPOSE I NEED to tell you that the hauntings became worse, señors. Became strange. He still pursued me in the night, my dead love, but he seemed to have changed; we seemed to have lost England and gone to places I'd never been. I'll tell you the dream that's clearest in my mind.

I was in a jungle like a Rousseau painting, you know, all those botanical specimens so carefully delineated and dead-eyed jaguars staring forth here and there like so many stuffed toys. Something was coming after me, crashing through the fever-green forest, and where he passed, the palms and ferns and bromeliads all shook to life, lost their neat arrangements, and became real, pulsing and shooting toward the sun.

I'm not sure I was making any effort to run from him.

Then he was coming across a clearing at me, and I could see him at last, the savage, was that a Mayan with his high cheekbones and long curved nose? No, how could I have thought so? This was another kind of naked savage. He was tattooed fearsomely, swirling blue spirals all over his white body, his pale-blue eyes glittering with deadly laughter, and he was on me with the grace and weight of a lion. I went over like a rag doll. What was my stern Protestant metamorphosing into? What atavistic madness was this? He had a flint knife, and it was a beautiful thing, beautifully worked, and as he searched for my heart,

I saw the fan palms waving above our twined bodies. I tried to tell him that the fan palm is the only member of the *Arecaceae* actually native to California, but I was distracted by the discovery that he had the front page of the London *Times* for January 6, 1863, tattooed on his chest.

I tried to read it as he was busily taking out my heart. Then we heard shots behind him, and he turned with a snarl. Looming above us was a vast blue pyramid, and from its base hunters were coming, sending lead singing through the air. He turned and looked back down at me, and I saw that his face was painted too, a pattern of red and white diagonals crossing on a blue field. No time, no time to do this properly! said somebody, and he rose above me and lifted the blade in both hands for the stroke of mercy.

But I was awake and moaning on my cot before he was able to give it, and blue light was crawling away, diminishing into darkness, leaving me miserably, eternally alive.

THE DAY THE ACTORS CAME, we were taken by surprise. We'd been alone in our canyon for so many days, it was hard to imagine a stagecoach ever stopping here again. But—

"Incoming," announced Einar, and with sour laughter we hurried down the canyon to see who was arriving, departing, or just passing through. We heard the shouting as the stage pulled up.

"Are you mad, man? Are you demented, have you quite taken leave of your senses?" said a stentorian baritone. "Press on! Press on, though wolves howl and birds of prey darken the air. D'you want to die of the peste, for God's sake?"

"Mister, if that wheel comes off when we're coming down the grade, it ain't gonna be the smallpox kills you," said the driver. "Now you just hush up and set tight. We'll be on our way again soon's we get the spare on."

"Ay, what a wreck," said Porfirio, crouching down to look at the wheel. "You want this thing repaired, señor?"

"It'll have to be." The driver handed off the reins to his partner and jumped down. "We can't get new ones from the Concord folks nohow, what with the war. You got any spares here?"

"Sí." Porfirio jerked his thumb at the shed. "You leave the bad one, and I'll see if I can have it ready when you come back down, huh?"

"Fair enough," the driver said, going to unhitch the team. "Though I'm half minded to stay up in Frisco, the way things is going. This ain't no business to be in right now. You heard about the Indian attack this summer?"

"Indians?" queried a soprano voice, and the baritone thundered out:

"Driver, you categorically assured me there were no savages to be encountered on this route!"

"Aw, shut your damn pie hole," the driver said.

"What Indian attack?" Einar asked, bracing the corner of the wagon as Porfirio settled the jack under it preparatory to taking off the broken wheel.

"Happened in Minnesota," said the driver, leading the first of the team to our watering trough. "Seems the Secessionists are paying 'em to make trouble. They been cutting down telegraph poles, too. You ask me, I think they're smart enough to figure out they can raise all the hell they like with the Army busy fighting itself. Whoever's behind it, I sure don't fancy being stuck out here with a mess of Indians and Mormons and who knows what all between me and Teaneck, New Jersey."

There was a noise like an asthmatic goose honking; it came from the passenger compartment. Juan Bautista and I looked at each other in puzzlement. He walked around to the other side of the stage to see if in fact it was a bird, but just as he disappeared, the last honk ended on a shrill indrawn breath and became evident as a fit of hysterics on the part of the soprano.

"Oh, we shall not survive! Ingraham, one cannot venture—into such *places*—without appalling consequence. Such venues. Such wretched venues, and such (for want of a better word) men!" she shrieked.

"Have courage, Caroline. It may be that we have escaped the Pale Rider in one form only to encounter him in another; but I say we *shall* reach the Golden Gate, though calamity leap headlong into our path," said the baritone. I walked around the wagon to see why Juan Bautista hadn't reappeared.

He was staring as though transfixed at a wicker birdcage, which was tied on the back under the trunk enclosure. The leather cover hadn't been fastened down properly, and a flap had blown back, exposing a gnarled and clutching claw the size of a fist. What was in there, a dragon?

Juan Bautista's face was stony with anger. He began to work on the knots that held the cage in place.

"Hey," I said uncertainly. "Should you be doing that?"

He didn't answer me. The knots were proving intractable, so he took out a knife and cut them. He hauled the cage out and down, exposing its occupant. The ranting from the passenger compartment stopped abruptly.

"Caroline, I believe our trunks are under attack," said the baritone, and the gilded head of a cane thrust the window flap aside. A face glared out at us. "I thought so! Boy, I shall prosecute you with the utmost force of the law. How dare you?" the baritone snarled. He was a thinly bearded gent in a very loud checked coat. His gray gloves matched his beaver hat, though.

"How dare *you*?" Juan Bautista shouted, trembling with anger. I took a step backward. I guess he was mad about the treatment of the occupant of the cage, who was a very, very large something with talons. The cage was way too small for it; it must have been stuffed in there with tremendous trouble, and had scarcely any room to move. Its head was sealed in a leather hood like falconers use, and its legs were bound; all it could move were its talons, which were constantly clenching and unclenching on the floor of the cage, nasty with its droppings. Not even a perch, and no water or food. Erich von Stroheim gronked and snaked his head sideways to peer down at it.

"Put that back at once," said the baritone.

"No," said Juan Bautista. "Do you know what this is? It's a *Haliaeetus leucocephalus*. Where did you get it?"

"You are mistaken, sir, that is a bald eagle, and it might interest you to know that it was a present to me from Chief Two Ducks of the Wyandotte Tribe on the occasion of my successful charity gala in Sudbury, Ontario," said the baritone with a sneer. "Its name is Mister Liberty, and if you don't immediately replace it, I shall be obliged to descend from this conveyance and beat you like the little thief you are."

Juan Bautista proceeded to wrench the cage apart with his bare hands. It was only a wicker cage, of course, but the baritone was so shocked, it took him a full ten seconds to roar: "Damn your impudence. Driver! Are there no laws to protect passengers on this line? Driver!" He leaned across and shouted out the other window.

The driver and Einar came around the side of the stage just in time to see Juan Bautista grab up the poor bird and run with him. Erich was jolted from his customary perch and flapped along above them, and the three disappeared in the general direction of Hollywood Boulevard.

"Oh," said Einar.

"Well, God damn," the driver said, grinning. "I guess you'll just have to file a Damages and Loss Report, mister. It will be reviewed by our claims representative, and when and if an award is made, you'll be compensated by the company in the amount of the registered value of the goods as reported in the parcel manifest or in an amount up to but not exceeding the approximate value of said goods as defined in paragraph 3, article 2A in said document."

"Blow it out your arse," the baritone said.

"Ingraham!" gasped the soprano.

"My apologies, madam." Ingraham gave me a peremptory tip of his hat. "Has the word *lawsuit* any meaning to you rustics? I see it has. You will make every effort to recover Mr. Liberty now, this moment, or I shall own you."

"Aw, that bird was about dead anyhow," said the driver.

"That is immaterial, sir. Are we to be deprived even of the services of a taxidermist? And are you aware with whom you speak? I, sir, am Ingraham Drew Culliman, of the Marlborough Theatre. Perhaps *now* you'll wish to avail yourself of a post horse in the pursuit of my personal property?" Ingraham's voice had risen to a frightening pitch.

"Never heard of you," the driver said.

"A liar as well as insolent. And if I were to mention that the rara avis in dispute was to be the centerpiece in my latest variety spectacle, the Salute to Liberty? That the magnificent emblem of our presently divided nation was to be held aloft by Mrs. Culliman (herself gowned as Martha Washington) at the climax of a musical tribute certain to raise the spirits and cheer the hearts of our boys in blue? There are those, sir, who might construe your detestable negligence as the next thing to treason, which, let me remind you, is a hanging offense." Ingraham brandished his cane.

The driver explained where he was minded to put that cane if Mr. Culliman shook it at him one more time, and added that Mr. Culliman was going to find it uncomfortable to sing or, for that matter, dance in any shows with the cane in that particular location.

"Hey, hey," objected Einar, as Ingraham took off his gloves to engage in fisticuffs with the driver. "Take it easy. I don't reckon we can get the bird back for you, but we'll be glad to pay you for him. How'd that suit?"

Immediately Ingraham put on his gloves again. "Well, of course the bird was a gift, but, taking into consideration the difficulty of obtaining another when we reach our destination, which is San Francisco, where rates are astronomical..."

"Remuneration in gold, Ingraham," Mrs. Culliman advised him.

"I'd say I couldn't accept less than a twenty-dollar gold piece," said Mr. Culliman, and leaned back on his cane and frowned magisterially at us.

Einar blanched, thinking of our budget. "It's a deal," he said in a hollow voice. We waited while he ran up to the inn and raided the emergency fund.

Mr. Culliman inspected the gold piece critically, nipping it with a careful incisor before tucking it in the watch pocket of his flowered waistcoat. "I daresay that'll suffice. One really ought to inform the police in a matter of such flagrant disregard for laws concerning personal property, but as it's the season of charity and goodwill toward men, I will let the matter rest without further prosecution." He touched his hat brim with the ferrule of his cane. "Driver! Pray see to it that our trunks are better secured before we proceed."

He vaulted back into the compartment and let the window flap fall. We could hear Caroline demanding to see the gold piece. The driver gave him a particular salute and lounged back against a boulder, rolling himself a cigarette.

"Is there trouble?" Porfirio asked, returning from the shed with a spare wheel. Einar and I shook our heads mutely.

Juan Bautista didn't return until three hours later. Erich was back on his customary shoulder perch, and the eagle was still clutched in Juan Bautista's arms. It had had the blinding hood removed, and it was a bald eagle all right, though a pretty sorry specimen to have cost so much. A lot of its feathers had been pulled out; and though I'm no judge of avian expressions, its eyes had a kind of fixed and glassy stare of rage that I'm sure live birds don't usually display. It made Porfirio's expression look mild by comparison.

One look at him, though, was enough to reduce Juan Bautista to tears.

"I tried to set him free," he said. "I wasn't going to bring him home. But he can't fly. Somebody broke his wings, and they healed wrong. Please! Let me try to fix him. I can do surgery that'll fix it so he doesn't hurt anymore. I won't keep him, I promise."

"The bald eagle will be on the endangered-species list by the middle of the next century, you know," Einar said helpfully.

Porfirio gritted his teeth and swallowed the fire and brimstone he'd been preparing to spill. "Why should I care?" he said, throwing up his arms. "Go ahead. The stink from sardines in your room is already enough to knock over a Turk, but you're the one who has to live in there. Maybe *this* one'll eat all the goddamn pelican chow I ordered."

In fact, the eagle seemed to like it. John Barrymore (so named after lengthy debate between Juan Bautista and Einar) was definitely not a normal bird. Not cute or whim_ al, either, after the months of abuse and neglect he'd suffered. Psychotic.

At least he didn't bite, and Juan Bautista managed to get him to stop pulling his own feathers out; but he destroyed every cage Juan Bautista made for him, no matter how roomy. Yet he never flew; he never even tried. He would stalk around like King Lear on the blasted heath, glaring at the whole world. Usually he followed Juan Bautista around, but occasionally he decided to travel his own path. It was unnerving, while reading the paper on one's cot, to look up into his accusatory stare not three feet away. The only thing that sent him into a homicidal frenzy was anyone attempting to pick him up, so rather than risk his talons, one had to lie there and yell for Juan Bautista to come coax him away. I got pretty tired of this after the third or fourth time. I don't know what the damn bird thought I'd ever done to him.

He was a symbol of many things, señors, not least of all this nation, crazed and self-destructive as it was. None of us could fly from that desolate place. Though the New Year arrived, there was a general feeling of the light going, waning, chilling, the feeling that we were journeying downward into darkness. The land sick, the people sick and crazy, certain ruin trundling toward us like a siege tower.

WHAT A TEDIOUS TIME this is," said Oscar, hitching up his trousers to protect the crease as he sat down. "I haven't sold anything but black dye in weeks. All my Christmas business vanished in quarantine; with so many funerals going on, nobody wanted to buy presents."

"At least your business will pick up eventually," I said, pouring myself a cup of black coffee. "Mine's going to hell without a return ticket. You should see it out in the temperate belt these days. I have to fight off the longhorns to get to my specimens. Everything's being grazed right down to the ground. Extinctions, honest-to-God extinctions happening right before my eyes. Or would be, if I wasn't collecting."

"Oh, surely not," he said. "Isn't this region prone to droughts? Wouldn't the local flora be resistant?"

"It's resistant to drought, all right, but not to being eaten by starving cattle." I sipped my coffee. It was bitter, but I drank it anyway. "Think of the way things looked this time last year. Remember how green everything was? The cattle herds do. They wander out every day, looking for the green. All their instincts are telling them to head for the salad bar after a long winter. Salad bar's closed, unfortunately."

Oscar sat straighter, struck with inspiration. "Ah, if only there were a rainmaking apparatus. Talk about supplying demand! Imagine how that would win the trust and affection of one's consumers."

I tilted the last bitter drops out on the dry earth. "If it didn't work, you'd need a fast horse or a good tar remover."

"Never happened to me," he said, waving a hand airily. "I am no charlatan. I carry nothing but merchandise of the highest quality."

"You *are* a good little machine," I said.

"The best," he replied with conviction. "How can you persuade mortals to trust you if you lie to yourself? And where's the passion, the suspense, the triumph of the whole business, if it's all a sham? Really, the field material is almost of secondary importance, because you can't obtain worthwhile data in an artificial situation. I've worked with partners whose heart just wasn't in the Deal, if you know what I'm saying. No focus on the act of enticement at all, merely on obtaining data. They might as well have *been* clockwork automatons, and don't you think the mortal customers didn't sense it. No, sirree. They froze up and hadn't two words to say about themselves."

"Basic characterization," I said in agreement, remembering what we were taught in school. "Believe in your character, and the mortals will, too."

Oscar held up an admonitory finger. "More than that. Believe what your character believes, and the illusion is unbreakable. A method guaranteed never to fail, under the most adverse circumstances. When the most important thing in the world to me is getting that gentleman or lady to make a purchase—when I have them craving it, whatever it is—their souls open, and they reveal all manner of secrets about themselves. They would never suspect I wasn't human, even if they saw gears and cogwheels flying out of my mouth."

"Well, but—really, we *are* human," I said uncomfortably.

"Just so!" He nodded his approval. "That's the attitude to take if you want a successful career, you may depend upon it."

I stared at him, and at last I asked, "So...have you always been stationed in the New World?"

"Native of this country, I'm proud to say!" He smiled in fond remembrance. "Born if not bred here. That Croatoan affair. No memories of a mortal life at all, of course—recruited as an infant. Orphaned, I gather. Some nasty business with the local redskins. No hard feelings, naturally. Quite an irony, wouldn't you say, that savages with stone tomahawks were the shapers of my destiny, with all its splendid artifice? I went straight back into the field after my graduation, too, never been back to a base since. Never wanted to! Why in blazes would I want to loll around idling, watching holos, when all the glamor and excitement's out here?"

"You find this glamorous?" I jerked a thumb at the bleak hills.

"Heavens, yes." He was incredulous I should even ask. "This is the very edge of the world! You can't go any farther out in America, not until we acquire Alaska and Hawaii. And what's my function here? To document the forces of civilization at work, as they transform this murderous wilderness into a place where decent folks would want to live. The more savage it is, the greater the challenge. It would be exciting enough if one were only a spectator; but look at me. I'm not only bearing witness to Manifest Destiny, I'm an apostle of it, by gum!"

I decided he was crazy too. "How do you mean?" I asked.

"By advancing the standard of living through the availability of fine merchandise, of course. With every labor-saving device or can of stove polish I sell, chaos is dealt another blow in this wilderness. Even when I don't actually conclude a transaction, even when those penniless folk stare openmouthed at the splendor of my wares but come not forth to buy, they go home with visions of a better world dancing in their heads." Oscar rose to his feet and swept off his hat.

"And they'll *desire* those visions, and there will be those among them who dare to improve their mortal lot, that they might purchase some measure of that splendor, some glittering prize, though it be but a fragment of the glorious whole. The idle will seek employment, the chronically hapless will become sober and industrious, and noble ambition will animate the frames of those who now lie torpid and indifferent to what they *might* have, if only they would rise to embrace it."

There was a breathless pause.

"Oscar," I said at last, "you will go far."

"Excelsior!" he said, and thrust his hat skyward as far as he could reach.

At this moment, we both noticed the approach of a vehicle. It was the wrong time of day for a stagecoach. Whatever it was, it had turned off the Camino Real and was rolling up our own little canyon, going right to the door of the inn. We turned to stare.

It was a fine two-horse open carriage, slightly antique, oxblood in color, with the arms of some grand old Spanish family blazoned on the body. It had been blazoned there an awfully long time ago, though, to judge from the way it had faded. A black man in a red coat drove it, and seated within was a mortal lady of our mutual acquaintance.

Oscar gasped. He had been in the act of returning his hat to his head, but now he swept it off and bowed double.

"Princess Rodiamantikoff," he said.

It was even she; but how changed. Gone were the Gypsy silks and cheap baubles. She wasn't more tastefully dressed, you understand, but certainly more expensively, and there was now a coherence and even a dignity to her ensemble. She'd found some good luck somewhere. Her plain face was fuller by a few square meals, but the blue eyes were still knife-sharp, unwavering, superfocused. She extended a regal arm, pointing at Oscar with her parasol as the carriage braked to a stop.

"It is he," she said. "At last we find you. Chief Running Deer and King Elisheazar have not searched cosmic ether in vain. You may approach us, sir, for we would discuss with you matter of trade."

The effect on Oscar was—well, it was indecent. He was beside the wagon at once, planting a fervent kiss on her outstretched hand. The black coachman looked at him askance.

"Your Highness!" Oscar said. "How pleased I am to see that your fortunes have improved. Doubtless loyal friends at the distant court have contrived to send you support of a material nature?"

"Naturally," she said grandly, lying through her teeth, if her pulse and respiration rate were any indication. "Not to mention certain assistance rendered by dear Spirit Guides and others in realms above who are anxious to see that great work goes forward."

"And what great work would that be, ma'am?" Oscar asked, terribly interested.

"Ushering in of new era," she said. "Epoch when unhappy multitudes gain peace and enlightenment through communication with world beyond. Secrets known only to arcane secret societies will at last be revealed to all! Futures foretold through modern methods of cartomancy passed on from ancient Egypt through Gypsy race. Loved ones who have passed over will send advice and encouragement through gifted individuals. We are pleased to be humble instrument of Spirits' will. Spirits have told us you were also instrument, bringing cards for entertainment purposes only."

"So Your Highness has improved her situation by telling fortunes?" Oscar's eyes were wide with fascination, his cameras rolling.

"Please." She raised a hand. "Grateful clients have presented tokens of esteem for messages received from beyond. We are now enabled to live in gracious home in better area of City of Angels. But now, Spirit Guides have advised we must prepare doorway to Spirit realm through construction of beautiful altar. Offerings will open pathway for clients to speak with loved ones through intercession of Spirits. Common household object of beautiful design must be used for this. Spirits have directed us to purchase from you beautiful cabinet whose gross material purpose is keeping pies. It will be consecrated to higher use through addition of sacred plates of metal from ancient Egypt, location of which revealed to us in trance."

"The pie safe!" I think Oscar leaped a foot in the air. "You wish to buy the Criterion Patented Brassbound Pie Safe."

She nodded demurely. "Do you deliver?"

He certainly did.

*Y*OU NEVER SAW A MAN, mortal or immortal, strut around so. It took us a few days to get all the ingredients for a New England boiled dinner together, during which time we were treated to multiple retellings of the story of the sale, with the hunt, the chase, and the astonishing moment of the kill. What a triumph for the good gentlemen of the Criterion company! What invaluable documentation of the development of spiritualism as a movement in America, throwing new light on its evolution on the West Coast!

The dinner itself consisted of a big chunk of beef brisket, boiled, with side bowls of boiled potatoes, boiled onions, boiled cabbage, and boiled parsnips. There was brown bread with raisins, but even that was water-cooked, steamed in a can over the coals, like a plum pudding. Everything was liberally buttered and mashed, with lots of salt and pepper, which it very much needed, especially the beef.

In honor of the occasion the meal was served indoors, on our rickety kitchen table made bright with a sheet of checked oilcloth. We crowded around, Oscar and Porfirio in our two chairs and Einar and I seated on kegs from the storeroom, basking in the steamy warmth. Juan Bautista was obliged to take his meals in his rooms nowadays, lest John Barrymore attempt to commit suicide in his absence, and Imarte was out on the prowl. It was pretty cheery in there, even with the Boiled Everything, especially after Porfirio brought out an earthenware jug he'd been keeping warm in a covered basket.

"Okay, Yankee man," he said, "it's time for a toast. Hot rum punch, courtesy of the house."

"Oh, my," said Oscar, rising unsteadily to his feet, doubtless feeling the powerful gravitational force exerted by his ingested supper. "And isn't this just the weather for it, too. I haven't had rum punch in decades. You're a prince, sir."

"Hell, we always knew you'd sell that thing," Porfirio lied, carefully tilting the jug to fill our graniteware mugs. Out jetted a stream of something as red as a streetwalker's dress, dotted by bits of orange peel and clove and fragrant with fiery rum. We howled in anticipation and raised our drinks high.

"To a radiantly successful mission, Oscar," Porfirio said. "Not only for unloading the pie safe, but for the commendation the Company has decided to grant you for the sheer volume of sociological material you compiled while you were trying."

"Surprise!" Einar and I yelled, and Oscar turned pink.

Porfirio held out a hand for dignity and order. "And what could be more appropriate in your honor," he said, "than a polycultural cocktail? The cranberry of New England, the orange of Old Spain, the peach of Georgia, spices from the Far East, and rum from Jamaica, all boiled and served as hot as your pursuit of the Willing Customer. We wish you many more, man." He threw back his head and gulped the drink down, and we followed his example.

Oscar actually got misty-eyed. "I'd no idea," he said. "A commendation? Imagine. All I've ever wished was to do my job, you know, to the best of my limited abilities. Setting aside false modesty, though"—and he stuck out his chest with pride—"I must say, when once I set my mind to accomplish a thing, I can't be beat."

"And what do we have for the winner?" Einar said, jumping to his feet. He gestured gracefully at an invisible prize. "Two months' all-expenses-paid vacation at that fabulous Company resort, Pacifica

Three, on the beautiful island of Molokai! You'll enjoy unlimited use of Company research facilities while dining on exotic tropical cuisine! When you're not lounging by the library pool, you can saddle up a pony and explore the island's natural wonders, or barter for anecdotal material at the friendly local leper colony. Other activities include windsurfing, spearfishing, and hot-air ballooning.

"But that's not all!" He turned and gestured in the other direction. "Tanned, relaxed, and refreshed, you'll return to an assignment personally selected by *you*. That's right. You may choose to go through either:

"Door number one, to the lush plains of the Oklahoma Territory, where you'll document consumerism in the developing settlement culture. Or,

"Door number two, just a canoe ride across to the beautiful Big Island of Hawaii, to report on the growing dependency of the native population on manufactured trade goods. Or,

"Door number three, to that all-male Queen of the Pacific Northwest, Seattle! You'll cheer (and record) as the arrival of female citizens and quality merchandise changes this lumber boomtown into an American metropolis."

Well, that was too much. Oscar's legs gave way under him, and he sat, put his head in his hands, and cried for sheer happiness. I could have cried too, from envy. How often do immortals get choices of anything? And here was Oscar, who'd cheerfully trundle his peddler's wagon into hell if the Company told him to, given the opportunity I'd been pining for. It just goes to show why one should do one's best to be a good little machine.

I was preparing to drink to his health as Porfirio poured us another libation from the jug, when we were all alerted to the approaching presence of a mortal on the immortal arm of Imarte.

Porfirio halted in mid pour, scanning, and we tuned in as well. No trouble; the mortal was in a happy, lustful mood, slightly drunk, and Imarte wasn't concerned.

"Why, sir, I declare I am simply in love with England," she was gushing. "I do feel that what we colonists gained in liberty was *quite* outweighed by our loss in culture. This must all seem so terribly rude to a gentleman like you-all."

"My dear lady, who can feel the want of social graces in your fair presence?" was the gallant if somewhat adenoidal reply. We heard an indrawn breath, and then: "By Jove! Is that rum punch perfuming the night air?"

"I believe it's some of the other lodgers here..." We heard her voice sharpen a little as she bustled after him, for he was coming down the passage to our kitchen like a devil after a soul. A moment later, he had stepped into the circle of lamplight, and we beheld a slightly weedy mortal youth clutching a leather valise to himself. He resembled Charles III of England, with the same sad, remote eyes; and their expression chilled further as he found himself in a room full of strangers. You could see him brightening, however, when he noticed our weapons and decided we were colorful and exotic.

"Oh, I say, though. Are you banditti?"

"No, señor, we are merely the staff here," Porfirio said. "You must be aware that it is advisable to carry firearms in Los Angeles."

"Quite!" Our visitor gave a horsey little giggle. "The code duello seems to rule in your streets; and may I say that, while I find the brevity of life here appalling, it certainly is lived with a manly lack of hypocrisy and cowardice."

We blinked at him. "Thank you," said Porfirio at last. "May we offer you a glass of punch, señor?"

"Yes, please. I shan't be sorry for the warmth." He set down his valise and rubbed his hands together. "For a tropical country it's devilish cold here o'nights, you know."

"Subtropical," I corrected him absently.

"What?" He turned to stare at me, but then his attention focused on the glass Porfirio was holding out to him. "Oh, now *that's* something like. To your good health, all." He raised his glass to us and drank deeply. Imarte scowled at us from the doorway behind him.

"Mr. Rubery, dear, recollect what happens when a man mixes his liquors. We don't want Bacchus's vine to make it difficult for us to offer myrtle to Venus, do we?" she told him rather acidly. He smiled into his empty glass, licked his chops, and turned to her with an awful leer.

"I've a constitution of iron, my dear. But let it never be said of me that I kept a lady waiting. Gentlemen, madam, I'm obliged to you for the potation." He gave us a nod and set down the glass. Sliding an arm around Imarte's waist, he let himself be pulled off in the direction of her bedroom.

"She's going to be mad as hell with us if he passes out before she can get him talking about secret plans," Einar said, grinning as he raised another toast to Oscar.

"He left his valise," I said, nudging it with my boot.

"Don't open it. It probably has one of those trick locks that spray tear gas, as in *From Russia, with Love*," he warned me.

"More likely a spare pair of socks and a set of embroidered hankies," said Oscar disdainfully. "What a prime example of a weak and decadent aristocracy. Did you see the way his teeth—"

What problem he had with Mr. Rubery's teeth I was never to learn, for at that moment we all picked up the signal we had come to dread: a mortal out there in the night, drunk and wrathful, putting the spurs to his poor horse. Cyrus Jackson.

"Two kilometers out and coming in fast," Einar announced, getting to his feet.

"Riding," said Porfirio, pulling out his gun and checking the chambers.

"You can't kill him," Oscar said, blowing out the lamp. The room glowed as we switched to infrared. "There's a mortal witness. That Britisher."

"Damn. You can't even shoot him with a trank," I said, following them out the back door. The valise was right where I could trip over it; impatiently I grabbed it up and shoved it into a cupboard. "The witness would still think we'd killed the guy."

"But I'm getting tired of Señor Cyrus Jackson," Porfirio growled.

"Tired of his staking us out all the damn time. I think the moment has come to nail his nasty ass to a wall."

"Uh-oh," said Einar, as we emerged into the clearing around the cookfire. Mr. Jackson's signal was growing louder and clearer as he galloped toward us, and it wasn't giving us the usual spectrum of his jealous misery and self-pity; it was off the scale. The man was in a homicidal rage. Einar leaned forward slightly, staring intently down the canyon. We heard the thunder of hoofbeats stop abruptly, and there was a thudding crash and a curse.

"I got his horse to throw him," Einar said. "And...shit, he's still coming."

There he was on visual now, a grotesque figure by infrared, crawling out of the bushes where he'd landed with the boneless impunity of a drunk and staggering to his feet. On he came, up our canyon trail, pulling his gun from its holster.

"It's your party, boys," I said, and winked out to the hillside, where I crouched down and did my best to resemble an ordinary rock formation. I still had a good view of the clearing, with the three of them standing undecided as the monster lurched toward them.

What's happening? Imarte broadcast in panic, having just noticed the approaching hazard.

Keep your Englishman quiet, Porfirio told her. *Maybe he should get his pants on, though.*

I'm staying inside with my birds, Juan Bautista transmitted from his room.

"We'd best get these poor creatures out of sight," Oscar said, nodding at the tethered mounts on which Imarte and Mr. Rubery had ridden in from Los Angeles. He took their bridles and led them off to the stable. "Might I suggest a timely visit from Michael Finn? I've a bottle of chloral hydrate I'd be most happy to contribute to the occasion."

"I don't think this guy's in any mood to sit down and have a drink with us," Porfirio said. "Thanks all the same."

"Smoke and mirrors, I guess, huh, chief?" Einar asked, rubbing his chin pensively. Porfirio nodded, and they winked out simultaneously, to reappear in the shadows on opposite sides of the clearing just as the mortal man came raving into sight.

He stopped when he saw the house. He stood swaying for a moment. His rage was building to a peak again. He groped around for the bottle he'd lost in his fall; when it failed to present itself, he let out an inarticulate roar.

A gasp from within the house, and some kind of half-smothered inquiry from Mr. Rubery, which fortunately Mr. Jackson was unable to hear. But he had recovered his bearings enough now to remember why he was there. Shambling forward, he addressed the house and drew a deep breath.

"Marthy!" he called. "You come on out of there, you faithless bitch!"

There was silence, at least as far as his mortal ears were concerned. I could hear the pounding of Mr. Rubery's terrified heart as he struggled to get back into his clothes.

"You come on out here where I've waited for you," roared Mr. Jackson. "You, no-good...you're a pitiless wanton. You're the goddamn woman in purple and scarlet, that's what you are. Marthy!"

I could hear Mr. Rubery whimpering, partly in terror and partly in pain as Imarte had hold of his arm in a viselike grip. In a low and exceedingly calm whisper she was explaining to him the dangers of heedless flight. Mr. Jackson, meanwhile, had leaned over backward until he looked likely to topple, staring in an accusatory way at the stars.

"I *defy* you stars!" he said, and hiccupped. "The way you looked down on me an' laughed. Marthy, ever' night I sat up there an' watched for you, an' waited for you, and it was so cold. You din't care none! Oh, Marthy, I'd 'a given you ever'thing that was mine, my good name and all, if you'd 'a loved me." At this point his gun went off accidentally, kicking up a spurt of dust in the starlight. He was thrown backward and fell on his ass.

At the sound of the gunshot, Mr. Rubery intensified his efforts to escape to such a degree that Imarte had to let go of his arm or break it. He blundered frantically down the passage into the kitchen, where he tripped over a chair with a crash. Even Mr. Jackson heard it, and he scrambled to his feet with an agility I would not have thought him capable of in his condition.

"All right, I know you're in there with her. Come out here, you no-good English nancy boy," he said. "You prancin' Ephebe! Bring him out, Marthy! Jesus God, woman, ain't it enough you've run my heart through with needles? Ain't I sat up there bleeding for you, crying in the dark with nobody to care?"

Mr. Rubery was going round and round in the kitchen like a trapped rat. Oh, he must have been hunting for his valise. Mr. Jackson thrust his head forward, peering at the house through narrowed eyes. He had to have been one hell of a hunter when he was sober, because even liquored up he was pinpointing Mr. Rubery's location as accurately as I was.

"I got you, limey coward," he snarled. "We go down to hell together, but you go first." And he started for the house with an unnervingly steady stride; at least, until Einar popped up beside him.

"Sorry, pal, you just crossed the line," he said, and winked out again. Mr. Jackson jumped and stared; he looked all around and then turned to look behind him.

Einar popped into view again, not an inch from his face. "You could drop the gun," he suggested. Instead Mr. Jackson swung it up and fired wildly at him—or at the place he'd been, for of course Einar winked away once more. Even with the echoing gunfire, though, we all heard the crash as Mr. Rubery got the kitchen door open.

"Enough is enough," said Porfirio, appearing behind Mr. Jackson with the empty frijole pot in his hands. When Mr. Jackson whirled about to see who was speaking, Einar popped up again and gave him a good push. As Mr. Jackson toppled backward, Porfirio shoved the pot down over his head. Mr. Jackson dropped his gun to clutch at the pot with both hands as he fell, and Einar kicked the weapon out of reach. Then Mr. Jackson was on his hands and knees in the dust, struggling blindly to rise and shaking his head, but the pot wouldn't come off.

The poker materialized in Einar's hand, and Porfirio had one of his iron ladles, and the two of them began to rain blows on the pot, alternating like clockwork figures striking the hours. As they did so, Mr. Rubery went running for his life through the sagebrush, bounding up the hill behind the inn at really amazing speed, and vanished over the ridge. Mr. Jackson kept trying to get up, but the deafening noise was too much for him. He collapsed at last, stunned and nerveless. When he'd stopped twitching, Porfirio and Einar stopped hitting the pot. Porfirio took out a little medikit book and peeled off a trank patch, which he stuck on Mr. Jackson's back, right where the shirttail had come out of the pants.

"That'll keep him out for twenty-four hours," said Porfirio, shoving the book back in his coat pocket. I climbed down from my place on the hillside as Imarte came raging out of the inn, stark naked.

"Is that miserable sot of a mortal finally finished with?" she said. "Mr. Rubery! Alfred, dear! Please don't be alarmed. 'Tis safe to return, dear, the wretch has expired."

"I don't think he can hear you," I said. "He's probably halfway to San Francisco by now."

She glared at me and swore an oath that would have made Cyrus the Persian blanch and cover his ears. "I CANNOT TOLERATE THESE WORKING CONDITIONS," she screamed, then said, when the air had cleared and the little green bats had stopped flying out of her mouth, "Do you know the chance I've just lost? Do you know who that boy was?"

"No, but I think he left his valise behind," I said. "It's in the kitchen cupboard behind the table."

"His valise!" She got an intense look in her eyes. "You're sure?" She turned and went bouncing off to the kitchen, with never a backward glance at Mr. Jackson.

We stood there in bemusement, until a snore from inside the frijole pot recalled us to our immediate problem.

"So, uh, chief," said Einar. "What do we do with this guy? The witness is gone. I guess he could just turn up dead in a ditch."

Porfirio made a sour face. "It's not like he killed anybody. Not here, tonight, anyway. On the other hand, he really needs to go far, far away and never bother us again."

"Don't kill him," I found myself saying, to my surprise, because I've always thought mortals with the If I Can't Have You Nobody Can Have You kind of obsession to be one of the lowest forms of life. "There must be a way to get him out of the picture without violence. We could shanghai him."

"An excellent suggestion," Oscar said, popping up beside us. "An involuntary sea cruise is just the thing for him."

"It's a long drive to San Pedro at this time of night," Porfirio said, sighing as he took off his hat and ran his hand through his hair.

"I'll take him," I offered, astonishing myself again. Why on earth was I sorry for this mortal?

"And I'll drive," Oscar said. "I've done this before, you know. Plenty of nasty fellows shipped out of New Bedford feet first when they made a nuisance of themselves around the Company safe house there, let me tell you. It's generally a humane and reliable way to dispose of unwanted mortals."

So Mr. Cyrus Jackson made his final exit from Hollywood at last, trussed and snoring in the back of Oscar's cart, and I heard a numbing five hours of speculation on which assignment Oscar ought to choose as we rattled across the night plain toward the sea.

In San Pedro, we circled warily around Banning's turf and made for the fishermen's huts on Rattlesnake Island, across from the old landing. Dark shacks on pilings, with a single lantern burning low and red—not a good place to find yourself at three in the morning. But Oscar drove straight up and hopped out unconcernedly.

"I'll fetch the blackguard. You go waken Señor Souza and make the arrangements."

I hated talking to mortals; but I crept up to the shack with the lantern and knocked timidly. After a long moment, the door was opened. I recognized the sleepy and unshaven face that peered out at me.

"Souza? The doctor has work for you," I said, using the standard phrase.

His eyes widened, and he nodded. "One moment please, señora," he replied, and ducked back inside. He emerged a moment later, trousered and shod, just as Oscar came bustling up with Mr. Jackson draped across his shoulders.

"Hello there," Oscar said brightly, in Portuguese so perfect, you'd have sworn he was born in Lisbon. "Has my friend explained about the evil and desperate man I'm wearing?"

Souza blinked and rubbed the bridge of his nose, just below his Company control implant. "No, señor. You'd like him drowned?"

"Not at all. No, sir, we simply think he needs a change of air. Now, unless I'm much mistaken, that ship over yonder's full of lumber. Is she going on a long voyage, by any chance?"

Souza raised his eyes to the open sea, where a schooner rode at anchor. He grinned, white teeth distinct in the gloom. "Yes, señor, the *Elg*. She is bound for Norway with the tide. Two of her able-bodied seamen killed in a fight in Los Angeles, too, I hear. Very sad."

"And this is your boat moored over here, is it not?" Oscar strolled out along the rickety pier.

"I am proud to say so, señor," replied Souza, strolling beside him.

"Capital." Oscar shrugged off Mr. Jackson and dumped him into the bottom of the boat, where he lay moaning. Souza leaped in and untied the mooring rope. A moment later he was rowing steadily out through the darkness in the direction of the *Elg*.

"Good riddance to bad rubbish," Oscar said, adjusting his lapels and shooting his cuffs. "Faugh, what a smell of rye whiskey. This coat wants laundering, wouldn't you say?"

"Very much," I agreed, and we climbed back into the cart and wheeled around to return to Hollywood.

Oscar took up the conversation again as though it hadn't been interrupted, and for the next five hours I gave my morose opinion in negatives or affirmatives on the merits of Hawaii over the Oklahoma Territories. Altogether it was an excellent thing for Cyrus Jackson that he wake up alive in a bunk on board the *Elg*, with no more Imarte to break his mortal heart for him.

The red sun was well above the horizon by the time we got back, and still Oscar hadn't made up his mind about where he wanted to be posted next. Nor had he decided by the time we saw him off, a week later. But Immortals don't get choices very often in their eternal lives, and who could blame him for lingering over his decision?

We did receive a holocard from him, later, though, all the way from sunny Molokai, and it may well be the last I ever see of that absurd little machine: pinkly sunburned, smiling and waving from the gondola of a hot-air balloon, the untamed world his oyster.

*U*NFORTUNATELY, in the same Company communiqué that had contained Oscar's commendation there was a memo of a less positive nature. It seemed that Juan Bautista's quota of rescued birds hadn't been met for several months in a row, though his budget allocation for maintenance had been exceeded to a remarkable degree.

"I know, I know!" he groaned, sinking into a chair, which brought Erich von Stroheim down to eye level with us. "It's not my fault, though. How am I supposed to go out and look for anything? I can't leave John Barrymore alone for two minutes, and I have to take Erich every place I go. Marie's the only one who'll stay where I tell her to."

"I warned you about this, Juanito," said Porfirio, shaking his head. "Didn't I warn you about this? Now you don't have a choice. You crate up the big birds and ship them off to HQ. They'll be all right. What's more important, you'll be able to get back to your work."

Juan Bautista's face went pale. "Please, just give me a little more time. I think I'm finally beginning to make some progress with John Barrymore. The microsurgery's all healed up, and lately he's even started to act like a normal bird sometimes. Please? One more month. As soon as the weather's better, I swear I'll send them away."

Porfirio leaned forward. "You don't seem to get it. This is not me telling you. This is Dr. Zeus *officially* telling you that you have screwed up. You're not doing your job. That's not acceptable, kid. You do understand that, don't you? And it doesn't take a lot of brains to figure out what your next move has to be, and you have brains to spare, thanks to Dr. Zeus. This is tough enough; don't make it tougher."

"What if I was able to catch up on my quota?" said Juan Bautista. "I know I've fallen behind, but it's not the birds' fault. I'll learn to manage my time better. I'll bring my work up to speed, you'll see. Couldn't I keep them just another month, if I was able to do that? Would one more month make any difference, if I was able to make the Company happy?"

This was too much for me. I had to slink out, so I didn't catch the rest of the conversation; but I gathered that Porfirio gave in again, because no big birds were crated up or shipped off in the next few days. All the stock of songbirds and little owls went, though, tagged in their wicker cages; and Juan Bautista was admirably industrious for a whole day in front of his room, weaving new cages for the new stock he had sworn to bring in.

Imarte was industrious, too. We never saw Alfred Rubery again, but he *had* left his valise behind. She spent days locked in her room with it, going over the contents in minute detail and making copies of what she found. We only saw her at mealtimes, and the transformation from whore to scribe was unsettling: inky fingers, disheveled hair, stained dressing gown. She looked radiantly happy, though, with whatever lode of cryptohistory she'd struck. I confess I was curious, but not curious enough to bring myself to ask her about it.

And Einar was certainly industrious. Longhorns were going for ridiculously low prices now, and he was acquiring them every day and conducting cattle minidrives into Los Angeles. Porfirio was always busy, of course. The one advantage to the drought was that no roads washed out that winter, and now that the smallpox epidemic was tapering off, the stagecoaches were running regularly again. Banning seemed to be deferring maintenance on the coaches, though, or maybe his regular crew had died of the pox, because there were repairs to be made at our smithy nearly every day.

I was the only one with nothing to do. Why was that, señors? There was nothing left for me to save. Everything that grew in the temperate belt had either been collected by me or grazed down to bare earth by starving cattle. There were no rarities left to find, unless I cared to venture into the Canyon of Lunacy again. But no prize on earth could have tempted me back into that place where I might glimpse the deadly city again, the future desolation.

Now, you would think, wouldn't you, that Dr. Zeus might give me a pat on the head and tell me to run along now, back to my beautiful green Ventana? I certainly thought so. I wasn't expecting commendations or prizes, or even thanks for a job well done; but I did expect a new posting, and none came, though I checked the Company directives pouch every time Einar returned from Los Diablos. Bureaucratic willfulness, or some subtle punishment to make me work harder, to improve my attitude? Why was I being ignored, señors? Was it simply that nobody noticed that I was stranded there, unable to do the work I'd been programmed for, the work I needed? The work that kept my demon at bay?

Or did the Company know? Did you know what would happen next? Did you know and sit there like God, silent, remorseless, useless? What happens if I sit here in silence, too? What if I never give you my all-important testimony, eh?

But of course you couldn't have known. You're stuck here in 1863, just like me. I don't imagine our masters up there in the future would tell you if they knew, either. No operative is ever told any personal detail of the Temporal Concordance. It's forbidden to tell. Though Lewis tried...Will you punish him, too?

More Theobromos? Well, thank you so very much. You damned well better anesthetize me now, if you want me to go on with this.

SO THERE WE WERE, ALL happily going about our work except for me. I sat huddled in my room most days, wrapped in a blanket and viewing holos hour after hour. Not as much fun as old-style cinema, overall. There is a pleasant sense of camaraderie with the rest of the audience, watching cinema. You know: throwing popcorn at the flat screen and cheering and sharing moments of excitement, like when Luke Skywalker is shooting down the bad guys pursuing the *Millennium Falcon,* or any part of *The Rocky Horror Picture Show.*

It's true that a holo takes you right into the center of the action; but that illusion is not always a good thing. The leeches scene from *The African Queen* comes shudderingly to mind. *Sunset Boulevard,* too. Who the hell wants to get unbearably close to Norma Desmond's scary eyes in that last scene? And let's not even talk about Hitchcock's films. Though it's no better, really, in the films you *want* to be a part of, because you're still isolated, you're like a ghost. No amount of technological cleverness can make Sean Connery take you in his arms, and no Good Witch will ever take you by the hand and welcome you to Oz. They won't see you, they won't hear you, because their reality is complete and you are not a part of it.

At last I gave it up and started following the war news again. Depressing, inconclusive, inaccurate, but at least it was really happening.

I feel badly that it absorbed my attention so much. If it hadn't, I might have noticed the noises in Juan Bautista's room that awful day.

Not that I could have done anything if I had, of course.

You see, encouraged by the progress that John Barrymore seemed to be making, Juan had taken to leaving him shut in his room when he went out on his collecting trips. Erich von Stroheim he kept in Einar's room, liberally dosed with bird dope of some kind, so the damn creature was quiet all day. He didn't like to do it, of course, but the idea was that it was only temporary, until he caught up on his quota and reassured Dr. Zeus that he too was a good little machine.

In my opinion he should have been doing this all along. It was no effort for Juan Bautista to catch birds: all he had to do was stand still, and the bloody things would light all over him. But he was seventeen! Sloppy and disorganized and stupid as youth will always be, no matter how cyberaugmented it's made. Perhaps that was why he filled his room to the ceiling with flimsy woven cages full of the miserable cheeping little things, and left a psychotic predator in there with them while he went out each day to hunt for more.

Do I have to tell you what happened, señors?

It was as bad as you could imagine. I heard his wail of horror when he opened his door. I came stumbling from my room in time to see John Barrymore bouncing clumsily out into the clearing. Porfirio and Einar emerged from the house too, and stopped dead at the sight of the eagle.

Not that he was covered with gore, or anything like that. Well, a little blood, and some few bright feathers from some little victim. He regained his composure and took a few paces sideways, cocking his head to stare at us in a puzzled way. But there was the most heartbroken sobbing from Juan Bautista's room.

The irony was that John Barrymore had been making progress. While he was sick and mad, he tried only to kill himself. It was when he began to heal that he felt the normal urge to do what predators do. But Juan Bautista was in no condition to appreciate this, as he emerged from his room with a little torn body in either hand.

"You *bastard,*" he screamed. "How could you do this?"

He ran at John Barrymore, who started and crouched in alarm. Then, with a wild flapping of wings, the big bird rose into the air and floated onto the roof of the inn. He looked down at us all, and we stood looking up at him with open mouths. Experimentally he beat his wings again, twice, three times, and we felt the rush of air in our faces as he nearly lifted off. Had the madness left any room for joy, when it vacated that narrow killer's skull of his? What was in his flat blank eyes, when he beat his wings again with a noise like a stiff breeze filling canvas? I don't know. In the next moment he leaned into the evening air and sailed away on spread wings, effortlessly, a long curve ascending. Up and up he went, high enough at last to catch the last light of the sun, and then he flew northward and was gone.

Marie Dressler had survived; she had managed to get into the clutter under Juan Bautista's bed and defend herself from there with her formidable old bill. And of course Erich von Stroheim was fine; he'd slept through it all in Einar's room. But the boy who loved them had changed.

Do you remember that terrible moment, señors, when the self-righteousness of your youth died? When all the stern warnings of your elders, ignored until the consequences abruptly came crashing down on your head, made you see in a flash that the warnings hadn't been unfair or mean-spirited or blind, they'd been *right?* All along your elders had been trying to tell you about the black joke that is life, trying to help you and save you from pain. But you insisted on running straight into the trap, mocking them as you ran, to the agony that was irreversible and permanent, with no one to blame, finally, but yourself.

It's not good to see yourself in the mirror then. Juan Bautista was reflected in the eyes of every one of the little dead birds he had to clean out of his room.

Next time Einar loaded up the wagon for the trip into Los Diablos, there were two big cages among his cargo. Marie sat patiently in hers, considering her new fate with a calculating eye; but Erich von

Stroheim croaked and hissed with anxiety, trying to muscle through the wire mesh that kept him from Juan Bautista. When the wagon started up and he found himself rolling away from the boy, he started up the piercing scream we knew all too well. Juan Bautista just stood there, watching, his face like stone. It took a long time and a lot of distance for the screams to fade to silence.

"It's better this way, muchacho," Porfirio said at last. "They'll be safe, they'll be happy, they'll have great lives in the Company aviary."

Juan Bautista nodded, but I knew what he was thinking: no way now he could kill them, either, with his well-meaning mistakes or unintentional neglect or selfish love. I wondered if he'd ever dare love anything mortal again. Some of us don't.

*I*T WAS MARCH 13, 1863. I was struggling back and forth between our galvanized bathtub and the nearest oak tree, carrying buckets of cold and slightly soapy water in my unending irrigation efforts, when I looked up to see Einar returning from Los Diablos in the wagon, trailing a cloud of dust several stories high. I squinted in the glare and frowned; he'd brought back a load of crates, something so heavy the wagon was low on its springs. Porfirio picked up the question I was broadcasting and came out to see.

"What the hell are those?" he said, wiping his floury hands on a dish towel. "He's brought back eight pianos? Where's the olive oil I ordered?"

"Wasn't room, chief," Einar called. "When I got to HQ, these guys were waiting for me. Ladies, I mean; they're eight tule elk does in stasis, and they've all been bred. I've got some marching orders. They're supposed to go over Tejon Pass out to Buttonwillow, to be released into the wild. You're tagged to assist me."

"Great," said Porfirio, throwing down the dish towel. "Just what I needed. A trip to beautiful Buttonwillow at this time of year."

I didn't envy them. If there was a place more desolate than Los Angeles, Buttonwillow was it; the only possible advantage being that there were almost no mortals there in this era.

Einar shrugged apologetically. "It shouldn't take us more than a week," he said. "We have to leave ASAP, though. 0500 hours tomorrow okay with you?"

Porfirio sighed. "That's life in the service. All right, tomorrow it is; I guess the pass is clear by now. No killer camels this time, huh?" Referring to the legend of deadly dromedaries haunting the mountains.

"That was just a joke, chief. Honest. But look at what else was waiting for me at HQ." Einar held up a big silver film can. "*Grand Hotel*, 1932! Greta Garbo, two Barrymores, Joan Crawford, Wallace Beery. We can have another night of the film festival when we get back, what do you say?"

I filled my bucket again and went trudging off to water the oak trees. How about Walt Disney's *Fantasia*, I wondered nastily. Weren't we all sorcerer's apprentices? Bucket-carrying brooms impossible to kill.

They left next morning in the bleak dark, bundled in their coats on the springboard of the wagon.

"You have plenty of supplies," Porfirio told Imarte and me. She had got up to see them off. "And there's most of a pot of fresh coffee on the fire over there. You ladies look after the kid, okay? And no cat fights in my absence, please."

Imarte and I looked at each other in disdain. "Wouldn't bother," I said.

"Don't give it a moment's thought," Imarte agreed.

He looked at us searchingly, his black eyes troubled. "No going out without wearing a loaded sidearm at all times, remember?"

"Hey, man, these are immortal girls," Einar said. "They can take care of themselves. Ciao, ladies; get your hankies laundered and ready, 'cause *Grand Hotel* has one of the really great tearjerker endings of all time!"

He gave a crack of his whip, and the wagon rolled away into the gloom, creaking under the weight of its improbable cargo. I hoped they wouldn't break an axle going over the Grapevine Grade. As though he had heard my thought—I wasn't broadcasting—Porfirio turned around in his seat and looked at me. What an uncertain look on his scarred devil's face. He was wearing it still when they turned onto El Camino Real and vanished from sight.

I stood there a moment longer, shivering in the mists. Then I remembered there was coffee. Imarte was already helping herself to the pot. I hurried to find my mug.

We managed to restrain ourselves from hair pulling and all that fun stuff, mostly because after she filled her mug she disappeared back into her room to continue her studies of the amazing secret-agent valise. Juan Bautista came moping out a while later, and I grilled him some beef for breakfast. He didn't stick around to talk; very shortly he disappeared up the canyon with half a dozen empty wicker cages, which had to be filled with endangered species. I knew a little of what he was feeling; he'd come to the place we all come to, sooner or later, when the work is all you have, all you can depend on.

So I was alone all day. There weren't even any passengers dismounting from the stages. It was a lovely, surreal feeling, all that peace and quiet. My ghost, too, left me quite alone. I made a stew of leftover grilled beef for supper, and built up the cookfire to a nice blaze afterward. In the interests of peace and harmony I broadcast a meal call to Imarte, and a moment later she actually emerged from the house.

"You prepared a meal?" she said in surprise.

"I know several recipes," I said. "Not that one can do a lot without olive oil."

"Goddess, that's true," she said, sounding astonished that we had found a common opinion. She made up for it by picking most of the chilies out of her dish, however, and flicking them into the dark. We sat there awhile in unpleasant silence, before she finally cleared her throat and spoke. "I believe I'll take the stage north tomorrow," she said.

"Really?" I asked. Where did she get off, leaving me with the responsibility of running the place? "You cleared it with Porfirio before he left, I suppose?"

"Oh, he knew I had a research trip to make," she said evasively. I just shrugged and kept eating. After a moment she gave up trying to keep her news to herself. "The contents of that valise contained the most incredible—"

"Is there any supper left?" asked Juan Bautista, appearing from the shadows. He was holding something bundled in his coat. I pretended not to notice as I ladled him a bowl of stew, but Imarte leaned forward and peered, frowning.

"Are you hiding something, child?"

"I'm—it's just a raven, that's all," he said. "She has a broken wing. I thought I could fix it with microsurgery. I seem to be pretty good at that."

She missed the bitterness of his last remark and sailed right on. "That's nice. Well, as I was saying, when I examined the contents of the valise—"

Juan Bautista's eyes widened with excitement. "Are you finally going to tell us what was in it? I've been wondering about that. Were there really, like, secret documents?"

"Incredibly secret," she said, her voice dropping to a dramatic whisper. "Lists of persons to be contacted, with their addresses. Communications from Judah Benjamin and John Bright. Letters of introduction. Documents pertaining to the Order of the Golden Circle. Drafts on the Bank of England, without countersignature, amounts to be filled in at the discretion of the bearer. Two pasteboard tubes filled with golden sovereigns, sealed with stamped wax. Timetables, instructions, and letters in coded phrases.

"Several letters of a most incriminating nature between a person named Greathouse and several Canadian nationals, to say nothing of some *very* interesting overtures from the Prime Minister to Benito Juárez." She leaned forward after an impressive pause. "Last but certainly not least, letters referring to some technological discovery, made in a place designated only by code. All written in a lovely violet ink, chosen undoubtedly not for its color but for the remarkable chemical properties that enable it to vanish without a trace when exposed to water."

"Wow," said Juan Bautista. "All you'd have to do is dip a page in water to get rid of the evidence? I guess he really *was* an English spy."

"A conspirator, I think," Imarte said judiciously. "Not spy material, or he'd have been back for the valise by now. But thanks to some cross-referencing of available data, I now have important information about just who these conspirators are. I found an invaluable text entitled 'The Great Diamond Hoax.' It purports to be a firsthand narrative, by one Asbury Harpending, of the true circumstances of what will be known as the Chapman Piracy Case, which I gather is the name the San Francisco papers will give my pet conspiracy when it resoundingly fails."

"You mean, they'll be caught?" I asked, glancing over at the little black thing in Juan Bautista's coat, which had stirred feebly.

"In a matter of hours," Imarte said. "If only I'd found Harpending's narrative sooner. It would appear that quite shortly our dear Mr. Rubery and his Secessionist friends will be cooling their heels in prison, thanks to some astonishing errors of judgment. My theory is that their bungling will be due to the loss of the vital information in the valise. Of course the plot fails, but somehow the British will manage to cover their involvement completely. I must know how! You can see this is important, I trust? It's absolutely necessary that the Company have a qualified observer on the scene. One of the most concerted covert efforts by a foreign power to overthrow an American government in this century, and somehow it will be made to seem nothing more than a boyish prank, a footnote in a minor chapter in history."

"I certainly won't stop you," I said. "Go, by all means. Have a grand time. And bring us back a loaf of sourdough bread." A little more flip than the occasion called for, particularly as I thought her obsession sounded kind of interesting for once; but she always brought out my worst side.

She narrowed her eyes at me. A chilly silence fell. It was finally broken by Juan Bautista, who said, "I was wondering..."

"What?" I turned my attention back to him.

"Did the Company ever try the immortality process on animals?"

"There are stories," I said. "It almost works, but not quite. Animals can be made smarter, or nearly immortal, but not all the way and not as smart as us. I know for a fact it was done with one of the higher primates, but the program never went further than the prototype."

"So you could make an animal as smart as a mortal human?"

"Sure you could," I said. "But why would anyone want to? Mortals are unhappy enough with the brains they have. Why inflict self-awareness on an animal?"

He didn't answer. Shortly after that, he went to bed, carefully cradling the little black thing in his bundled coat. Imarte flounced off too, doubtless to pack her bag for her trip to San Francisco. I stayed up a while, looking at the stars. I could hear Juan Bautista playing his guitar in his room. It was the first time he'd touched it in days.

PART THREE

*M*ARCH 15, 1863. A day to remember, señors.

I woke early and was quite happy grinding coffee beans, grilling beef. I thought to myself that perhaps there was a future for me in the food service industry, if the Company had no further use for me as a botanist. Juan Bautista ate hurriedly and vanished into the brown wilderness, so I was the only one there to see Imarte off when she came out to meet the stagecoach, bag in hand. She was all tarted up again, hair curled and ink stains scrubbed away, corseted for action.

"I'm on my way," she said. "It's unlikely I'll return before the end of the month. Convey my apologies to Porfirio, but I'm certain he'll understand why this was necessary when I have a chance to explain it to him."

"Fine with me," I said. "Aren't you taking the secret valise, though?"

"No, of course not!" She shifted her bag to her other hand and leaned close to lower her voice, though we were the only living souls for a good six kilometers around. "That material is far too incriminating to carry abroad. I rather imagine some sort of effort will be made to recover it, so I've left it in plain sight in my room. Should any suspicious-looking persons call, let them take it. I've made a detailed copy of everything."

"We're not going to be visited by angry Union Army troops or police, are we?" I asked.

"A ridiculous idea. At this particular point in time my conspirators are blissfully unaware of any trouble brewing for them, and my research indicates that the attention of the law will be focused entirely on their activities in San Francisco. The fact that the conspirators also had a cabal in Los Angeles seems to have disappeared in the Historical Event Shadow," she said, glancing at her chronophase. "We're perfectly safe. Now, if you'll excuse me, I have a stagecoach to catch."

I watched her go sashaying down the trail, scarlet ribbons and curls bouncing, Immortal Babylon insatiably after a good time. The fact that her pleasure derived from history rather than from pretty boys made it no less delicious. A deeper and more subtle pleasure, no doubt. If there really are gods and goddesses, this must be how they amuse themselves, not with the pettiness of individual men but with the sins of nations, the follies of kings.

So I had the inn to myself. I wandered into the storeroom and poked through Porfirio's groceries. I found a cake of Theobromos and made off with the whole thing, luxuriating in a sense of selfishness. But wait, there was more: six months of back issues of *Punch* I'd never got around to reading, and nobody to complain about the way I folded them. I dug them out from under Porfirio's bed and settled in the kitchen, putting my feet up on a chair. Should I make myself another pot of coffee? Should I eat all the Theobromos now or save half for later? Maybe I'd eat a whole cone of piloncillo sugar too. Oh, the sins I could indulge in with nobody to see.

But even as I turned my attention to the latest nasty caricature of Abraham Lincoln, I picked up the signal of a mortal approaching. So much for blessed solitude.

I ignored it as long as I could, which wasn't very long. What the hell was this mortal doing? I set down the papers, got up, and went outside.

It was a male, very much in control of his thoughts and emotions, wary but not particularly afraid or even disturbed. No, he was concentrating intently on his activity of the moment, which seemed to be the covert surveillance of our humble establishment. I faded back into the doorway and scanned.

Yes, there he was on the ridgeline, a barely visible figure having a nice leisurely look at us through a pair of field glasses. They were all I could distinguish on visual alone. Infrared in broad daylight gave me a sketchy little scarlet ghost, but judging from the proportions, he was large. There were large animal readings, too; the man must have had a horse tethered just out of sight.

Over the next hour he worked his way around our canyon, studying us from all sides. I gave up and went indoors, deciding he was after the valise. He was welcome to it, as far as I was concerned. He didn't read like a mortal intent on violence, so I settled back in the kitchen, put my feet up again, and resumed my perusal of the British funny papers. I did make sure that my gun belt was fastened properly and my Navy revolver was loose in its holster, though.

Was he going to have his look and go sneakily away, leaving me in peace? No, damn it, here he was again, riding up the trail on horseback like a proper visitor. He was going to come to the door. I had him on audio now; there were the plodding hoofbeats of his horse; I could hear his breathing and his heartbeat. There was something unsettling about them. I eased my gun from its holster and held it concealed behind the copy of *Punch* I had been reading. I hoped I wouldn't have to blow a hole through that comic poem about highwaymen. He was a *very* large man, too. Would one bullet stop him?

"Hello? Is anyone here?" he called out.

And his words might have been a bullet through me, such an impact they had on this immortal body I wear, señors. I jerked as though I'd taken a hit, cursing silently and wondering whether I was having some sort of malfunction, some electronic seizure. My chair squeaked a good two inches backward. I did a self-diagnostic in the fraction of a second it took for the echo of his words to die away, but found nothing wrong.

The man heard the noise my chair made and was coming to the

door. Angrily I got to my feet, holstering my weapon—why, I don't know—and tossing away the papers. Every defensive sense I had was activated. There, he had stepped through the doorway and halted, looking into the kitchen at me.

A big mortal indeed, absurdly so, even without the tall hat he was in the act of removing. He wore the tailored clothing of a Continental gentleman, in subtle tones of gray and brown that had just incidentally made him nearly impossible to see in the underbrush. You couldn't have told he'd been out there crawling around in the purple sage, though; not a wrinkle nor a stain on the man, not a single twig in his lank fair hair.

He was even wearing gloves; at least the hand that held the Spanish-English phrasebook was gloved. He was wearing a gun, too, though that was discreetly holstered under his left arm and would have been invisible to another mortal. He smiled at me with a great deal of charm and no little confidence. When he smiled, his pale-blue eyes narrowed and his high wide cheekbones seemed to slant upward, which made his long broken nose look longer.

He was, señors, the living image of the man I had last seen bound to a stake, screaming in flames, three centuries ago and half the world away. How could I not know him, my one and only lover? He had died in those flames, and my human heart had gone into the fire with him and become the charred thing it was. But here he was now, he'd smashed through the barrier of dreams and come to claim me in no more hauntings but in living flesh. My doom had come upon me, as the lady in the poem said.

"Please excuse me, señorita," he said in perfect Castilian Spanish. He pretended to read from the phrasebook. "Is this the inn where one may meet the coach to San Francisco?"

It was the same voice, too, that dark tenor of such power, such beauty. When he'd preached to the avid spectators from the flames, even they had been moved to tears.

I found myself perfectly calm. Well, I wasn't a mortal woman who might have fainted or wept, was I? I was the same cyborg creature who'd watched Nicholas Harpole die, and I knew he was dead, and this man could not be my lover miraculously returned to me. "I speak English, señor," I said.

"Do you?" he replied. "How very convenient for us both." His smile widened, and the phrasebook disappeared into his pocket with a single graceful movement. Dear God help me, he was an Englishman. Not *my* Englishman, of course. I was going to be rational about this if it killed me.

Who did I think he was, you ask? Give me more Theobromos, and I'll tell you my friend Joseph's theory of genetic stability.

Thanks so much. Joseph calls it the English Character Actor Phenomenon. Have you ever had occasion to watch a lot of British cinema, or look at British portraits or photographs? You may have noticed that many of the faces are identical, though separated by decades or even centuries. Compare a cast photo of the D'Oyly Carte company from 1885 with one from 1973, for example. Some of them could be the same people, as immortal as we are. Of course they're not; and there's no need to grope for a mystical reason to explain the resemblance, either. It's a simple matter of genetics on a rather small island. There are only so many faces, only so many physical types in that gene pool. You can find the same sort of recurring appearances in other communities that tend to disapprove of marriage outside one's race.

Older operatives with countless lifetimes behind them—like Joseph, for example, whose theory this is—are always running into people who could be identical twins to mortals they knew centuries earlier. I'm told one gets over the surprise fairly soon. Perhaps I would, too.

"By your leave, señorita," said the mortal man, holding my gaze steadily as he stepped forward with a caution that indicated he'd noticed my weapon and taken my measure. "I believe we have acquaintances in common. I was informed at the Bella Union Hotel that there was a well-spoken daughter of joy who kept a private house at this location. Have I the pleasure of her company?"

"No, señor," I said. "She is away. I do not expect her return for some days."

"Ah." He tilted his head a little to one side, considering me. "You are perhaps in her employ?"

I blinked at him. It actually took me a moment to realize that this magnificent stranger was asking me to have sex with him. He thought I was a whore, my long-lost beloved.

On the other hand, I had been celibate for just over three centuries now, and the nearness of his mortal flesh and the sound of his voice were more than I could bear.

Why not? Why deny myself this thing?

"Yes," I said.

"Very well," he said, drawing off his remaining glove and tucking it in his hat with the other one. "I trust you have the afternoon free? Where may we be undisturbed?"

I led him into Imarte's room without a word.

The light flickered over his eyes as he took in the dimensions of the room, rapidly noting placement of doors and windows, locking mechanisms, possible traps. He was *scanning*, señors, as ably as one of us, if without electronic assistance. He spotted the valise under Imarte's table—no change in his expression at all—and turned his attention to me with nothing but expectant and straightforward lust. Had I always been able to read him like this? But I was so young when I met my man, and so many years of hard living since then had sharpened my perceptions.

"What is your pleasure, señor?" I asked after an awkward pause. Wasn't that what whores said?

He drew his eyebrows together slightly. "Well, under the circumstances, I believe it's customary for one to undress," he said, just a hint of irony in that well-bred voice. Undress, right. I unbuckled my gun belt, and he held out his hand to take it. "Allow me."

He hung it over a chair, well out of my reach. I watched as he turned back to me, and our eyes met, acknowledging that he'd scored the first touch. He stepped back a pace to indicate that I should proceed.

So I took them off, the drab and convenient garments of my life, the long walking skirt with its slightly muddy hem, the plain dark blouse and bodice, the battered high-topped boots and threadbare black stockings. My lingerie was a disgrace, shabby gray cotton I'd mended with pack thread; but I had never expected to sleep with anyone again. It just goes to show that you ought to invest in good underwear, because you never know, do you, when a long-dead lover will pop up and whisk you into bed. At least my flesh was presentable: to all appearances that of the same eighteen-year-old girl who'd loved the man in England. Immortality has that much consolation.

He watched me intently, and only when he'd seen that I had no other weapons concealed in any other possible place did the good red blood rise into his face, and a certain ready warmth into his eyes.

"Charming" was all he said; and setting down his hat and gloves, he shrugged out of his coat. There was his holster, for anyone to see, with a revolver snugly tucked away in it. He acknowledged my stare with a frank smile. "Lest one fall amongst thieves whilst traveling," he explained. He took it off and hung it on the chair next to mine, but rather closer to the bed. While removing his boots, he was able to get a good look under the bed and satisfy himself that nobody was lurking there. Off came his waistcoat with its watch in the little pocket, off came his flowing tie; and that was as undressed as he was going to get, except for letting his suspenders down and unbuttoning where necessary. What a pity; I wondered if the rest of him was eerily identical to Nicholas Harpole. What I could see as he unbuttoned was gorgeously the same.

We sank down on the counterpane together and, yes, if this wasn't the same man, there was something wildly wrong with the universe. He kissed like Nicholas, used his hands with the same masterful expertise, played my body like a rare instrument just as Nicholas had done, as though I were something beautiful.

There was only one moment of trouble, when an expression of amazement crossed his face, and he rose on his elbows and gave me a sharp wondering look; but the music was playing too sweetly to stop the dance now, and we went leaping on. I didn't try to guess what he was thinking. Would *you* have?

I won't describe the physical pleasure. You wouldn't believe it, señors. I don't know that I believed it myself. One moment the world had been the sad ordinary place I'd lived in for the better part of three centuries, and the next it had shattered and fallen away like an image painted on glass, a dreary illusion gone forever. If this day was possible, then angels might exist, fairies too, miracles and wonders, even a loving God.

I think we made love for hours. He was a determined sensualist, as perfect and as tireless as one of us, and seemed intent on exhausting me, which of course he couldn't do, except emotionally. A long while later, I lay weeping silently, curled against him. He leaned up on one elbow to regard me.

My God, the same dear face, flushed in the same way after his pleasure. His eyes were sharp and considering; and yet I could sense no desire to harm me, though I'd detected at least three more weapons concealed on his person during our lovemaking. What on earth was he, a professional assassin?

Well, why else would he be carrying all those weapons? He'd been sent for the valise, and I was the only witness.

This realization hit me like a thunderbolt, in the precise moment that he casually draped an arm over me and pulled me close again. Without apparent effort on his part I found myself caught against him, my arms securely pinioned and the weight of his big body holding me down. If I'd been a mortal woman, I couldn't have escaped. My heart raced all the same.

He looked into my eyes, probing for something. "That was delightful, my dear," he told me suavely. "But you're not a whore, are you?"

"No, señor," I said. "My apologies for the deception."

"You were in fact a virgin, were you not?" He sounded regretful, not for my lost innocence but because he was afraid there might have to be a death in this room, and he was sincerely hoping it wouldn't be necessary.

I stared. I couldn't tell him that if I seemed a virgin, it might be because I hadn't slept with anybody since March 1555. Did you know our bodily regeneration was that thorough? I hadn't known. "Yes, señor, I was," I answered.

He smiled slightly. "I don't flatter myself that my personal attractions led you to sacrifice something of such value to a young lady. Why, then, did you lie to me concerning your...vocation?"

What he intended to do next depended on my answer to that question. What was the right answer? No way to tell him the truth. At least I was in fair control of myself. Time was when even a mortal in a temper would have had me winking out in nervous terror. Killer apes, I'd called them; but this was a killer angel. You may think he was a monster, señors, prepared as he was to quietly kill a woman he'd just pleasured; but I tell you it maddened me with new desire, and isn't *that* monstrous? But who in the hell knows what's clean or unclean in love?

"I needed the money, señor," I lied, as frankly as I knew how. "Bereavement has left me a pauper, without refuge. In the past few days my situation has become desperate. The whore of this place is absent, I told you the truth of that; and when you came inquiring for her, it appeared that fate had placed a terrible opportunity before me. You seemed like a decent man, señor."

"Or at least a wealthy one?" He raised one eyebrow and studied me. His body was relaxing. "And this, then, was the occasion of your fall from grace? I trust you won't take offense if I observe that you don't seem suited for this occupation. Are you aware you never even set me a price, my dear? Pleasant as our dalliance was—and believe me, señorita, it was a pleasure indeed—I think this is not the life for you."

He was amused. He was deciding there was no need for unpleasantness. He wasn't through with me yet, though. Was I disappointed?

"What price ought I to have charged, señor?" I asked.

He smiled wryly. "The price of a good dowry in this backward country, or whatever donation the nearest convent requires to take in a novice. I believe I have a fair idea of the exchange rate at the present time. I'll leave that sum in gold; but you must promise me you'll use it for the one purpose or the other, as your inclination directs. Harlotry's a dangerous business."

He was a professional killer, and so far as he knew, I was a wretched nonentity he might just as easily have discarded, by one means or another. Instead he had opted to *do the decent thing.* Who was this man? Who sent him here, to this miserable place? Queen Victoria's Foreign Office?

"Thank you, señor" was all I could think to say.

He smiled again and kissed me, releasing my arms. "There's a good girl. Now, shall we seal the bargain with a toast? What wine or spirits does the resident strumpet keep here?" He rolled off me and sat up.

"There's aguardiente," I said.

"Your local brandy, yes. That'll do. Fetch us a bottle of the best and two glasses, and we'll drink to your future as an honest woman."

I hastened to obey, so readily that I was on my way back from the pantry with the bottle and glasses before I remembered that I was stark naked. He smiled engagingly at me as I scurried back to him where he lounged against the headboard of the bed. He was concealing something in one hand, however.

"Many thanks," he said, taking the bottle and one of the glasses. He poured a drink for me, dispensing a white powder into my glass as he did so with beautifully neat sleight of hand. It dissolved without a trace in the aguardiente. He handed me my glass and poured one for himself. "Back into bed, now. Climb under the blankets. There's rather a chill in the air."

There certainly was. I analyzed the contents of my glass, smiling ingenuously at him. Not poison, at least; something to make me sleep. Sleep while he did what? Made off with the valise, of course. What was I going to do now?

"To your good health and moral reclamation," he said, lifting his glass. I lifted mine too. He drank, but as soon as he saw that I wasn't drinking with him, his attention was fixed on me again.

"Perhaps you don't indulge in spirits, my dear?" he inquired, in a way as delicate as the perfect spring mechanism of a steel trap.

"Not often," I said, lowering my glass. I leaned affectionately on his right arm. "Never mind, señor. You know, it's only just occurred to me how you must have come to hear of this place. You must be a friend of Mr. Alfred Rubery."

Ha, that startled him. Nobody but a cyborg who was reading his pulse and skin conductivity could have told, however. His eyes narrowed in that dangerous smile.

"The young ass," he said. "Yes, he was quite taken with Madam Martha."

"I hope he was able to get back to his hotel safely? Really, señor, you'd have laughed if you were here to see it. A perfect farce! Except that he really was in danger of being shot by the jealous lover. He barely escaped with his clothing as it was. In fact..." I looked around the room as though searching, then pointed a finger at the valise as though I'd only just discovered it. "There it is, señor, that's Mr. Rubery's valise. He left it here in his haste. We expected he'd send for it, but ever so many days have passed. I assume he's afraid to come back here. Would you perhaps be so kind as to take it with you when you return to the Bella Union?"

"Anything to oblige a lady," he said, kissing my hand, all cozy gallantry, but there was a coldly inquiring look in his eyes. Had I overplayed the scene? Had I swung too quickly from vulnerable waif to cheerful servant girl? I rather think I had. He looked again at the glass I wasn't touching and sighed. I had given him a way to exit gracefully with the valise, but something about me rang false, and he couldn't afford to leave a loose end.

Damn. I do *not* interact gracefully with mortals. They can always tell.

"This is all quite pleasant," he said, getting his right arm free and sliding it around me snugly. "And may I say, my dear, that you speak English beautifully? I am really quite astonished at your command of the language."

Oh dear.

"My mother was English," I temporized. It was happening again; three hundred years, and another tissue of lies to conceal what I truly was. Talk about déjà vu.

"Was she?" He had another sip of his aguardiente. "How did she come to be here, might one ask?"

How indeed. Pirates? Kidnapping? Shipwreck?

"She came in search of her brother," I said carefully. "He emigrated, you see, señor, first to America and then to Texas, when the Mexican government was inviting settlers to farm the land. He sent word that he had a fine farm and was prospering. Her parents died, and there had been some thievery by solicitors—what, I never knew precisely, but she was left nearly penniless. She wrote to her brother to expect her and spent the little she had inherited to buy passage to Texas."

He was nodding thoughtfully. Nothing improbably romantic, nothing that clashed with geographical or historical facts.

"Unfortunately," I continued, "it appeared that her brother had exaggerated his success. He had become, in fact, little more than a beggar. The New World had failed to reform the prodigal vices of his youth. His parents were well-born, you understand, small gentry of an old family, but not rich. Yet he lived as though he had a fortune to inherit, drinking and gambling. That was why he'd been obliged to emigrate in the first place." I monitored his reactions to my story. Was that all right, that little intimation of good bloodlines to appeal to his English snobbery? Yes, he was accepting it.

"So, she arrived in Texas and found that her brother was not only not prosperous but sitting in the village prison for vagrancy, and all her prospects were dashed forever. I am afraid she quite collapsed. Luckily, as she sat weeping in the street, she drew the attention of a gentleman who had come to Texas to see to some business affairs he had there. He was a kind and gallant man, and he rescued her from her plight.

"That man was my father, Don Rodrigo Mendoza. He was not a Mexican, you understand, señor, he was born in Old Spain, the youngest son of a house of ancient valor but no fortune. All his parents could procure for him was an officer's commission, and he made the best of it. He came with the army to New Spain and won a grant of land in Alta California from his king. After the Revolution he remained here; there was nothing in Europe to draw him back, and he had come to love this New World." There, a little more aristocratic ancestry, a father who was an officer and a gentleman. How was he taking that? He was still listening.

"My father was no longer a young man when he befriended my mother, but such was their love that he married her and brought her back to Alta California with him. They lived happily at his rancho near"—what was the most remote and unlikely spot I could think of?—"San Luis Obispo. I was born there, and they had no other children. I was educated in all that a lady of property need learn, and more, for my father had a great admiration for classical studies. I also had to learn what it is to manage an estate. We thought we would always be happy, but the coming of the Americans ruined my father's fortunes, and we lost our home." My Englishman was quite interested by that, to judge from his heart rate and respiration; but he merely made a sympathetic noise. I drew breath and went on.

"The shame killed him, señor. To be cheated out of what he had won with his sword, by shrewd Yankee traders. And my mother did not long survive him, such was her grief. I was left with the clothes on my back and a determination to live. For five years I have won my bread by honest means, cooking and cleaning for strangers; and if it was menial work that my own maids would have scorned to do, when I was a cosseted child, at least I had the satisfaction of knowing that I had never descended into another kind of shame." How was that playing? Pretty well. His pupils were dilated; always a sure sign he was moved about something.

At least, that had been true for Nicholas Harpole, who was not this man.

"Two years I have been the cook at this station, señor, and it has been enough to keep me. But times are hard, señor, surely you know that. The American war, the floods, and then the smallpox, and now the drought. Men run mad, and this land is dying. I have not been paid in weeks. Can you blame me for the despair that led me to this bed? The inn is nearly deserted now, and I fear it will be abandoned soon. Where shall I go then? How am I to live?"

There, I'd written myself a role to play. This was Hollywood, after all. Though the slight tremor in my voice was genuine. My fear and misery were real enough; if they could be made to convince this glorious stranger of my sincerity, so much the better. But had I convinced him?

Maybe.

He was excited about something I'd said, intrigued, not suspicious. His blood was racing. And now he turned to look down into my eyes, and there was a genuine emotion visible for a second behind the smooth opportunistic facade. Was it sympathy? Not love by a long shot, but a good start; and a damned sight better than the reluctant intent to kill me. Yes, we were coming along splendidly.

"Where will you go?" he said, taking my face in his fine strong hands and kissing me. "Why, wherever in this wide world you please, with such a brave heart. You've no need to sell yourself to strangers, my dear; you can make your own terms for a husband. If you once catch the eye of a man of property, your fortune's made, and he's a damned lucky fellow!"

Well, *that* rang false, though I doubt a mortal girl could have told. He wanted something from me. Some detail of my pathetic story had suggested an opportunity to him. What did I care? I loved the taste of his mouth.

"You are married, I suppose," I sighed.

"I? No. My line of work prevents that indulgence; travel, you know. And I'm no man of property, unfortunately. No, my dear, you can do better for yourself than me; but if you'll allow me to come to your assistance, I think there are certain measures that can be taken to ease your entry into better society." He looked deep into my eyes, and the fact that he had thought of a use for me didn't make his smile any less sincere. "Upon my word I do."

"I am in no position to refuse assistance, señor," I told him guardedly.

"No, poor child, and God knows that's none of your doing," he said, settling me gently into the pillows. How persuasive and silken his voice, and how nicely he smiled with that wide humorous mouth of his. "See here: I represent the interests of Imperial Export of London. My firm would pay handsomely for the exclusive rights to supply British manufactured goods to the inhabitants of this coast. That's not our main object, however. You may be aware that British textile industries have suffered from the American conflict. Cotton production in the Southern states (on which our mills depend) has come to a virtual halt, and the little that is being produced is blockaded. Meanwhile our researches indicate that the prevailing weather in this part of California would be ideal for cotton.

"At the present time, the vast pastoral ranchos of your childhood lie fallow and desolate, mortgaged to unscrupulous Yankee moneylenders, and the hereditary gentry of your people are impoverished—not merely by debt but also by the present drought, which has driven the price of cattle down so far as to ruin them. Your countrymen have exchanged independence for a dubious citizenship in a nation that despises them. How they must regret signing the treaty of Guadalupe Hidalgo," he said, not too theatrically, and had another sip of brandy.

"Assuredly they do," I said. "But what is to be done? Were we able to defend ourselves? Our cavalry was magnificent, señor, but we were something short on weapons. Perhaps before gold was discovered here we might have driven them out; after that, never in the world. The United States of America won't relinquish California willingly. We must resign ourselves to being a conquered people."

How intently he was listening to me. His face didn't show it, though, as he moved his hand idly along my thigh.

"And if this Civil War of theirs should alter the situation in your favor...?"

"I try not to hope for anything these days, señor," I said, watching his hand. "Life is so uncertain."

"How very true. But consider what might happen if a benevolent interest were to buy up the debts of your countrymen. What if they found themselves once again in free and clear possession of their lands, with that same benevolent interest offering to lease their abundant acreage at handsome terms for a new industry?"

"The British want to grow cotton here, señor?" I asked, drawing my brows together. I was beginning to understand Imarte's blather about the fascination of secret history. "But...where would you get the workers, señor? Most of the Indian population has been wiped out. Who would pick this cotton?"

"Not Negro slaves, certainly," he said, smiling as his hand traveled. "But former slaves have a great deal of agricultural expertise, and if they were offered good wages for honest employment, I daresay many of them would find their way here. Irrigation would present a difficulty, but one easily surmounted by the best engineers an empire could provide. All this remains to be worked out. At the present time, my principal interest is in arranging to meet with the prominent rancheros of your father's race and determining whether they might be interested in Imperial Export's offer. I truly feel that such an arrangement would be in California's best interests.

"And," he continued, tracing the curve of my shoulder with a finger, "if I were to engage in negotiations with a representative of the displaced ruling class at my side, one who could advise me as to local customs and relationships...my chances of success would be greatly improved." Had his teeth always been that long? Yes, in that saturnine smile. I realized that it looked strange to me because I'd so seldom seen my poor godly Nicholas laugh. We'd been happy, though, at least at first...

"I don't know if I could be as much use to you as all that, señor," I felt obliged to say. "It's hardly as though I have the ear of Pío Pico. I'm a cook in a stagecoach inn, nothing more."

"But you know the land, you know the people," he said. "And you yourself are one of the deposed *gentes de razón*. Your experience with the Yankees is common to them all. Should they not be more readily disposed to listen to my offer of better treatment at British hands if you added your charming voice to mine?"

I smiled at him and stretched. "Am I to be your Malinche, señor? You know the story? She was born near Campeche, where your English pirates used to make so merry. Long before that time, however, the Aztecs enslaved her people and were exacting cruel tribute from them. One day Cortés came from the sea and offered to free her people. She became his interpreter, and led him into Aztec lands to overthrow her tribe's oppressors. Are you planning a revolution, señor?"

"Nothing so uncivilized." He took my hand and kissed the fingertips. "Surely there's been enough blood shed in this poor country. Wouldn't you like to live in a city where you could walk down the streets without fear of being shot? I can assure you, in her native land your mother had no need to wear a pistol. Order and safety and the rule of law, that's the blessing of a modern empire."

"That was what the Yankees promised us, too," I said lazily, tickling him. He arched his back and reached for my hair.

"Well, can one really expect better from Brother Jonathan?" He loosed the end of my long braid. "His nation of liberty was founded on the backs of Negro slaves and at the cost of exterminating the aborigines. As far as I can tell, the Yankee's idea of freedom is his right to carry a pistol with which he may shoot strangers in the street. No wonder his Union has crumbled. My expectation is that it will shortly expire of its own viciousness; and when that happens, California will have the chance to begin anew."

"Under Britain's guidance."

"Of course," he said, unraveling the serpentine twists of my braid.

It all seemed like a great idea to me, except for the fact that I knew it would never happen, thanks to whatever critical mistakes Mr. Rubery was even now in the act of making. All because he had set his valise down in the wrong spot. But why shouldn't I go along with it? What a splendid ride it would be, with this polished and dangerous mortal man, and who cared when it came to a stop? I had no idea what bizarre decision of God's had placed my lover in my arms again, in defiance of reason and death; but now that I had him back, damned if I would ever let him go again.

"Exigua pars est vitae quam nos vivimus," I said.

To my astonishment, he looked blank and then furrowed his brow. "Brief is that part of life..." he translated haltingly.

"The part of life we actually live is too short," I said in English. I switched to the Latin in which I'd flirted with Nicholas Harpole centuries past. "What is this, young man, have you forgotten your grammar?"

In schoolboy Latin, with several pauses, he said, "The sword, when it is not drawn daily, rusts." He leaned back and looked at me, and there was that flicker of real feeling again for a second. Was it grudging respect I saw there? Maybe even the beginning of admiration? "You *have* had a classical education. And your memory is better than mine, I fear. Tell me, can you actually shoot with that pistol of yours?"

"To kill," I said.

What a gleam came into his eyes. I had him now, and he was determined to have me. My hair coiled in his fingers like snakes as he pulled my face close for a kiss.

"Madness, to leave you scrubbing pots for vaqueros," he murmured. "You'll have a house in London, if that's your pleasure, or rule a plantation here that would be the envy of some queens. I've the wherewithal to free you from this miserable life, my girl, if you'll accept my offer on Imperial Export's behalf. And consider the benefit to your countrymen, Señorita Mendoza. What, pray, is your Christian name?"

"Dolores," I said, because that was what I'd been using for the last few decades or so. Then I remembered that my mother was supposed to have been English. "Dolores Alice Elizabeth Mendoza."

"Delighted to make your acquaintance," he said. "Allow me to introduce myself. Edward Alton Bell-Fairfax."

"Charmed, Señor Bell-Fairfax." Dear God, what a Victorian name. It suited him, though. "I'd be lying if I told you your offer of financial assistance didn't attract me, and I seldom lie, señor," I said, and bit his lower lip gently. "But I rather imagine the Americans will have something to say about the Verdugos and the Picos signing lucrative contracts with a foreign power."

He took my untasted glass and set it atop the headboard. Rising to lean over me, he took my two hands in his own. "Let me make an analogy, if I may," he said. "I think of California as a beautiful girl, lost beyond the mountains. In her veins runs the mingled blood of the Latins, passionate and heroic, and the cooler blood of the pragmatic races. Now, she is nominally under the protection of her two stepbrothers, the lantern-jawed gentlemen Jonathan"— he took my left hand and stretched it out above my head—"and Sam"—he took my right hand and stretched it out too, and lowered his face inches from mine. He went on. "But they have not dealt with her in a brotherly fashion, have in fact spent her inheritance recklessly. This would be bad enough; but Jonathan and Sam are now locked in a fratricidal struggle, tumbling perhaps to their destruction. And what of the lovely California?"

What indeed, I wondered, as our lips met in a fierce kiss. He rose on his elbows again. "Who will defend her? For she must be defended. Cruel eyes watch from the howling wasteland and plot her ravishment. To the south is the French beast, and his contemptible lackey the Austrian." He raised one hand and brought it down, down, threatening my left breast. "What they have planned for the fair maiden is too terrible to be imagined, except in the mind of a lascivious Frenchman.

And what is this to the north?" He lifted his other hand and poised it over my right breast. "Dimly seen on the horizon, shambling down from the region of ice and snow where he is monarch, the Russian bear. What is his intention? What has it ever been, my dear, but rape and pillage?

"Who will defend her from them?" he said, leaning down to me, laughter glinting in his wicked eyes. "She cannot flee to the east—savages bar the way, and Mormons, only too eager to seize her. She cannot flee to the west, either. But she has one friend, I assure you, one stout friend who will rise to help her, who will bring her peace and contentment, who will look after her best interests, and invest her dowry wisely. And that stalwart stands ready to crown her with the wealth of a prosperous empire, if only she will raise her eyes to him."

We embraced. In the subsequent tumult the brandy glass was knocked from its place on the headboard, and it fell behind the bed and shattered, so the sweet narcotic spilled out. And the whole time, I swear to you, a little brass band was playing "Rule Britannia" in the air just above our frantic bodies.

And that was how I became a double agent, señors, a spy in the pay of Her Britannic Majesty. And, you know something? I'm not sorry. I wish it *had* worked out. Would Lower Canada have been so bad, really? But the laws of nations count for nothing, in the end. The only law that matters is the one that states that history cannot be changed.

W̶E DECIDED I SHOULD accompany him back into Los Angeles, where Mr. Edward Alton Bell-Fairfax had some correspondence to look to, since he had only just arrived yesterday from Veracruz. Then the first order of business would be to find me some clothing suitable to my role as Imperial Export's cultural liaison. Following that, we would make a brief sea voyage across the channel to Catalina Island. It seemed that there were some other representatives of Imperial Export on the island, doing scientific research for possible investment proposals. They had made quite a comfortable camp there, away from the gunfire and generally insalubrious air of Los Diablos. Perhaps we might stay over there a few days, while we planned a strategy for gaining the support of the rancheros.

Once we had managed to pry ourselves apart, I got dressed first and went out to leave a note on the credenza in my room. This also gave Edward a discreet opportunity to go through the valise and make sure that all its contents were as they ought to be. I realized with a start that we'd been in bed a lot longer than I'd imagined; the sun had already dipped down behind the ridge. That surprise was minor compared to my shock at encountering Juan Bautista, coming down the canyon with a couple of wicker cages. He seemed like a ghost, so unreal had my former life become in the last few hours.

He stopped and stared at me, openmouthed. "Is something wrong? You look different."

"Nothing's wrong," I said. "But I'm going into the field for a while myself. I may not be back any time soon. Let the others know everything's okay." After all, if Imarte could do it, why couldn't I? But Juan Bautista had noticed Edward's horse, and was lifting his head and scanning.

"Who's the mortal?" he said. "And—hey! Who's going to fix dinner tonight?"

"Fix your own damned dinner," I snapped. "Look, you know that special research Imarte's doing? About the English? Well, tell her I'm following up a lead for her. Tell her I'll bring her back some invaluable first-person narratives."

"But you're a botanist," he said.

"Have you noticed there are no plants left to study around here? I'm making myself useful, that's all. And if you want to do the same, why don't you go saddle me a horse?" I said, putting every ounce of authority I had into the request. He nodded meekly and set down his cages, hurrying off to obey. And it seemed to me, señors, that my reason was a perfectly valid one. I was indeed contributing to another operative's research. Perhaps even you would have accepted that as an excuse. If only the rest hadn't happened.

Edward emerged from the inn, fully dressed, hat in one hand and valise in the other. He had to duck to avoid the top of the doorway. "With whom were you speaking, Señorita Mendoza?" he asked politely.

"The stable boy. Only an Indian, señor, and he knows nothing," I said. "He's fetching me a horse."

"Good," he said, and set his hat on his head, which made him nearly seven feet tall. Just like Nicholas. The extraordinary height must have been something of a disadvantage for a spy. He went to fasten the valise securely into a saddlebag. When he had made fast the buckles and straps, he vaulted easily into the saddle and sat, reins in one gloved hand, waiting as Juan Bautista led out my horse. It took me a moment to notice Juan Bautista standing there helpfully, ready to give me a foot up onto my own mount.

Edward Alton Bell-Fairfax looked like a god in the saddle. I had a moment of lurching terror as I realized how much I loved this man, whoever he was. His long-ago death had blasted my immortal life. What would it do to me, if it should happen again?

But this wasn't the same man, was it? He was certainly no saint and martyr, as my Nicholas had been. Subtle, politic, quite capable of a double cross, I should think, and certainly of cold-blooded murder if duty required it. He hadn't expressed any religious opinions, and I'd be willing to bet he had none, to be in his line of work. Could I be happy with this man?

I was insanely happy.

And that is, finally, the only reason I can give you for why I swung into the saddle, snarled, "There's cold beef in the pantry" to Juan Bautista in Spanish, and rode away with Edward Alton Bell-Fairfax.

We went at a swift canter through the slanting red sunlight, toward the place that would one day be black towers blighting the sky but for now was only the adobe sprawl I'd come to loathe so much. We were shot at only twice, and both times Edward sent off a lead riposte with a speed that was breathtaking, for a mortal. We made such good time that the sun was setting as we rode down Calle Principal.

Edward made for the telegraph office while I waited in the saddle. He emerged with a communication he'd received on flimsy paper. I read it upside down without his noticing.

E. A. BELL-FAIRFAX, REP. IMPERIAL EXPORT CO.
YOURS OF 14TH REC'D 11:PM. BEST REGARDS FROM
GOLDEN GATE. SUCCESSFULLY RECOVERED FROM LA
GRIPPE AND LOOK FORWARD TO PROFITABLE
VENTURE WITH CHAPMAN. A. RUBERY, SALES MGR.

Edward exhaled angrily, but there was a certain satisfaction in his eyes as he mounted again, and we ventured once more into the mean streets.

"Good news, señor?" I asked.

"Tolerably good," he said. "It seems my young idiot of a friend has managed to succeed in his affairs, against my expectations. Alfred never had much head for business. Privilege tends to soften the brain, or so I've observed."

I reflected on that opinion. "I should have thought *you* were a member of the privileged classes, señor."

"Hardly, my dear. My ancestry's good enough; but will you understand if I explain that my birth represented a certain inconvenience for my parents? I trust that won't dismay you. My upbringing was discreetly anonymous, and my inheritance is nil. So I've had to shift for myself rather. Another reason I'm not a suitable husband, by the way," he added slyly. My God, that was Nicholas to the life, that trick of talking out of the side of his mouth when he was being ironical.

"Señor, your excellent qualities outweigh any consideration of clerical sanction," I said with an airy wave of my hand. He was grinning, about to answer, when his expression suddenly changed, became ice-cold. I followed his gaze but could see nothing except a pair of men hurrying into the Bella Union Hotel down the street. That was our destination too. Yet now Edward pulled abruptly on his horse's reins and spurred down a side street. I followed silently. A few more streets over, and he turned in his saddle to address me.

All the easy warmth of the day's pleasure had gone, with all the high color from his face. There was a look of strain in his eyes, though his voice was composed when he spoke.

"My dear, I'm afraid there's been a change of plan. Regrettable, but it can't be helped. There were two gentlemen entering the Bella Union just now—perhaps you saw them? I know them, unfortunately, and their presence indicates that they know I'm here. It would appear our friend Mr. Rubery made a few more blunders than I thought. Please accept this as a token of my esteem." He reached into his saddlebag and drew out a small leather pouch. He passed it to me over my horse's neck; it was heavy for its size. "That should enable you to find a more hospitable corner of the world in which to live. I believe you're clever enough to see that my presence shall shortly be a very dangerous place indeed, so I'd advise you to ride, and quickly."

"Not in this life, señor," I said in a low voice, leaning forward in the saddle. "I know the country, as you said, and I think you need a swift way out of here. You can't go back to the Bella Union. Will those men think to look for you at the stagecoach inn when you fail to return to your room?"

"Possibly," he said. "I must assume they've already discovered certain things. You're owed an explanation. You'll have it if you can get us both out of here alive."

"Follow," I said, and urged my horse forward. He followed, to my relief, and I immediately accessed a detailed street map. There was a narrow alley that ran along the base of the long low hill, and we made for that and galloped its length, behind its houses out of town. We encountered nobody but a dead man; our mounts slowed to pick their delicate way over him where he lay staring placidly at the new stars, and we sped on as the twilight deepened.

So back toward Hollywood, but not the way we'd come. I found us a route over torn earth, where cattle and vaqueros had passed in the dozens, and widened my scanning range to eight kilometers. Nobody was following us; nobody was lying in wait for us. The people whose delight it was to lie in the underbrush and take potshots at passersby were evidently on their dinner breaks. So far, so good. We made a wide turn, avoiding Cahuenga Pass, and rode for a winding canyon about a mile west of it.

About a kilometer in, there was a great branching sycamore tree near a spring that bubbled out of the sand, and we reined in under the shadows there. The tree was occasionally used to hang thieves, and so local residents tended to avoid the area after dark. "Well, Señor Bell-Fairfax?" I said.

"Well, Señorita Mendoza," he said. "You were indeed correct in your assumption that what's left of the Yankee government wouldn't approve of our plans for profitable trade with the locals. Apparently certain agents in the employ of Mr. Allan Pinkerton have got wind of something, doubtless thanks to Mr. Rubery's lack of discretion."

So this was how it had failed? "The game is over, then, señor?" I asked, hoping we'd make the best of a bad business and get out of the heat.

"By no means," he said, "since we were able to escape with our lives. Our proposal for your countrymen will simply be delayed, and they may be even more willing to listen by that time. If you're still game, of course?"

"I am." Though I didn't like his persistence in the face of danger. Better to give it up, go home, live to spy another day. "What about getting over to Catalina Island?"

"Hm. That's compromised now. I had engaged a reliable fellow to take me across tomorrow evening, but if my room has been searched, I daresay he'll be watched." He looked thoughtful in the darkness, but the color had returned to his face. After a moment he turned, surveying the night. He couldn't have been able to see anything; to a mortal the black shadow would have been complete and impenetrable. "I'm afraid I must impose on your bravery and your hospitality a while longer, my dear. I'd like to move on. We need a secure retreat with a decent view of the surrounding countryside. Do you know of any such?"

"I think I know a place," I said, and we rode on up the canyon.

It twisted steeply for a few miles, and we followed a sandy creek bed under black avenues of trees. There was no water there now, but cool air currents flowed past our faces in the darkness until we emerged, riding straight uphill toward rimrock. To one side below us a splendid view of the plain opened out, and there was a tiny cluster of yellow lights to show us where the village of Sherman slept. I wondered if Señora Berreyesa had survived the smallpox. What a lifetime ago that had been.

We stopped climbing and made our way north through the hill-
tops, keeping well below the rimrock, and our horses picked their way
carefully through black sliding piles of scree. I found a trail to take us
around and down, until we emerged on another view: the San Fernando Valley lying vast and silent in the darkness. There below us was
the northern end of Cahuenga Pass, beyond was the gigantic wall
of Mount Hollywood, and far, far out on the valley floor was the
tumbled ruin of what had been Mission San Fernando, its graceful ar-
cade broken open to the stars. Not that a mortal could have made it
out at that distance. I remembered chatting with a friar in its tidy mission garden, once, and felt a pang of loneliness.

"My compliments," whispered Edward beside me. "A fine panoramic view. All we need is a defensible spot." How could he tell
there was a fine panoramic view? I was seeing it by infrared, but he
was a mortal man.

"Up here," I murmured, gesturing to a small steep hill like a tur-
ret that was crowned with a stand of trees. We rode up into the cover
they provided. On the other side of the hill was a little terrace,
wooded and dropping to a rocky saddleback ridge. To either edge the
land fell sharply away in deep canyons. Below us, nearly invisible in
the night and the trees, was a rough square of leaning wooden huts.

"You want a defensible spot?" I said to Edward. "This was one of
Fremont's outposts. It's been abandoned for years. Nobody for miles
but Cielo the farmer, and he won't be able to see us from his house."

Edward nodded.

I let him reconnoiter while I gathered wood for a fire. I'd told him
the literal truth, we really were the only people for kilometers except
for Mr. Cielo; so he returned satisfied as to our security. The largest of
the buildings had a crude stone hearth, and I cleared it enough to start
a small fire. No furniture left, but at least the creaking plank floor was
dry. Edward saw to our horses and then came in and sat down beside
me, carrying the saddlebag. He pulled out his watch and looked at it.

"Twenty-four hours," he said, with some satisfaction.

"Is that significant, señor?" I asked.

"Yes, I think so," he said, closing the watch and slipping it back into his waistcoat pocket. Without explaining further, he took out the valise and opened it. "I daresay you examined the contents of this whilst it was left at your inn?"

"No, señor," I said truthfully. "But I'm fairly sure Martha went through it."

"Yes, I'd gathered someone had. Damn." He looked up as an idea struck him. "Where has that intriguing lady got to, by the way? You said she was gone; where did she go?"

"San Francisco," I answered.

He stopped in the act of taking out the neat little stoppered bottle of violet ink. "When?" he said in a voice too calm.

"Just this morning, señor," I said. "If you'd arrived two hours earlier, you'd have met her."

He relaxed visibly, but his expression was still grim.

"Now, I wonder," he said, pulling a pen from an inner pocket and removing the cap that protected the nib. "I wonder how well you're acquainted with the lady."

"Quite well, señor."

"She had rather a reputation at the Bella Union as a sympathizer with the Secessionist cause, and was reputed to have had a particular fondness for Britons. I assume this was how Mr. Rubery chanced to be enjoying her favors at the moment her jealous friend stepped on-stage." He pulled out a sheaf of papers, half sheets that appeared to be printed in the same violet ink, and thumbed through them carefully. "Was the lady what she seemed to be, in your opinion?"

"I don't think she's a Federal spy, señor. I think she serves her own interests, like most whores."

"Yet she made no attempt to pilfer the contents of this valise." He held up the sheaf. "These are drafts on the Bank of England; useless without a countersignature, but a dedicated thief would attempt to forge one. And there's a considerable sum in coin as well, but apart from prising up the seal to look at it, she left that quite untouched. She may also have read through certain other papers here, the idea of which is rather unsettling." He rested the valise on his knee to use as a writing surface. Dipping his pen in the violet ink, he selected a draft and filled out an amount. He signed it with a flourish and carefully put his pen back in his inner breast pocket. "I put the question to you: having examined these things, what was the lady's object in departing for San Francisco this morning?"

"She didn't say," I lied, looking thoughtful. "If she was intending to betray your cause, I should imagine she'd have taken the valise straight to Fort Drum down here. Would she have learned from the papers that your friend was now in San Francisco?"

"Yes," he said, waving the check in the air to dry it.

"Well, then, perhaps she's gone up there to blackmail him. That might explain why she left the valise."

"It might well." He stared into the fire. "In which case, we have nothing to fear from that quarter, at least at present."

"We haven't?"

"No," he said. Groping with his free hand, he pulled a kind of envelope of oilcloth out of the valise. It was exactly big enough for a half sheet. He tucked the check inside and handed it to me. "There, my dear. Less immediately negotiable than the gold, but if we should be separated, this will get you to London, where you'll find you have friends. Take care not to get it wet; even perspiration is enough to make that ink vanish like a dream."

"You're too generous, señor," I said, opening it to peer at the amount. My jaw dropped. I had to read twice before I was sure. I looked at him in confusion. "Señor! That's—it is too much."

He gave a brief shake of his head, putting away the contents of the valise. "You may well earn it before this business is done. Let me tell you honestly that your life may stand at hazard, Señorita Mendoza. I shall certainly think no less of you if you wish to withdraw at this point and travel elsewhere. Indeed, I'm obliged to tell you it's in your best interests to do so at once. The money's yours, regardless." He reached back into the saddlebag and brought out a small box.

"This is more than a matter of trade, isn't it?" I said.

Edward looked at me for a long moment before he answered. "It is a game of nations," he said. He drew his gun from its holster and opened the box, which contained small tools, ammunition, and a chamois cloth. Methodically he removed the remaining bullets from his gun and began to clean it.

I watched him awhile before I spoke again. "I suspected as much. Well. Señor, I will not leave you. This involves my honor, after all."

He was shaking his head. "That won't do, my dear. Marriage is really not—"

"You mistake my meaning," I said. "You are a stranger in my country, and you have shown me kindness, and now our common enemies hunt for you. I will not leave your side, señor, while I can be of use to you. That's my honor, and I won't surrender it." Only lines spoken by the character I was playing; but I meant them all the same.

Real emotion in his eyes again, before the cold businesslike look returned. What kind of man lay behind the role *he* was playing? "Señorita, you do credit to your father's sword," he said. "By God, I hope we can win through to London."

"What are our chances?" I settled back, hoping he couldn't hear the way my heart was pounding.

He took up his gun again and spun the empty cylinders. "Not poor, I think," he said, reloading. Oh, his heart was pounding too. "If we can avoid capture for another day or so, and if we can get across to Santa Catalina Island, we'll do very well indeed. The difficulty will be finding a vessel to take us."

I remembered Señor Souza and his dark house on its pilings.

"I can manage that, señor," I said. "I know a fisherman with a house on the slough, below the old landing place."

"His name?" Edward gave the weapon a final inspection and returned it to its holster.

"Souza. A Portuguese gentleman. There was a doctor who resided at the inn for a while, to whom he's indebted. I'll call in a favor on his behalf."

"Can you?" Edward said, putting away the box. He leaned back and stretched out his long legs. "Then we'll hope for the best and prepare for the worst, and God defend the right."

Flames were dancing in his eyes. Flames running up his shirt, sputtering in his fair hair, Nicholas had stared at me until the agony broke his concentration...

I had to close my eyes and draw a deep breath. When I opened them, Edward was sitting forward and frowning at me. "Are you well, señorita?" he asked.

I stared at him. "Do you believe in God, señor?"

He looked disconcerted. "I suppose so," he said at length. "Certainly religion is a civilizing influence, if it's not taken too far. I imagine you're a Roman Catholic?"

"I was born one," I said, which was the truth.

"I won't offend you, then. But I think we can agree that zealots of any persuasion do a great deal of harm. All the same, men need commandments of some kind."

"Do you think there's a true religion?"

"Do I? Yes, the C. of E., I suppose. But if I were a Hottentot, I'd tell you that my great wooden idol was better than anyone else's. I doubt that distinct creeds matter much, so long as civilized behavior is observed." He looked at me askance. "Is the matter of doctrine very important to you, my dear?"

No, this man wasn't one to die for his God, and I'd have to remember to thank God for it, next time I believed in Him. I wasn't sure I didn't believe in Him right now. Could my lover have been reconstituted *without* the faith that had killed him?

In my relief I stammered, "Not to me, señor, but I feared it might matter to you." I drew breath and temporized. "My mother owned an English book about Protestant martyrs, *Foxe's Acts and Monuments*. You understand, she became a Catholic when she married my father, but since this book had been given to her as a girl, she kept it for sentiment's sake. Well, I read it when I was learning to read English, and what a terrible business. Such hatred the Catholics and Protestants felt for each other! So I drew the conclusion that Englishmen might feel strongly on the matter even now."

"And many do," he admitted. "But that was three centuries ago. If all nations brooded interminably on old scores, there'd never be an end to the vengeance. Most of the Catholics I've known have been reasonably decent chaps. A certain amount of tolerance is essential to civilized behavior. Barbarity is the force to be fought, not differences of dogma. Wouldn't you agree?"

"Yes!" How direct, how enlightened. Nicholas's intellect and humanity, everything I'd adored in him, without his late medieval prejudices.

Possibly encouraged by my enthralled look, Edward continued: "Religion has its place, certainly, in reinforcing ethical behavior amongst the masses, but any sufficiently enlightened secular laws will have the same effect. After all, most of the creeds of the world have essentially the same purpose, have they not? To enjoin men to be what we call moral, which is to say *civilized*. A civilized man obeys the rule of law, he acknowledges that he must not injure his neighbors, and if injured by them, he must appeal to law for satisfaction rather than indulge in burning their houses over their heads as they sleep. Civilization is the ideal for which we strive, with so little perceptible success; yet we do succeed, in inches and over years.

"Consider." He sat forward, resting his elbows on his knees, and the intensity of his eyes made my heart flame. "What was Britain when the Romans found her? A wilderness of howling savages. And Rome, a thousand times more civilized, yet was so barbaric, she held spectacles of slaughter for her citizens, and her rulers were guilty of the most hideous crimes.

"Still, the Pax Romana tamed the wilderness, taught the savages, and, as imperfect as she was, Rome sent the idea of civilization working throughout the world. Even her fall into decadence could not stay the forces she had set in motion."

"Other people were what we'd call civilized, before Rome," I said with effort. His voice was so magnificent, I hated to interrupt him.

"Certainly. The Greeks, in fact, were more so. They lacked, however, Rome's peculiar genius at organization and her insistence that civilization be spread. That, in my opinion, was Rome's great contribution to the world, and that is the inheritance she passed on to Britain: the moral imperative to bring the rule of law to barbarians, through the operative mechanisms of empire." He moved closer to me. There was a purpose to all this, of course: he wanted to win me to his government's side. But look how his eyes glowed. All the easy, deceitful charm had fallen away, and passionate conviction was shining out of them like light.

"That is the cause in which I labor. What force can bring the greatest good to the greatest number of men? Only the modern empire, with its constitution to guarantee their individual rights, and its power to bring them prosperity. A missionary may persuade a painted savage to worship a cross rather than an idol; but he will not make laws that send that savage's children to school, where they might learn to make the desert they inhabit another Eden by means of the advanced sciences. He may persuade his flock to love one another for his God's sake, but he'll invariably urge them to slaughter any neighboring tribe that still worships stone idols. This is the failure of religion as a force for the common welfare," he said.

"Señor, you have the truth of it," I said from my heart. How had Victorian England brought forth a man like this? "And surely this is the way to a better world, is it not, this secular enlightenment? Even the Americans have deduced this, with their separation of church and state."

"Ah, the Yankees." He sneered elegantly. "What have they achieved but violent chaos? And I'll tell you why, my dear. Liberty (as they conceive of it) and loyalty are opposing concepts. Having rebelled against the hereditary ruler who was the embodiment of their nation, to what will they be loyal? Their flag? But see what has happened now: half the nation, asserting its liberty to keep slaves, has rebelled and taken up arms to defend that liberty. It won't end there, either, you know. Any brute will demand his right to be a law unto himself, beating his wife and his children as he pleases, and defend that right with his father's rifle and think himself a patriot." He used his big hands so well when he spoke, with graceful economical gestures to make his point.

"The difficulty, I think, is that liberty is too abstract an idea for human nature to grasp. It is too easily twisted into lawlessness, as has happened in America. Most men are incapable of reverencing a mere principle; that principle must be embodied in a living person to effectively hold their allegiance. This is where empire inspires, and democracy fails in inspiration: love of one's monarch."

What a spell he was weaving, jarred only by my mental image of dumpy little Victoria and her priggish prince. No, I certainly couldn't agree with him on that one. But he swept on and took my breath away by saying:

"Mind you, royals and their attendant baggage of toadies, cretins, and thieves are seldom an inspiring lot in and of themselves, but in a constitutional commonwealth they need not be. I believe that my sovereign has deplorable taste in art, is devoid of much talent to rule, and certainly couldn't compete with Venus for beauty. But she in her person is the empire personified, the driving force of civilization, and as such I serve her, reverence her, and will, when necessity commands, die for her."

The wickedly confidential way in which he said this was so delightful that it took a moment for the last part to sink in on me.

"I trust, señor, you've no intention of dying soon," I said.

His eyes narrowed, and he shrugged. "No intention at all. But my occupation carries that risk, always. I imagine I came rather close to the awful specter this evening. Certainly I'd hate to lose my life as the result of some fool's incompetence. Should there come a time, however, when my death would serve the purpose of empire, then I hope I will die without hesitation. As the bard of Avon says, 'Live we how we

can, yet die we must.' And that being the inevitable case, one can at least
have the satisfaction of accomplishing something with one's death."

It has probably already occurred to you, señors, but it was only at
that moment that I realized that this *was* the same man I had loved.
He had exactly the same inner drive that had got him burned at the
stake; only the focus of his devotion had shifted. As I stared at him in
horror, he leaned back and went on:

"I don't imagine I'd much care to live to decrepit old age, to tell
you the truth. End one's days being pushed about in a bath chair? Not
for me. Better a brief life lived intensely, with a keen appreciation of
its pleasures." He gave me a meaningful smile. "It's no more than the
bargain soldiers make, after all, self-sacrifice for the greater good."

He was the perfect operative. Brilliant intellect, no life of his own,
utterly focused on his duty to make the world a better place, thoroughly convinced that his masters were wise and good. He was just
what I was supposed to be.

"But—isn't human sacrifice one of the barbarisms you're working to put an end to?" I protested, rising up on my knees. "Whether
willing or unwilling? And how can you *know*, señor, that your death
will really have accomplished anything? Secrets of espionage are the
most transitory. And who can ever say how history will play out?
Consider, consider those same English martyrs!"

I felt my voice shaking and tried desperately to control it, but
everything I'd wanted to say to him for three hundred years came
howling up from my heart. "They let themselves be burned in droves,
señor, and for what? They died for *nothing*. If they'd only kept their
mouths shut and lain low, they'd have lived to see a better day, because in short order Bloody Mary died and Elizabeth succeeded her,
and restored their stupid Protestant faith to power. So how can you
know, señor, that you wouldn't be throwing your life away, that you
wouldn't serve your cause better as a living man?"

Was I convincing him, señors? No, I was only arousing him. He
found the throb of my voice, the firelight on my hair, and the angry

blood in my cheeks exciting. But he did make an effort to reply seriously rather than simply grab me and pull me down.

"I am astonished at how well you know English history, my dear," he said. "Granting your point—without foreknowledge of history, what else could those Protestant heroes have done? Nor can you say with real certainty that their deaths accomplished nothing. If they hadn't died as bravely as they did, if they had not so publicly denounced Mary's tyranny, might not her husband Philip of Spain have been emboldened to seize the crown after her death? Setting aside the immediate salvation that martyrdom is reputed to confer on the martyr." His eyes glinted, reflecting fire.

How could I tell him that *I* had known how history was going to play out, and I'd failed to save him, even so? He continued:

"The instinct to preserve life is natural for your sex, my dear; it's a fine and appropriate womanly inclination. And when the ideal is reached at last and the world is civilized, I trust there shall be no more need of martyrs to die in any cause. At present, however, we live in a world that requires certain regrettable actions in order to bring about the better world we desire. I myself have been required to commit crimes, to do things I would certainly rather have avoided. And when my blood must be shed to atone for those acts, then at least I'll face oblivion with a clean score. It works out, you see."

"In the minds of wicked old men who make governments, it works out," I said in despair. "They know they can always count on a ready supply of brave men who'll die for a cause, like you, and so they continue to wage wars and spend lives to keep themselves in power. But if all the heroes refused to play that great game, what then, señor? If the nations had no means of waging war on one another, wouldn't they be obliged to find some more civilized means of settling their differences?"

I thought he wasn't listening to me, so hungry were his eyes. Even now he was moving forward with one hand out to wind it in my hair and pull my face close to his. He kissed greedily, but when we came up for air he growled:

"No, my dear, they wouldn't. Come, come, do you suppose the politicians are the only ones responsible for wars? When one shepherd will steal his neighbor's flock, when one child will pick up a stone to fling at a child from the next village over? Things are by no means so simply drawn as you imagine, and the causes of war are far too complicated to gloss over with a pacifist cliché."

He bore me backward, and we wrestled as he very adroitly unbuttoned and unhooked. "If all the statesmen in the world signed a universal peace tomorrow, some spiteful fool would find a way to bare his bum at his former enemies, and the whole misery would begin all over again. It will take a great deal more subtle work, over a much longer period of time, to bring peace to the world."

And of course he was right about that, and I *had* used a pacifist cliché. Really, what other man could argue like that while in the throes of carnal passion? Only one I'd ever known, a long time ago in a land far away.

Edward put his face close to mine and looked into my eyes, and I was so spellbound by his gaze and the music of his voice, I very nearly missed the meaning of his words, which would have been a pity, because it was extraordinary.

"And *when* there is peace at last, and *when* men are no longer distracted by the ravages of war and crime, then the real work begins. Mankind has grasped at science and invention to improve his lot; when he truly understands that he can wield those tools to improve *himself*, he will lay the cornerstone of the earthly paradise," Edward said. "What might not science achieve, in a world where a nation's resources weren't continually drained by strife? What if that nation made a remarkable discovery, one that gave new meaning to old legends of a golden age? What if it were possible to utterly change the human condition? What if it were possible to put an end forever to disease? To age? To death itself? And where will men ever make those discoveries but in a stable and peaceful empire?"

How did he know? Was the man a bloody prophet? How could he foresee so clearly what the future would hold once the Company was founded? And how the hell could he prophesy so, with our hearts thundering against each other and our bodies locked in the most intimate embrace? I didn't know, I had never known, but just so had my lover spoken three centuries before. And now as then, I fled from the meaning of his words and lost myself in the worship of his magnificent mortal flesh.

So we burned together beside that little fire, in the leaning ruin of Fremont's outpost, and the shades of Manifest Destiny and Imperialism looked on with sardonic smiles. If the flames had risen and consumed us in each other's arms, señors, we'd have felt no pain. If only we were lying there now, our quiet ashes mingled together!

I opened my eyes and saw him, in the chilly morning light. For a moment I thought I was lying in a garret room in England, awake at last after a nightmare of terrible sorrow and interminable length. But no, this was my new lover, who by an amazing coincidence was identical in every respect to Nicholas. Limited gene pool indeed! I had never once in all the intervening centuries met another mortal with his face. He wasn't conventionally handsome, with that broken nose and that wide mouth; but the combination of features that would have made another man a leering gargoyle were elegant in Edward-who-had-been-Nicholas. Part of the trick was the way he used his face, the responsive liveliness of expression, the movement of his eyes. He fascinated, he charmed, he *moved* well, and one never realized that the big man didn't quite look human—something odd in the angle of the cheekbones, in the way the head sat on the powerful neck. But he hid his strangeness far better than I, who looked human.

It was going to be tricky keeping him alive and safe, in his line of work, but I could do it, if I stayed by him the rest of his life. How to manage that? I'd find some way. Porfirio had his pet mortals, didn't he? The Company let him go to them, stay with them, help them when they needed his help. All I'd need do is learn clever makeup skills, appear to age with Edward as he aged.

Full body appliance makeup to make me look like an old woman with my clothes off obviously wouldn't work. What then, live with him as is and hope for the best? The best would be some mortal disease felling him comparatively early, before he could notice that his hair was graying while I still looked eighteen.

If I took the chance and lived an idyll with him, and if he loved me enough, might I gradually let him in on my little secret? But look what had happened the last time he discovered I wasn't human.

But we were in the modern era now, and this was a man with a strong belief in the virtues of science, unlikely to attribute my inexplicable abilities to Satan. Maybe I could explain, maybe he could be brought to understand, maybe he could become one of Dr. Zeus's paid mortals with a control implant...

No. But something would suggest itself, something could be worked out. Who knows, perhaps we'd live blissfully awhile and then lose interest in each other, as so many mortals did, as *we* might have if he'd lived, and go our separate ways without pain. Perhaps fate had brought him back for just that closure on the events of 1555, to heal my life at last.

When he opened his eyes, though, I stopped thinking.

"Good morning, my dear," he said, alert at once. The charm went on as though a switch had been flipped, and his courtly smirk acknowledged that he'd very much enjoyed my company last night, wink wink, squeeze squeeze, yet his eyes also tracked around the room. Saddlebags still there, weapons still there, no intruders. Having ticked these off his mental list, he smiled down at me. "I trust you slept well?"

"Very well indeed, señor," I said, smiling back at him, but I had logistical problems of my own: here was a mortal man who'd been without food or water for at least twenty hours. "Though the land of dreams is a poor place to visit after one has been to heaven."

"Ah, but *I* was in paradise all night," he said gallantly, getting to his feet and offering me his hand to rise. "Now, my dear, our first business is to feed and water the horses. Where did the redoubtable John Charles Fremont attend to such things?"

I accessed a topographical survey. The nearest water should be a little creek flowing down a ravine just over our turreted hill. What was this footnote? Future site of Harrison Ford residence? I made a mental note not to download map information from Einar again. Movie star homes, my foot. Was the damn creek there in time of drought, that was the information I needed. I smiled prettily at Edward and pointed vaguely north. "Woman's intuition tells me, señor, that there is a spring in yonder canyon."

We led the horses to where there was a little green forage. But the spring had dwindled to a seep, an uninviting trickle in a black muddy bog at the canyon bottom, full of amoebic guests that wouldn't bother a horse but would be only too happy to give a mortal dysentery. We had to prise up a couple of big rocks and grub out a hole for the water to collect in so the horses could drink. No bullwhip-wielding hero showed up to offer us assistance, but it was 1863, after all. My own hero produced a canteen from his saddlebag and offered it to me.

"You'll find it brackish, I'm afraid, but safe," he said. How did he know about the shigella I had detected here? And see how expertly he was avoiding the poison oak as he looked for a clean place to sit down. He settled on a boulder at the approximate location of what would one day be Mr. Ford's front step, and nonchalantly proceeded to shave himself with a clasp knife that appeared in his hand out of nowhere.

I was distracted from my awestruck contemplation of this feat (no soap, no water, and he didn't nick himself once) by an annoying little signal pulsing through the ether.

Mendoza?

What is it, Juan Bautista? I'm busy.

Are you coming back today?

No. Fix your own breakfast. Wait, this is important. I need you to put some food together and bring it up to me. Make it look as though you'd fixed yourself a very large picnic lunch. I'm going to lead my mortal friend back in your direction, and we're going to just accidentally on purpose run into you as you're out hunting, okay?

What's going on?

I'm doing fieldwork for Imarte.

Hey, is that guy a real British secret agent? Like in the James Bond movies?

Uh, yes, I guess he is.

Edward was standing up, neatly folding away the clasp knife. A day and a night of living rough in the field, and he hadn't so much as a smudge on those fawn wool trousers of his. Whatever secret device kept James Bond's tuxedo impeccably pressed, it seemed to have been already in use by the British secret service in 1863.

Neat! Can I help with whatever it is you're doing?

No, just bring us food. And this is secret, okay, J. B.? I'm trying to keep this man out of danger while I find out more about his plot.

Right.

I'll broadcast a directional signal as we come. Do your best to look surprised when you meet us. Spanish only, and remember, he probably understands it as well as you do, so watch what you say.

Gotcha.

Edward was coming toward me. "Well, my dear," he said. "I find nothing especially edible hereabouts, with the possible exception of rattlesnakes. What are the chances we might purchase food from that farmer you mentioned?"

"He is an inhospitable man," I said. It might have been true, too, for all I knew. "I recollect a farm near the Rodeo de Las Aguas where they are friendlier. It would be our wisest course to keep to the heights and work our way over there. We will pass near the stagecoach inn, but not near enough to be seen. Does that suit you, señor?"

"Very well indeed," he said.

We saddled our horses and rode out, working our way back in the direction of the inn, with me broadcasting a steady signal to Juan Bautista. As we were edging our way down onto what would one day be Mulholland Drive, I spotted him lounging ever-so-casually against a rock.

"Ay," he said in Mexican Spanish. "Señora Mendoza, I was afraid when you did not return last night. I am out hunting, as you see." He waved one of our rifles unconvincingly. Edward raised an eyebrow at him.

"And I am safe, as *you* see. Is that food you have in your basket, boy?" I said.

"Oh, yes—I packed myself a lunch." Juan Bautista was trying not to stare at Edward. "It's a very good lunch."

"Well, listen to me, I'm going to ask you for it. My friend here is a kind gentleman who is being pursued by thieves. We had to flee Los Diablos last night, and he has had nothing to eat. We would go back to the inn for a meal, but I am afraid they may come looking for him there."

"Oh, they have already," Juan Bautista said.

"What?" *What? Why the hell didn't you tell me?*

I thought you knew. "Yes, señora, two Yankee men. They said they were the friends of the Englishman who had been there. They came to collect the valise he left behind. I pretended not to understand them because, as you know, I do not trust the Yankee oppressors of our people." Juan Bautista gave the rifle a dramatic flourish.

I turned to look at Edward. His face was a perfect mask of polite incomprehension, but he had turned pale. "Señor," I told him, "the boy says that two Yankee men came to the inn asking for the valise an Englishman left there. He doesn't like Yankees, so he wouldn't speak with them."

"Really," Edward drawled. He made an odd little gesture that I would have taken for a shrug, if I hadn't known where all his concealed weapons were. He was quietly assuring himself each was in place. "Ask him when they were at the inn."

"When was this, Juanito?"

You're scared, aren't you? What's wrong? "It was this morning, señora, just after first light."

They'll kill him if they find him. "And are they still there now, boy?"

"No, señora, but I think they did not go far away. I think they are hiding to watch the stagecoach come and go, but, as you know, I am an Indian and white men cannot conceal themselves from me." *Can I help? Can I be your Indian guide? Please? I could throw the bad guys off the scent if they followed us.*

God damn it, this isn't a movie. "He says they were here at dawn," I told Edward. "He says they left, but he thinks they're still hiding in the pass, waiting for you to come."

Edward just nodded. I was feeling a slow anger building in him, sullen and exasperated. Not much fear, though for all he knew the Yankees might have had him in their sights at that very moment. But *I* was terrified for him, señors.

"I think you ought to ambush and kill those Yankees, Juanito," I said. "I assure you they are very bad men."

Juan Bautista did a good job of looking crafty. "Perhaps that can be arranged, señora." *So what do you want me to do about them, really?*

Like I said.

That shook Juan Bautista's little world. Even though Einar had been nailing mortal hides to the wall for months. After all, wasn't this Los Angeles, where such things were done every day? The boy shuffled his feet and looked at the ground. *Mendoza, I can't kill mortals.*

Why not? James Bond does.

Edward apparently came to some kind of decision, because he looked up at this point and said, "Thank the boy and tell him to go on with his business. If he meets the Yankees again, on no account is he to mention that he's seen me. But he should avoid them if he can, because they are very dangerous men."

"Give me that food now," I told Juan Bautista. "My friend offers his thanks and says to stay away from those Yankees, but don't tell them about him if you do encounter them. I assume this means he does not wish them to die. What a pity. However, your soul is free of two mortal sins. How fortunate for you."

Juan Bautista was too unnerved to play back. He just handed me the lunch basket and muttered, "Good day, good fortune on your journey," before vanishing into the sagebrush.

I hefted the basket and flashed Edward a brittle smile. "The boy has kindly surrendered his luncheon repast to our greater need. Poor fare, señor, but sustaining. I suggest we find a secure place to eat and revise our plans."

He shook his head grimly. "If I were a free man, we'd be riding for San Francisco this moment. Unfortunately I have a duty to salvage what I can from Rubery's incompetence."

This gave me an idea, but all I said was "One cannot make decisions on an empty stomach. Let us ride back to the high ground, señor."

We returned to the vicinity of Fremont's outpost and stopped in a grove of oak trees on the saddleback ridge just below. We still had a good view of the north end of the pass, but from a more sheltered spot. If anyone tracking us should find our previous night's camp, we'd have warning of their presence and a reasonably clear shot at them.

I unpacked the basket. Left to himself, Juan Bautista had grilled beef and made severely deformed tortillas for supper last night, and we had lots of the leftovers. He had also included a jug of water, a jar of olives, some cheese, a can of sardines, and a couple of cakes of Theobromos.

I should mention that I didn't have to explain any of the food to Edward, or show him how to roll up a filling in a tortilla. He'd learned how, somewhere. Perhaps in secret agent school; more likely in Veracruz, whatever he'd been doing there. From his saddlebag, he drew out an immense white handkerchief and spread it across his lap. I watched in amazement as he made himself sardine tacos and ate them without getting one spot of oil on those immaculate clothes.

"As regards this plan, señor," I said at length, when we'd consumed half the contents of the basket and neatly packed the rest for later. "As I said: my honor will not permit me to leave you. But clearly we are dealing in matters of life and death now. For your sake, I will be my father's sword at the throat of your enemies. Yet I begin to question whether your government is wise enough to rule the world. What fool ever trusted your Mr. Rubery with important papers?"

Yes, that touched a nerve. What a cold, bleak look in his eyes as he stared out at Cahuenga Pass, and how well I remembered the bitter anger that pulled the corners of his mouth down. He mastered his temper, though, and turned to face me with a rueful smile and a shrug.

"I can't deny the truth, my dear, particularly in this instance, since we're facing considerable danger as a result of it. I have at least the satisfaction of pointing out that well-born imbeciles tend to get themselves killed before they manage to breed, leaving room for men of ability to replace them. And not all well-born men are idiots! I can assure you that there is an office in Whitehall where a very wise and noble man makes national policy, one whose judgment I'd utterly trust, for all that he's seldom quoted in the *Times*. That same man who made the decision to give Alfred a task he was barely fit for had the foresight to send me after him, guessing no doubt that Alfred would make the wretched mess he has."

I shook my head. "Why send the boy in the first place? If your people think you're expendable, their aristocratic brains are no better than Mr. Rubery's. I'll grant you, the idea of this land in peace and prosperity under British rule is a splendid one. I'd die myself if that would bring it into being. But I don't see how it can be accomplished now, do you? Martha must have gone straight to the Yankees and told them about the valise; or if she did not, some other indiscretion of Mr. Rubery's put them on the scent. They surely know everything now. I don't see how your masters can blame you for pulling out and saving what you can of the affair."

"Ah, but the Yankees *don't* know everything now," he said. He pushed his lank hair back from his forehead with the flat of his hand and set his hat straight on his head. "If they did, they wouldn't be after the valise. Whatever else we do, it mustn't fall into their hands."

"Shouldn't we destroy the papers, then?" I asked.

"No. If we can salvage any part of this, we'll need them. And, my dear, the game's not over yet. Alfred's an idiot, but at least he's a British idiot, and despite the business with the valise he's managed to accomplish successfully another part of his task." He glanced down involuntarily at his watch pocket. "So. All we need do is evade our Yankee opposite numbers until we can get across to Santa Catalina Island. My compliments to Abraham Lincoln, I must say. Certainly no one thought he had the resources to spend anything on counterespionage in this corner of the nation. But he can't keep it up for long, I think. And if the Union loses to the Confederacy, it won't matter whether he knows about us or not." He rose to his feet briskly and extended his hand to me. "We'll triumph yet. Are you still game, my love?"

My love. The earth wobbled in its orbit, just for a second, there. Against all my better judgment I let him pull me to my feet, and tried to look every inch the fearless secret agent's girlfriend. "I'll go with you, señor!"

So much for my attempt to seduce him away from his duty. He was unstoppable, señors, and he always had been. What an operative he'd have made for Dr. Zeus, eh? Our agents are always so adroit at stepping in and whisking away unwanted children. Where were they when Nicholas Harpole made his unwelcome entrance into this world, or Edward Alton Bell-Fairfax? Sublime bastards both of them, with a courage and determination and nobility of character I'd never possessed. What imbecile chance selected me for immortality, when *he* could have made so much better use of an eternal life? He didn't fit the optimum physical parameters, I'll admit; and that was absolutely the only bar I could see.

Consider his ability to inspire. I had been lost in the dark wood, on this wretched posting, and despair owned me. I'd seen at last the future we'd all been promised, and I knew it for the hard and ugly thing it was. I'd seen the madness that descends on older immortals, and it wasn't an enjoyable prospect to contemplate for myself. Nevertheless, others of my kind have in their differing ways found a certain happiness, a sense of purpose, even love. I had my work; but the work dried up, like the seasonal streams of this accursed place, and in its absence I had glimpsed the hideous dry void it covered. What if the Company gave me new work? The void was still there. Besides, I had now the growing suspicion that the work was meaningless, a pointless series of tasks devised to keep busy a thing that couldn't die, since its creators could find no way to unsay the spell that had set it in motion.

But this man walked back into my life and changed everything.

Surely, I thought, his mere existence argued that there was a greater power than the Company, that there was more going on here than our pitiful creators imagined! You see? There might be a point to this eternal life business after all, a purpose and a meaning I couldn't see. Had he not come back to me, like a good angel in my darkest hour, and started my dead heart beating again?

Theobromos, please. Thank you. You want to know what we did next, not listen to my opinions. I see, though, that some of you recognize the feeling. Yes, and some of you are as frightened of the future as I am. Your eyes give it away. So much the worse for you. What's the old saying, don't rejoice at my troubles, because when they're old news, yours will have just started? You have no refuge, any more than I; unbearable Time is master of us all, who thought we had defeated him. Will he treat you with more charity than he's treated me?

We rode, señors, by devious and careful paths, down from that ridge and quickly across the grade to Dark Canyon Road. The plan was to work our way around behind Mount Hollywood, then cut across the lands of the old haunted rancho on the other side, crossing the river at some point. Los Angeles being what it was, this could be done with dry shoes most years; especially so in this year of drought. Edward looked around him in wonder as our horses picked their way through the sand and river cobbles.

"But—this is the principal river in southern California," he murmured.

"So it is," I said. "Not at its best just now, unfortunately. In a normal year, however, it is at least two feet across. Sometimes even three."

He frowned and fell silent. I imagine he was wondering how even the most brilliant British engineers could irrigate this desolation to the point where cotton could be grown.

"Wheat might grow here, señor," I said helpfully. "Cotton, never, unless you bring water down from the north. Plenty of water up there. It's a green paradise; parts of it even look like your England. You would like it there."

He wasn't comforted. Perhaps he was beginning to doubt the feasibility of the grand design after all. In a pigeonhole in some fine antique oaken desk in Whitehall, there was a map of southern California; and some Briton had looked at this wavy line that described itself as a river and made plans accordingly, without understanding that Los Angeles never plays by the rules, whether of geography, law, or anything else.

And of course I knew, I who rode faithful at his side, that the whole business would fall to pieces anyway. Even now Alfred Rubery was probably sitting in a San Francisco jail, having been unable to get any part of his mission right. The British would never own California. Edward and I would at least enjoy a holiday on Catalina Island first. But when the piracy case hit the world newspapers, surely Britain would throw in the towel and call its operatives home.

And what would we do then? What would I do in England, on which I'd turned my back with the earnest hope that the island sink entirely into the sea? I hadn't seen the place since before the Industrial Revolution. It had been crude, cold, and violent, still largely medieval then, with all the attendant lustful bawdiness that implied. What would I make of the new Victorian propriety? What would I make of the mill towns and mine towns that had turned the green fields black? There were railways there now, and canals, and no one was burned at the stake anymore; all peace and prosperity. Except for the workhouses, of course, and the children freezing in alleyways and drinking gin to warm themselves, and the typhus and tuberculosis...But what other nation in the world hadn't the same problems, or worse? No gunfights in the public streets, at least.

It occurred to me that I'd like to go to Rochester, to the open place near the cathedral where Nicholas was burned. To walk there in my Victorian clothes, on the arm of my Victorian Nicholas, and laugh in the face of Death.

I'd have to make some accommodation to the Company, explain my actions and propose a plan that would serve its interests as well as mine. Hadn't they been understanding of Porfirio's needs? After all the years I'd served them, surely they could afford to make some allowances for me. Yes, and it should even be possible to break the truth to Edward. What was the Company, after all, but the ultimate expression of the civilizing force to which he'd dedicated his life? And if he too should become a double agent? Oh, but of a much higher order than a flunky like Souza. It would have worked, señors. We could have made it work.

So I rode over that barren ground, with my head in the rainy clouds of England.

We went up into the foothills to avoid Sonoratown as we approached Los Angeles, though scanning from a distance, I could tell that it was virtually deserted. Best to be safe. We climbed, screened by laurel and oak scrub, until we were peering down on the city we'd left in such haste only the night before. It looked flat and desolate, the whole scene filtered through a yellow haze of dust raised by cattle and horses. Terrible dust, for of course there'd been no rain. And the smell of manure rose up, and of roofing tar, and mesquite smoke, and, faintly under all these, the smell of death.

But out on the horizon, what was that poking up blue into the high clean air?

"Catalina Island, señor," I said, stretching out an arm. "If only we could fly there."

His face was somber as he surveyed the distance, and his gaze dropped back down to the uninviting prospect below us. "I must warn you, my dear, that our road to the sea will be watched. It would be pleasant to think that they've simply posted a man to observe the stage line to San Pedro; but I rather think they know I've got wind of them by now. Is there a fairly straight route to the sea that avoids the pueblo?"

There would be, when the 710 freeway was built. I accessed information hurriedly and superimposed a twentieth-century grid over the present-day map. No reason why we couldn't follow the freeway route through the sagebrush and sand. It would take us right down to the future site of Long Beach, just south of Souza's landing. I plotted a course and nodded. "This way, señor," I said, urging my horse forward, and Edward followed.

So we went down across the wide plain, keeping the smoke of Los Angeles on our right, through a wilderness that would one day be East Los Angeles and various urban housing tracts called Maywood, Bell Gardens, South Gate, Downey, Compton. Such orderly Yankee names for a place that was now only a desert of trampled earth and bleaching cattle bones. Would there be an interval of little Yankee towns with gardens and cottages here too? And would they too vanish in their time, asphalted over, shadowed by the steel towers that would themselves vanish in the urban wars? And what pair of lovers would one day pick their way across a desolation not of sagebrush but of rust and broken paving, under a poisoned sky, past the bleaching bones of men? Full circle for this place, but not for me. With any luck I'd never see Los Angeles again. I'd be off to Great Britain. I'd have to find some way of persuading Edward to give up this nonsense about dying for Queen and country, though...

We had gone on our way about an hour when I edged my horse close enough to speak to Edward in a low voice.

"A question, señor. You understand that I have every confidence in your ability, and absolute faith in your word. To look at the matter coldly, however—what shall I do if we do not succeed? What will the Yankees do if they apprehend us?"

He gave a brief, humorless laugh. "My government is in no position to come to my assistance. The Yankees, for their part, cannot fight a war with Britain just at the present moment, being preoccupied with rather more pressing matters. They'd dearly love to obtain all the particulars of our business here, make no mistake about that. But I doubt very much they'll go to the trouble of declaring me persona non grata and paying my passage home. Much more likely, I'll quietly vanish into a shallow grave, and the contents of the valise will be forwarded to Washington. This is, you understand, the worst possible chance; but it is a possibility. All the more reason to avoid capture, my dear." He looked up and gave me a brisk smile, cold and bright as the winter sun. "Are you reconsidering your offer? I should, if I were you. You see what it is to be a pawn on this particular chessboard."

I might demoralize him, but I couldn't dissuade him.

With his gloved hand he reached over and took mine, and held it tight. "Dolores," he said. He stopped and drew breath. "I don't know what impression of me you've formed in the last twenty-four hours, but I think you see clearly enough that I'm unlikely to end my days quietly. Men in my profession do not. Women in my profession (and there are a few) are as much at risk, indeed at risk of worse. I will never marry you, I will never settle in a pleasant cottage by the sea with you, and we will never raise children together. You are clearly intelligent enough to have perceived this."

"I know, señor. Your life is not your own."

He gripped my hand more tightly and went on. "And it's not that it isn't a glorious life. Giving yourself to a noble cause. True, sometimes one must disregard certain moral considerations to achieve a desired end. One might go to a great deal of trouble to obtain a useful tool, sharp and bright and perfect for the job, a really remarkable tool to find in so unlikely a place. One might have no intention of discarding that tool, either, when its use had been served—though the use might well destroy the tool. A man who seduces a girl into prostitution is vile enough; what would you call a man who persuades a girl to risk her life?"

"Not a liar, at all events," I said with a shrug. "Your conscience should give you a rest, señor. I understand the danger here."

"But I did not, twenty-four hours ago. The ground has shifted since then. Don't share a shallow grave with me, my dear."

"I have no intention of dying," I replied. "And you're not a dead man yet. Catalina, señor, look at it out there, isn't it beautiful? Only a few more miles of this hideous desert, and then it's all blue water. We'll make it, and then we'll have all the time in the world to discuss what further use I can be to Imperial Export."

"By God," he said, looking away from me. "If only we'd met some other place or time."

We had. It hadn't worked out; would it work out now?

We rode on in silence.

I WANTED TO ASK HIM about himself, to find out where he'd been born, who those highborn relations were who had hushed up his birth but evidently found him some back entrance into the corridors of power. The secret child grew up into a secret man, terrifically useful but never to be publicly acknowledged. And when his usefulness ended? When he finally failed to accomplish a task that had been set for him, or began to question the wisdom of the masters who paid him, as I think he must already have begun to do? How did any secret service reward an agent who couldn't do the job, whether through his fault or through the folly of his superiors? Silence and abandonment, disappearance without a trace. I knew that much. Within our own Company there were always rumors that certain operatives had been retired, though nobody knew what that involved exactly.... It's unsafe to inquire after fellow immortals one hasn't seen in a while. I guess I'm going to find out where bad cyborgs go, eh, señors?

But I couldn't ask Edward anything, about his personal life or our plans once we got to Catalina, for a number of reasons. The most immediate reason being that we were trying to cross a dangerous place quickly and in silence.

I could access the historical record, though.

It was so easy, it never occurred to me. All I had to do was access the files I was given codes for when I came to California. I was given whole libraries full of stuff on its history, its future, much more detailed information than I ever bothered to use. When you spend most of your time in a coastal mountain range miles from the nearest mortal soul, you don't need to know who will run for third mayor of Pasadena. But was Edward Alton Bell-Fairfax mentioned in the history of California? Perhaps in some connection with Catalina Island? There would be no mention of me, of course. No Dr. Zeus operative is ever given information about his or her own future, so if I appeared in any footnote in the historical record, it would have been carefully excised from my files.

But I might find references to Edward. I set my primary consciousness to automatic scan and focused on the material behind my eyes.

California, Channel Islands, Santa Catalina Island. One of eight channel islands. Geology: crystalline metamorphic rock, principally quartzite, also steatite, lead, silver—only traces of gold. Botany: several rare endemics (how fascinating, why hadn't I ever been sent there?). Zoology: biggest predator a small fox; goats introduced by the Spanish doing very well. Ornithology, archaeology...nothing I wanted here.

Any record of British involvement? I scanned the records of ownership.

The Indians first, obviously, for about 30,000 years. Thirty *thousand*? Wasn't that a little early? And what was this nonsense about sunken continents, reports of white Indians, and seven-foot-tall skeletons found in the oldest burial mounds? Then assorted Spanish galleons stopping by for souvenirs over the next couple of centuries, doing no harm for once. Russian fur hunters, Yankee sea captains, meddling Franciscans finally causing the place to be abandoned by its native population, who went over to the mission communities on the mainland, where they all died of smallpox.

First owner to hold any kind of title, thanks to Juan Rodríguez Cabrillo: King Charles of Aragon and Castile, later the Emperor Charles, father of my old acquaintance Philip II of Spain, husband of that very same Mary Tudor who had my Nicholas burned at the stake. Small world. And then subsequent kings of Spain, until the Revolution in 1822, when Mexico claimed it. Modern times, now: when Pio Pico was dodging the invading Yankees, he granted title to the island to his friend Thomas M. Robbins. That was in 1846.

Robbins sold the island to José Maria Covarrubias in 1850, and in 1853 it passed out of his hands, sold to one Albert Packard of San Francisco, who had it now and would keep it until at least 1864.

But here the records grew confusing, incomplete. Somebody named Eugene L. Sullivan was claiming part title as early as 1858. And who was this James H. Ray claiming to be Packard's agent, traveling back east *now*, 1863, and bragging to potential investors that he "about had a deal with John Bull"? British parties were interested in buying the property, if clear title could be established. And here was Ray buying out Packard's interest in the island and immediately selling shares in the title to a consortium of men with fairly British-sounding names. Were they the Britons Ray had boasted about? Good Lord, by next year they would own Catalina Island.

I scanned further, fascinated. No—they wouldn't hold the place long. Here was the American government stepping in and seizing the island, ordering everybody off. They'd build a Union Army barracks over there. When would this happen?

January 1, 1864. Nine months from now. A General West would arrive with Union troops, forcibly remove all settlers—including the Albion Mining Syndicate, who had developed an area on a defensible bay and named it Queen City—and build a Union Army barracks at the narrow isthmus that connected the two halves of the island. Under government orders, West would name the two opposing bays Catalina Harbor and Union Harbor. The schooner *Jessup* would be outfitted with a pivot gun and put into service as an armed supply vessel for the Union troops there. In short, Civil War or no Civil War, Abraham Lincoln would find the time and resources to come down on any funny business on Catalina Island like a ton of bricks. Why?

I sped through document titles and froze on one: "Winfield Scott

Hancock's Threat Evaluation. Survey Performed on Orders of Edwin M. Stanton, Secretary of War, November 26, 1863." Eight months from now.

So something that happened within the next eight months would cause the secretary of war in far-off Washington to order a survey of Catalina Island with national defense in mind. I scanned the report. What had Hancock found?

That the population of the island consisted of a few squatter families who had been there since the 1850s, sheepherders and fishermen only—and approximately one hundred miners (most of whom were British nationals), who arrived abruptly, proceeded to fortify a little crescent-shaped harbor, and engaged in no observable mining activity.

That the island's coast was rife with small, accessible harbors, many of which had adequate capacity for vessels of war. Hancock felt the island had dangerous potential for a military base: "any major maritime power" could, with minimal ordnance, control the entire coastline of California from a base on that island, preferably one located in the two-square-mile area around the isthmus. What major maritime power? The Confederacy, desperately dodging blockades or busy hunting Union ships in the Atlantic? It hadn't the wherewithal to send a fleet around Cape Horn. Britain, though, had ships all over the Pacific, and as recently as 1842 the U.S. was so afraid that Britain was going to make a play for California that they'd rushed ashore and prematurely raised the Stars and Stripes at Monterey, which, by an inconvenient little quirk of international law, still happened to belong to Mexico.

What a sharp-eyed fellow he'd been, this Winfield Scott Hancock, and how quickly the secretary of war had acted on his request. Whatever tipped off the secretary of war to order the survey in the first place (doubtless something relating to Mr. Rubery's big mouth, or possibly even Mr. James H. Ray's), in less than a year the whole British plot would come unraveled, and Catalina Island would be firmly under the control of the U.S. government. What a shame, though at least it seemed to have happened without any bloodshed. No mention of any Edward Alton Bell-Fairfax.

Quite an interesting little episode in local history. Imarte had been right: it was all utterly fascinating. So that was the end of British attempts on Catalina...

Wait a minute: what was this? The U.S. government would pull out its forces in September 1864. None of the miners would ever return to the island to press their claims (not surprising, since no substantial amount of gold had ever been located), and a man named James Lick would seek out the consortium members and purchase their titles to the island. There was a lot of correspondence from certain parties in the Department of Indian Affairs, who thought the island would be a great place to dump the unwanted Indian population of Humboldt County, but this would never come to anything, because of the fact (or perhaps in spite of the fact) that Catalina Island had almost no fresh water or arable land, and also because James Lick would be by this time the sole and legal owner, with a clear title.

And here was Lick, in 1872, the Army long out of the picture, offering an option on the island to a Major Max von Stroble. The major would go to London to form an English syndicate to take up the option. Curiously, on the morning he was to sign the papers and collect the money, he would be found dead in his hotel room.

What the hell? And next? Here was George Shatto, the developer, buying the island from Lick in 1887 and selling an option to an *English mining syndicate*. With the money he would receive, Shatto would busy himself laying out the little resort town of Avalon. But there would be problems: the English were supposedly mining silver this time, but then they would leave suddenly, and Shatto would default on payments and lose the island. Shortly afterward, he would reportedly fall from the back of a moving train.

The island would revert to the Lick trustees, who would sell it in 1892 to the Banning brothers. And who were they? The sons of our present staunch pro-Union stagecoach tycoon Phineas Banning, the little boys who'd grow to manhood in that nice mansion being built above San Pedro even now. William, Joseph, and Hancock Banning, the youngest having been named for his father's good friend Winfield Scott Hancock, who'd written the threat estimate fingering the British. Very small world.

So the island would remain firmly in American hands from then on, though the Bannings would experience some trouble: fighting on the waterfront, mysterious sabotage attempts, and arson in 1915 that would destroy the Hotel Metropole (where Harry Houdini stayed) and most of the resort buildings. In the end, the brothers would be bought out by the millionaire Wrigley, of chewing gum fame, who would rebuild Avalon along grander lines. Oh, look: here was a reference to a visit by the Chronos Photo-Play Company, for the purposes of shooting a movie. Chronos Photo-Play was an early alias for Dr. Zeus's entertainment division. I wondered if Einar would be involved in that.

Decades of peace and prosperity for Avalon, then, a pretty little resort town dreaming in the island sun, all its bizarre history long forgotten. No more mysterious deaths, no more British strangers lurking around. The only bit of trivia to stand out of the record was that Wrigley would pay to have an extensive geologic survey done and then suppress the results...

What was going on here?

For half a century, in absolute silence and in deadly earnest, two world powers would wrestle for control of this tiny island. At the beginning, its strategic importance was undeniable. But why would the British keep coming back, long after they'd lost any chance of adding it to their empire? What would they be looking for that required engineering and mining teams? What would Wrigley's geologic survey reveal? Not gold, which had never been found in enough quantity to merit attention of this kind. Not the various buried treasures reported to be there: every island had its tales of buried treasure. What were the British after? What had Imarte told me, something about letters referring to an astonishing technological discovery, made at a place designated only by code. Was the place Catalina? Had they unearthed something there they wanted to study?

Did Edward know?

I remembered his face above me by firelight, shining with the sweat of passion, while he said something about a remarkable discovery, one that might enable men to defeat death. What did Edward know?

I scanned forward through the records. With the Second World War, the strangeness would begin again. The island would be closed to the public once more, and the OSS, forerunner of the CIA, would be quartered there. Oh my. There would be rumors of visits by Allied scientists, particularly the British, and of classified projects at science bases in the island's interior. From that time onward, access to the island's interior would be strictly controlled, even after the war, when the resort areas reopened. A conservancy would be formed in 1972, closing off most of the island to anyone but authorized residents. Access to certain areas was completely restricted, the reason given being that these were rare ecosystems where endemic plants thrived.

I noticed something interesting in the successive editions of the island's history. The earlier works said the Union Army barracks were built to discourage Confederate sympathizers who might try to turn privateer, which doubtless related to whatever Mr. Rubery had been involved in. But later editions began to change the story: the barracks were built to patrol the Indian reservation that had been planned for the island. Still later, the story was that the barracks were built to guard against opium smugglers, and later still (by which point mortals were clearly losing their grasp of history) that they were built to prevent bootleggers from bringing in cases of whiskey.

The same thing happened with the successive maps. Here was one from 1912, nicely detailed, showing a lot of the interior features: the old mine adits and in particular Silver Canyon, where the English would work until their swift departure in 1887. Perhaps they got what they were after. But here was a map from 1938—where were the mines? And here was one from 1976, with interior roads and hiking trails but few other features. Silver Canyon was not marked. Over this I superimposed a map published by the conservancy in 1982. There was *nothing* on the map in that section of the island, not even topographical lines to show ridges or streams, though they appeared everywhere else. The Silver Canyon region was white, blank, featureless. Who was taking such pains to obliterate its memory?

Ah, but a cross-reference in the text indicated the conservancy's involvement with a twentieth-century holding company for Dr. Zeus.

Here were the records for the twenty-first century, and the UFO sightings that would begin on Catalina Island—over the Silver Canyon area, by the way. We all know, of course, that UFO sightings will be a gigantic hoax, costumed nonsense to conceal Company experiments in some cases and mass hysteria in all others. We know that, because the Company told us so. Although nobody ever bothered to explain to me about those little pale men I ran into back in 1860, or why all the material I collected on that job was confiscated. But doubt the Company's word? Inconceivable.

In any case, the Company was surely responsible for those sightings on the island, because here was name after corporate name becoming entangled in the conservancy's affairs, and nearly every one of them was some pseudonym of Dr. Zeus. And it was undoubtedly Dr. Zeus who would provide the islanders with the armament enabling them to close their harbor to mainland vessels after the Second Civil War broke out in mid century, Dr. Zeus who would patrol their waters for them, Dr. Zeus who would develop the advanced agrarian technology that would make them self-sufficient when foodstuffs could no longer be imported from the poisoned mainland.

And it would be Dr. Zeus who established the secret libraries and archives there. When Los Angeles is the toxic, riot-ridden hell it will become, Catalina Island, like sixth-century Ireland, will be a peaceful and remote sanctuary beyond the sea, where knowledge is preserved and research conducted.

Look at the names: Olympian Technologies, Kronos Diversified,

Jupiter Cyberceuticals, Lightning-A Company, Jovian Integrated Systems. Every one of them the Company. Will the Company be behind the bizarre incidents that occur on Catalina Island in the twenty-second century? The rash of Kaspar Hausers who come wandering down onto the golf course in Avalon over a three-month period in 2136, babbling in no known language? The weeping man, found floating off Long Point in a fishing boat of antique design, who says his name is Emilio Machado and swears it is the year 1901? The persistent rumors that a Scots actor, famous for his adventure films of the twentieth century, is somehow still alive and well and can be glimpsed occasionally dining at the Avalon Country Club? What is Dr. Zeus up to?

Señors, if I wasn't meant to know these things, I should never have been given the access codes. Or was it simply that nobody ever thought that one of us would reference this particular subject matter, connect this particular chain of events? I'm fairly sure I wasn't supposed to find out that the CEOs of Olympian Technologies, Jupiter Cyberceuticals, and the rest are, to a man and woman, loyal subjects of Henry X of England. But that must be a coincidence. We were always taught that Dr. Zeus was a multinational entity, drawing the best brains in science and finance from every nation on Earth. There are undoubtedly plenty of Czechs and Kenyans, too, on the board of directors. Anyway...

I raised my eyes to the distant island; it loomed out there like a dream, as I had seen it every day and night of my sojourn here. I turned to Edward Alton Bell-Fairfax, who was now ten times the enigma he had been before. I opened my mouth to ask him a question.

But I never did ask him, because at that moment I picked up the signal of the mortal man approaching through the brush ahead of us. My head snapped around, and I focused on him. Mortal male, two meters tall, thirty to thirty-five years of age, sober, approximately 270 pounds, blood pressure slightly elevated, brainwave pattern suggesting he was hunting. Mounted, and urging his horse forward at a brisk trot. Armed. Rifle and two Navy revolvers.

"Edward," I said in a low voice, "we'd better get off the trail." He looked at me sharply but turned his horse's head at once, and we found our way down a gully and into the partial shade of a scrub oak.

If only he hadn't been so tall.

The mortal must have caught a glimpse of that tall hat, because he sent a bullet whistling through the sagebrush at us. That was no more than conversation in Los Angeles, and it missed by a good ten feet. But here he came, galloping after it, emitting the signal I'd come to know too well: a mortal after blood.

We slid from our saddles, and I found myself flattened between Edward and an undercut clay bank, where the storms of 1862 had hollowed out a space. The clay was just about the same color as those miraculous trousers of his, which were still spotless, by the way. Edward's gun was already in his hand. Damn, here still came the mortal, and even if he didn't spot me and Chameleon Man, he'd see the horses.

He did, too; he saw them first. A long searching stare along the gully, and he saw Edward as well. He grinned in delight, taking in the details of Edward's appearance, his tailored clothing.

"Now I just bet you're that limey bastard," he said. "Let me hear you say something, friend. Talk for me." And he raised the barrel of his rifle.

Bang. Just like in the movies, a red dot appeared in the center of his forehead and a dark red drop ran down. Just like that. He sat there a moment in the saddle, his grin frozen, then fell slowly to one side. His horse didn't appreciate that at all; it stepped clear of him and kicked impatiently to clear his dead foot from the stirrup.

Edward rolled away and looked at me in astonishment. "Good shot, my dear," he said.

That was when I realized I had just killed a mortal. The gun was there in my hand, a bullet gone from the cylinder.

We don't do such things. Einar's mad, he doesn't count; Porfirio had immediately saved the life of the only person I ever saw him shoot. We don't kill. We reason, we run away, we lie to our attackers or confuse them or project illusions to hide ourselves, but we never, ever rob them of their miserable brief lives, because we have so much and they have so little. Unlike us, they have mothers who mourn for them. They have families who starve.

I was crushed with such a sense of sin as I had never felt in my wretched long life. I was a true Angeleno now, wasn't I? At last I'd fired a gun at a total stranger, and blown him away too. But no audience cheered for me, as would have happened in the movies.

Edward took the gun from my nerveless hand, stroked back my hair, looked straight into my eyes. "Dolores, my dear. This was your first time, I think?"

Nice of him, to help a lady so gently on the occasion of retching after her first kill.

"My apologies, señor," I murmured at last.

He waved a dismissive hand. "It quite shocks the system," he said, "the first time. But I think you ought not to take this up as steady work, however good your aim. One can accustom oneself to the act of necessary murder, but does one wish to?"

Yes indeed, something to be seriously considered by the young woman contemplating her entrance into Victorian society.

We mounted and rode on.

The sun was dropping into the west now, and we were nearing San Pedro and the probable cordon, so the danger was greater than ever. We arrived at Long Beach before it was quite dark, splashing across the slough. I wondered if D. W. Griffith's men would plant palm trees here one day, preparing the scene for the desperate chariot race to warn Babylon.

It seemed preferable to wait until full cover of night before making our way to Souza's. Accordingly we found a dry stream bed under an oak tree along the outskirts of Señor Tempe's rancho and reined in there, to dismount for a while.

Edward jumped down first and put up his hands to catch me as I slid from my saddle. I fell into his arms. The brief hold became an embrace, and without quite meaning to we were kissing hungrily. It was going to happen again; nothing we could do about it, other than unlock for a moment as Edward staggered over to loop the horses' reins around an oak branch. He came back, breathing hard. I knelt in the sand; he swept off his hat and knelt beside me.

And really it was like prayer, señors, desperate prayer for forgiveness, an appeal for mercy, an act of life in that deadly place. I gave him pleasure to atone for the death I'd given the stranger. He gave me absolution for what I'd done, and found his own blessing of acquittal in my arms. Violent prayer, struggle and assault, shuddering ecstatic confirmation that we were still alive, though without our bower walls were dogs and enchanters, whoremongers and murderers.

We lay there afterward, looking up awhile at the red evening sky through the black leaves.

"What are you?" Edward whispered.

"Your mate," I said. "As meaningless as that is, for us both. We'll never marry. We'll never settle in a cottage by the sea. We'll never raise children. Death and time stalk us like a pair of hounds. But we were formed in the mind of God from the same piece of steel, for what purpose I cannot imagine."

He was silent for a while. His hand traveled up and closed on my breast. "Death and time," he said at last. "What would our life be like, if we could live?"

"Oh, we'd make the world the place it should have been," I answered with a grand wave. "We'd blaze across the sky like meteors, and our masters would look upon us and tremble. We'd bring down the palace of Death as though it were so many cards. You'd take the flaming sword and smash the lock on the gates to Eden, and let our children into the garden. I'd teach them how to grow corn, and you'd give them laws. Everything would begin again, except sorrow."

He laughed, softly. "So it would," he said. "And then, perhaps, the world could look after its own affairs for a while. Imagine not having to justify one's existence, ever, to anybody."

"Imagine having the freedom to travel where one wished."

"Imagine having the time," he sighed, and I sighed with him. Somewhere out in the evening a sea bird cried, a high thin far-off piping, a lonely sound.

Perhaps it made the moment too surreal, brought home to him just how strange our conversation was. I felt his mood changing, his wariness returning.

"Dolores Alice Elizabeth Mendoza," he said musingly. "You're far too young to understand this business as well as you do, and to kill with such precision. But for your age, I could imagine you were one of Juárez's agents, or even that buffoon Napoleon's, though I can't see how or why. You were certainly a virgin, and yet I've known Eastern whores with less expertise in the arts of love. Less enthusiasm, too. What am I to make of you, my dear?"

I lay very still. "You might accept the truth as I told it to you," I said. Of all the mortals in that English hall, long ago, Nicholas had been the only one to suspect what I was. It had been a game between us, a delightful game of question and evasion, until he discovered the truth. Then he tried to kill me.

"Well, my love, but it doesn't quite convince," said Edward. "I add together all the figures you've given me, and they simply don't produce the sum of you." He stretched luxuriously, in that motion bringing at least two of his concealed weapons into place for immediate deployment. "A sensible man in my line of work would have disposed of you—by some means or other—hours ago. I am, however, reluctant to lose such a charming companion. And it is a fact that your objective and mine would seem to coincide." He smiled, narrow-eyed, waiting to see what I would say.

I gave the faintest of shrugs, a tilt of the head, and spoke in the most reasonable of voices. "Señor. If my intent were to betray you, I might easily have led you to the Yankees by now. If my intent were to secure the contents of the valise—I had all the time in the world to do that when it sat at the inn, before ever you came looking for it. If you find my knowledge or my skill with a pistol remarkable, all I can tell you is that there's not much for a well-born girl to do in San Luis Obispo, save read and practice shooting at targets or the occasional bandit. I believe it's customary for a gentleman to accept a lady's word without question, is it not?"

"It is," he said. "Though I expect you'll appreciate the difficulty I'm in just now, my love, as regards the luxury of trusting anyone."

"I do." I looked up into his eyes. The pupils were dilated, enormous. He really did not want to kill me. "I point out that you have little choice in the matter, señor."

His dark smile deepened, melting me, even with the point of his hidden knife inches from my heart. "So the question remains: What are you? I find myself with a price on my head in a foreign land. My associates have bungled and miscalculated to such a degree that I may well be unlikely to escape with my life. I'm in a very narrow little corner indeed, and my only ally is a remarkable young lady who seems, by some unlikely trick of metempsychosis, to be a fused reincarnation of Boadicea and Cleopatra. A very bad business. And I can't for the life of me think why you're not having a fit of hysterics now, or angry tears."

"Metempsychosis," I said thoughtfully. "Now, that was Pythagoras's theory of the transmigration of souls, was it not? Rebirth, after death, in a new body. Possibly I trust you because we were lovers once, in some previous life. Possibly you trust me for the same reason. It makes as much sense as anything else, señor."

He drew a deep breath and struck the earth beside my head with the flat of his hand. "Now, how in hell do you know what metempsychosis means? Whoever you are," he said, "whoever you've been, if we get out of this with our lives, I *will* marry you. See if you can keep the truth from me then!"

The stars came out, and the chill of evening set in, but we didn't notice. What stamina he had. And what good fortune for us that no bounty hunters chanced to come near that particular oak tree, on that night of the sixteenth of March, 1863.

Much later we arose and rode out again, and I led us through the marshy tidelands and the shallow sea of reeds by scanning for solid ground along Rattlesnake Island. If we made noise, the frogs and the night creatures made more; and so we came in safety to the huts of the fishermen, and I was so grateful to ride up onto the causeway and behold Souza's night lamp burning.

"I will talk for us," I told Edward as I rapped softly on the door. He nodded, and when Souza opened and peered out, I said in Portuguese, "The doctor has a request to make of you, Souza. This gentleman and I need to go across to the big island out there, in silence and secret. When can you take us?"

He yawned and rubbed his eyes. "With the tide, lady. Six hours more."

"Have you a secure place we can rest until then?" I asked.

Of course he had; it was a Company safe house, after all. He bowed us through his low door and showed us to the little closet of a room kept for Dr. Zeus agents who were passing through. Not spacious, but the low, wide bed was clean and dry. There was a chair, on which Edward deposited his saddlebag; there were a washstand and a table with a candlestick on it. Souza lit the candle for us and went to see to our horses. We undressed by candlelight—it flickered, from a little draft coming through the plank walls off the sea—and we sat up by its light long enough to make a late supper out of the last of Juan Bautista's picnic lunch. We barely spoke for exhaustion.

Edward got up once, to make certain the door was secured to his standards, and I lay in bed and watched him. Not one mark, not one scar on his body, same as Nicholas. Really rather remarkable for a man in his profession. But, then, he seemed to be as perceptive of danger as an immortal. Anybody who ever contemplated sending a bullet or knife his way must have been fatally beaten to the draw.

And what was he? I was a woman of mystery to him, but his existence posed a far greater question. Setting aside for a moment that we were somehow in bed together again after three centuries had passed—how was he connected to the technocrats who would one day found my own Company?

I opened my mouth to ask him, but somehow the only question that popped out was "How did you break your nose?"

He turned, peering at me curiously. Naked there by candlelight, no Victorian trappings, and he was Nicholas in every line.

"I've never broken my nose," he replied, coming back to get into bed beside me. He believed what he was saying, too. I lifted my hand to his face and ran my thumb along the irregularity in the bridge that had always so fascinated me.

"But it *has* been broken, just here," I insisted. I could feel the scar in the cartilage, an old injury, healed long ago. "You must have noticed."

"I've noticed the ugly fellow in my shaving mirror, yes, but he's looked that way as long as I remember," Edward said wryly. "It's a family feature, I assume. I'm not sufficiently acquainted with my relations to know. But I assure you, my dear, I've never taken a blow to the face. One of the few advantages of being exceptionally tall; it's difficult for one's assailants to reach so far."

"Ah," I said. I'd never asked how Nicholas broke his nose. He'd had quite a reputation as a university brawler, and I assumed he did it in a fight. "Perhaps you broke it in infancy, then, and don't remember?"

"Perhaps," he said, yawning. He leaned up on his elbow and blew out the candle, and drew me into his arms. We snuggled into safety, there in that room where the wind sighed in the corners, bearing on it the smell and the sound of the sea. Sleep came at once.

We were almost there, señors.

MARCH 17, 1863. I had no nightmares, I seemed to have had no sleep at all before there came the discreet knock and Souza's apologetic murmur advising us that the tide had turned. There was a lingering impression that I'd been having an earnest conversation with someone about Catalina Island and its absurd history, going over and over the cryptic records. The person, who must have been Edward, was patiently explaining that everything was all right because we were really on the same side after all, that the office that employed him would hand on its discovery to the first cabal that would become Dr. Zeus, and that the contents of document D... the *what*?

I opened my eyes groggily, shivering, reaching for the shreds of memories, and of course they disintegrated into meaninglessness. I saw no blue light in the room, though. Edward's arm came out of the darkness, bracing around my shoulders. How hot his skin was.

"Wake up, my love," he said. "We've a crossing to make."

We washed and dressed, and he didn't take the trouble to shave, this time. Every concealed weapon had miraculously found its way into place again, though, and his gloves and hat were firmly on as we stepped out into the morning darkness.

Wide black sky, wide black horizon, and the glint of water between the waving reeds. Freshening wind and the promise of morning, much more of a smack of the sea and less of tidal mud. Souza was crouched in his boat, clearing away nets for seating space. He rose up and offered me his hand into the boat.

"We need to leave now," he said. I nodded and made room for Edward, who stepped in easily and silently and placed his saddlebag among the nets. Souza cast off and bent to his oars. We moved out, bearing well to the east of Dead Man's Island. Slowly we worked our way out of the shallows, past that island of bad reputation, and at length we felt the pull of the tide taking us into deep water. The wind rose. Edward helped Souza run up our little sail, Point Fermin began to recede behind us, and the black threat of the mainland dwindled away.

We had done it, we had got clear. The sky began to pale with morning, and we could see the island now, fair across open water, twenty miles out. I was making for a destiny of which I'd never dreamed, with the missing half of my soul beside me, and it didn't matter what we came to in the end. The morning shone with more promise than any I'd known in my long life.

Edward was leaning back on his saddlebag, watching the mainland shrink. He turned a speculative eye on Souza; then sat up and addressed me in his awkward Latin.

"The fisherman," he asked. "Does he speak my tongue?"

"No, he does not," I replied.

"Good." He continued in English, but kept his voice low all the same. "I estimate we'll make landfall shortly before noon, if this breeze continues steady. Friends will be waiting for us there."

"Englishmen conducting their scientific studies, yes, you told me," I said, smiling at him. And they must have made one hell of a scientific discovery, to judge from the tug-of-war that the British and Americans would be playing soon. Whatever it was, Edward and I would have flown to some further safety by then.

"Ye-es," Edward said. "And some others. Assuming he managed to find a competent pilot on his own, Mr. Rubery and a party of friends should also be arriving, at very nearly the same moment we do. You may be rather surprised at the company he keeps."

"Why, señor?" I asked, folding my hands in my lap and looking expectantly at him. Now would come his explanation of the piracy business.

"There will be certain American gentlemen with Alfred," Edward said, sitting up to face me, "who are under the impression that Her Majesty's government will assist them in a privateering venture in aid of the Confederacy, and that my colleagues on the island have been preparing a base for them from which they may prey on the Pacific Mail steamers. This is, of course, not precisely the case; but we aren't anxious that they should learn the truth immediately."

Asbury Harpending, that was the fool's name.

"It will be useful, in the event that they are caught," Edward continued, "to have the venture assumed to be a purely Confederate conspiracy. We will endeavor to supply them with all they need to make a fearful reputation for themselves, and with any luck their depredations will help push the War of Secession to a speedy conclusion. With funds from the San Francisco Mint cut off, Lincoln will surely sue for peace."

And California would be up for grabs, isolated on a distant coast.

"At this point," Edward said, smiling a cold smile, "there will be certain changes of plan suggested for the privateers. It is to be hoped, by that time, that Southern gentlemen will form only a minority of the crew—having been replaced gradually by gentlemen adventurers of Californian birth, whom I shall have recruited with your able assistance, my dear. We can also expect fresh numbers of my countrymen, once the American hostilities have ended and they can move with greater openness."

He leaned forward and spoke more quietly, and so smoothly. "But there will be an interval during which great tact and persuasion are called for, to convince the enthusiasts of the erstwhile Confederacy that a change of loyalties is in their best interests. It will fall to me to attempt this conversion, on a case-by-case basis. Those Southern gentlemen who cannot be induced to exchange the Stars and Bars for the Union Jack will meet with unfortunate accidents, and I regret to say that the arrangements for those accidents will also fall to me." He looked into my eyes, reading my reaction.

Yes, I know, it was murder he was talking about, but of tobacco-chewing bastards who trafficked in black slaves and had the temerity to dress up their shame in plumes and epaulets. I'd seen those belligerent Southern boys in the bar of the Bella Union. Someone might urge mercy for their kind, but it wouldn't be me. I nodded for him to continue.

"Shortly thereafter, my dear, you and I will have a number of journeys to make," he said. "If we can persuade certain persons of certain things—for example, that a league of amity between Great Britain and Mexico would benefit both parties—then various and assorted efforts by several persons in several countries should bear fruit. That being the case, happy days will ensue. And I will at last be more than Alfred Rubery's long shadow, and you will be whatever you choose to be, in whatever country you choose to reside."

"I may choose to travel, señor," I said, giving him my most meaningful look. He smiled and settled his tall hat more securely on his head, for the wind was blowing strongly now. Souza politely ignored us, leaning on the tiller.

I had no doubt Edward could talk Confederate privateers into supporting the cause of Britain, or persuade Benito Juárez that Her Majesty desired to assist him. The mystery, to me, was why a man with his abilities hadn't gone further. But being illegitimate put the wrong sort of stripe on his old school tie, and that carried so much negative weight with the English. It meant that superb men like Edward lived and died in obscurity, while their nation was run by second-rate boobs who'd lose that empire he was working so hard for. Eventually. Years from now.

Or would they?

This particular plan was already defeated—there would be no British-backed privateers stalking the Pacific Mail—but what about the other part of the plot, involving some discovery the British had made on the island? How would Dr. Zeus become involved? There was every indication that England—in that far-off future when it was no longer even the United Kingdom—would somehow slip into the director's chair at Dr. Zeus. And Dr. Zeus *did* rule the world. Secretly, of course. Would they be able to do this because of what they'd found on Catalina Island in 1862? And what could they possibly have found?

"I've never been to this island," I said. "Though of course I have heard the stories." This was a prompt, but it didn't work.

"What stories would those be, my dear?" Edward asked, extending his hand and clasping mine.

Damn. I sped through reference files. Any old farrago of nonsense would do to get the conversational ball rolling.

"The Indians used to believe that there was once a great continent here in the West, which drowned in much the same way as we believe Plato's Atlantis did," I said. "The Indians claimed there were white men who lived there, extraordinarily tall. They called the place Lemuria."

Edward looked puzzled. "Unusual name. Were there lemurs there as well?"

"I've no idea. In any case, these islands in the channel are thought to be the highest mountaintops of the submerged continent, the only part to survive the deluge. The white men who lived there were unable to prevent the sinking of their world, but they were mechanically brilliant—so the stories say—and produced engines of genius that far surpassed the modern railway or ironclad warship."

Ha, Edward reacted to that, if only in the pulse of his blood. His face showed nothing, however. "What an extraordinary story," he said. "I suppose it's all nonsense, though."

They *had* found something, and he knew about it. Was it some kind of technology? But whose? There had never been any real Lemurians.

I shrugged. "The Indians used to tell fantastic tales. The priests discouraged it, of course, as a lot of superstitious nonsense."

"As well they might," Edward said. "Though there is a growing opinion that the mythologies of primitive peoples ought to be collected and studied. Conquering races tend to destroy such things, to their own loss. Science now indicates that what were once thought to be fantastical myths may well have some basis in historical fact."

"For example?" I asked, sitting forward in anticipation.

He removed his tall hat and pushed his hair back from his forehead before setting the hat on his head again. "In Dover, I was recently shown the complete skeleton of an antediluvian monster, fossilized in solid rock. Educated persons had dismissed accounts of dragons as no more than fairy stories. And yet here was the leviathan himself, and any reasonably observant peasant must conclude it was a real creature that had lived once. And so it had: not galloping after knights and virgins, but sporting in vanished seas."

"An ichthyosaur," I said in disappointment. He wasn't going to tell me what they'd found on the island.

"That was its name, to be sure," he said, squinting at me in the sunlight. "Don't tell me you were trained in palaeozoology as well!"

"No, of course not," I said. "I saw an article in a San Francisco newspaper."

He nodded slowly, a speculative look on his face. "I do look forward," he said, "to the leisure for more of these conversations with you, my dear."

So much for artlessly digging information out of him. How much did he know about what had been found? I was never to find out. But I daresay you know, señors.

The sun was well up now, the little boat sped on and on, and with each hour the island became more than a blue outline. We could see the steep canyons and vast mountains in the interior. We were going directly across, in the shortest line, to the west end of the island: not near the future site of Avalon, but to the double harbor where the Union Army would build its barracks soon. From the sea, you might think Catalina was two islands here, a little range just west of the main mass; but they were connected by a half mile of level isthmus just above sea level, making a neck you could cross in five minutes' lazy walk.

It looked brown and dry, terribly overgrazed by sheep—not like a place you'd find fascinating endemic species of plants. But, then, there was more to this island than met the eye, wasn't there?

Edward took out his field glasses and scanned, and I scanned right with him. A few miles west of the isthmus was where the construction was going on. It was no simple field camp. I could see where they were preparing gun emplacements, and really the little bay they'd chosen was superbly suited for a defensive position. Neat field shelters and some kind of equipment, too, though it didn't look like anything connected with mining. A couple of plumes of smoke: small tidy breakfast fires, I'd bet, preparing kippers and whatever else Englishmen were eating for breakfast these days. I shuddered at the memory of the sardine tacos. Could I see the mysterious Silver Canyon from here?

No, it was back on the windward side of the island. Well, perhaps I'd have a chance to explore the area on foot.

I became aware that Edward had turned beside me and was peering at the far western end of the island, up the coast from the fortifications. I turned too.

There was a ship out there, rolling at anchor, her sails furled.

"Ah," said Edward with satisfaction. "Now, what should this be but the good ship *Chapman*, bearing her crew of traitors and pirates? And the slightly competent Alfred Rubery. Have the boatsman change course. Let's go cheer on the gallant Confederate cause, shall we?"

I gave the order to Souza, but my heart was in my mouth. That couldn't be the *Chapman*, because history had recorded that Rubery and the other conspirators were caught before they could leave San Francisco Bay. They should be in jail cells by now. So there was no way the *Chapman* could be arriving here at its appointed rendezvous, right on schedule. But if that ship wasn't the *Chapman*, what was it?

"Why is she just sitting out there, señor?" I asked. "Oughtn't she have moored in the bay before the camp?"

He shrugged. "Alfred may be following orders at last. He was to wait until I came aboard before taking her into the bay. I'd have been here by now, if all had fallen out as planned. So there he waits, like an obedient boy, for me to bring the valise and further orders. I daresay he'll be glad to see the money. It's rather difficult to recruit a crew on promises."

I scanned the ship. There was a crew on board, but at this range I couldn't tell much more. Nothing to do but sit and wait as we sped across the blue water; nothing but access the historical record.

I hurried through data files. What was the source Imarte found? *The Great Diamond Hoax*, here it was. And other stirring incidents, supposedly, in the life of Asbury Harpending. Just who was Harpending?

Liar, traitor, and swindler, according to historians; scion of a fine old Kentucky family of wealthy landowners, according to himself, as well as a philanthropic speculator, developer, and crusader for truth. In this year of 1863 he was only about twenty-one, though, with a long career of shady dealing before him.

I sped through the chapters. Here were the abortive attempts to stage a Confederate uprising, failed because of hysteria, lack of nerve, and the discovery of the Comstock lode. Just as Imarte had said. Here were the gallant Confederate sympathizers attempting to regroup with an eye to privateering, under the leadership of Harpending. Here Mr. Rubery entered the picture—callow British youth (I'll say) with a sympathy for Southern aristocracy and a love of adventure. Even Harpending made him out to be something of an idiot; though I wondered how much of the privateering scheme had come into shape *after* they met and not before, and whether Harpending was really their leader.

They spent money feverishly, buying the *Chapman,* buying cutlasses, cannons, firearms, and ammunition, and probably a Jolly Roger and cocked hats too. There was no mention of Rubery's making a trip to Veracruz to obtain more funds, but he must have done so, with a stopover in Los Angeles on his way back. Thanks to Cyrus Jackson's jealous passion, Rubery fled back to San Francisco empty-handed; and not only had he left the money behind, he'd come away without the list of contacts who would have helped the next part of the plan along.

For here it was in print: the conspirators were unable to find a navigator anywhere in San Francisco. They'd made inquiries, they'd had friends and acquaintances make inquiries for them; and word had evidently gotten around to the authorities that a band of young men with known Confederate sympathies was looking for an able-bodied navigator likewise eager to overthrow the Union government.

So one came forward, courtesy of the San Francisco Police Department, a man named William Law (surely a broad hint if ever there was one). The conspirators took Law into their confidence. He signed on readily and just as readily took all details of the plot to Captain of Police I. W. Lees.

Lees, being a wise man, opted to wait until all the birds were in the net. If Edward could read this, his hair would go gray. Law went along with all the preparations and agreed to be on board the *Chapman* well before her scheduled sailing time of eleven o'clock in the evening of March 14, 1863. That had been the meaning of the coded telegram Edward picked up the following day.

At ten o'clock on the 14th, I had been sitting in front of the cookfire, listening to Juan Bautista play his guitar. Edward had just arrived from Veracruz and was settling into his room at the Bella Union. And Alfred Rubery and Asbury Harpending were just going on board the *Chapman* and discovering that Law was nowhere to be found.

Was this enough to warn them off? No, they left a sentry to watch for Law and went to bed in their bunks on the *Chapman*. The trusty sentinel dozed off too, it seemed, because the next thing they knew, it was broad daylight on March 15 and the U.S. warship *Cyane* had her guns trained on them. Boatloads of marines were bearing down on them from all sides, to say nothing of a tugboat full of San Francisco police.

And then? Off to Alcatraz with them for interrogation, at just about the time Edward was watching me undress.

News of the foiled plot went out over the telegraph that same day, to the whole world, as Edward and I lay in bed together. If we'd been in any other city, we'd have heard the newsboys crying the story under our windows; but we were in a coaching inn on the edge of nowhere, and we never knew a thing.

What did Rubery tell the police, under interrogation? Something to occasion those two Pinkerton men to go hurrying into the Bella Union as Edward and I approached it that evening? Were they tipped off by an alert telegraph operator, who compared the names on Edward's yet unclaimed message with the names in the breaking story? I cringed inside. No wonder there were bounty hunters after us the following day. Everyone must know now, Queen Victoria on her distant throne must know by now. Everyone knew but Edward.

I fast-forwarded through the details, desperate to see what would happen. The conspirators would be convicted of treason. Possibly because it would seem so obviously a stupidly boyish game, they would be sentenced to fines and imprisonment instead of death. Alfred Rubery's Parliamentary uncle would step in and wheedle a free pardon for him from Abraham Lincoln. Rubery would be thrown out of the country all the same, though, shipped out on one of the Pacific Mail steamers and transferred to a British vessel at Panama.

And that would be the end of the matter.

No villainous British plot to invade the state would ever be publicly uncovered, no scandal of foreign nationals preparing fortifications on Catalina Island. No mention at all of an Edward Alton Bell-Fairfax.

And yet the secretary of war would know enough to send the Army to Catalina. How would he make the connection between a bunch of silly young men wanting to play pirates for the Confederacy, all the way up there in San Francisco, and the activities of certain Britons on an obscure island off the coast of Los Angeles? All Harpending ever said in his memoirs was that they had a general plan to base themselves in some islands *off the coast of Mexico*. But then, he hadn't known about the whole plot, had he? And had he protested when he discovered the use to which his pirate ship was to be put, my smiling Edward would have been there to slip an inconspicuous knife between his ribs.

Did the authorities tell Alfred Rubery that he faced the prospect of being shot as a spy? He must have sung like a damned canary.

We were near the ship now, and there wasn't a soul on deck. She looked as deserted as the *Mary Celeste*. I realized, as we drew near, that whoever had anchored her in that particular little cove chose the spot with coy discretion: we were able to spot her from the open sea, but the men at the British camp on the other side of Arrow Point could have no idea she was there.

There were men on board, alive, alert, and waiting for us.

"Edward," I said, "this isn't right."

He didn't lower his field glasses, for he was studying the ship intently. "Not right? Moral qualms, my dear?"

How could I tell him what I knew? "Not that—there's something the matter here. Why isn't your friend on deck, watching for you?"

"That's a good question," he said, slowly adjusting the long focus. "How can you tell there's no one on deck at this distance, my dear?"

It was like a faceful of ice water, señors. He hadn't mentioned what he was seeing, and he knew I had no field glasses of my own. There was a sadness in his face when he lowered the glasses to look at me, but a certain shivery distance, too.

Nothing to do but brazen it out.

"I have trained eyesight," I explained, as though impatiently. "I was raised to count cattle on hills five miles away, señor. Can't your English shepherds do the same? Look." I pointed to the ship. "See the stain on her jib sail? See the red rag tied to her wheel? The three belaying pins on that rail there at the left, and the five at the right? Look there, that's a brown pelican lighting on her aft deck now. Stupid creature expects someone to toss it a fish. Do you see it, señor?"

"Yes," he said, looking through the glasses again.

"And do you see a living soul on deck?"

"No, my dear, I don't."

"And does that seem reasonable to you?"

"No, it doesn't." He lowered the glasses and looked at me again, not quite sure what to think. "You never cease to amaze me, Dolores. It should make our continued acquaintance interesting indeed. However—Alfred hasn't much experience with maritime customs such as leaving a watch on duty. Neither, I suspect, have his fellow privateers. They may all be belowdecks playing whist." He looked through the glasses again. "Or there may be something wrong. I doubt it, though. Sails reefed, anchor down, everything in order, both boats there."

"How do you even know that's Mr. Rubery's ship?" I was in agony. Nearer we flew and nearer, across the lovely clear water, closer to the ones who were waiting for us.

"That is another good question," he said coolly. He didn't know what to make of my terror, but he wasn't about to panic himself. "Let's just see, shall we? You!" he addressed Souza in Spanish. "Take us in, under her stern."

Souza looked inquiringly at me—though he understood Spanish perfectly well—and I nodded weakly. We made straight for her now, then angled around so that we were coming in with a good view of the aft cabin. There was her name, in big blocky letters: J. M. CHAPMAN. Her boarding ladder was down, in open invitation.

Behind my eyes, a line of text jumped out at me, Harpending peevishly complaining that the name of the vessel was the plain *Chapman*, though for some reason journalists had seen fit to refer to it in all the papers as the *J. M. Chapman*.

"It's she," said Edward briskly. He said to Souza, "Bring her alongside."

I stared up at the painted name. Freshly painted name. Wait, no. The J. and the M. and the CH were duller; only the APMAN gleamed with new enamel. I subjected it to infrared scanning and saw, underneath, the letters ISHOLM. This ship had been the *J. M. Chisholm* not long ago. Who had altered her name, and why?

"Señor," I said, keeping my voice as reasonable as I could. "Call it woman's intuition. I fear treachery here. What if Mr. Rubery has met with some misfortune?"

Edward gave me a long speculative look. "Then he'll need my assistance," he said. "In any case, it's my duty to find him. Are you frightened, Dolores? You needn't go on board if you are. This shouldn't take long."

He took up his saddlebag and caught hold of the ladder, climbing nimbly despite his awkward grip. I sat there and watched him a dull moment, before rising and scrambling after with a sob of desperation. If I couldn't prevent him from walking into the trap, perhaps I could get him out of it. Perhaps nothing very bad would happen after all. Mr. Rubery, twit that he was, would come out of this with no more than a slap on the wrist and deportation, so perhaps Edward and I would escape once more, sailing free into the sunset after amazing adventures.

We boarded the *J. M. Chapman* and stood on her empty deck. All sunlight and silence, but for the creaking of the rigging and the sough of breakers on the shore nearby.

"Edward," I whispered. "There are mortal men below decks."

He raised an eyebrow. "*Mortal* men?" he said, smiling a little. He set off down the deck and then halted, turning to me with the strangest look in his eyes. "What did you—?"

Yes, señors, I'd given myself away. Not that it mattered, however.

With only the slightest sound, the door of the aft cabin opened, and a man emerged. He was a clean-shaven nondescript in a neat gray suit, smiling as he leveled a pistol at Edward. "Commander Bell-Fairfax?" He had a pleasant flat American voice. "You're under arrest, sir. Could you set down that bag, please?"

Edward went white as a sheet, but he smiled that cold and narrow-eyed smile.

"Ah," he said. "This bag?" He set it down very carefully. He opened it. The Pinkerton agent made a sharp little noise, stepped toward him, thrusting out his pistol—but Edward held up both hands in a pacifying motion and slowly drew out the valise.

"This is what you want, I expect," he said, and held it up. The agent smiled and stepped forward, holding out his hand.

Edward shot him.

I had the American's pistol out of his hand before he fell. "Jump!" I screamed to Edward, for I could hear the men below hatches boiling from beneath us, coming up on deck as the wounded agent rolled and cried for help. I turned to see Edward composedly opening the valise and scattering its contents over the side, papers fluttering and falling, and the lovely violet ink blurring and melting away to nothing as soon as the pages settled on the water. The Americans would never learn the whole truth now. They'd get the island, but they wouldn't know what its secret was or where, and the British would find a way to creep back and take it from under their noses.

"Jump, for God's sake!" I ran to him, but the bullets got there first.

It didn't happen in picturesque slow motion. He neither jerked nor spun about. He coughed once, with the first hit; then he squared his big back and took the shots, doing his best to ignore them as he sent the last of the papers into the sea and dropped the valise after them. He pushed himself around to face me and the crew of Pinkerton agents who had surrounded us.

He met my gaze with an ironical smile. Oh, he was falling; his legs weren't working anymore. He toppled forward, and I caught him, and we sank to the deck in a welter of bright blood. His hat came off and rolled away.

I was sobbing, catching my breath in ugly little cries as I rocked him in my arms, trying to get enough air for a scream. Blood was coming up out of his mouth. He gave one grimace of pain and he stiffened; but then something seemed to get easier, and he opened his eyes and peered up at me with an inquiring expression, as though I had just made a remark he didn't quite hear and was hoping I'd repeat it.

The world had shrunk to that little space on the deck. Our enemies might have been a circle of statues, for all we noticed them. His world was shrinking even faster; he was fighting to keep his eyes focused on mine.

"Wh—what *are* you?" he asked, quietly, as though we were lying in a green garden somewhere and no blood was running down his chin.

The only gift I could give him now was the truth. My throat was like stone, but I got the words out, whispering to him.

"I'm not a mortal woman, *mi amor*. But it was science and medicine that made me so, not magic. I exist because your masters discovered something that enabled them to make immortal creatures like me, to do their work for them here in the past. They *will* create a race that can never age nor die, just as you said. This is what you have bought with your life."

He was knitting his brows, his breath was rasping and wet as he strained to hear me. Suddenly there was comprehension in his eyes, and they brightened. He gave a gurgling chuckle. He knew.

I fought to suck in a breath. His death was coming for him. I leaned closer and said, "Listen to me, my love. I'm trapped by centuries, I can't follow you. Come back for me and break my chains. Set me free. Will you set me free?"

He nodded. He looked into my eyes, trying to say something. He had neither the strength nor the time. A wind gusted across the deck toward us. His soul slipped away with it.

I bent over him, hiding his dead face with my hair.

"I hear no sound but your silenced voice," I murmured. "I feel no heat but the fire that burns you, I draw no breath but you come into me, before me, behind me, you are the sea and the rock!"

"Johnston's dead," someone announced. "Who's this woman?"

"The whore from the Bella Union, ain't she?" someone else said.

"God damn," said a voice directly above me. "I guess you could say this didn't turn out so well. What'll we do with this one?" A booted foot tapped Edward's leg.

"Weight the body," someone said. "We'll put out to sea and drop him in the channel. No evidence, gentlemen."

"Come on, girlie, get up." A hand closed on my wrist. "You're under arrest."

I don't really have a clear memory of what happened next, señors, only a few impressions. I remember seeing Souza in the distance, rowing away for his life. I remember the Americans screaming and trying to hide. If you want the details, you can check my video transmission. I know what I must have done; because when that longboat full of British voices came around the point to see what was going on, I remember throwing human heads at them. And an arm. I didn't kill the Englishmen, though, I'm fairly certain. I think they retreated in some haste. And then of course your security operatives came and found me, doubtless because poor Souza's control implant was broadcasting his horror.

And that's it, señors, that's the end of the story. I had a second chance to save my love, and I failed. I took unauthorized leave and I committed murder. I did find out a great many interesting things about the genesis of our Company, but I have a feeling that the information was classified, not for my eyes at all.

I was a bad machine.

But I've told you the truth, señors, every word. Now, you wouldn't have one more piece of Theobromos to spare, would you, for a poor old thing like me?

*H*OW VERY EMBARRASSING to read one's own testimony. If the hearing panel hadn't given me so much Theobromos, I'd have told them the story in half the time.

As it was, I lay in the worst case of theobromine poisoning I'd ever had, for three days and three nights, before they came for me and gave me to understand there would be no trial, no further action. I was only to be sent off to my new posting immediately. I was still groggy when they helped me into the silver box, and I heard the hiss, breathed in the yellow gas, and was abruptly *here*.

And where exactly is here? Ah, that's the cream of the jest. I crawled out of the box and wandered around in bewilderment for several minutes before I found the crates and dispatch case that had been sent with me. I fumbled open the seal and read my orders.

I am now the managing operative of a Dr. Zeus agricultural station, located—where else?—on Catalina Island, and the present year is 153,020 B.C.E. I am in fact the sole personnel assigned to this station, but after all I'm an immortal with unlimited strength, so I find myself adequate for the job. Plenty of heavy equipment I can drive, plenty of supplies sent as I request them. No company at all.

Is it my job to collect the rare endemic species that grow here and nurture them along? Not exactly. My assignment is to grow produce for the Company's Day Six resort on Santa Cruz Island, some miles north of here. I supply the salad bars of wealthy twenty-fourth-century vacationers, who pay out a considerable chunk of their income to be herded into cramped shuttles and thrown back through time to an unspoiled and unpolluted paradise where they can sport-fish, have their holos taken with dwarf woolly mammoths, or just relax by the pool. I read that in a brochure somebody dropped on the loading dock where I deliver the crates of radicchio, squash blossoms, and endive that I raise. I never stay to watch the ship arrive. I don't like talking to people.

My heart aches when I think of the Ventana and Big Sur. I can never go back there again. I'm forbidden to leave this garden I've made. And some violence has been done to my electronic memory, I fear. Something's been deleted. I can't access all those fascinating historical records of this island now, nor the successive altered maps. They don't seem to have realized that the information still exists in my human memory. But since I can't download the information to another operative, maybe they don't care, especially as I'm unlikely to see anyone I know back here. Even Joseph won't be born for a hundred thousand years. Longer for Lewis and the others. No way at all to talk about my discoveries, which is undoubtedly why I've been put so far in the past.

All things considered, though, the Company has treated me very well. One door closes, another one opens. This is a beautiful island right now, not at all the dry and rocky place it will become. There are immense forests here, ironwoods the equal of any sequoias you might find on the mainland, deep groves of mahogany trees, great spreading oaks and pines. Very little flat land, but what there is I have covered with neat green rows of vegetables, tidy orchards, and a small area for my own botanical experiments. No animals bigger than the little fox. Plenty of birds. No mortals at all... yet.

I'm to watch for them, though. This is very, very secret. Really I shouldn't be writing it down here, but who the hell will ever see? I'm to watch for certain people, odd-looking people with pale skins, who will arrive one day. They will not be Ancient Lemurians. It is expected they will arrive in well-designed oared galleys or perhaps even in gliders of some kind. It is expected they will settle in the Silver Canyon region. It is expected they will dig themselves in under a mountain and hide there, safe from marauding Neanderthal or Cro-Magnon primitives. I'm to report their arrival to the Company at once, and then I'm to monitor them unobtrusively for the next few centuries. When they've reached a certain level of technological development, when a certain energy signature begins to appear, I'm to alert Dr. Zeus. I suspect the Company will come in and slaughter them, then, and make off with their peculiar inventions.

Talk about piracy. But the Company won't take everything. Something will be deliberately left for the British to find in 1862 or whenever, some bit of machinery that will be hidden away in a military laboratory for decades, until some Briton finally discovers how to make it work, and gains thereby insight into certain dimensional principles that enable him to solve the problem of time travel. Dr. Zeus will have guaranteed its own birth, built the foundation of its empire. And Edward will have been the sacrificed hero whose blood mortared its cornerstone.

Pretty sneaky, eh?

It was a few centuries before I could bring myself to climb over to the west end of this island and look down into the anchorage where Edward died. I half-expected to see the ship lying there, and his poor mortal body sprawled on the deck. But none of that's happened yet. Thousands of years yet before the acorns fall that will grow into the trees that make up the timbers of the *J. M. Chapman* of fatal memory. Edward's distant ancestors are at this time knapping flints for hand axes. I would bet, though, that in some tribe on some cold green island there is one very tall savage who has learned how to put a wooden handle on his ax, or perhaps to draw reindeer on his cave wall. It will so unnerve his fellow cavemen that they'll grab him at the next spring equinox and sacrifice him to their gods. Perhaps some wretched little proto-Celtic girl will weep for him and wring her hands, too.

Who knows? We may have been in this dance since time began, and could never see the pattern until Dr. Zeus made me an immortal, unable to die or to forget. When Nicholas died, I was still too young to see what was going on. This last time with Edward gave them away, however. I don't believe in reincarnation, but surely even the Hindus don't imagine it works like this. What's the point? The same man circling through lives like a blazing comet, always returning on the same course, meeting the same inevitable doom before he vanishes into darkness, serving somebody's purpose with his death but never his own. The game is fixed. Whoever is running it—and I can guess at the identity, though not the reason—it's fixed.

But now at least I know.

I don't expect I'll see him again for a while. But I will see him again. He will come back and set me free, because he said he would. And it may not be on our next encounter, or the next, but one day the pattern of his sacrifice and death will be broken. We will make something better than this, he and I, and God help our masters if they try to prevent us.

In the meanwhile I tend my rows of corn and tomatoes, or wander on this narrow cobblestone crescent and admire the blue sea, or sit outside my shelter at night and watch the sky. I'm patient; I can wait.

He will come again.

CPSIA information can be obtained at www.ICGtesting.com
Printed in the USA
LVOW07s1027160815

450305LV00002B/261/P

9 780765 315304